Dungeon Royale

Also by Lexi Blake

EROTIC ROMANCE

Masters And Mercenaries
The Dom Who Loved Me
The Men With The Golden Cuffs
A Dom Is Forever
On Her Master's Secret Service
Sanctum: A Masters and Mercenaries Novella
Love and Let Die
Unconditional: A Masters and Mercenaries Novella
Dungeon Royale
Dungeon Games: A Masters and Mercenaries Novella, *Coming May 13, 2014*
A View to a Thrill, *Coming August 19, 2014*

Masters Of Ménage (by Shayla Black and Lexi Blake)
Their Virgin Captive
Their Virgin's Secret
Their Virgin Concubine
Their Virgin Princess
Their Virgin Hostage
Their Virgin Secretary, *Coming April 15, 2014*

CONTEMPORARY WESTERN ROMANCE

Wild Western Nights
Leaving Camelot, Coming Soon

URBAN FANTASY

Thieves
Steal the Light
Steal the Day
Steal the Moon
Steal the Sun, *Coming March 18, 2014*
Steal the Night, *Coming June 2014*

"I can always trust Lexi Blake's Dominants to leave me breathless...and in love. If you want sensual, exciting BDSM wrapped in an awesome love story, then look for a Lexi Blake book."
~Cherise Sinclair USA Today Bestselling author

"Lexi Blake's MASTERS AND MERCENARIES series is beautifully written and deliciously hot. She's got a real way with both action and sex. I also love the way Blake writes her gorgeous Dom heroes--they make me want to do bad, bad things. Her heroines are intelligent and gutsy ladies whose taste for submission definitely does not make them dish rags. Can't wait for the next book!"
~Angela Knight, New York Times bestselling author

"A Dom is Forever is action packed, both in the bedroom and out. Expect agents, spies, guns, killing and lots of kink as Liam goes after the mysterious Mr. Black and finds his past and his future... The action and espionage keep this story moving along quickly while the sex and kink provides a totally different type of interest. Everything is very well balanced and flows together wonderfully."
~A Night Owl "Top Pick", Terri, Night Owl Erotica

"A Dom Is Forever is everything that is good in erotic romance. The story was fast-paced and suspenseful, the characters were flawed but made me root for them every step of the way, and the hotness factor was off the charts mostly due to a bad boy Dom with a penchant for dirty talk."
~Rho, The Romance Reviews

"A good read that kept me on my toes, guessing until the big reveal, and thinking survival skills should be a must for all men."
~Chris, Night Owl Reviews

"I can't get enough of the Masters and Mercenaries Series! Love and Let Die is Lexi Blake at her best! She writes erotic romantic suspense like no other, and I am always extremely excited when she has something new for us! Intense, heart pounding, and erotically fulfilling, I could not put this book down."

"Certain authors and series are on my auto-buy list. Lexi Blake and her Masters & Mercenaries series is at the top of that list... this book offered everything I love about a Masters & Mercenaries book – alpha men, hot sex and sweet loving… As long as Ms. Blake continues to offer such high quality books, I'll be right there, ready to read."

"I have absolutely fallen in love with this series. Spies, espionage, and intrigue all packaged up in a hot dominant male package. All the men at McKay-Taggart are smoking hot and the women are amazingly strong sexy submissives."

Dungeon Royale

Masters and Mercenaries, Book 6

Lexi Blake

Dungeon Royale
Masters and Mercenaries, Book 6
Lexi Blake

Published by DLZ Entertainment LLC

Copyright 2014 DLZ Entertainment LLC
Edited by Chloe Vale and Kasi Alexander
ISBN: 978-1-937608-22-4

McKay-Taggart logo design by Charity Hendry

Foreword

This is my first book with two British leads and set entirely in foreign countries. I've been to many of the sites I talk about in this book. I would be remiss if I didn't thank the amazing tour guides and citizens of Helsinki, Finland and Berlin, Germany for making me feel so welcome and sparking my imagination.

As I said before, both the hero and heroine of this novel are British, and I've attempted to capture the flavor of their language. Yes, we all speak English, but anyone who has traveled to London knows we do it in very different ways. If you want an example, just look up what the Brits think of the word "fanny." You won't carry a fanny pack in London again, just saying. Because I'm just a Texas girl, I reached out to some friends for help in making Damon and Penny as realistic as possible.

I would like to say a huge thank you to Fiona Archer for her contribution to this book. I couldn't have done it without you. And big hugs to the girls across the pond—the women of Naughty Book Club on Facebook were so helpful and warm in pointing me in the right direction when it came to British slang. Another big thank you to Katija Rothbächer for her help with the German and Finnish translations.

If I do anything right concerning the dialect in this book, the credit goes to them. All errors belong to me. I thank you for reading and hope you enjoy Damon and Penny's story.

Prologue

London, England

Dying was a messy business.

The coppery smell of blood filled his senses. It was so damn strong. He'd been surrounded by blood before, covered in it a few times when he'd been with the SAS, but this was different.

This was his blood.

And his death.

Get the fuck up, Knight. You're not bleeding out here on your desk. This is not how you end.

He couldn't breathe. A rattle came out of his chest as he attempted to take a deep breath. It sounded like the rusty old furnace from his childhood, the one that heated his grandfather's hunting cabin in Scotland. He'd adored that old man. His grandfather died when Damon was eight. One more loss.

Would he see his grandfather again?

After everything he'd done in his life? Not bloody likely.

Through sheer force of will, he pushed off the desktop where he'd been slumped for what seemed like an eternity.

Phone. He needed a phone. Fucking bastard had taken his phone. Basil Champion the third had been his partner and his closest friend for the last ten years. He was also the man who had put a bullet in his lung. He was thorough. The arsehole had taken his mobile and his laptop.

Everything ached. Each and every move felt like the last. There was no grace to his walk. He stumbled, falling to the floor.

No air. No fucking air. His lungs wouldn't work.

He stared up at the ceiling. He loved this club. He'd spent every dime he had to make it into an odd type of home. It was supposed to be a place where he could be himself, where he could one day live with his sub. He wasn't sure he ever wanted a wife, but he'd considered taking a permanent sub and housing her in The Garden where they could live free of the constraints of the vanilla world.

Now he wondered why he'd waited. He was dying and no one would care. He'd held himself apart for so long, waiting for the perfect woman. Now he kind of wished he'd found any woman. His parents were dead and his partner turned out to be an international terrorist, so there wouldn't be anyone weeping at his funeral.

Now that he thought about it, no one would likely show up at all.

He should have asked her out. The blonde. Penelope. He watched her when he was in the office. She was a pretty girl with a smile like sunshine. Until recently. She didn't smile much anymore.

"Damon? Is something going on? The front door was left open," a masculine voice said from the hallway.

A spark went through him. James Turner. He was a Dom here at The Garden. Usually the place was closed down at this time of day, but James had keys.

There was a squeak as the door opened. He tried to shift his head, but his muscles had stopped moving.

Suddenly James was beside him, staring down at him. "Knight? What the hell happened? I'm calling 999 right now. Hold on." He had a phone in his hand. "Yes, I have an emergency. It looks like a gunshot wound."

No one at The Garden knew he worked for MI6 with the exception of Baz. He would simply die and there would be nothing more of him. The periphery of his vision began to fade.

The world started to move in an odd set of flashes. Blessed darkness would come and then a flash of pain and light.

The medic holding his hand to his chest, pressing down.

The world going in and out of focus as he was lifted up.

The sounds of sirens as he was taken away.

"His BP is dropping. Damn it all. He's in arrest."

"Big bastard is a fighter, that one. He coded three times on our way in."

He caught sight of a nurse holding some form of anesthetic mask over his face. She was blonde, curvy. Funny. She looked a lot like Penelope. Such a pretty thing. A translator. He'd heard her speaking Danish over the phone. It had gotten him hot. *Not for me. Not for me.* He told himself that all the time. She was rather kind to everyone around her. She'd made him a cake for his birthday. No one else had remembered his birthday and he'd never even told her she was pretty. Never asked her out to lunch. Never done the thing he really wanted to do—never pulled her close and planted his lips on hers.

Because he was a bastard who would break her so he'd kept his distance and now he would likely never know how truly sweet she was. He'd worked with her for years and she had no idea he watched her.

"Just hold on, Mr. Knight," the nurse was saying.

As the anesthetic took control, his last thought was about a girl with blonde hair and a sweet smile.

* * * *

Penelope Cash stood in the cemetery on the outskirts of London, rain beating against the umbrella she held, and wondered when the rush of relief would come. She'd taken care of her mother for five years. She'd handled every bit of horror that the dementia had thrown at her. She'd worked to pay for the day nurse and had not a pence left to show for what should have been years of saving.

So where was the relief?

She stared down at the grave they would soon place her mother in and all she could see was the vibrant woman she'd been. All she could see was the mother who had taken her to the cinema and told her stories at night. The woman who had kept them all together until disease had torn her apart.

There was no relief to be had, only an aching sadness. Her mother had effectively died years before, replaced with a woman who screamed at night and pointed at horrors that weren't there.

"Hey, love, are you coming back to Diana's?" Her brother, George, slipped an arm around her shoulders.

She sighed. She loved Diana, but she didn't think she could handle being at her perfect sister's house today. It reminded her far too much of everything she'd lost. How could she watch Diana and her babies and her husband? She very likely would never have a family of her own. There had only ever been Peter who had been interested in her, and now he was gone.

"I think I'll go to the office for a while." Work was numbing, blissfully so. When she was translating a document or analyzing a code, she wasn't thinking about everything she'd denied herself over the years.

And when she caught sight of Damon Knight, she could sigh and daydream a little. Her own James Bond.

"Do you hate us, Pen?"

She nearly sighed. It was very much like her brother to bring up their family problems on a day like this. "Of course not."

She turned away, hoping he would let it all drop. He could go to Diana's and drink her excellent wine and pretend that he was in mourning. *Damn it all.* She didn't want to hate him. Tears blurred her vision.

"I wouldn't blame you if you did." He fell into step beside her, his normally handsome face a bit worn and weary. "I think I hate myself a little today. I know Diana does."

"I don't want to talk about this now, George."

He stopped her, his hand reaching out. "You never want to talk about it, Pen. You seem to think that if you let it go, it will just float away and we'll never have to deal with it. I loved Mum. I know I didn't show it the way you did, but I loved her and I realized something last night. I realized that the way I prove it is by keeping this family together."

George had been constant. Even after their mum had lost the ability to recognize him, he'd come to visit twice a week, making the long train ride from Oxford to London without fail. Diana had paid as much as they could toward Mum's care and brought meals by on occasion. They had tried.

But they hadn't been forced to live with the daily struggles. They had their own families.

"If I let you, you'll drift away from us, Pen. I don't want that. I don't want to end up like the other families I've seen break apart after their parents die. Sure we would probably see each other this Christmas, but you would make up an excuse to miss Easter and then time would do the rest. I know the burden you carried. I know you carried it alone. You have every right to hate us. We didn't do everything we could have. I should have moved back."

And given up his work? Should Diana have left her children at home to stay with their mother? Should she have put that pressure on her marriage? Penny knew how hard it was for a relationship to survive that kind of burden. When she really looked at it, she'd driven Peter away because she wouldn't make time for him. First there had been her father's long battle with cancer and then her mother's dementia. She'd made choices. Perhaps they'd been the right ones, but they'd led to her engagement dying a slow, pitiful death.

"It doesn't matter now, George. I don't blame you. You did what you could."

"It does matter. Damn it, I don't want you to end up a bitter old woman. It's the last thing Mum would want."

Penny stopped cold and turned back to her brother. His suit was plastered to his lanky body, his normally perfect hair bedraggled. There was no mistaking the fire in his eyes.

She felt a spark of her own. "I'm thirty-two. I'm hardly old."

But she felt every single one of those days.

"You don't date. When Diana and I offered to watch Mum so you could go out, you always turned us down. You don't go out with friends. God, I don't even know if you have friends. I'm worried because I don't think Mum dying is going to change anything for you. I think you'll just go on the same way. I think it's gotten easy for you to be alone. I think it's gotten easier for you to be angry than it is for you to forgive us. We weren't as good as you, Pen. If it had been left up to me and Diana, she would have gone to a nursing home a long time ago."

They had argued it was the best place for her, but Penny couldn't send her mum to one of those places that reeked of urine and death and utter despair.

God, the last few months, it had been how her own home smelled.

Dying was a horrible business. Even when the death wasn't her own.

"Come out to dinner with us. Just you and me and Diana. We'll tell everyone else to take a hike. Just the three of us."

"I want to go home." She just wanted to be alone. She wanted to shut the door of her house and…what? Mourn? Wallow in self-pity? Eat ice cream and pretend like she wasn't turning in to exactly what George was afraid of?

She'd stopped smiling. She used to bake cakes for her fellow employees and go to lunch with the "girls," as she called them. She used to laugh and let them tease her about her crush on Damon.

It had all gotten to be too much. Even she could break.

Could she put herself back together? She'd made the choice to put her life on hold to take care of her parents. Could she find the girl she'd been?

George stared at her, his arms open. She could be mad at him or she could choose another path.

A sudden memory hit her. Her younger brother slugging an upperclassman at their school because he'd called Penny ugly. Diana had been there, holding her hand and promising her that everything would be all right. George had taken a black eye and Diana had taught her everything she knew about makeup.

They had been a little gang, the three of them. No one else could understand what it meant to have lost their parents. Others could sympathize, but they couldn't understand the uniqueness of her grief.

She'd been strong for years and never quite realized what it had cost her. No smiles. No tears. No anything.

Grief hit her like a wave, rolling across her and bringing an odd sense of peace.

She let the umbrella fall away and stepped into her brother's arms.

For the first time in years, she allowed herself to truly feel.

Chapter One

MI6 Headquarters
Seven months later

"**W**hat are you trying to say, Nigel?" Damon Knight looked across the wide, solid desk at the man who had been his handler for the last ten years. The very air seemed to have stilled around him.

Nigel sat forward, his graying hair perfectly coiffed and his eyes serious. They had come up through the ranks together, but Nigel had taken the analyst route while Damon liked to be in the field. He was rather afraid his wishes weren't going to be taken into account now.

"Have you looked at the reports from the medical team?" Nigel asked.

Fuck. A hole was opening up in front of him and he wasn't even close to being ready. He didn't need to read the medical reports to know what was in them. "I'm perfectly fit."

It had been seven months since his partner, his best friend, had walked into his office at The Garden and put a bullet in his chest. He'd sat there, bleeding out at his desk, visions of murder and revenge running through his dying brain.

And a deep regret that no one would miss him.

It had only been luck that one of the Doms at his club had dropped by to set up a scene for the evening. Otherwise, he would be dead.

"Not according to these reports you aren't." Nigel set the folder between them. "According to this, you're permanently incapacitated. You lost an enormous amount of blood. There was some question about how long you were technically dead."

He couldn't help but answer through clenched teeth. "I'm not brain damaged."

"Of course not, but it had to have affected you."

"I'm not suffering from bloody PTSD." He'd gone through every counseling session they'd forced on him. When the bloody hell had the Secret Intelligence Service become a bunch of psychobabbling, talk-about-their-feelings wankers?

He might have spent too much time with Ian Taggart, but the man had a point. Spies should have nerves of steel. If they didn't, if they required weekly hour-long sessions to discuss their feelings, they bloody well shouldn't be spies.

Nigel frowned. "Fine, let's talk about the physical damage then. That bullet tore apart your left lung. The doctors were forced to remove a portion of it."

"The good news is, I have a spare." They had only been forced to remove a small portion of his left lung. Unfortunately, MI6 preferred its agents to have full lung capacity. No matter how hard he worked out, he always hit a wall.

He didn't mention the other problems he was having, the problems the doctors in Dallas had discovered with his heart. If Nigel knew about those, he wouldn't be sitting here talking about assignments.

Nigel sat back. "Damon, you know how much we all want this to work. No one on the team wants to see you out of the field. You've been our most effective agent since the moment you walked through the doors."

Ah, there was a "but" coming. Damon could feel it. He just didn't want to hear it. "Excellent. I'm very glad to hear it because I am ready to get back in the field. I have some thoughts about information building on The Collective."

Seven bloody months. He'd spent seven months recovering, waiting, thinking. And plotting his revenge. He was ready to start again, ready to do just about anything that brought him one step closer to getting his hands around Basil Champion's throat.

"Yes, I found your file on them very interesting." Nigel's fingers drummed along the thick file folder he'd turned over.

Damon had spent his recovery time in Dallas with Adam Miles and Charlotte and Chelsea Dennis, using their brilliant computer skills to find absolutely everything he could about the shadowy organization known only as The Collective. As far as he could tell, they were a secret organization run by some of the world's largest corporations and richest men. They used secret agents culled from intelligence agencies across the globe to manipulate the world economies to suit their companies.

He'd put together everything they'd been able to find, and none of it was completely solid. It was all conjecture, and he was pretty sure Nigel was starting to think he was a conspiracy nut.

"Perhaps it's not concrete, but you know that an operative has to listen to his gut. This is me. I'm listening to my gut and my gut says this is real and Baz is involved."

"You know the chief is fairly certain that Champion was a double."

It took everything Knight had not to groan. "He wasn't working for MSS."

The theory was that Basil Champion had turned and started to work with Chinese intelligence.

"It would explain the influx of cash you found."

"But it does nothing to explain why he left when he did. He chose to blow up his career because he realized that Ian Taggart had found out about The Collective. Hell, the man practically told me he was offered Nelson's job." Eli Nelson had been a CIA operative recruited by The Collective. He'd run guns where it suited the corporations involved to keep civil wars going in order to spike prices on oil and other resources. He'd stolen technology plans from non-Collective companies. As far as Damon could tell, Nelson had planned and carried out a couple of terrorist plots that had aided the corporate bottom line. After the Taggarts had sent Nelson to his just rewards, Baz had become their go-to guy.

"The CIA believes Nelson was also working for MSS," Nigel explained.

Damon slapped a frustrated hand against the desk. "Tennessee Smith wants you to believe that. He's hiding something. Damn it. You don't have to believe me now. You just have to give me some tech staff so I can prove it. I'll find him, Nigel. I'll find that bastard if it's the last thing I do."

"How do you feel about moving into training?"

"I feel rabidly, violently opposed to it." He wasn't going to be relegated to the training gym. No. He didn't want to spend his time training recruits for the life that should have been his. He damn straight wasn't going to invest in a bunch of idiots who would likely get themselves killed. "I'm not a trainer. I'm never going to be a trainer, Nigel." He stood, his head swimming just a tad because it really was rather hard to breathe in this building. He couldn't imagine being chained to a desk day after day. It would be a living purgatory. "You'll have my resignation on your desk by noon."

He had absolutely no idea what he would do. The decision he needed to make about his future was here, and despite having seven months to think about it, he wasn't close to being ready for the outcome. Somehow he'd always thought he wouldn't be forced to face it.

He'd been sure he would die in the field like a good double *0* should, not get retired like a useless object.

He was thirty-nine years old and he had absolutely no idea what to do with the rest of his bloody life.

"Damon, please sit down. I might have a solution."

"What? I grow a new lung? Has tech managed to do that yet?" He could hear the bitterness dripping from his voice. Maybe he'd end up being one of those old men in a pub, barking at the world around him.

"We've had a situation come up, and you might be the only one who can take over."

He stopped, pulling his hand back off the door handle. "Is it an operation?"

Nigel gestured to the seat in front of him. "Yes, though it's not as dangerous as you're used to. It's fairly simple. We have intelligence that a known terrorist will be attempting to come into England using a cruise ship."

He snorted a little, settling back in his seat. "Even cruise ships require passports."

"Not in every port they don't."

He hadn't thought about it like that. A cruise ship required proper documentation to get on the boat. It depended on the port of call from there. Damon wasn't knowledgeable about their security protocols. He'd never been a holiday-type chap. If he went to a country, he wasn't sight-seeing. He was hunting. If Damon had been running a cruise ship, he would have required proper identification, including thumbprint scans, facial recognition, and routine pat downs for everyone getting on board.

There was a reason he didn't get invited to a lot of parties.

"What exactly do you mean? You think he's going to wander up from the beach on some island and make his way to London?"

"We believe he's targeted a very specific cruise. Cruises are usually full of children. This particular cruise is going to be all adult. It gives the target more of a chance to find someone he can change places with. We believe he intends to target someone with a legitimate passport, wait until he gets off the boat, and then kill the man and take his place. All he needs in most ports is a card the ship requires to get back on the boat."

It could work. "He would have to have someone on the inside."

"Yes. We believe he's got an English woman working for him, but we haven't figured out a name yet. Our source isn't particularly close to the heart of this group."

"What's the group?"

"It's a bit odd. We think this agent is working with Nature's Core."

He groaned. Nature's Core was an all-encompassing lefty group who thought the world would be a better place if the banking system was shut down. They fought against everything from new technology to CEO pay scales. They were normally quite peaceful, just obnoxious. "Then it's not a terrorist group. What are they going to do? Protest us to death? I will admit the smell they get after a month camping out in Hyde Park can be rather noxious."

"They're using Nature's Core as a screen to throw us off. Our source is absolutely certain that this operative is going to attempt to enter England with biological weapons."

Nigel was trying to send him on a wild goose chase. "How is he going to do that? Surely they have some security."

"They do, but if he got small amounts in every port, he might be able to either sneak them on board or claim that they're medicinal. Security won't know the difference between a biological agent and a vial of insulin if it is done properly. And no one will check his bags as he gets off the ship in Dover."

"If you know which ship it would come in on, why don't we just lock it down and search the place?"

"It's a two thousand passenger ship, Knight. And all he has to do is toss the package overboard. We need to catch him in the act. I want you to go on board, identify the target and his assistant, get control of the package, and bring everyone in for questioning."

It didn't sound too difficult. "Fine. Why does it have to be me?"

"Because the cruise ship is the Royale. It's the top of the line ship in the VIP Cruise Line. They're known for their specialty cruises."

"Like a GLBT cruise?" He'd heard of the company. They were a party line, very adult-experience oriented.

"Yes. Or their new alternate lifestyle cruise."

Damon sat forward, arching his brow. Seriously? "Are you telling me there's a bloody BDSM cruise running out of Dover?"

"Yes. I know you keep your lifestyle private, but I think you can see why you're perfect for this job. We have very little time to prepare. No more than a week and a half before you need to have a team on board." Nigel glanced out his window and then refocused on Damon. "If you can prove yourself here, perhaps I can convince the higher-ups to disregard the medical reports. The truth is you wouldn't be considered for this job except the two agents we had working it were involved in an auto accident. Harris broke both legs and Keller's face looks like one big bloody bruise. I obviously can't send her in as a submissive."

Nigel knew about his lifestyle, but they hadn't talked much about it besides Damon being forced to prove it didn't impact his security clearance. Other than that, Nigel hadn't wanted to know much.

"Why wasn't I brought in on this operation? I can't imagine you have anyone who understands the lifestyle better than I do." He reached for the folder Nigel was pushing across the desk. He ran through the particulars including the fact that the cruise was a twelve-day Baltic tour that went across Northern Europe.

He spoke Russian, but he would need a partner who spoke German at the very least, Danish and Finnish preferably.

"We began the operation before you were cleared for duty," Nigel explained.

It seemed a simple enough operation, but he would need more than one set of eyes. And he only had a week to prepare, so he would need his own people. He wasn't close to anyone here. Well, anyone who hadn't turned out to be a traitorous bastard. "Do you already have support in place?"

"This was Harris's operation. He wanted to do it quietly." The tightness of Nigel's voice told Damon he didn't agree.

Which was good because Harris was a bloody idiot. How did he expect to watch over an entire ship without backup? But then Harris had always been an arrogant prick who couldn't find his head because it was usually shoved up his arse.

"I'd like to bring in my own team. I'll want to put a couple on staff. Have we made contact with the cruise line?" It was a piece of shit assignment, but if it got him back in the field, he would work it with everything he had.

"We're stretched a bit thin, Knight. With Harris and Keller out of the picture for a bit, I was thinking about sending in a couple of analysts."

Good god. That would be perfectly dreadful. He needed operatives. He needed people who would take the shot when they needed to. Analysts would sit down and go through all the reasons why they shouldn't fire the gun before maybe taking the shot.

"I believe I have a friend who owes me, and he won't need to be brought up to speed about the lifestyle." He'd done Ian Taggart a favor by not hauling his information broker wife back to England. Ian and Charlotte would be perfect as long as he could keep them from having sex all over the ship.

And Taggart came with a whole crew he wouldn't have to train.

"Does he have a woman you can take in as your sub?"

Damn, it was weird to hear Nigel say the word "sub" and not mean something nautical by it. Damon ran through the women of McKay-Taggart. If he had to spend any amount of time playing in public with a sub, there was the chance of sex, the possibility that they would look odd if they weren't sexual in some fashion. He rather thought Ian would protest if he used his wife, and Alex would just shoot him first and ask questions later once Eve's name left his mouth. The rest all recently had babies.

Chelsea? She was smart and a bit ruthless and so uncomfortable with her own body that she would never work.

And it would be so much better to have someone who spoke a couple of languages.

"What about the blonde?" He tossed it out casually, not wanting Nigel to know how anxious he was. Penelope worked in translations. She was an analyst. Pretty, petite, perfectly round with nice-sized breasts and an ass that he could squeeze. Sweet. Submissive. His groin, dead since the accident, gave a good flare of life.

A quizzical look crossed Nigel's face. "Blonde? We have a few."

How did he not give himself away here? "She's a translator. Not sure what she translates. German, maybe. Curly blonde hair. She's complete shit at dressing herself. Pretty girl, but she doesn't know it."

"Are you talking about Penelope Cash?" Nigel's mouth practically hung open.

Penny Cash. God, her parents must have hated her. "I believe so. She would work."

"You want to take Penelope Cash on a fetish cruise? Well, uhm, she actually speaks German, Danish, and Finnish and her Russian is fairly good."

"She sounds perfect." She was a mouse, a cute little mouse who obviously needed a very good fuck. She was kind and sweet and a bit of a doormat. He might be able to teach her a thing or two. And he might be able to break out of his rut. Seven months and not a single erection. He was a bit worried that it didn't work anymore.

"All right. I suppose it's your team, but she's very quiet. I don't know that she'll suit you at all."

She was quiet, submissive. She wouldn't give him hell in the field. He should be able to control her. He didn't need a woman he had to worry would disobey him. He needed a sub, and from what he'd seen, Penelope fit the bill better than anyone else in the office. Coupled with the fact that she spoke the languages and he could halfway see himself fucking her—she was practically perfect.

It wasn't that he was really attracted to her. It was just that she was his type. That was all. He would have to keep an emotional distance from her. No, the fact that he'd thought about her when he'd almost died had been random. She'd simply been kind to him and he liked to reward kindness. In this particular case, he might reward her kindness with multiple orgasms.

"She's not married, is she?" He hadn't seen her in seven months. A lot could happen. He'd heard she'd been engaged at one point. That wouldn't suit. He really would likely have to screw her and possibly in a public setting. It didn't bother him at all. He could fuck with an audience all day, but some husbands might object.

He didn't like the thought of her having a husband.

"Penelope? No. I don't believe she even dates."

Excellent, then no one would get in the way. "Perfect."

"Well, you have to convince her first."

Damon huffed, allowing a bit of his arrogance to show. He might have lost a step or two physically, but the bullet hadn't taken his charm. "I think I can handle one small female."

She wouldn't turn down the chance to serve Queen and country. Of course, in serving Queen and country, she would find herself serving him. His cock stirred for the first time in forever.

Yes, going back to the field would be good for him.

* * * *

"I'm sorry. What did you say, sir?" Penny asked because she couldn't possibly have heard him right. No. He hadn't said what she'd thought he'd said.

Nigel Crowe hadn't just told her he was partnering her with Damon Knight and putting them in the field together where they would pose as lovers. He hadn't said that because that would be utterly ridiculous.

And she really wished Damon Knight wasn't standing behind him, looming over the proceedings like a gloriously dark angel. The man was far too big, too grim, too gorgeous for her to be able to breathe in the same room with him.

The head of the double *0* program shook his head. "I seem to be having an enormous amount of difficulty making myself plain today."

She was screwing up. She was a bloody translator. She understood words and their nuances in many different languages, but nothing was computing today.

"He meant what he said." Knight's voice was like rich dark chocolate. It seemed to flow from those gorgeous lips of his to caress her skin as though he was talking only to her, and no one else in the world mattered. She'd never had that deep voice turned specifically on her. Oh, he'd said the occasional hello before and once he'd thanked her for baking him a cake—though he hadn't eaten it—but she'd never held an actual long conversation with him.

Which was good because apparently she struggled with the power of speech around the man. Their whole relationship involved him asking her to translate things and her acting like a drooling idiot.

"Miss Cash, this is an operation of the highest priority, though we believe there is very little risk to your person," Nigel explained.

"I'll take care of you." Knight had his arms crossed over his chest, those stark gray eyes pinning her to the chair.

"I don't understand. I'm a translator." She didn't go into the field. The entire idea was silly.

"You passed your physical." Knight seemed to have taken over the meeting. Though he didn't move an inch, there was something active about the way he stood and stared at her. He was like a large predatory cat just waiting for her to make the wrong move so he could attack.

So he could jump on her. His body on hers. Her body under his. He was so big, would she even be able to breathe if he gave her his full weight? He had to be sixteen and a half stone, and every bit of it was pure muscle. She'd seen him without a shirt once. He'd been in a training room, running on a treadmill, sweat glistening off his perfectly formed chest. He looked a bit like she suspected Greek gods would have looked.

She'd heard all the horrible stories about his injury seven months before, but, god, he looked healthy today. Good enough to eat.

"You didn't pass your physical?" Knight asked, one dark brow rising.

God, how long had she been sitting there staring at him like an idiot? "No, I passed."

Barely. Though she had been hitting the gym a bit in the last several months. Exercise was supposed to be good for lifting the spirits. It had lifted her rear at least.

"Excellent. And you passed the firearms courses. I don't expect that you should have to actually use one, but you'll be issued a sidearm." He moved suddenly, his big body uncoiling as he reached for a file folder. "This is the basic information about the operation. Obviously, it's for your eyes only."

She stared at the folder like it might bite her. "I'm a translator."

"Who seems to be having a bit of trouble with English today," Knight quipped. "Yes, you're a translator. That's why I need you. This operation is going to take us to Germany, Denmark, and Finland. You speak the languages."

She was freakishly good with languages, and she'd been raised in a home where several had been spoken. Her grandmother had grown up in a small town in Finland and spoke Finnish around her constantly. Her father's family was German. She'd picked up the language in summers spent in Bavaria. She'd learned Danish because her brother had bet her she couldn't. But there was a problem with the scenario Knight laid out. "Almost everyone in those countries speaks English, you know."

A superior huff came out of Knight's mouth. "Yes, darling, they do. They are spectacularly well educated. So smart, in fact, that they tend to speak their own languages when they don't want the idiot Brits to know what they're saying. I don't suspect that they'll switch to English when they discuss their nefarious plans. We have twenty suspects. We're going to bug their rooms. I doubt those conversations will conveniently take place in English. And there's the fact that if we need to follow the suspects into the countryside, the farther you get from the cities, the more likely I'll need a translator."

She finally took the file and flipped through it. "I thought you said this was a potential terrorist. Shouldn't you be looking for someone who speaks the Middle Eastern languages?"

"Yes, because all terrorists are Middle Eastern."

God, she sounded like a complete idiot. "I know that. Uhm, you think this is tied to Nature's Core?"

"Yes," Nigel said.

"Not at all," Knight interjected. Then a smooth smile crossed that perfect face of his. He was a hard-looking man, his face all angles and roughhewn planes, but when he smiled he damn near took her breath away. "I mean, yes. Yes. The files explain it. And Nature's Core is a German group. So you can see why I need a woman who speaks German."

"To pretend to be your lover." The words sounded dumb. He was gorgeous and sophisticated. The suit he was currently wearing likely had a designer label attached. She was wearing a shapeless skirt and a cardie that she'd probably picked up at a car boot sale. She had kinky blonde hair and wore glasses. She was a bit overweight. Just a bit.

She set the file back down on Nigel's desk. She couldn't read it when all her brain was thinking about was Damon Knight.

He moved again, walking around Crowe's desk and coming to stand right in front of her. She was taken by how he seemed to occupy the space around him. There was no way to ignore Damon Knight unless he wanted her to. He reached out and took her hand in his.

And her heart rate tripled.

"I think it won't be such a challenge, love."

Dear god, she'd actually become quite…excited. She could feel herself getting moist and hot, her female parts softening right up the minute he touched her. It was deeply disconcerting since she hadn't actually had that reaction to a man in…ever.

She hadn't had sex in several years. She couldn't even pretend to be the type of woman who would share a bed with Damon Knight. And if she was right, she actually would be sharing a bed with him. They would be going on this cruise together, and he would likely insist on keeping up all appearances and that meant one bed.

One bed that she would share with him, lying beside him, feeling the heat of his body.

Not being alone for once.

"What do you say, darling? Let's go on a cruise." He was using charm on her now. He should have stuck with the grim reaper act because she could turn down charm.

She pulled her hand from his. "I can't."

"Why not?"

"I'm not a field agent, Mr. Knight. I'm a translator. I listen in on conversations and translate them."

He got to one knee in front of her so they were almost on the same level. He took her hand back, sliding it palm up between both of his. She was suddenly surrounded by warmth. "I know it sounds a bit frightening. We've lost agents in the past, but this is going to be different. I promise you. I'll take care of you in every way. While the operation is a priority, I will put your safety and security above everything else. Do you understand? I'm going to make sure that nothing bad happens to you. It's going to be my goal to ensure that you have a pleasurable experience. It's a cruise, Penelope. For the most part, we're going to relax and let the support staff do their jobs. You're going to be there in case I need your talents, but your primary job is to give me a reason to be on that boat. I can't go on without a female. You'll be my girl, you see. You'll be with me and that means that I'll always be around to protect you."

His every word seemed to sink into her skin, drawing her into those eyes. If he kept it up, her tongue would be on the floor or trying to get into his mouth because he was so close, all she could think about was kissing him.

She couldn't. She couldn't kiss him because it was ridiculous and she would look like an utter twit. No. She wasn't this person. She wasn't the girl who took on assignments and pretended to be a double 0's girl. She was the type of girl who went home at night and had tea and watched telly.

Penny stood, unable to be close to him a moment longer. "I'm sorry. You'll have to find someone else."

His face hardened, eyes going dark. He'd gone from charm to menace in an instant, and Penny had to wonder which one was the act and which was the real Damon Knight. She rather thought she was looking at him now. "There isn't anyone else. I'm out of time. I need at least ten days to get you properly trained and ready to go. We need to start by Monday, so I'm going to give you the weekend to think about this and come to the proper conclusion."

"Juliet speaks German." He hadn't moved an inch toward her, but she suddenly felt stalked. She took a step toward the door, wanting to flee. If Nigel Crowe hadn't been in the room, she likely would have, but she needed to keep her job and that meant showing some small amount of backbone.

"No." Knight gave no explanation, just a sharp shake of his head.

Crowe stood with a sigh. "Unfortunately, I've looked into this, Miss Cash. You really are the only one with the proper credentials. We are in a bit of a bind here. Perhaps you could reconsider. I understand that it might seem distasteful to you..."

Knight snorted, an oddly aristocratic sound. "She's scared out of her mind, Nige, and I rather think it isn't about taking a bullet. She's not stupid. She knows I'll keep her safe. So that makes me wonder what really frightens her. I think she's a prudish chit and she's worried I'll get her knickers off."

Lexi Blake

Now there wasn't any thought to backing off. There was the real
Damon Knight, and she was so happy he'd finally shown up.
Arrogant. A bit mean. Yes, that she could handle. "Did you ever stop
to wonder if perhaps I'm simply not interested in even pretending to
sleep with you?"

"No. Not once."

"Maybe I don't like men, Mr. Knight." The minute she said it
she wanted to take it back, but it wasn't the first time her
stubbornness had gotten her in trouble. If SIS wanted to fire her for
being a pseudo lesbian, let them.

"Oh, you like men, love. And you like me. Why do you think I
got so close to you? Why do you think I slid my thumb over your
pulse? Because I needed to know how I affected your heart rate. I
needed to see how your eyes dilated the minute I touched you. And I
definitely wanted to know if I could get a whiff of arousal coming
from between your thighs."

"You bastard." She could feel her cheeks flushing, shame
threatening to overtake her because she knew just how aroused she'd
gotten. Still was. God, she had to be sick to still find the man
attractive.

His face softened slightly. "It's all right. It's nothing at all to be
ashamed of. I know we tend to devalue sexuality in this country, but
I think it's a lovely thing. If it makes you feel better, come here and
bump up against me. You'll find I've got a hard-on."

She couldn't help it. Her eyes went there. Sure enough, his
slacks had tented. Impressively.

"I had the same reaction." His voice was all seduction now. "It's
all right. Let's go somewhere and talk about this. I was wrong to
approach you in such a crass manner. I'll be honest. I'm usually
much smoother than that. Give me a chance to take you to lunch and
we can be civilized."

But it was all an act. He could wear a thousand pound suit, but
there was a predator underneath it. One she couldn't handle. If she
walked out with him, he would very likely smooth talk her in to
agreeing and she would be underneath him by the time the boat left
Dover.

30

And what the hell was wrong with that?

What was wrong with having an adventure? What was wrong with having an affair? She'd lived her whole life serving the people around her. What exactly was wrong with doing one completely insane thing?

"Knight, back off." Nigel was standing, his face a grim mask. "I believe you've done enough damage for the day. Let the girl go."

Knight's face went a polite blank. "Of course."

He stepped around her, making sure he didn't poke her with the erection that was still obvious. He opened the door and closed it behind him without saying another word.

"You'll forgive him. He's not himself." Nigel smoothed his tie down. "He's struggling with the fact that his career is changing. This operation was important to him."

"I'm sorry." Her heart was still racing.

Nigel held a hand up. "I'll attempt to find someone else."

She nodded and turned, her hand on the knob, the same place he'd touched just moments before. "How likely is it that you'll find someone in time?"

"Highly unlikely. We'll have to figure something else out. But you don't need to worry about that. Just continue your work. And it would be nice if you didn't mention Knight's state of…well, perhaps you could pretend he didn't proposition you in my office."

"Of course." She wasn't about to bring him up on sexual harassment charges. She had no illusions who would win that battle.

Or would he? He'd been injured. His career was changing? That could only mean that SIS wasn't sure of his status. He'd been shot. Everyone had talked about it, but no one in her department knew exactly how bad it had been. He'd been gone for months. She'd been so lost in her own grief after her mum died that she hadn't thought about him in forever. Well, not in anything but a fantasy way. She probably had never really thought about who he was as a man. Beyond his gorgeous face and his amazing body, there was still a man under there.

How hard would it be for a man like Knight to know that his whole career depended on one translator?

"I'll give you my answer on Monday."

Crowe sat up straighter. "I rather thought you'd already given me your answer."

"Do you really think you can't find anyone else?"

"I believe we won't find anyone as qualified as you, but Miss Cash, you should understand that this is going to be a very, how should I put it, a very intimate operation. This cruise that the target is on is a cruise for people in what many would call a sexually deviant lifestyle. I really didn't think Knight should even ask you, but he insisted."

She had to work to make sure her jaw didn't drop open. "What sort of sexually deviant lifestyle? Is it one large orgy? A swinging thing?"

"No. Not at all. I've rather heard many of these men are deeply possessive of their partners. That doesn't mean you wouldn't see public sex, but Knight certainly wouldn't ask you to sleep with anyone, well, anyone except him, very likely." Crowe, who had overseen more bloody missions than Penny could even count, seemed deeply awkward talking about sex. She thought he'd rather be discussing the terrorist plot. "It wasn't well done of him to ask you. I tried to explain that to him."

It wasn't well done of him to ask her on the mission or to ask her on an operation that might include having sex with him to keep up their cover? She wasn't sure she liked the sound of either. It was perverse. Crowe was supporting her position, but now she felt a well of stubborn will rise up. "Well, I am a member of this organization. I do have security clearance. And I knew that I could be asked to go into the field if I was needed."

"Yes, of course, but this isn't the type of operation you should be on. You're a nice young lady. You certainly shouldn't be exposed to that sort of thing."

That sort of thing? Sex? He thought she shouldn't be exposed to sex? Well, it wasn't like she hadn't thought the same thing, but it hurt. "Is the lifestyle situation detailed in the report?"

He picked up the file. "There is information on it, yes."

"And Mr. Knight knows about this lifestyle?" She had to admit she was curious. Curious about everything.

And she owed it to Mr. Knight to at least read the file. She couldn't do it herself, but perhaps they weren't thinking of everyone. Maybe she could help them find someone who would be suitable. "I'll take a look at it."

"If you're sure." He let her take the folder. "But obviously no one expects you to accept." He emphasized the "you."

And she felt that deep sense of completely unrealistic outrage again. "We'll see."

Before she turned, she thought she caught just a hint of a smile and wondered if Nigel Crowe wasn't playing her for everything she was worth.

And she suddenly wondered if it just might work.

Chapter Two

He'd fucked up royally.

Damon stood in the middle of Paddington station, the Saturday crowd milling around him, the smells of coffee and baked goods filling the space, and considered the problem he'd created for himself.

He'd completely lost his cool. He'd damn near rubbed his cock all over Penelope Cash and then wondered why on earth she didn't want to work with him. The entire afternoon before had been a classic fuckup. He'd been a tosser and she'd been a prude. Well, at least on the outside she'd been a prude.

Why didn't she want to work with him? He hadn't been insane. He really had felt her pulse, seen her eyes dilate, gotten a hint of the sweetest arousal coming from between her legs.

If he'd slid his hands up that plug-ugly skirt she'd been wearing, if he'd caressed her thighs and made his way to her pussy, he was damn sure he would have found her wet and squirming. And all right in Nigel's office. How would she respond to him when he got her in a dungeon?

There was a whooshing sound that signaled the arrival of the train he'd been waiting on.

Paddington station was a massive hub, a testament to the power of London transport. To his right, he could get to the Tube and go just about anywhere in London proper. But the train platforms in front of him led to the rest of England, and more importantly to Heathrow.

The Heathrow Express pulled into the station, stopping quietly, its shiny silver doors opening with almost a preternatural quiet.

What came out of the train wasn't quiet. What came out of the train was likely to be a pain in his arse.

"I'm just saying you didn't separate Li from his newborn." A big man with military-cut dark hair and broad shoulders was complaining as he muscled out with a duffel bag over one arm and a massive suitcase handle in the other.

Ian Taggart had his own baggage. "Li doesn't have a partner. If you wanted to get paternity leave—god, I just vomited a little—then you should have manned up and gotten your own girl. Adam won the battle fair and square. He gets to stay with the wife and rug rat."

"It wasn't a fucking battle. It was rock, paper, scissors, damn it. I think Adam cheated." Jacob Dean frowned as he looked up and finally caught sight of Damon. "Hey. You suck. Don't you have like a whole fucking country of Brits to do your job for you? You have to hire us?"

So not everyone was happy with the assignment. Lovely. "Sorry about that."

"I have a kid who's going to grow up while I'm gone, thanks to you. I need some coffee. Your immigration officers suck." Jake walked off, his every move a testament to his annoyance.

Ian just grinned as though he loved the chaos.

The rest of the crew had stepped off the train and were rearranging their baggage. Charlotte Taggart smiled as she looked around the station, her blue eyes taking in everything. Simon Weston had seen it all. He had come home and didn't exactly look happy about it. Jesse Murdoch rubbed his eyes as though he'd just woken from a nap.

And then there was Chelsea Dennis. She pulled her suitcase out of the train, the last one to leave. She was a petite woman, twenty-seven years old. She favored her left leg. He recalled she'd had both legs broken quite badly, but the left had never healed properly and she walked with a limp. Pretty enough, though there was a darkness about her, like a cloud followed her around.

God, so unlike Penelope. She was a little light even though she obviously didn't know it. Her light wasn't brilliantly bright like Charlotte Taggart's. She didn't light up the room when she walked into it, but a man could look at Penelope Cash and know that she would try her damnedest to take care of him.

No one took care of him. No one ever had really. Not since his parents had died.

Fuck. He wasn't a child. He didn't need someone to take bloody care of him. He just needed a sub, and like it or not, Chelsea Dennis might be the answer to his problems.

Taggart stepped up, his hand out. "Knight. Good to see you. Sorry about Jake. He's had a rough day. He got a pat down at security. I'm pretty sure Adam arranged that. He's been pissy about it ever since."

Damon clasped his friend's hand. Yes, Big Tag was a pain in the arse, but he'd been a damn fine friend. It had been Ian's home he'd gone to once he'd gotten out of hospital. It had been Ian who pushed him to get strong, who hadn't given him a minute's pity.

Penelope likely would have held his hand and baked him biscuits. Yeah, he didn't need that.

"I'm sorry about dragging Dean away." He couldn't even understand the idea of ankle biters or changing nappies. Jacob Dean was a stone-cold killer. He'd moved through the ranks of US Special Forces, gaining the nickname Ghost for how quietly he could move, how easily he brought death to the enemy.

Now he wasn't quiet. He was bitching at some poor shopkeeper about his coffee.

"I told him he should have read his job description. It plainly states that he's an *International* Super Spy," Taggart explained. "If he'd wanted to stay in Dallas, he should have applied for *Regional* Super Spy."

Jesse pulled his jacket open. "Big Tag made us badges and everything."

Sure enough he was wearing a cheeky name tag. *Jesse Murdoch—International Super Spy.*

Sometimes he didn't understand the Americans. "Well, thanks for coming so quickly anyway."

"We had a choice?" Weston asked, buttoning his suit coat. He wasn't wearing a cheeky name tag. He was dressed to the nines, his suit impeccably tailored without a hint of wrinkling. The bastard must have changed. No one could get through a nine-hour overnight flight, hours in immigration and customs, and still look as perfect as Simon Weston. He glanced around the station as though looking for whatever was going to try to kill him next.

"Simon, chill," Taggart ordered with a smile on his face. "It's all good. Charlie here isn't in Brit jail and we had a nice first-class flight."

It was time to fuck with Taggart. "I'm so sorry, Tag. You do understand that we're not actually reimbursing you for that. The deal was that you would do us some favors. Favors that don't include any exchange of cash."

Ian turned the funniest shade of red.

His wife stepped up, a frown on her pretty face. She put a hand on her husband's shoulder as though physically restraining him. "He's joking, baby. I already got the paperwork started. Now follow Jacob and get some coffee. We'll expense that, too."

Ian pointed a single finger Damon's way. "I will kill you and bury you. Don't think I won't."

He stormed off, and Damon couldn't help but chuckle.

Charlotte turned that frown to Damon. "Don't tease him. Do you know what the rest of us have been through? Do you have any idea what a first-class flight costs at the last minute? He's turned into a penny-pinching asshole. He yelled at me the other day for buying raspberries for four dollars. Four freaking dollars. I've heard lectures on getting nickeled-and-dimed for months and all because we had to write you an enormous check. So you will pay for everything while we are here. Are we understood, Knight?"

She was awfully cute when she was mad. And she had written SIS a massive check in exchange for keeping her very nice arse out of jail. She'd also given them information the analysts were still going through. She'd been The Broker, a powerful information dealer. "Yes, ma'am."

She nodded slightly and seemed to catch sight of something. "Oh, thank god. The champagne bar is open. You're paying for that, too. Let's go, Chels."

Simon followed the women, Jesse yawning at his side.

Damon watched as they walked away and realized why he'd really called them in.

He'd wanted a team. Even if he didn't really belong to the team, he wanted one around him.

Thirty minutes later, he, Ian, and Charlotte were ensconced in the limo Damon had hired to take the Taggarts to their very posh London hotel. The others had scattered, taking up their respective covers, though they would all come together at The Garden later.

He pulled out the documentation he'd had made up for them. "Here are your passports and itinerary. I think you'll find the hotel adequate."

Taggart took the files but didn't look at them. Instead his eyes narrowed. "What's wrong with this op?"

"Besides the fact that the previous operation leader and his partner were in an accident?"

"Yes, besides that. Now that we're alone, I want you to level with me." Taggart always could read between the lines. It was what had made him a brilliant Agency asset.

There was so much wrong about it, but Damon knew where to start. "I don't know, but it seems odd that Nature's Core suddenly decided to get violent."

Charlotte put a hand on her husband's thigh, the motion so subtle it was obviously not even conscious. "Didn't a couple of kids get hurt in a demonstration in Frankfurt a few months ago?"

Taggart ran his hand around the back of her seat. "It's not the same, baby. That was a protest that got out of hand. This is different. This is far more sophisticated. They've always been against biological testing, but now they want to unleash a bioweapon in London? It makes one wonder exactly who's in charge."

This was the other reason he wanted Tag with him—because he was a paranoid bastard. "We suspect one of the women on the cruise is working with the terrorist cell. I asked Adam to check into the registry and find anyone with strong corporate or intelligence ties."

"Fuck me. You think it's Baz."

"No. I worry it may be The Collective." Baz didn't matter. The Collective was all that mattered. If Baz got caught in the net, it would be outstanding. But he wasn't going to allow his anger to rule him. Emotion was not his friend. He needed to remain cold, calculating.

Taggart turned thoughtful. "And MI6 doesn't believe The Collective exists. What the fuck is Ten thinking? I read that report he submitted. It's a load of BS. He's playing some angle."

"Have you thought about the fact that Ten might be working with them?" It was his greatest fear. Tennessee Smith ran a great deal of the CIA's field operations. If he was corrupt, they were all screwed.

"I can't believe it." Taggart shook his head. "He's playing some angle, but he's not with them. I know that fucker. He's perfectly capable of sleeping with anything with female parts—and I do mean anything. I'm pretty sure I caught him with a goat once."

"Ian!" Charlotte said.

Taggart shrugged. "That woman needed a shave. It's all I'm saying. The point is, Ten is loyal. So something else is going on. He's also not an idiot. If he thought he might have a leak, he would want that person to feel safe and he can't do that if he runs around proclaiming he's found out the truth. Could that be what's happening with MI6?"

"No. They really are idiots." He sighed. Taggart deserved to know the whole truth about what he was getting into. "They're trying to get me to retire."

"Excellent." Taggart clapped his hands together. "I'm thinking about opening a New York office. When can you start?"

Everyone wanted him behind a bloody desk. "I'm not retiring and I'm not managing an office for you."

"Come on, Knight. I promise to send someone to assassinate you at least once a month. It'll keep your adrenaline up. It's not so bad,

39

man. Hell, I'm lying. It's horrible. You get to sit around and listen to everyone whine constantly. 'I need time off. My wife is giving birth. I can't sleep with that target in order to get information because I'm a faithful husband.' God, they constantly whine at me."

"You were wrong to ask Li to sleep with that woman." Charlotte shook her head.

"Well, I really needed her computer and she liked Irish guys. Is it my fault everyone's getting married? I'm relying on Simon and Jesse as my man meat. And when I need a pretty girl, I have to hire Karina. Do you know what she charged me last time? Two hundred dollars an hour. She charged me two hundred fucking dollars an hour to sit in the bar and flirt while Adam retrieved the stolen corporate data. I could have hired a prostitute for less and she would have blown the dude. The point is, I need Knight because he won't ever get married, and therefore I can throw him out there when I need someone to charm the ladies."

Charlotte stared at her husband for a moment and then a brilliant smile crossed her face. "You should be so glad I love you."

"I am, baby. You're the only one who gets my charm." He winked his wife's way and then gestured to Damon. "But Knight here is a different story. If we can convince him to work for us, we won't have to worry about beefcake any more. Simon gets touchy about being seen as a sexual object. Jesse is fine if the lady in question wants a fairly attractive insane idiot, but you're a gold mine, man."

"I think you're overestimating my charms, mate. That brings me to my second problem. And just to make things clear, I would never work for you. I would murder you first. You're an obnoxious nutter, so you can take your whole job offer and piss off."

Taggart shrugged as though he'd expected nothing less. "All right, then. What's problem number two?"

He hated to admit to it but Taggart might be his solution. He'd managed to get Chelsea clearance to work the technical side of the op despite her sister's problems with several major intelligence agencies. Damon had actually tried to hire Charlotte the year before, but she'd chosen to stay with her husband. "I need a sub."

"You have a club. Pick one."

"It's not that easy. The submissives at the club won't pass with SIS. I need a trained female, or one who at least brings something to the operation other than looking good when I spank her." Penelope likely would have looked lovely. Her bum was a thing of beauty no matter how hard she tried to hide it. That was a big, gorgeous arse on the woman.

"And there's no one at MI6?" Taggart used the American version of the Secret Intelligence Service. It had once been called Military Intelligence. The sixth section was the foreign section. Hence MI6. James Bond and a rash of like films and movies kept the old moniker alive.

"Yes. I found one, but she doesn't want the job." He'd been turned down by an uptight translator. Some Lothario he was.

"How can she turn it down if she's an operative?" Charlotte asked.

"She isn't. She's a translator. She's never been in the field before, but she's got all the proper requirements and I believe she's actually quite submissive. She's single, so I don't have to worry about a husband. Her name is Penelope, and she speaks most of the languages we need."

"And you don't mind fucking her?"

"Ian." It seemed like Taggart's wife said his name a lot.

"Well, that's what we're talking about," Taggart shot back. "We can't go on a massive floating dungeon and not get physical."

"No. I wouldn't mind fucking her," Damon replied. He'd actually sort of looked forward to it. "But it's obvious she doesn't want the job, so I need to ask you about Chelsea."

Both Taggarts stopped, staring at him for a minute.

"My sister?" Charlotte asked.

"The bitch from hell?" Ian offered and immediately moved out of his wife's reach. "She doesn't like me, baby. She calls me Satan. It hurts my feelings."

She growled a little. "You don't have feelings. And no. She is not going to play your sub, especially when there might be sex involved. No way."

"It should be up to her," Ian said quietly, turning serious. "You can't protect her forever. The only reason she's working this operation is Serena convinced her to take Adam's place so he could stay home and help take care of Tristan. Jake should be shot for letting them pick that name. That boy is going to get his ass kicked starting in preschool. If Serena hadn't convinced her, she would still be sitting at home brooding about whatever the fuck it is she broods about. She needs a job, and she won't take one with me."

"It's not like she's going to go to the supermarket and get a job sacking groceries, Ian. But she's not an operative," Charlotte complained.

"She's not trained," Taggart replied. "But I wouldn't hesitate to send her into the field. From a strictly business standpoint, she's made of the right stuff to be a successful field operative."

Which meant she was cold, calculating. Like they were. Unlike Penelope Cash, who he would have to watch over. He would very likely not need to protect Chelsea Dennis. She could handle herself. It would be better that way. It really would. "So we can talk to her about it?"

Ian leaned forward, his business face on. "You'll get pushback from Simon. There's something odd going on with them. She'll need to go to the shooting range and prove she can handle a gun. And I would watch her closely. Not because I'm worried about her. I don't know where her loyalties really lie."

"How can you talk about her like that?" Charlotte asked.

"Because I'm being the boss right now, Charlie. This is an op, and it's an operation you're involved in. I have to make sure it runs properly. I would never put you in this position because you're far too emotional. You work with me and me alone because I don't trust your safety to anyone else. Chelsea is different. Chelsea can handle herself. God knows she'll put her own safety first. She'll be fine."

Charlotte got a little teary. "She's not like that. You just don't know her. Please, Ian."

Damon waited as they seemed to wage a small but important war.

Taggart's mouth became a flat line, and he looked back at

Damon. "No. Chelsea can't go in the field. She's strictly tech."

Charlotte turned and hugged him, whispering a "thank you."

Ian Taggart was well and truly caught, and it fucked up Damon's day.

"Sorry, man. You need to talk to that girl again," Ian said, leaning into his wife, giving her the comfort she seemed to require. "If she's perfect, then you'll just have to convince her. Bring her to the club. If she's submissive, she'll be curious. You need to use that curiosity. Let Charlie talk to her. She's awfully persuasive."

Damon stared out as the limo slowed, caught in the never-ending London traffic. To his right, Hyde Park looked peaceful, tourists and locals milling about on a nice Saturday. Not a care in the world.

What was Penelope Cash doing?

And how was he going to convince her?

* * * *

Penny closed her laptop, her face heated, her heart pounding. *Submission. Dominance. Discipline.*

If she took this assignment, she would find out just what those words meant. Kinky sex stuff. It was kinky, weird sex stuff. Distasteful. She should march right back into Nigel's office and shove his file in his face and tell him she was a lady and she wouldn't be used as a prostitute.

Except it wasn't really distasteful and she was rapidly discovering she wasn't the prude everyone thought she was.

She'd known that. She'd never cared what people did in their own bedrooms. Or dungeons. Or playrooms. Or wherever people wanted to do the consensual things they did. She just didn't think she wanted that for herself. She'd always imagined herself with a nice man, a quiet intellectual who she could talk to and raise a family with.

Of course, she'd had that man. Peter had been kind and quiet and should have been perfect. So why had she avoided sex with him after a couple of months of being engaged? She told herself that it was because her mother had gotten sick, but there had been chances to see him, chances to keep their relationship together, and she'd let them all drift by. By the time he'd left her, she'd actually felt grateful.

Her mobile trilled, the sound surprising her a bit. She looked down. Her sister. Diana was trying. Trying hard, and it wasn't like she hadn't lost anything. "Hello, Diana."

"Pen. I wanted to ring to see if you need any help packing. I'll see you at the wedding, but I can come down today if you need me. I know how much work there is to do. I really think you're going to be happier, but you know you can stay as long as you want. George and I don't mind. The house is yours."

She felt a small smile crease her lips up. "I want to go with something smaller, and I'm going to split the money with you."

They'd been having this argument for months, but it made her feel oddly secure. There was a lot of money in the house, but her siblings weren't fighting her. She was having to fight to get them to take their portions. George was handling the legalities, and Diana had pitched in.

It made her realize how much she'd pushed her siblings away, how much she'd taken on her own shoulders.

She got up and walked to the largest of the three bedrooms. Her parents' room. She'd put it off long enough, and now she was packing up her mother's things, keeping a few items, but giving away the clothes and knickknacks that represented her mother's life. She pushed the speaker phone option and continued talking to her sister as she worked, emptying the dresser. "I'm fine, Diana. I'm almost done. There's just the bedroom and then the kitchen. I'll be ready to put it on the market in a couple of weeks."

"All right. I just want to make sure I'm helping."

She was overcompensating. "She knew you loved her, Diana. You came every week."

"She didn't know me at all at the end, Pen. And George and I let you take the load. I should have moved her in with me."

Around the children? Her mother could get violent when she had an episode. "No. Please let it go. I don't want to talk about this. We've discussed it and you've apologized."

"Fine, I'll let it go for now. I'll see you tomorrow, right? You won't leave me and George alone with the horrible Hendersons, will you?"

Their cousin, Beatrice Cash-Henderson, was marrying some posh nob and Penny had gotten dragged into the wedding. It was being held at some expensive club where Bea and her nasty sisters would lord it over the rest of the family.

And she'd promised to go.

"I think I feel a bout of Ebola coming on, Diana."

"Oh, don't you do that. There is no hemorrhagic fever in London. You're going and that's that. I'll see you there. Do you want me to get you a date? I met a nice doctor the other day. He works at University College. I think you would like him."

Her skin nearly crawled. The last time Diana had tried to set her up had been with an accountant who spent the entire night bemoaning the British tax system. "No. Oh, no. I'm fine going by myself."

It would be miserable because everyone would ask her who she was seeing and why she'd let Peter go, and oh, did she really want to become an old maid and everyone knew some nice man they wanted to set her up with. Then there were a few who really thought she was a lesbian and tried to set her up with a nice lady.

It was the burden of being single and in her thirties.

She should date, but all she could think about now was Damon Knight and his devil's bargain.

Diana chatted on for another few moments and then they hung up. Penny was left alone with the sum of her mother's life. She took a long breath. Soon this house would belong to someone else. Some other group of kids would run and play in the garden in the back. They would fight and share secrets and grow up right here where she had.

It was odd to think that she'd spent her whole life in one place and now her future was somewhere else. It was a bit frightening.

She could stay here. George and Diana wouldn't mind. She would be comfortable here. She could move right into her mother's room and nothing would change.

Her hand came up against something hard in the last drawer. Odd. The dresser only had clothes in it. She pulled it free. It was a small notebook. A long sigh came from her chest. Her mother's recipe book.

A sheen of tears hit her eyes as she sat back on the bed and started to flip through her mum's personal versions of Yorkshire pudding, pot roast, popovers. All her favorites. The book had gone missing a year before and she'd been worried that her mother had lost it.

The recipes were written in her mum's steady hand, each one a memory for Penny.

Until she got to the last page. It wasn't a recipe she found there. It was a letter.

My Dearest Heart,

I'm lucid now. The times that I remember are getting further and further between and I need to talk to you but you're at work. The nurse is kind, but I don't trust her to remember what I need to say to you. George and Diana will be fine. They took after your father. They'll find themselves and forge their own lives, but I am so worried about you, my Penny.

I know you've put life on hold to take care of me, and I can't thank you enough. I wish it weren't necessary. But I fear that you will continue to put your life on hold. Much as I did.

There is always an excuse to not do something. I wanted to go to university. I wanted to teach. But it was always something I would do next year or after the children were grown or after your father was settled. Tomorrow never comes when you keep telling it no.

I loved your father, loved you children, but I wanted more. I wanted something for myself. I fear if you continue down this path, you will have nothing for you, dear girl, and that would be a tragedy.

I'm going to leave this out and hope you find it. If you don't, then you will likely discover this after I'm gone and I want you to stop grieving. Stop it this instant. Do one thing for me. I will only ask one thing more of you, my darling girl.

Say yes.

Say yes to one thing that frightens you, that intrigues, that you think you can't do. Say yes and don't look back. It will or it won't be, but you'll never know if you don't say yes.

Her mother's handwriting became indecipherable, the script turning into doodles as the dementia had obviously overtaken her again.

But the words had penetrated Penny's soul. She stared though she couldn't see through her tears.

If she stayed here she would never start her life. She would never begin that essential piece of a life—the part where she had no idea what the next day would bring. She'd gotten comfortable with the daily rituals of serving her family.

It was time to figure out who the hell she was, and she couldn't do it here. She couldn't do it if she was always, always so afraid.

Her mother had sent her a lifeline, a prayer for her.

Without another thought, without letting her brain take back over, she found her phone. The number she needed had been left in the file, and she dialed it with shaking hands.

One chance. If she didn't do this, she likely would wake up tomorrow and come up with some excuse to go back to her safe life, but some decisions had to come from emotion, from instinct—from love.

The phone rang once and then again.

"This is Knight." His deep voice rumbled into her ear.

If she did this, she would likely have sex with him. She would know what it meant to be Damon Knight's lover.

"Penelope? Darling, are you there?" He was back to oozing charm. He must have seen her name on his caller identification.

"Yes." She said it.

"Yes, what?"

"Yes."

She could practically hear his satisfaction. "Yes. You said yes."

"I'll see you Monday." When he'd said they had to start training. God, she was going to let him train her. In kinky things. In things that made her heart pound. Maybe she would finally understand what sex meant.

She hung up before he could say another word.

Clutching the tiny notebook, she sat down and cried, the tears somehow purifying.

Penelope Cash was finally and truly ready to begin.

Chapter Three

Penny picked up a glass of white wine with a sigh. The reception had just begun but she was wondering if there was a way out. She wanted to get home. She had roughly eighteen hours before she was supposed to begin her rather odd training with Damon Knight, and she'd spent every spare minute reading up on the Internet about Dominance and submission.

She stepped behind one of the large potted palms decorating the space. Her aunt and uncle had spared no expense in celebrating their daughter's wedding, but Penny couldn't keep her mind on it.

What would it feel like when Damon Knight's hands were on her body? She'd had one lover her entire life and they hadn't exactly set the world on fire.

Damon was doing this for a mission. It wasn't because he was desperate for her body. She had to remember that.

Still, every single word she'd read the night before made her scared. And every single word called to her.

She couldn't be submissive. The images and words were playing through her mind even as she began to hear the conversations around her. Her family. They were a truly European family with members from across the EU. There were at least five different languages being spoken. Unfortunately, she understood most of them.

"Das arme Mädchen ist hübsch genug. Ich verstehe nicht, warum sie keinen Mann findet."

Translation. *The poor girl is pretty enough. I don't understand why she can't get a man.*

Her aunt Angela. She was a widow who seemed to spend all her time gossiping and traveling amongst the family. And she almost always traveled with her sister, Aunt Edda.

"Nun, wenn sie einen Ehemann bekommen will, muß sie ein wenig abnehmen. Männer mögen keine beleibten Frauen."

Translation. *Well, if she wants to find a husband, she needs to lose some weight. Men don't like portly women.*

She moved away, walking toward the bar. It looked like she would need something stronger.

"Hän on ruumiinrakenteeltaan äitinsä kaltainen."

Translation. *She's built like her mother, that one is.*

"Ainakin Diana muistuttaa meidän sukuhaaraamme."

Translation. *At least Diana took after our side of the family.*

Embarrassment flashed through her system. Two elderly women sat, hats perched on their silvery heads, drinking tea and gossiping about the people around them.

Gossiping about her.

Did anyone remember she spoke several different languages? Including the Finnish her father's cousins were speaking now. She had a good mind to walk right up to them and tell them off in Finnish.

She turned away, catching sight of her sister and brother-in-law dancing together, smiles on their faces. George was standing next to his impossibly gorgeous boyfriend.

When she'd been a child, they'd called her a changeling. Diana and George were tall and statuesque. Penny had been short and could never get a handle on her weight. Her blonde hair kinked and never laid sleek and beautiful the way Diana's did.

"The poor girl couldn't even find a date."

She didn't need to translate that. It was spoken with a perfect British accent. Apparently her relatives didn't think she could hear either.

She took a long drink and decided to head out. She smiled at the waiter who took her glass, but refused another. She didn't have to stand there and take it. There was plenty to do at home. No one would miss her.

"Hello, Pen."

She turned and Peter was standing there, looking at her, his blandly handsome face smiling down.

"Hello, Peter."

He was dressed in a suit that was slightly too big for his lanky frame. There was not an ounce of muscle on Peter Bolling. Now that she really looked at him, he resembled a baby bird, his face soft and round, his body long and ridiculously lean.

She'd slept with him. She probably weighed more than him.

She was practically petite compared to Damon Knight.

His thin lips curled up in a semi smile. "It's good to see you."

"You, too." Polite. That was what she needed to be. She would be polite and he would go away.

Why on earth was he even here? She glanced around and realized the answer to her question. Beatrice wasn't paying attention to her bridegroom. She was leaning in, whispering to her sister and pointing at Penny.

Bitch. She'd set up the meeting.

Penny had absolutely no idea why her cousin hated her, but Bea had worked hard to make her life as much of a living hell as possible. From childhood, the woman had teased and bullied her about everything from her weight, to the way she dressed, to her lack of a boyfriend.

So she gave Peter a brilliant smile. Well, she hoped it was. "You look good."

If Bea thought she was going to break down, she was wrong. She had to be strong. She was going into the field soon. She couldn't be some girl who cried the minute she saw her ex.

Now that she was standing here looking at him, she had to wonder why she'd ever cried over him. He'd been her fiancé, her only lover, and she hadn't really thought about him in over a year.

He smoothed down the lapels of his suit. "Yes, well, I have been working out, you see. I've been promoted. And I suppose you heard about me and Susana."

Susana Henderson? Her cousin? "No. I hadn't heard anything."

He flushed a bit. "Oh. I thought someone would tell you and all. Uhm. Susana and I are seeing each other."

"We're doing a bit more than seeing each other," a saccharine-sweet voice said. Susana was tall, her blonde hair stick-straight and lush. She was always perfectly made up and dressed as though she'd walked off a fashion runway. "We're getting married."

She showed off a magnificent ring, at least two carats.

When they'd been engaged, he'd claimed she didn't need a ring. He'd convinced her they should save their money in order to purchase a flat of their own.

She felt her face heat as she realized everyone was looking at her, whispering behind their hands. George was making his way toward them, a worried look on his face.

"Sorry you had to find out this way," Susana said in a way that let Penny know she wasn't sorry at all. "No one wanted to tell you. Everyone feels sorry for you because they know you can't keep a man yourself, but I'm sick of not being able to celebrate. I'm not going to let you ruin my happy time."

"Susana! Peter." Bea made her way over, a sly smile on her face. "Oh, let me see that ring."

Everyone knew Peter hadn't bought a ring for her. That's what they would all be talking about now. Poor Penny. She didn't even warrant a ring from her fiancé.

"I'll let you get on with it, then." Penny took a step back, desperately wanting to get out of the situation.

Her heel slid on the marble floor, and before she could catch herself, she landed on her bum, her dress bunching around her knees.

Tears filled her eyes. Everyone was looking at her. She was a thirty-two-year-old woman, but in that moment she was back to being the awkward girl who watched as the world passed her by.

"Pen?" Her brother was suddenly at her side. "What the hell happened?"

Humiliation threatened to overtake her, but she tried to put a stupid smile on her face. "I just slipped. I might have rolled my ankle a bit."

George got down to one knee. "Don't move. Let Harry take a look at your ankle."

Harry, George's incredibly handsome boyfriend, was also a doctor. He dropped down beside her, pressing past the now burgeoning crowd. "Let me just check, Penny. It looks perfectly fine, but tell me if anything hurts."

"Good god, who the hell is that?" George asked, his eyes wide. "Harry, you know I love you, but I'm afraid I've just seen an actual Greek god."

Penny looked up as the crowd began to part, everyone looking to the new guy.

Damon Knight's suit fit him perfectly, as though it had been custom made to fit his massive, muscled body. The dark suit contrasted with the pristinely white dress shirt and blue silk of his tie. Dark haired, with deep gray eyes, he didn't walk into the ballroom. He strode in like a lazy panther looking about for his supper.

"That's not a Greek god," Harry said with a smile. "That's sex on two legs, mate. If you can manage to sleep with that, I'll high-five you. Unfortunately, I don't think he's looking for a boy."

Damon turned, his every movement graceful and masculine. His eyes searched the crowd, not paying a bit of attention to the stir he was causing. He ignored the women who sent him looks, brushed past the waiters. He was on the hunt. Damon Knight was looking for someone. He was looking for her.

His eyes flared when he finally found his prey, and she would have sworn she saw anger there. She was fairly certain it wasn't directed toward her, but a nervous thrill flared up as he stalked across the ballroom.

"Hello, darling." He reached out a hand. "Had I known you were going to be treated like this, I would have gotten here sooner."

She was almost afraid to take that hand, but something about the deep quality of his voice had her moving before she could properly think it over. "I slipped."

"Really?" George asked, getting to his feet. He stared Peter's way. "It's interesting that you tripped just as this arsehole shows up."

"Oh, Georgie, you know Pen has always been a clumsy cow," Bea said, her eyes not leaving Damon. "How do you know Penny?"

The humiliation didn't seem to end today. She hadn't wanted Damon to see her like this, to see how everyone viewed her. He would very likely rethink her place as his partner.

She expected him to help haul her to her feet, but he simply gripped her hand, leaned down, and picked her up in one strong move. He cradled her body to his chest. She clutched her purse, not wanting to drop it.

His eyes found hers, a startling heat in them. "Are you all right?"

She managed to nod. She'd never been held like this, up against a man, his strength bolstering hers. Being held by Damon made her feel petite, feminine.

Damon turned to Bea, cuddling Penny close. His voice was arctic cold as he replied. "I know your cousin because I'm her lover. I'm taking her to the washroom so I can make sure she isn't hurt. When I return, I expect you to be pleasant and polite or we shall have a problem, you and I."

Even Bea, known for being the Queen Bitch of the World, backed off.

Damon turned to Peter, who shrank back. "Seriously, Penelope? You almost married that?"

"We didn't actually set a date." There was a breathless quality to her voice. What the hell was happening?

"You couldn't have handled her, little boy. Go home." Damon walked off, carrying her toward the posh-looking set of washrooms.

Everyone was still watching her, wondering very likely if she'd paid an escort because there was simply no way they fit together.

"I'm fine, Mr. Knight."

"Damon, darling. You call your lover by his Christian name. Unless we're playing, and then you may call me Sir or Master. I would prefer Master. I won't have time to earn the title with you, but it's for the best." He didn't hesitate, simply moved toward where he wanted to go, and the crowds parted for him.

The way he said "lover" practically made her shiver.

He kicked in the door to the loo, though it was more a grand suite of rooms complete with six women standing in front of a mirror doing their makeup. "Out."

"Damon, this is the women's room." Even as she spoke, the women were rushing to get out. One huffed and began to say something about rudeness. The look in Damon's eyes had her fleeing like the devil was on her heels.

He set her on the counter top, her legs dangling, before he turned the lock on the door with a decisive click. He placed her purse on the settee opposite them. "Stay there."

"Damon, you can't just take over the loo."

He walked back to the stalls, checking each to make sure they were alone. "I just did. As for selecting the women's room, well, you've never seen a men's room. Trust me. I made the right choice. Smells so much better in here. Do you want to explain to me why you were allowing that woman to humiliate you?"

"She's my cousin."

"That means she gets to behave like a horrible bitch around you? Thank god I don't have any family." He got to one knee and gently pulled her shoe off. The minute his big hand encased her skin in warmth, she shivered the tiniest bit. Harry had just done the same thing, but his hands hadn't made her want to soften and curl up against him.

She had to be stronger than that. "What was I supposed to do, Mr…Damon? If I had said something back to her, I would have caused a bigger scene."

He studied her ankle, turning her foot in his palm, and then lightly running his hands up her leg to her knee.

Thank god, she'd shaved. And why did having a hand on her leg seem to make her core heat and melt?

"Sometimes it's all right to cause a scene. Life isn't a series of polite encounters. She wasn't playing nice, so why should you?"

He didn't understand. He couldn't possibly. She turned her mind to a more immediate question. "How did you find me?"

His hand moved to her other foot, as careful with this one as the first. "I tagged your mobile. I then did a complete analysis of you, your family, and your friends. According to your sister's social media postings, there was a wedding today. Your raging-bitch cousin sent some of her friends e-mails detailing how much fun she was going to have with you and that they should watch to see how you embarrass yourself at this particular event. She thinks she's going to Thailand for her honeymoon."

He had the evilest smile on his face as he said the last bit. It made him look like a very gorgeous, ridiculously sexy devil.

It also frightened her a bit. "What do you mean she 'thinks' she is?"

And it was gone, replaced with what she was coming to think of as his "male model" smile. "Nothing at all. I wish her the best. So, we shall start your training today."

"What? You said we would wait until Monday."

"I said you had until Monday to say yes. You said yes yesterday. There's no need to wait. I came to collect you."

"Collect me? Am I going somewhere?"

"Oh, I've already moved you into my place."

"You did what?" The question came out in a slightly panicked screech.

He sighed a little, his eyes hooded as though he expected a fight and wasn't particularly looking forward to it. "I had a team go through your place, pack up your things, and move them to my club in Chelsea. The rest of the house is being moved to storage, and I already found you an estate agent."

She shook her head. He was upending her life and he'd managed to do it all in a manner of hours. "You can't just move me. And I already have an estate agent."

"No, you had a front for the Ukrainian mob."

"I did?"

"Yes, darling. You really need to let the tech boys do their job. I have them run searches on everyone in my life. By the way, your florist is dealing prescription drugs out of the back of her store. You buy a bouquet from her every Monday. Scotland Yard is raiding her tomorrow. The good news is, we have a very nice one in Kensington station. I'll take you there on the way back home."

He was missing the point. They hadn't made this deal. "You can't just walk in and move me."

"I did. Actually it was rather difficult to figure which clothes were yours and which were your mum's."

"I already packed up Mum's things."

"Oh, well. Not a problem then. I was going to buy you new ones anyway. I'm going to kiss you now, Penelope."

"What?"

"You seem to have an enormously hard time understanding me today. We're going to have to work on our communication skills." He moved right between her legs, spreading her knees and making a place for himself there. One minute she was utterly gobsmacked by the chaos he'd brought into her life in a couple of hours' time, and the next, she couldn't manage to breathe. He invaded her space, looming over her. Despite the fact that she was sitting on the counter, he still looked down at her. His hands slid her skirt up, making her gasp a little. "You said yes. That means you're mine, Penelope. You're my partner and my submissive. I take care of what's mine."

She swallowed, forcing herself to look into those stormy eyes of his. He was so close she could smell the scent of his aftershave, feel the heat his big body gave off. "For the mission."

"I don't know about that," he returned, his voice deepening. "If this goes well, I get to go back out in the field. It's always good to have a cover. Men are less threatening when they have a woman with them. If you like fieldwork, there's no reason you can't come with me. Especially if you're properly trained. Tell me how much your siblings know."

She shook her head before finally realizing what he was asking. His fingers worked their way into her hair, smoothing it back, forcing her to keep eye contact with him. "Oh, about work, you mean. Everyone in my family thinks I work for Reeding Corporation in their publishing arm. They think I translate books."

Reeding Corporation was one of several companies that fronted for SIS. When she'd hired on, she'd signed documentation that stated she would never expose who she truly worked for.

"Excellent. If they research me they'll discover I'm an executive at Reeding. We've been having an affair for the last three months. You were worried about your position at the company and the fact that I'm your superior, but I transferred to another department and now we're free to be open about our relationship."

"I don't know that they'll believe we're lovers."

"Of course, they will. I'm very persuasive, love. Now, I'm going to kiss you and I'm going to put my hand in your knickers. You are wearing knickers, aren't you?"

"Of course."

He shuddered. "Not anymore. Knickers are strictly forbidden. I told you I would likely get into your knickers, but what I really meant was I can't tolerate them and you're not to wear them at all anymore. I've done you the enormous service of making it easy on you and tossing the ones you had in the house out."

His right hand brushed against her breast. The nipple responded by peaking immediately, as if it were a magnet drawn to Damon's skin.

"You can't toss my knickers out, Damon. And you can't put your hand there. We're in the ladies' room for heaven's sake."

"Here's the first rule, love. Don't tell me what I can't do." His mouth closed over hers, heat flashing through her system.

His mouth was sweet on hers, not an outright assault at first. This was persuasion. Seduction. His lips teased at hers, playing and coaxing.

And his hand made its way down, skimming across her waist to her thigh.

"Let me in, Penelope." He whispered the words against her mouth.

Drugged. This was what it felt like to be drugged. She'd been tipsy before, but no wine had ever made her feel as out of control as Damon's kiss.

Out of control and yet oddly safe. Safe enough to take a chance.

On his next pass, she opened for him, allowing him in, and the kiss morphed in a heartbeat from sweet to overpowering.

She could practically feel the change in him. He surged in, a marauder gaining territory. His tongue commanded hers, sliding over and around, his left hand tangling in her hair and getting her at the angle he wanted. Captured. She felt the moment he turned from seduction to Dominance, and now she understood completely why they capitalized the word. Damon didn't merely kiss her. She'd been kissed before, casual brushes of lips to hers, fumblings that ended in embarrassment, long attempts at bringing up desire.

This wasn't a kiss. This was possession.

He'd said she belonged to him for the course of the mission, and now she understood what he meant. He meant to invade every inch of her life, putting his stamp on her. If she proceeded, he would take over. He would run her life and she would be forced to fight him for every inch of freedom she might have.

"That's right, love. You touch me. I want you to touch me. If you belong to me, then my body is yours, too."

She hadn't realized her hands were moving. She'd cupped his bum even as his fingers slid along the leg band of her knickers, under and over, tickling against her female flesh.

He'd said exactly the right thing. He hadn't made her self-conscious. He'd told her he would give as good as he got. It wasn't some declaration of love, but she'd had that before and it proved false. Damon Knight was offering her something different. He was offering her the chance to explore without shame.

She cupped Damon Knight's arse and, god, it was a magnificent piece of work. Those cheeks were made of steel, but there was a bloody generous portion of them. She could sink her nails into them when he worked over her. Damon Knight likely wouldn't tell her she was too rough with him the way Peter had.

She pulled back.

"What?"

"I just thought about Peter. He said I was too hard on him. I don't mean to be."

Damon's face hardened, his eyes darkening. He pushed his pelvis forward, letting her feel every ridiculously long inch of his cock. "Don't you hold back on me. Sex isn't polite, Penelope. Sex is dirty and nasty and raw. I want you rough. I'm a bloody man and you're going to treat me like one. And I'm going to show you just how much of a woman you are."

His thumb slid over her clit, and she nearly screamed in pleasure.

Damon took the opportunity to forage deep. His tongue slid against hers. She let her hands cup that amazing bum of his even as his fingers played in her pussy.

Pussy. She couldn't think of it as a vagina, and fanny seemed adolescent. It was a pussy and it was readying itself for Damon Knight's cock.

"Do you like that, Penelope?" He slid his thumb back over her clit. "You seem to. You're wet. Were you thinking of me before? Or were you thinking of him?"

"Who?" She seriously couldn't think about anything except Damon. When she arched her back, she could feel the hard line of his erection against her belly. She hadn't had sex in over two years, but now she was about to have at it in a washroom at her cousin's wedding.

"Good." His thumb stayed on her clit but his fingers parted her labia, teasing into her channel. "I want you focused on me. Tell me how it feels. Tell me what you like."

She was pretty sure he wasn't talking about what she liked to eat or watch on telly. "I don't really know what I like, Damon." She gasped as his fingers curled up inside her, stroking deep. "I like that. I really like that."

He growled a little, pulling his fingers back out and then slowly, so slowly, pressing deep again. "You're not a prude at all, are you? No prude gets so fucking wet in such a small amount of time. You're soaking my hand."

Embarrassment flared. "I'm sorry."

He nipped her ear, a sharp tingly pain that somehow seemed to have a straight shot to her pussy. "Apologize again and I'll spank you right here and now. Your pussy is hot and wet, and I like it that way. I'll try to keep it that way as much as possible over the next few weeks. You read the materials I gave you?"

"Yes."

He sighed and suddenly his fingers were gone, and she felt a flash of pain as he twisted her clit between his thumb and forefinger. The sensation flared and then she felt flush with heat and another wave of that wet arousal seemed to flow through her pussy.

"Sir or Master when we're playing. I'll give you a tweak every time you forget."

"Yes, Master. I read it, Master." He'd told her he preferred Master. She could barely speak because his fingers were teasing again, keeping her on the edge of pleasure. Even the pain threatened to send her over the edge. It wasn't real pain, just a torture tactic to bring her more pleasure.

"And you respond beautifully to discipline, Penelope." His mouth was right at her ear. "Do you understand why your pussy clenched down on my fingers when I nipped your ear?"

"Because the pain is tied to pleasure."

"Because you're submissive, love. Not just sexually." His fingers found their way inside again, and she practically sighed. "You're a soft little thing. You like to take care of the people around you. You're that woman who remembers everyone's birthday. You're the one everyone cries to and complains to because you always listen. You're the one who never asks for anything in return, but I'm going to teach you to ask me for this. You're going to ask me to let you come, Penelope. You're going to ask your Master to please fuck you with his fingers and toy with your clit and allow you to come all over his hand."

"Please, Master." Somehow with his hands playing her body like a finely tuned instrument, it didn't seem wrong to ask him. It didn't seem wrong to say dirty things and expect pleasure. He was right. She tried very hard to be everything to everyone, and most of the time they didn't even think to invite her to the pub after work. She deserved a bit of pleasure. She deserved what he was willing to give her. "Please let me come. Please fuck me with your fingers and toy with my clit and let me come on your hand."

The kiss he placed on her cheek was oddly tender, and she could feel him smile against her skin. "Very good, love. Your Master is pleased, and he will grant your very polite request. Come for me."

His fingers curled up, one and then two taking up all the space. She felt filled and stretched as his fingers worked their magic. Over and over he plunged deep, fucking inside her as she pressed against him, begging for more.

His thumb pressed hard against her clit and she went flying. Pleasure pounded through her starting at her core and pouring through her body, making her blood sing, her skin come alive.

She was still shaking with it as he gently pulled his fingers out of her pussy and very deliberately brought them to his mouth. He sucked his fingers inside, licking off the arousal as his eyes watched her.

"You taste like sweet cream, Penelope."

"Everyone calls me Penny." It was stupid. He was licking her arousal off his skin and that was all she could think to say?

He took a step back and then turned on the water at the sink, washing his hands. "I'm not everyone. I'll wait for you outside. Ditch the knickers, Penelope. You won't want to wear them now. They're soaked. I'll know if you're still wearing them and you'll discover that not all discipline is about pleasure."

She managed to nod.

He smiled, a simple turn of his lips that seemed to somehow light up the bloody room. "Now you look like a girl who just fucked her lover. That should make them believe our cover. I'll meet you outside. Don't take too long. I think we should have a dance before we leave. Explain to your siblings that we're going on holiday in a week or so. We don't want them to think you're missing now, do we?"

He unlocked the door, and she was alone again.

Cover. He'd done it all to establish their cover. She'd just come apart in his arms and he'd been thinking about how best to fool her relatives.

The door opened again and Penny forced herself off the counter.

"What on earth?" Her elderly aunt frowned her way. She'd come in with three other relatives, all of them scowling in deep disapproval. "You look like a trollop, girl. Your whole generation has gone to the dogs. In my day, the washroom was for washing and other things that ladies do not talk about. It was certainly not for whatever that man was doing to you."

Penny couldn't help it. Laughter bubbled up. She was thirty-two and finally getting lectured on how immoral she was.

It was a new day. Penelope Cash was a bad girl. Penelope Cash was Damon Knight's girl.

Even if only for a while.

"You'll have to forgive me, Aunt Edith." Right there in the middle of the posh loo, she wiggled out of her very soaked knickers. "I'm not allowed to wear these."

"Good god!"

She tossed them in the trash, collected her purse and walked out, her head held high.

Chapter Four

Damon forced himself to walk away from the washroom door when all he really wanted to do was lock the door again and get his cock inside Penelope Cash's ridiculously tight pussy.

She'd been so fucking hot. She'd damn near singed his hands, and the way she looked when her body had tightened and she'd creamed all over his fingers had nearly unmanned him. He'd almost come in his slacks like an untried teenager.

He hadn't expected her to be so beautiful, so open. Her whole face changed when she came. She softened up the moment he touched her, her face losing the stoic look she normally wore. She looked younger, fucking gorgeous.

He wanted to see her breasts. He hadn't even gotten a peek yet. When he got her to The Garden, he was going to strip her down and inspect every inch of her.

"Would you mind explaining exactly who you are and what you're doing with my sister?"

Ah, the troops were swarming. He turned and Diana Cash-Holden, aged twenty-nine, married to an accountant, mother of two girls, was bearing down on him. Diana was the middle child, well educated, but she had to have spent her school years in the shadow of her near genius-level sister. As far as he could tell from the profile he'd worked up on her, she wasn't a bad woman, simply very busy.

In a matter of seconds, he decided just how to deal with Diana.

"I'm dating her. I'm taking care of her. She's been lonely since your mum died."

Diana flushed slightly, obviously feeling guilty about not spending enough time with her sister. That was exactly the reaction he'd been looking for. "Yes. She's been working quite a lot. She hasn't mentioned you at all. I do ring her a bit."

"She's private, and we work together so we had a few things to iron out before we went public." Out of the corner of his eye, he caught George Cash striding up, obviously willing to pile on the new guy. He rapidly went through everything he knew about Penelope's brother. He was the youngest, came out as gay during his teen years, but it seemed to have been smooth enough. He was a solicitor working for various human rights groups. It was obvious that he thought Damon might be in violation of a few.

"Where is Penny?" George asked, his eyes narrowed.

"I'm here," she called out.

Fuck. His cock stirred again because she looked soft and pretty with her hair tousled and her dress a bit wrinkled. Her blue eyes were still wide and innocent though. He was fairly certain nothing was going to change that. He could likely fuck her a thousand times and she would still look at him with those wide, innocent eyes.

He had to protect her. She wasn't a seasoned operative who knew what the game was. Of course if she had been, she'd likely have turned him down altogether because of his limitations.

It struck him suddenly that Penelope Cash might be his ticket back to the field in more ways than one.

George held out a hand. "Penny, come over here. Let me get you a drink and maybe we can sit down and talk."

That was not going to happen. He had plans for the afternoon and they didn't involve sitting around with Penelope's siblings. He was sure Penelope would defend them and go on about how much each had going on in their lives, but they'd left her to bear the weight of her mother's care, and he wasn't open to excuses. They'd had their chance to shelter and protect their sister from the big bad wolf, and now the big bad wolf was going to eat her alive and make her happy while he was doing it.

He was going to get his mouth on her pussy and not leave for a very long time.

It was just part of her training. That was all it was. The fact that his cock was truly engaged was a plus in his opinion, but at the heart of it, having sex with Penelope Cash was a necessity. It would bond her to him, make her trust him so if everything went to hell, she would obey him without question.

It was time to start testing the fragile bond he'd begun to forge with his sub.

"Darling, you're feeling better?" He opened his arm, silently requesting she come to him.

It left her with a choice—the brother she'd known for years or the man who'd held her, touched her.

She practically fell over herself to get to Damon. "I'm much better now."

Wrapping an arm possessively around her shoulders, he looked back at her brother. He told himself the warmth he felt was all about a job well done. It had nothing to do with satisfaction that she'd chosen him. "Excellent. I was just telling your brother about how we met."

She flushed sweetly. "He was my boss. It's why I didn't talk about it. He took a transfer so now we can openly date. I'm sorry I didn't tell you about him. Damon. His name is Damon."

Damon held a hand out. "Damon Knight. It's nice to meet you."

Penelope made introductions all around. He put on his most charming face and managed to finesse his way out of the family situation in less than twenty minutes. After the dance he'd promised Penelope, he took her hand and made his good-byes, wishing Beatrice and her new husband all the best of luck.

The bitch would need it since he'd placed her on a Thai terrorist watch list, and she was scheduled to be picked up and questioned the minute her plane touched down.

She would probably get out of it. Eventually.

"I don't understand why I have to leave my home." Penelope's fingers were threaded through his as they walked along Bishopsgate. The late afternoon sun was high in the sky, only the tiniest pinch of a chill in the air, but Penelope shivered.

He eased out of his suit coat, placing it around her shoulders before clasping her hand again. The weekend crowds were hustling around them and he didn't intend to lose her.

She stopped, her hands on the coat. "Oh, I'm fine. I'm sure you're cold as well. You don't have to."

He stared, not minding that he was stopping foot traffic. "Leave the coat on, Penelope."

Her blue eyes were almost the same color as the sky and just as bright. "Is this one of those Dominant things?"

It seemed like forever since he'd had to truly train a submissive. Most of the ones he'd played with in the last few years already understood everything about the lifestyle. "It's one of those polite things. What kind of household did you grow up in that you think a man should allow his female to be cold so he can remain warm?"

She pulled the coat around her, the material practically swallowing her frame. "My father was a college professor. I have to admit, he wasn't big on manners per se. Not that he wasn't polite, but he was often thinking of other things. Mum, god rest her soul, was a bit of a feminist."

"Keep the coat on," he commanded, taking her hand again and beginning to walk toward Liverpool Street. "And this is precisely why you're moving in with me. We can't have these sorts of arguments on the boat. We're supposed to be a D/s couple."

"So it is one of those Dominant things." A cheeky grin curled her lips up.

Oh, she was going to be enormous fun to spank. "We're going into intensive training, and that means I want access to you twenty-four seven until we get on that boat. I want you to get comfortable with the team I have backing us up. They're Americans, so they take some getting used to. I especially want you to spend time with Charlotte. She's going in with her husband as another couple on holiday."

"She's pretending to be a sub, too?"

Charlotte didn't have to pretend, which made her practically perfect to help educate Penelope. "She's Ian Taggart's wife and his submissive. She's also a well-trained operative. I brought her in to help teach you about the lifestyle. She can answer all your questions from the submissive's point of view."

She turned a little, her eyes lighting up in a way he believed they wouldn't have before the incident in the washroom. She needed intimacy to open up. "When do I get my gun?"

"I've rethought that part of the operation. If you prove to me that you can use one, perhaps." He wasn't sure he liked the idea of an armed Penelope. She would just as likely shoot herself as she would anyone else. As though to prove his point, she nearly tripped on a perfectly even piece of the pavement. He caught her easily and then picked up the brooch that had come unpinned.

"Oh, sorry. I'm always losing things like that." She pinned the brooch back on and steadied herself. She seemed to be having trouble with the tiny kitten heels she was wearing. Subs at The Garden were given the choice of stilettos or bare feet. He could guess which one Penelope would choose. But then he rather liked the fact that she only came up to his shoulders. It allowed him to tuck her easily against his body when he held her.

She turned and her handbag nearly took the head off a corgi. "Sorry!"

She might never get a gun. He pulled her away before she could kill a passerby with that purse of hers. "You evaded my question before. Why do you let those women humiliate you?"

She frowned, and he almost wished he hadn't asked the question. "I didn't want to cause a scene. It's always that way with the Henderson side of the family. I still go to events because we're related, but I try to stay away from her. She's a bully. I don't let her get to me."

But it was obvious she did. He rather hated the sad look on her face. "And what on earth were you thinking to do with that tiny man?"

A ripple of laughter went through her. "He's six foot, Damon. He's hardly tiny."

"He might weigh six stone soaking wet. I could break him with one hand." He couldn't help but laugh a bit thinking about what she'd said before. "Did that idiot really say you were too rough with him during sex?"

She turned the sweetest shade of pink. "Damon, we're in public."

He stopped at the corner. "Penelope, no one is listening. They're off in their own worlds. We can safely talk about your very sad former fiancé. How did you meet him?"

The light changed from red to yellow to green. She kept up as he crossed the street, staying firmly in what Londoners called the zebra walk. "I met him through a mutual friend. We went on a blind date and didn't hate each other, so when he asked again, I said yes."

He was actually a bit surprised the idiot had managed to ask her. He would bet that Peter was almost as subby as Penelope. His e-mails to his fiancée showed a pitiful habit of begging to be forgiven for the most innocuous of flaws. His bride-to-be sent him text after text of things for him to do for her and vicious messages when he didn't do them properly.

He and Penelope would have been a nightmare together.

She needed a firm hand and someone patient enough to retrain her to find worth in her own strengths and actions.

She needed someone who would teach her just how good sex could be.

"He wasn't the right man for you."

"Obviously not." She frowned a little. "I don't pine for him. But I will admit, it hurt that he bought her a ring. He wouldn't buy me a ring. He said it was too expensive. Not practical. He was a very practical fellow. I think that's what hurt most today. Everyone knew he didn't think I was good enough for a ring."

He stopped in the middle of the walk. She'd been honest. She likely would struggle to be anything else. His earlier intimacy had the intended effect. She had softened toward him and he needed to bring her even closer for his plans to work. He pulled her into his arms and hugged her against him, lending his warmth. "He's an idiot, darling. And that cousin of yours will make him miserable. According to her texts, she's cheating on him anyway."

Her head came up. "You have to stop that. You can't invade people's privacy like that."

"Of course I can." He really didn't see the problem. The means were there at hand, and the boys in tech were easily bribed with pizza.

Turning into Liverpool Street station, he glanced back and noticed she'd already pulled her Oyster card.

They walked toward the underground. Damon guided her to the Central Line escalators, placing her in front of him as the crowd rushed by on the left.

It was a long ride, the escalator on a steep embankment. He ran an arm around her waist. "Do you miss him?"

"No. I didn't really love him. I think I just wanted to start," she explained. She leaned back into him, naturally falling in to intimacy the moment he gave her the choice. How hard had it been for her to go without the physical affection she so obviously required? "I spent all my time studying when I was younger. My father pushed me to excel."

She'd passed her A and O levels brilliantly. He'd looked through her school records. When she'd gone to university and proven her skills in languages, SIS had recruited her. She'd likely been a lonely girl trying hard to please a distant father. At school she would have been in the shadow of her showier siblings when it came to making friends.

It wasn't a surprise she'd tried to search out a relationship.

He wondered if she knew Nigel had considered her for field training. Likely not. By then her mother had been diagnosed and she was considered too risky for a high-level clearance. Somehow her brilliance had gotten lost in the shuffle of daily work and poorly timed family issues.

"I suppose I just fell in with him really," she explained. "It was easy. And then it wasn't. Mum got sick and I had to take care of her."

So many would have let her go to a facility, but not Penny. She'd taken on everything herself and everyone had let her.

"He left you?" If Peter had been a man, he would have married her immediately and moved in to help her out.

"We drifted apart and one day he realized he wanted something more than I could give him."

She sounded wistful. She alone had proven to be the difficult one to profile. He'd found enough information on everyone in her life to write books on all of them, but she was a bit elusive. Apart from cheery e-mails she sent to friends and texts to her siblings that included an enormous amount of emoticons, she was fairly quiet. Her social networking profile seemed to be nothing but a way to like and comment on photos of her nieces. She talked on her mobile to her family and a few friends. As far as he could tell, she lived a rather blameless life.

Was he doing the right thing by bringing her into the field? She was sweet and soft and his world could tear a person up. If she'd made it through proper SIS training, she'd likely be harder. He didn't have the time to put her through it, didn't even want to. He liked her soft.

He took a long breath and caught her scent. God, she still smelled like sex, and he knew in a moment that it didn't matter. He wanted her. He wanted something sweet in his bloody life and he'd have her. He would protect her. "Did you ditch the knickers? I'll warn you, if I find out you haven't, I intend to spank you, love."

He felt her shiver against him. "I took them off in the loo. I threw them away."

He could picture her rushing to the stalls to comply before anyone saw her. "That must have been quite difficult. Those stalls are very tight. I'm proud of you, Penelope. I think we'll get on quite well together."

Her face tipped toward his. "Oh, I didn't go into the stalls. My perfectly horrid aunt accused me of being a trollop, so I took them off in the salon and tossed them away right in front of her. It was all quite scandalous. Maybe she can put that in her yearly holiday card."

Her cheeks were stained with pink, but she held her head up.

One orgasm and his sub was turning into a cheeky brat.

She stepped off the escalator and moved toward the platform, the wind from a departing train blowing her hair back. "Oh, no. I dropped my card."

He turned to see if he could still catch it.

And that was when he saw him.

Basil Champion the third stood right in front of the escalator, his eyes trained on Damon. "You look good for a dead man."

Chapter Five

Damon stood stock-still, almost unable to believe his eyes.

Baz. The man who'd been his best mate for ten years, who'd helped him found The Garden, who had stood beside him and fought back their enemies.

Now Baz was the enemy.

Baz leaned against the large median that divided the escalators. It was a shiny metallic, roughly two feet wide. All around him people were getting on or off the escalators, a crowd protecting him. "Come on, Damon. Surely you have something to say to me. It's been almost a year after all. And look at you all up and moving about. I knew you'd pull through. Oh, did your girl there drop this?"

He held up the blue and white card Penelope had dropped.

"Damon, I think we should call the police." She started to move, pulling out her mobile. "You're wanted for attempted murder, Mr. Champion."

Baz threw back his head and laughed. He was dressed in all black, a ball cap on his head. He would blend into the crowd, easily moving about the city. Damon doubted that the CCTVs would pick up his face. He was too well trained. SIS had made sure of that. "Good god, man. You're shagging the help. How the mighty have fallen. Get rid of the girl. We need to talk."

Damon reached out, pulling Penelope behind him. This was one of those things he intended to avoid later. He would teach her to always stay behind him in a dangerous situation. "You don't move a muscle. That's an order."

"But Damon, I can't get a signal," she complained. "We need to find the authorities."

The authorities wouldn't be able to handle Baz. They would only cause trouble and this was between him and his ex-mate. He needed to get Penelope somewhere safe. "And I need you to keep your mouth shut for a moment. This is none of your concern. Get on the next train toward Holborn. Change to Piccadilly and a friend of mine will be waiting for you at Gloucester Road. Do you understand my instructions?"

Her hand clutched his arm. "Damon, I can't leave you."

Anger and fear were a toxic mix in his system. "You bloody well can, and if you can't follow orders then I have absolutely no use for you. Are we understood? I am your superior and I expect to be obeyed without question, so you will move your arse and if I find out you've called anyone, I'll make your life a living hell and you know I can do it."

He knew he'd been too harsh, but she was standing right in front of a hardened killer who wouldn't think twice about slitting her throat if he thought it would get to Damon. He couldn't be gentle with her.

And damn it, she was supposed to obey. He glanced briefly at her, enough to see that she'd gone bright red, tears shining in her eyes, but her mouth remained stubbornly closed and she nodded.

"I need my card." She moved toward Baz, holding her hand out as though he would just politely give it back to her and not use her as a hostage.

Damon gripped her wrist, pulling her back. "Bloody well take mine and get the fuck out of here."

"You're being terribly rude, Damon. I hope he doesn't shoot you again, but only because I'm a better person than you." She turned and walked off.

Baz chuckled. "Isn't she that stick-up-her-arse translator? She's gotten a bit cheeky. Maybe you took the stick out and replaced it with something more personal, eh, mate? You always did like the chunky ones."

"Give me one reason I don't kill you right here." Because now that Penelope was out of the line of fire, he couldn't think of a single good one.

And he was definitely getting her a gun and making sure she knew how to use it.

Baz twirled his finger, gesturing to the large crowds around them. "Well, first of all, you don't really want me to open fire on all these very nice people. And then there's all the CCTVs. I don't think Nigel wants his golden boy featured on telly. Or maybe that would solve his problem. They don't want you in the field, you know. You're used goods, done up and all that fun stuff."

He needed to stay calm, but he felt his anger rising, a real visceral element threatening to take over his body. "You don't know a damn thing."

Baz shrugged negligently. "Course I do. I read your medical records. When I need a good laugh, I read them again. They're my favorite bedtime story. You can't seriously think we don't still have people at SIS, do you? As for that, I work for a company that has even better access than SIS. Taggart's crew did a good job hiding your medical records. SIS doesn't even know you saw a doctor in Dallas. You know, the one who found the issue with your heart. It's getting worse, isn't it?"

He thought Adam Miles had hidden those files. The doctors who had saved his life hadn't found the damage to his heart. It had only been once he saw a specialist in Dallas that the true extent of the damage had been discovered. Taggart had helped him hide it from Nigel, but it looked like the news was out. "That's really none of your business, is it?"

"It's all my business. But don't worry that I'll tattle. I like the idea of playing this game with you." He stopped for moment, his eyes looking up and down Damon, making him uncomfortable in a way only Baz ever could. "I meant what I said though. You really do look good."

He tried to ignore Baz's personal comments, sticking on the more professional statements he'd made. The thought turned his blood cold. He'd been gone for months. He hadn't really thought about the fact that there could be more moles. He couldn't even convince Nigel that The Collective existed. "If you have people in SIS, I promise you I'll find them."

"Maybe you already have." His eyes drifted to where Penelope had disappeared. "She would be the perfect mole, you know. She's so innocent looking no one would suspect her. Maybe your new girl is really working with me. After all, how else did I find you so quickly?"

If there was one thing he knew, it was that Penelope Cash couldn't betray a fly, much less her country. "Don't bother. I won't believe a bloody thing you say about her."

"It's worth a try. Think about it. She really is perfect. She's smart. She's always in the office. She could get access to your records and no one would suspect her because she's such a sweet little thing."

He wasn't going to allow Baz to drone on. "I'm going to bring you in. I promise. If it's the last thing I do, I'm going to be the one who takes you down."

Baz's eyes went oddly blank and the smile on his face dimmed. "It would be fitting, of course. You know I didn't really want to shoot you. I had to. I had to try to keep my place in SIS. I'm not as valuable on the outside."

His heart was racing, adrenaline beginning to pound through his system. He kept his eyes on Baz, ready for any kind of movement from him. "I'm so sorry to have wrecked your plans."

"I think I didn't finish the job because I didn't really want to. You know the drill. Two to the chest. One to the head. I couldn't do it." Baz took a long breath. "I knew it was a mistake the minute I walked out, but I couldn't make myself go back and finish the job."

He was supposed to feel sympathetic because Baz had only shot him once? Had only taken out one of his lungs? "What are you doing here?"

He needed to get his hands on him. He could wrestle him to the ground and…what? Get him to HQ? The British Transport Police would show up and he didn't exactly carry an SIS card on him. They would both get shoved into lockup while things got sorted out.

"I told you. We need to talk."

That would be a mistake. Baz was a snake. One didn't sit about and talk to a snake. One stepped on it before it managed to bite. "We have nothing to talk about."

His smile was back. "I think we do. We need to have a sit-down, and if you don't give me what I want, I'll have to do something drastic to convince you. I've been watching you. You like the girl. Let's talk about what happened to the last girl you fancied. Jane. I think that was her name. She was prettier than this one. You're slumming, mate."

Damon had been the one to bury Jane. She hadn't had any family past the one she'd found at The Garden. He'd trained her, hired her to work, allowed her to live in the building. He'd fucked her when it was convenient. He certainly hadn't loved her, but he'd been fond of the girl. She'd been his responsibility, under his care, and Baz had taken her life because she'd been in the wrong place at the wrong time.

The need to wrap his hands around Baz's throat was overwhelming. It took everything Damon had not to move on him. He heard the train whoosh in. Penelope would be safe on the train. She would be on her way to the station where Taggart was waiting for them. She could tell him what had happened, and Taggart would come.

And then he could deal with Baz.

"Why don't we go somewhere quiet and have this talk of yours?" The minute he got Baz out of the crowd, he would pull the knife he had in an ankle strap and slit the fucker's throat.

Baz's dark eyes rolled. "I'm not going to be alone with you, Damon. I'm not that stupid, and it wouldn't go the way you think it would."

"I'm not going to stand here in the middle of the station and conduct business." He needed to get Baz away from so many potential hostages.

"Fine. I'll make it simple for you then. I need you to get me in to see Nigel. It's serious. We have a major problem, and I'm the only one who can help. Tell him it concerns the assignment on the ship."

The train pulled away, the sound accompanied by a rush of air.

Penelope was gone, and there was no way Damon would allow Baz into SIS headquarters or within a mile of Nigel.

Baz's eyes trailed to the escalators, narrowing. They were filled with travelers.

Damon remained still. He would only have one shot at him. The crowd would slow him down. "If you want to talk, this is how to do it. Surrender yourself and we'll have a chat. The only way you see Nigel is from behind bars."

Baz's jaw tightened, eyes hardening. "That's not going to happen. We will talk, Damon. On my terms. And tell your girlfriend that I'll be seeing her."

In an instant, he took off, but not on the escalator stairs. No, he leapt onto the metallic median that divided them and started running up at a near-impossible angle.

Damon followed, gracefully hauling his body onto the median. He stared up for the merest moment before starting to climb.

Everyone was watching, turning, and shouts began as Baz moved easily up toward the station above. The minute he got to ground level, he would be able to lose himself on the streets.

Damon followed but his dress shoes were already slipping.

And he could feel his body failing.

Baz stopped halfway up, turning slightly. "Don't even bother. These aren't exactly shoes you can get in a store. One of the perks of my job. Our tech guys are far better than yours."

He stood there, grinning down as Damon struggled.

"Are your lungs burning already? How's the old ticker working?"

God, he wished Baz hadn't found those records. Damon managed to move another three feet before slipping again. Rage poured through him and he pushed on, jumping to the escalator steps when a spot opened. The steps were moving in the opposite direction of where he needed to go. "Move!"

The crowd shifted, trying to get out of his way, but he was fighting an uphill battle.

His lungs burned, his heart pumping. He pushed, dragging oxygen in, forcing it down as he ran.

And Baz just stood there and laughed. "It's not going to work, mate. You're done for. You should let them put you out to pasture because I might not have taken your life when I shot you, but I damn sure took your balls."

He was almost there. Blood pounded in his ears, blocking out everything except the sound of his heart threatening to explode.

"Tell your slag if she wants a real man, I can take care of her," Baz shouted, his arms out as though embracing the chaos he'd wrought.

Damon pressed on. All he could see, think of, was getting his hands wrapped around Baz's throat. He would stop him. He would make sure Baz never got near Penelope. The very idea of him getting his hands on her served to fuel Damon's rage.

So close. The pain in his chest sharpened, but he ignored it. He could push past it. The weakness was nothing. He could do it. He could make it. He was stronger than this.

The world narrowed to just him and Baz, his vision closing in on his enemy. A black fog played at the edge of his consciousness, but it didn't matter. He would get the fucker. He would...

Baz winked down at him, turned and ran up the escalator, his shoes clinging to the metal, making it possible for him to run.

Damon pushed on. He just needed to get to the top. When he got to the top, he would call the tech boys and figure out how to track him. They would take over the CCTVs. If they just kept him in sights, they wouldn't need to see his face. Hell, Chelsea was very likely watching him. She'd been playing with hacking the CCTVs when he'd left and she'd promised to track him. She was smart. She would keep him in her sights.

He could still do this.

His legs moved, working to get him up the mountain he seemed to be climbing. His arms pumped. His vision began to fade.

A lightheadedness took over.

The world went gray, and he fell back.

Pain flared through his system, his head pounding.

"Damon? Damon?" An insistent feminine voice pulled him from the fog.

He opened his eyes, and Penelope was staring down at him, a worried look on her face. "What happened?"

One minute he'd been closing in on Baz, and the next he was looking up at someone who should be at Gloucester station by now. He seemed to be at the bottom of the escalators, lying on the floor, his head in Penelope's lap.

"You fell. You almost got to the top and then you just fell back. If someone hadn't caught you, you would have tumbled down the entire way." She smoothed his hair back, her palm cool against his skin.

It felt nice. And wrong. She wasn't supposed to be here.

Damon forced himself to sit up though his head was reeling. "You disobeyed me."

She remained kneeling on the ground, her hand coming out to drag him back to her. "Lie back down. A medic is on his way. I couldn't find a transport officer. They're apparently dealing with some sort of threat."

So Baz had covered all his bases. He'd set up a distraction to keep the police at bay. But a medic would come. A medic who would write a report that would find its way to SIS and give them one more reason to pull him out of the field. He coughed, forcing his damaged lungs to work. Every breath ached, but he had to get out of here before that medic showed up.

And he was viciously angry at her. It wasn't fair, but she was the only one around to take the brunt of his rage.

He tried to tamp it down as he got to his feet and straightened his shirt, ignoring the stares of people around him. "Let's go. There's a train coming in now."

He didn't care where it went. He would get on it and make his way home where he intended to make it very clear to his new partner exactly who was in charge.

"Damon!" She followed after him, reaching for his hand. The

train pulled to a stop. It was going the wrong way but anything would do. "You need to see someone. You fainted."

He gripped her wrist, pulling her onto the train.

Mind the gap between the platform and the train.

The ever-present reminder not to fall between the cracks echoed through the station as the doors closed. That's what would happen to him if Penelope had her way. He would fall through SIS's gap. He would be an operative without a mission, useless and meaningless. He would go back to his former life. Nothingness.

That wasn't going to happen. He couldn't let it.

The doors closed, and he herded her to the back of the train where the bench seat was open. "Sit down."

There was fire in her eyes as she looked up at him. "I know you're angry that I didn't obey, but I couldn't leave you behind. There was no way I could get on a train and leave you behind with that man. He nearly killed you before."

"And what exactly did you think you could do? He wasn't going to start speaking German. I didn't need a translator."

"I thought at least I could be with you," she said, her eyes sliding away from him. "I couldn't stand the thought of you being alone. I think you should see someone, Damon."

He kept his voice low, barely above a whisper as he took the seat beside her. One long agonizing breath and he felt more in control, at least able to speak to her without frightening the others on the train. He'd brought enough attention to himself this afternoon. Still, he had a point to make with her. "I think you should mind your own business. And if you tell anyone at SIS that I fainted…"

Her own face was a careful blank. "Yes, you'll ruin my life. I am well aware of that. You've properly threatened me, Mr. Knight. If you prefer to kill yourself, who am I to care? Now, I would like very much to go home and be done with this charade."

His heart was starting to squeeze again. "I told you. You're coming with me."

She stared straight ahead. "I don't very well want to come with you anymore."

Because he'd hurt her feelings. She was a stubborn thing. He hadn't counted on that. Damn it all, he needed her. If she walked away, the whole operation very likely got shelved. "Ah, so you don't get your way and the operation is finished."

A little huff came out of her throat, and she finally turned his way. "That's not fair."

"None of this is fair, Penelope," he shot back. "You know how much is riding on you and the very first time I don't do exactly what you want, you threaten the entire job. I really didn't expect that from you."

She was a person who wanted to please, needed it. It was precisely what attracted him to her, but it was also a weakness he would use against her.

"I didn't say I wouldn't work, and I know why you're intimidating me. You don't want me to say anything to Nigel. He doesn't realize just how bad your lungs are."

No one knew. He didn't even really understand what the problem was. "He doesn't realize it's affecting my heart, too. Baz nicked it when he shot me. The real damage wasn't apparent until later. I had a second surgery in the States. It should be fine, but it's not."

"And you won't see a doctor because it would go on your reports. You're mad, you know."

"I'm trying to keep my job." He ground the words out. No one understood, but then they didn't have to. It was his bloody problem.

"At the cost of your life?"

"My job is my life, Penelope. It's all I have. I will fight for it. I'll fight you and anyone else who thinks to take it away from me."

They sat in silence for two stops, the train moving beneath them in a familiar rhythm. He knew he should be thinking about Baz and what he was going to tell Nigel. SIS had to know about him being in London. He would have to explain how he lost the bugger in the crowd.

He should have been plotting out just how he would handle the situation, but all he could think about was how much he wanted Penelope to look at him again. Not with tears in her eyes. He wanted her to look at him the way she had at the wedding, like he meant something to her.

He'd had plenty of women who wanted him, used him for a good time in bed. Penelope was the only one who looked at him like he was worthy of something more, like he would really protect her, would take care of her in a way that didn't involve shagging.

"Are you really all right?" she asked.

He turned to look at her. Even in profile, she looked soft. She had no place in his world. He was going to hurt her in the end. It would be so much better if he let her go. But he wasn't going to do that. He couldn't do it. He wasn't going to let her get away from him.

He slid his hand into hers, lacing their fingers together. She tried to pull away, but he placed his other over hers, trapping her, holding her. "I'm fine now, darling. Let's get home and put this behind us. We have a job to do, after all."

She stared ahead, but he felt her relax.

The train rolled on, and he rather wished they didn't have to get off.

Chapter Six

Penny looked up at the unassuming building in front of her. "This is some sort of sex club?"

Damon smiled at her, right back to his charming self. It was as though he'd never yelled at her, never threatened her. How could she trust a man who could look so perfect? "It's my home. I live in apartments on the sixth floor. It's only a sex club four nights a week."

"It sucks, Knight. Charlie wants me to put plants all over Sanctum now. I knew this trip would blow." Ian Taggart was a big man who seemed to hate everything. He'd been especially mad that they were late getting to the station, and then he and Damon had a private talk while she bought a few items for the night at Boots and he'd been even angrier when she'd returned.

Apparently Basil Champion had enemies on both sides of the pond.

Damon stepped forward, pulling out a keycard and slipping it through the reader on the door. "I can't help it if my club is better than your club, mate."

This Taggart person was apparently a Dom as well. He was massive and so fit it hurt to look at him. His face was gorgeous, but the man himself seemed so dark she was a little afraid of him.

"Your club is not better. You just have time to garden and shit,"

Taggart said irritably. She moved out of his way to let him enter, but he stopped, his eyes narrowing on her. "Are you nervous about going in? Expecting to be shot?"

"Tag?" Damon asked.

Taggart shrugged. "I expect to be shot all the time. I don't understand why she thinks I'm going to go first unless she wants me to get killed instead of her."

"Of course not," she said, shocked he would think that.

Taggart loomed over her. "Submissives go first unless there is some kind of danger and then I would absolutely be murdered before you. I would go first and Damon would protect your back. We're safe in the club, so you go first. You need to train her better. She's been running wild all afternoon."

"Running wild?" She didn't see how anyone could accuse her of that.

"Yes. You nearly got lost in the crowd at the station. You just walked off. That would have been a time for you to stay between us. You charged through and didn't pay attention when I tried to open the door for you, and I didn't like the way you constantly walked on the road side of the sidewalk. You're not my sub, but I don't buy for a second that you and Damon are involved. Otherwise, you would have let him take care of you."

"I was hard on her when Baz showed up so I let it go," Damon said, but it was easy to see he was embarrassed.

And looking back, she could see he'd tried. He'd herded her away from the street several times. He'd tried to get in front of her at the station. She'd wanted to prove that he hadn't really hurt her. She'd been stubborn, and he was trying to protect her.

He was brutally confusing.

She entered the club first, ready to see a real look into Damon Knight's soul. This was his private sanctuary. He ran the club when he was in the country and had a manager when he was out. He lived here and played here.

The lobby was lovely but a bit bland. It was nothing she hadn't seen in a nice hotel. She was disappointed. She'd expected to see his dirty side. She'd expected whips and chains and those St. Andrew's

Cross things. She didn't like to think about just how interested she was in those.

If the last twenty-four hours had taught her anything, it was that she had to climb out of her shell. She couldn't pretend like sex wasn't important. She was tired of her existence. It wasn't a life. For years she'd been a slave to duty. It was time to figure out what she wanted. She wanted love and intimacy. She wouldn't find that from Knight. But she might figure out what she wanted from a lover.

Damon locked the door behind them. "When we're running, we have someone working the front desk. We don't open again until Wednesday night, so we have a few days for you to get used to the club and everything that goes with it."

"All right. So we'll practice a bit before we're on display, huh?" There were no windows. The place was lit with tasteful wall sconces and recessed lights. It was plain. Ordinary.

Vanilla. Wasn't that the word they used?

Taggart walked to a carved wooden door that required another keycard. Naturally Damon would be paranoid about security. Taggart slid his card through and the door opened. He turned to her with a pointed stare as he held the door open. "I should warn you both that Charlie's been a brat and she's being punished, though she doesn't really view it as punishment. It's really more like I'm getting something out of it."

She was about to ask what kind of punishment his wife had earned when she walked through the door and into the club.

She stared, her mouth dropping open. She'd expected salacious, something a bit smutty. She hadn't expected beautiful.

The entire space was covered in rich, green plants. The floor in the lobby had been a plush carpet, but now it gave way to a natural stone walkway that wound around the showroom.

She was Alice and she'd just fallen into Wonderland.

"The light is all natural." Damon walked up behind her, his voice hushed as though this was a sacred place to him. "It comes through the ceiling. The building itself is rectangular, but when I bought it, I had the atrium built in to accommodate the garden. The floors above all look down on the dungeon."

It was magical. She walked up to a large tree that was just right in the middle of the dungeon floor. She touched it, running her palm along the trunk, making sure it was real. "It's beautiful, Damon."

"It's a pain in the ass. My Dom in Residence would quit if I told him he had to take care of a bunch of trees." Ian Taggart shook his head and walked away.

Damon pointed around the space, showing her where the entrances and the exits were. She watched as Taggart went up the lift toward the guest quarters.

"Wait until you see it at night," Damon said. "All the flowering plants are night bloomers. When the moon is full, the entire place is alive with blooms. It's quite lovely. During nice weather, I open the dome at the top and let fresh air in."

She'd known he was wealthy, but this place put her so far out of his league it was ridiculous. Just buying a building in Chelsea would have cost more than she would make in a lifetime, but the renovations he'd done had to be in the millions. "How could you afford this?"

He stared up at the massive skylights that apparently moved like a stadium dome. The sun lit the planes of his face, touched his hair, making it shine. "My parents left me with quite a bit when they died. What my guardians didn't manage to blow through, I spent on this place." His eyes came down, hooded, cautious. "I really did sink almost everything I have into The Garden. I've got a comfortable income, but I'm not fabulously wealthy like my father was. My guardians spent the majority of it."

She hadn't pried into his life. Though she'd always been fascinated by him, it felt like an invasion of his privacy to read his files. Not that he'd given her the same courtesy. "When did your parents die?"

"I was seven." He walked the edge of the room, running his hands through the thick vines that covered the walls. "I went to my grandfather in Scotland for a while. He died. Then I went to a cousin who paid for a series of nannies and boarding schools. By the time I was ready to go to university, the money was almost gone. I took what was left and put it in investments while I went into the Army.

By the time I got out, I could afford this place."

The military part she did know about. Damon had not only gone into the Army, he'd been decorated for valor in military actions in both Sierra Leone and Afghanistan. By the time he'd been sent to Afghanistan, he'd been Special Air Service, a commando. He'd been recruited to SIS from there. He'd spent his entire adult life as a soldier of some sort. He wasn't ready to give it up. Though she'd hated the way he'd talked to her, she could understand it on some level. He didn't think he had anything else to offer the world except his skills as an operative.

She followed him, watching his every move. Now that she wasn't completely distracted by the beauty of the place, she could see that there were small staged areas among the natural settings. The St. Andrew's Crosses were placed strategically around the room. There were several spaces with dungeon-looking apparatuses, and in the back she saw something that looked like a lounge with a large, decadent-looking bar dominating the space. "It seems like a lot of room for just one man. I know you have the club here on the bottom, but there must be ten floors."

"Only six. And I don't live alone."

"Oh." Did he have a girlfriend here? That stopped her in her tracks. She knew he'd do just about anything for a mission, but she hadn't considered that he would compartmentalize so thoroughly that he could bring in a partner he was going to sleep with when he had a woman living with him.

He stared at her for a moment. "You don't think much of me, do you? I don't keep a wife or a sub here. I meant I have a friend who runs the club when I'm not around. Like Taggart, I have a Dom in Residence. His name is Reg and he keeps his two subs with him. They're poly. I'm sure that will make you think less of me, too."

She stopped. He was doing it again. She'd begun to notice just how good he was at manipulating her. She was pretty sure he did it to everyone around him. He wasn't a man who just faced a relationship issue head on. He tried to sneak around them to get his way without having to compromise. He was so beautiful, and he controlled his world with an iron fist. She wondered if anyone ever even thought to challenge him. It was right there—the instinct to apologize, to try to make the gorgeous, distant man feel better, but she pushed it aside. "It doesn't bother me at all. As long as everyone is consenting adults, I think they should do as they please. You'll have to try again."

"Try again?"

"Yes. You're manipulating me in to giving you some outcome you want. I would rather you simply asked. I don't like manipulations."

A bitter laugh came from his mouth. "Then you're in the wrong business."

"Perhaps," she allowed. "I never meant to leave the confines of my desk. It's much simpler there. I understand that you might have to manipulate situations in your job, but I'm not your job. I'm supposed to be your partner, but I think you telling me that was another manipulation. You're very good at using the right words to get the intended outcome. I'm not your partner, am I?"

"No."

"I'm a prop."

He frowned, his eyes finding hers. "You're upset that I was hard on you."

She understood why he'd been hard on her. He'd been in the moment and he hadn't had time to figure out how to ease her in to giving him what he wanted. She didn't like it, but it had pointed out the reality of her situation. "No, I'm simply trying to get to the truth of the matter."

"You were hurt that we were intimate and then I was mean to you."

"Of course. I'm female. I'm rather inexperienced. Sex was definitely the right way to manipulate me. If the incident with Mr. Champion had occurred a few days down the line, after you'd gotten me into bed, I likely would have brushed it away because I would have been so eager to continue the relationship."

Those gorgeous lips turned into a sullen pout. Unfortunately, it didn't make him any less attractive. "But of course you're not now."

"Well, now I've come to the conclusion that it's not a relationship. It was foolish to pretend it was." But she had. It had only been a day since she'd accepted his offer and she'd been daydreaming about having him around.

"So I've made you angry and you're going to shut down the operation."

That was at the heart of it. This was his operation, the one that would get him back in the field, the one that proved he could still handle himself, that he was still a man.

"No. I'm going to continue because I read the file and it's important that we succeed. I'm going to continue the operation and your training for a variety of reasons."

A single brow arched over gray eyes. "Oh, I would love to hear your reasons."

This was the part she'd decided on the train ride. She'd analyzed the situation and come to a couple of conclusions. She couldn't walk away, but she intended to get something out of it. "One, because it's important for the mission. You're right. We do have to look the part, and that means I need to learn to be a proper submissive."

"Very logical. And your other reason?"

Ah, the harder part to admit. But she was done with hiding behind books. "Because I think I might like it. Because I would like to explore this lifestyle and perhaps at the end of this mission, I could meet someone who could help me continue my journey. You were right about a few things. I do let people walk on me. I want to feel better about myself so I can stand up. I'm not a bad person. I'm actually quite good, and it's time I started asking for what I want. That's what all this business is about at the heart of it. It's about communication and trust. I want those things, Mr. Knight. I crave them. So I'm going to make you a new deal. I will stay on and learn your ways and you will give me access to the place after we're done."

"So you can find a bloody Dom?" The question came out on an angry huff.

"Why shouldn't I? Am I not worthy of one?"

He stalked toward her, crossing the space in long, lean movements. "Now who's manipulating whom? I had my hands inside your cunt not three hours ago, and now you're asking me to find you another man?"

She was quite shocked at the vulgar word coming out of his mouth. He'd used dirty language around her but there had been tenderness to it. He was angry now, and he wasn't trying to hide it. Penelope started to take a step back, but if she'd learned anything at all today it was that she needed to stand her ground if he was ever going to think of her as anything but a prop. "You did that because you wanted to establish our cover. Don't act like you're hurt because this is all about the mission."

He stopped about a foot away, and just for a moment she thought he might explode. Just for a moment she thought he might need to, but he calmed, soothing out the rough edges of his expression and he was silky smooth again. She could already see him thinking, working up another strategy. "Of course. I'll show you the rest of the place and then you can get started. I've arranged for us to spend the early evening with Charlotte and Ian and their friends. You can meet the crew and get used to them. I need to go and call Nigel."

"You're going to tell him about Champion?"

"Yes."

But he wouldn't tell him why he hadn't brought him in. He wouldn't mention that he'd passed out from lack of oxygen and a possible heart problem.

Should she make a call of her own?

They had some time. She could think about it. It wasn't her place to worry about him. He'd made that plain. It was her place to do her job and that was to give him cover and translate what he needed her to.

"How are you going to explain the CCTV tapes? Surely he'll see them."

"I've already handled it," he replied. "Taggart's team includes its own tech. He called and she's already broken into the feed at Liverpool station. I believe they'll find that portion of the tape has damage to it. They won't be able to view it."

"How could she do that?"

"She's quite good. I don't ask tech how they do what they do. I just expect them to do it." He was quiet for a moment. "I was trying to protect you."

Finally something real. She'd heard him talking to his enemy. After she'd walked off, she'd stayed behind the wall and listened. Basil Champion was a horrible person who had tried to use her against him.

"Did you believe him? What he said about me? Not the part about me being a slag."

His face went red, and she watched as his hands twitched. "I'll kill him for that."

"It's fine, Damon. It was a refreshing change actually. Usually when people insult me it's about the fact that I can't get a date, not that I'm a dirty whore."

"Like I said, I'll kill him."

She shook her head. She'd immediately understood what Champion was doing, but it seemed to have eluded Damon. "They're just words. And he didn't really mean them. He was doing the same thing you do. He was manipulating you. He was trying to get you as angry as possible so you would make a mistake. I meant did you believe him when he talked about me being dirty in a non-sexual way?"

He'd claimed he didn't believe she could be working for The Collective, but had he really believed it?

He laughed, a release of tension. "No. Not for a second. If there's one thing I understand, it's that you're not the betraying type." His eyes focused on her again. "It's why I want you."

"For the mission."

He remained silent, his look telling her what he wanted her to know.

If only she could believe him, but he was so good at giving a person what they wanted. If she was going to get out of this with a whole heart, she had to guard it herself. "I'd like to see the rest of the place."

He gestured to the lift. "Of course."

She followed him, wishing the lift was slightly larger because she was so close to him their fingers touched.

She forced herself to move away, not trusting that she wouldn't hold his hand.

* * * *

Twenty minutes later, he'd shown her the guest floor. He walked beside her, putting off the time when he would have to tell her that she wasn't staying on this floor. He didn't want another argument. Since her pronouncement that she wanted to explore BDSM and find her own Dom, she'd been talking about all the ways they could pretend to be a couple without actually having sex.

Like he was going to allow that to happen.

The trouble was his charm wasn't working. She seemed to see right through it. There had been a moment down in the dungeon when he'd been sure she'd seen right through him, past all his defenses, right down to the fact that he was still a lonely boy who'd been left to fend for himself.

It was pathetic.

"The common rooms are just ahead," he explained.

"I'm sure they're lovely. Everything is lovely, Damon." Her eyes glowed with pleasure, and he wondered how difficult it had been for her in that tiny town house where everything had been utilitarian and drab. Even her bedroom had been spartan, with just a bed and a dresser and a well-organized bookshelf. He'd gone with the clean-up team himself because he'd wanted to see where she lived. Yet again, Penelope Cash proved elusive because he was sure that tiny dull room wasn't who this woman was on the inside.

And he'd been right because she delighted in the theater of his home. She'd looked around the dungeon with wonder, and he'd wished they were here for different reasons. He'd love to chase her through the garden, catch her, drag her to the soft earth and hear her gasp when he penetrated her.

The woman might just drive him mad.

They were interrupted by raucous laughter coming from a large living area.

"Come along," Damon said, his tone still serious. He'd been meticulously polite, showing her his building and explaining how it worked. There was a whole floor of offices and a large conference room where they would all meet tomorrow to go over the particulars of the mission. The second and third floors were part of the club, including privacy rooms for members who preferred to play without eyes upon them. The time they had spent together had been awkward, with none of the seemingly easy intimacy from before.

He wanted that back so badly, and he couldn't even fool himself in to thinking it was all about the operation. He'd enjoyed the day with her.

Then Baz had shown up and it had all gone to hell. He showed her into the guest lounge where Tag and his crew were gathered. "Good evening, everyone. I'd like you to meet the last member of our crew. This is…"

"Pen? Good god. He didn't tell me your name, just said he'd found someone who would work." Simon Weston stood up, his handsome face smiling with obvious shock.

And Penelope—shy, retiring Penelope—squealed like a schoolgirl and flew across the room, practically jumping into the bugger's arms. "Simon, it's so good to see you!"

He chuckled and pulled her up into a bear hug. "You, too, love. I'm so sorry I left like I did. I didn't even say good-bye."

"So you know each other then?" It was an understatement. They obviously knew each other. Perhaps quite well. The idea of Simon bloody Weston getting his overly aristocratic hands on Penelope made him want to shred the bugger. He and Simon had worked together for two years, though Damon never spent a lot of time with him. Simon had worked undercover most of his career, using his society connections to move easily in the business and social worlds.

Penelope turned but kept her arm around Simon's waist. "When he worked for SIS, we were paired for a few cases. I translated for him."

"She was fantastic. An amazing code breaker. I was working with the Agency on a terror cell in Malaysia. Pen here didn't even speak the bloody language, but she cracked the code in forty-eight hours." The bastard kept his arm around her shoulder, winking down at her.

Penelope's smile nearly lit up the room. It was good she was happy with someone. "It was a fairly simple code."

Damon had worked with her a few times as well. He knew how competent she was, but he'd also been smart enough to stay away from her. She'd been engaged at first and then she'd had trouble and then...well, then he'd been almost dead.

The truth was he likely never would have approached her because he knew how dangerous his life could be. And he knew how much she would need from a man. Commitment. Tenderness. Things he wasn't sure he could give her.

"She helped out when I worked at United One Fund, too." Simon looked down at her affectionately. "She's being humble. Don't believe her. She's fabulous."

Damon had worked that particular op as well. Simon had been undercover for a suspected arms dealer who was running a charity as a front for his illegal activities. Now that he thought about it, Nigel had assigned Penny to work on the man's code, which she'd discovered was buried in letters from potential donors. Simon had fucked up the op, and he'd hired on with Ian.

Simon hugged her again, pulling her up so her toes didn't touch the ground. "It is so good to see you."

"You can unhand her now. She can stand perfectly fine on her own." Damon's tone held a bite of ice.

Simon eased her to the floor, still chuckling. "And of course I know her, Knight. I made it a point to get to know the girl who made the best biscuits and cakes. I remember she made you a cake. Chocolate, I believe. It was delicious. You wouldn't know. You didn't even try a bite."

He'd hoped no one had noticed. He was allergic to gluten. That sounded stupid. It was just another bloody weakness. Naturally Simon lasered in on it. Damon was pretty sure the man blamed him for the reprimand that led to Simon leaving SIS.

"It's fine. Not everyone likes cake." Penelope smiled brightly, obviously trying to defuse the situation. She turned to the rest of the room. "Hello again, Mr. Taggart."

"God, that makes me sound old. Call me Ian or bastard or son of a bitch. I answer to them all." Taggart was sitting in a big wingback chair looking like a king on a throne, and there was a naked woman with strawberry blonde hair at his feet. So that was Charlotte's punishment. He waited to see how Penelope would take it. None of the others in the room seemed even vaguely distracted by the fact that their boss's wife wasn't clothed, but Penelope wasn't used to the lifestyle.

"Hello." She nodded and smiled, but he could sense the shock in her.

Charlotte grinned up at her. "Hey. How's it going? Sorry about the way-too-much-of-me part. I mouthed off and this was how Ian chose to punish me."

"Yeah, because you're so not an exhibitionist, baby." Taggart petted his wife's hair and suddenly didn't look like he wanted to murder everyone around him.

The only other female in the room walked with a slight limp. Chelsea Dennis was dressed in jeans and a turtleneck, despite the fact that it wasn't exactly chilly. She gave Penelope a tight-lipped smile. "Hello. I'm the non-exhibitionist of the family. That's my sister, Charlotte. Only Satan calls her Charlie. I'm here to work tech. I'm Chelsea, by the way. And yes, I know. I'm Chelsea in Chelsea. Jesse already made the joke about forty times."

"I think it's funny," Jesse Murdoch, the newest member of McKay-Taggart, said. He was a younger man with sandy blond hair and a ready smile. "Simon finally got into Chelsea, too. He's been trying really hard for months to get into Chelsea."

Simon reached out, his hand coming up to slam the side of Jesse's head, but the younger man was quite fast. He rolled off the couch and was on his feet before the smack caught him.

"I'm so used to that by now." He reached out, offering her a big hand. "Jesse Murdoch. I'm pure muscle. Like all muscle. How are you doing today?"

He was practically a bloody infant.

"Why don't you kill him?" Damon asked Simon. He was a bit sick of men touching his sub. Oh, she might be fighting him at the moment, but she was under his roof and his command.

"Ian won't let me," Simon replied.

"He's amusing," Taggart allowed. "But if he doesn't stop hitting on another man's sub, I'm going to throw his ass to the dogs. Mind your manners, PTSD."

There was a reason he got on with Tag.

Jesse Murdoch smiled down at her, looking impossibly young. "She's not wearing a collar, boss. And don't mind the nickname. My PTSD is way better. I haven't tried to kill anyone in like a year."

Murdoch was a stray Tag had picked up. He'd been in the military and gotten his arse captured in the Middle East. His unit had been executed one by one and even after he'd been rescued, there had been rumors that he'd turned. Damon didn't believe it, but he also didn't want the puppy making eyes at Penelope.

Taggart glared Jesse's way. "She's off limits. She's Damon's cover and everyone is going to respect that including you, Weston. I don't care what relationship you had with the girl before. She's his for the duration of the op. The minute I find one of you fuckers poaching, I'll let Damon have you, and he's not as forgiving as Sean. I told you that story and this one will not end the same way."

Murdoch held his hands up. "You can't blame a guy for trying."

"I certainly can. I can also viciously murder him and bury the body," Damon muttered.

"Damon!" Penelope said, frowning his way.

Tag laughed. "Oh, shit, man. They're serious when they say your name with just the right amount of indignation. American accent. British accent. It's all the same pissed-off wife."

Penelope flushed. It was his turn to smooth over the situation. And how better to diffuse an awkward situation than by bringing up bad news?

"Did you explain that Baz is back?"

Charlotte's head came off her husband's lap. "I am going to kill that fucker. I'm going to tear his balls off with my bare hands, and then I'll shove them down his throat."

Tag put a hand on her hair, gently moving her back down. "You're so sexy when you're violent. Down, Charlie. Down. We have to figure out why the fuckwad's here. Jake! Stop watching your progeny make poop and get your ass in here."

Jake Dean walked in, holding his tablet and frowning his boss's way. "He's not pooping. He's sleeping, and you're going to wake him up. Hush."

"Nah," a feminine voice said from the tablet. "I'm pretty sure he's doing both, babe. He smells so bad."

Jake's face turned tender as he looked down at the screen. "I wish I was there."

A sarcastic male voice took over. "God, Jake, I don't know if you do. I swear since he started on solids, I've smelled things I never thought existed. Hey, tell Big Tag that I'm sending him those files as soon as I change Tristan."

"About time," Tag yelled toward the tablet. "I've been waiting for days."

A loud, healthy cry came from the tablet and Jake frowned. "Now you've done it. Bye. I love you guys." He flicked off the tablet. "Give Adam a break. He's going into the office every day and he's had very little sleep."

Tag shook his head. "He should have thought about that before he decided to have a kid. Now, since you've been MIA all afternoon, you missed the news that our special friend is back."

Jake looked over at Damon. "Are you fucking kidding me?"

It was time to get settled in because it was going to be a long night. Now that Penelope was here and everyone had an adequate amount of sleep, it was time to start going over the operation and all the shit that went with it. Jesse and Jake were taking positions as crew members and would be leaving to join the boat soon. Simon and Chelsea would work on the boat as well, but wouldn't join the ship until it docked in Dover.

"I'm afraid not." He took the seat across from Taggart, another big wingback near the fireplace. Tag looked perfectly happy with a sub at his feet, and the image curled a nasty wedge of jealousy in Damon's gut. It never had before, but he hated the fact that Penelope was settling in beside Simon on the couch. She was his, damn it. Even if he only had her for the duration of the op, she was bloody well his. "Penelope?"

She looked over at him. "Yes?"

"Your place is here." He gestured to his lap. "I told you we begin your training now. Come along."

"You want me to sit in your lap?"

He wished they didn't have to do this in front of everyone, but he wasn't about to back down. There was a reason to begin now. It would be easier to get her used to him now than it would be to get on the ship and expect her to fall in with him. And, damn it, he wanted her close to him and away from Weston. He wanted her curled up in his lap, naked, but he'd take what he could get. "Yes. When we're on board and together, I expect you to be connected to me in some way. You'll spend the next week watching Ian and Charlotte. We need to look as comfortable as they do."

She stood, but he could see the trepidation on her face. He waited patiently as everyone resettled. Jake took her former place next to Simon. Chelsea settled in on one of the barstools, but there was no way to mistake where her eyes went. She was looking between Simon and Penelope as though trying to figure out exactly what was going on. If he needed an ally to keep those two apart, he likely had one in her. Jesse got another beer from the fridge and took the last seat, propping his booted feet up on the table in front of him.

Bloody American barbarians.

But he forgot about all of it as a sweet English rose settled herself on his lap. His cock sprang to attention the second he caught her scent. She bit her bottom lip and wriggled around, her soft ass moving and settling in and making him want to fuck so badly, he thought he might just carry her away and have it done with. Once he'd screwed her a couple of times, he'd be able to think clearly. He'd be able to think about something other than her.

It was only because she'd denied him. Surely that was it. He so rarely didn't get a woman he wanted, and she was proving a bit elusive.

Stupid bastard. He didn't just want her. He could attempt to lie to himself but deep down, he knew the truth. He liked her. He wanted her to like him back.

And his cock definitely wanted her to change her mind about the whole no-real-sex thing. His cock was coming up with a hundred different ways to defeat that line of thinking.

She finally settled down, though her back was ramrod straight and she couldn't possibly be comfortable.

He shifted, forcing her to move, bringing her in closer contact so her head drifted to his shoulder and her legs didn't dangle off his knees. He brought her fully across his lap, her only option for balance being relaxation and him.

"So let me explain what's going on with Baz." He began to speak as Penelope finally let her body go limp in his. He cuddled her close as he explained the situation and everything that needed to happen. About halfway through the conversation, he noticed her even breathing and the way her head was deadweight on his shoulder.

She'd fallen asleep, resting in his arms.

He still had a shot and he was going to take it.

* * * *

Some field agent she was turning out to be. She'd fallen asleep on her partner's lap and had to be awakened for supper. Damon had been smiling down at her as he kissed her nose and brought her out of a perfectly pleasant dream.

She'd been curled up on him, practically drooling on his shirt. She'd started out very awkward and feeling completely ridiculous, and somewhere along the way the deep sound of his voice and the strength of his arms around her had made her feel safe and warm and she'd just kind of completely fallen asleep.

She was fairly certain she'd blushed all the way through the supper he'd had catered in. He'd ordered her to sit by him, and he'd served her throughout the meal. He'd poured her wine and made sure she had everything she'd wanted. Ian had treated his wife in a similar fashion, though she'd been sitting in his lap the whole time. It had been so weird at first and then it had seemed oddly normal.

It made her wonder what it would feel like to sit in Damon's lap and let him feed her.

Now she stood in front of the lift trying to process the words he

100

was saying.

"We're on the sixth floor. We can walk up the stairs if you like, but the lift lets out straight in front of my rooms."

Yes and that was a problem. "Your rooms?"

A short sigh puffed from his mouth. "Penelope, you knew you would have to sleep with me. It's best to get it out of the way."

She took a step back. "I told you I don't think it's a good idea to have sex."

"Good god, do you really think I'm going to jump on you? I'm not going to rape you, Penelope. We have to share a room on the boat. Are you planning on making me sleep on the floor?"

Because he would never, ever allow her to do so. The man didn't like her walking next to the street when he was around. He wouldn't allow her to sleep on the floor. If she was stubborn about the sleeping arrangements, it would cost him and not her, and she didn't think that was a manipulation on his part. She was starting to figure out which parts of him belonged to Damon and which were the agent who refused to fail at a mission.

"No." She was going to have to do it. She was going to have to lie in bed next to him and pretend she didn't want to go any further with him.

Because she really did.

Despite what she'd said earlier, seeing him among his friends had shown her a different side to the man. Though he still held himself apart, it was so easy to see that he wanted to belong. Maybe no one else could tell since his expression almost never changed, but there was a way he held himself that let her know when he was feeling out of sorts, apart. She knew because she felt that way most of the time.

Or she could just be fooling herself again.

The lift doors opened, and he gestured her inside. Of course he would. He knew how to play the gentleman, but she wasn't used to it. He entered behind her and the doors closed.

"What are your thoughts on the possible weapon?" He pressed the button for six.

She might have fallen asleep during the discussion, but at least she'd read the materials. She might not say anything that hadn't already been said, but she did have some thoughts.

"I'm worried it's sarin." Sarin gas was a nerve agent. "This group might be attempting to mimic the 1995 Tokyo subway attacks that killed thirteen people. The cult that organized the attack used very basic means of diffusion. They wouldn't need to smuggle in more than the gas. It might be difficult to get that on board the boat. They would need quite a bit of it. I know it's lethal, but it dissipates quickly. And why would they need a certain individual? Why not just send the bloke through as a tourist and mail the gas? It could be done."

The doors opened again. It did seem a bit elaborate when a simple plan was always best.

Damon led her this time, a keycard in his hand. "I have a card for you, too. It's with your things. My apartments are locked at all times. So is my office. I work in both places. I upped my security after I nearly got killed in my own bloody home."

The door swung open, but Penelope was caught by the moonlight shining down on the atrium. She stepped up to the railing, turning her head up and then looking down. Even from this height, she could see the flowers had opened. Gorgeous white blooms dotted the dungeon below.

This was Damon's fantasy. Darkness that brought about light.

"Do you like it?" He was standing behind her, so close she could feel the heat of his body, but he didn't reach out to touch her.

"I love it." She'd never seen anything like it. Decadent. Beautiful.

He moved to stand beside her, leaning on the railing, his eyes on the dungeon below. "I was trying to protect you. I know I was harsh, but he killed a woman who worked for me. He killed her here. I couldn't stand the thought that he might hurt you."

"I understand that."

"Do you?" He finally turned to her, his hand coming up to brush back her hair. "I don't think you do. Until you've really known violence, you can't conceive of it. I'm going to try to make sure this all runs smoothly so you don't have to understand."

Despite her best intentions, she was back to feeling comfortable around him. It was easy. Somehow, they fit now in a way they hadn't before, as though his near-death experience had fundamentally changed him. He wasn't softer, not at all. He was more serious, more willing to look at her and really see her. "Why do you and Simon not get along?"

"A couple of reasons," he explained. "I ran the op that led to him leaving SIS. He fucked up and believed the wrong man."

"You fired him?"

"No. Nigel reprimanded him and he quit. I know you're friends with him and he's a pleasant enough chap, but he's led a rather charmed life. He always seemed to me like he was a rich boy playing at being an agent. Tag seems to have toughened him up. He got the jump on me last year."

She couldn't imagine anyone getting the jump on Damon, but Simon did seem harder, more dangerous than she'd remembered him. And he'd spent much of the evening staring at the girl with the limp like he could eat her alive.

Her mind flashed back to that moment in the washroom. Damon had tasted her. He'd put his fingers to his lips, the ones he'd brought her to orgasm with, and he'd tasted her.

She was going to sleep beside Damon Knight. Was she really going to hold him off in bed?

She was worried she had to or she would spend the rest of her life mourning him. He was reckless with his own life, dedicated to a career that didn't offer a lot of longevity. Even if he decided to keep her as a partner, it wouldn't be love.

Penelope Cash wanted to be loved. Like Charlotte and Ian Taggart. She wanted to know why that ridiculously hard man softened when he looked at his wife. She wanted to know why Charlotte was so comfortable in her skin.

Damon might be able to give her some of what she needed, but he would never love her the way she wanted.

"Have I lost you?" Damon asked, the sweetest smile on his face.

"Sorry. I'm tired." The day had been exhausting, and she was looking at several weeks of being intimate with a man she shouldn't give in to.

"Of course. Come on, then. Your things are in my rooms." He opened the door and allowed her in. "The bathroom is in the back. I'll use the guest bathroom for now. I'm going to shower. I'll be in there awhile."

She nodded and walked through the hall toward the room he'd gestured to. Damon's inner sanctum was lush and beautiful, like the dungeon. She peeked through an open door and found what had to be his office. Dominated by a huge masculine-looking desk, the office was filled with books. A single light had been left on, and she could see him there working by himself.

She knew she should leave, but she couldn't help herself. She stepped into the office. There was exactly one picture frame in the entire room. It was sitting on the desk. Penelope moved around so she could get a glimpse of what Damon thought worthy to frame. The rest of the building contained artwork and prints, but this was smaller, more personal.

Her heart clenched a little. It was an old photo. A man, a woman, and a child of maybe four years. The toddler was male and had the most exuberant smile on his face. His arms were up as though this was a kid who embraced everything around him. His parents both had a hand on him, keeping him safe and loved.

God, this was Damon before his parents had died. He'd been adored and protected, and it all had been taken from him in a single day.

What had that been like? Her father had been distant. Her mother had loved her, but never asked for more. And yet she'd always had a support network. Damon hadn't. He'd been that kid in the photo and then he'd been lost.

A lost boy.

Was he still lost and searching for someone who could bring him home?

It didn't matter. It didn't. The tears in her eyes didn't mean anything. She forced herself out of the room. She made her way to the bedroom.

Decadence predominated. Damon's bedroom was large and his

bed was huge and sultry. She shook her head, trying not to think about all the things he could do to her there.

Her trunk was sitting beside the left-hand side of the bed. He'd left it open. A sense of the familiar washed over her as she knelt beside it. She looked through the trunk but couldn't find her gowns. She had a dozen or so night shifts, and none of them seemed to be here.

Bastard. No underwear. No gowns.

She sighed. She wasn't going to be defeated so easily. She'd need to buy more. She went to his dresser and opened a couple of drawers before she found his white undershirts. They would do. She pulled one free and strode to the loo.

Naturally, his loo was larger than her bedroom at home. There was a separate bath and shower. That didn't happen in London real estate, but she was sure it was normal for Damon Knight. She turned on the hot water, undressed, and stepped in.

Pure pleasure flowed across her skin. Heat suffused her, and she wished she could make worse choices. Damon would be here with her if she wasn't so fucking practical. She could be with him if she didn't overthink absolutely everything.

Penelope quickly washed off, ready to slide in between the sheets and sleep. Tomorrow she would have to figure out what to do, but tonight she would sleep.

After turning off the shower, she dried off and slipped Damon's shirt over her head, trying not to think about how he smelled. Clean and masculine, with just a hint of spice.

The shirt enveloped her, hitting her just a tiny bit above her knees.

She walked into the bedroom and stopped because she wasn't alone.

Damon was standing in front of the bed, his hands pulling down the comforter and sheet.

He was completely and utterly and gorgeously naked, his backside on full display. No bum should look that good. It shouldn't make her mouth water, her insides slide against each other in a long, slow dive to arousal.

"You're naked." It might be the dumbest thing she'd ever said. It was obvious he was naked since he wasn't wearing any clothing. His cock had been laying against his muscular thigh, but the minute he'd turned and looked at her, it had started to rise.

"It's how I sleep." He seemed to ignore his dick, pulling the sheets down and fluffing the pillows. He drew them back and moved onto the bed, his body long and lean on the perfectly white sheets. He laid his head against the white pillow, making his hair look even darker than before. He didn't bother to cover his body. All of it— from his perfect hair, to his ridiculously cut chest, to a six-pack to die for, to his muscular legs—were on display.

She couldn't stand there and drool. She moved to the opposite side of the bed. She noticed he'd taken the side closest to the door. To protect her.

God, he was so hard to resist. He was an obnoxious mix of perfect man and selfish child. "You can't go to bed like that."

His eyes narrowed, staring at her. "You keep telling me all the things I can't do. I don't like it. Do I need to remind you that I'm in charge? I'm the senior agent. I'm the Dom. You're the sub. If you can't remember that, we're going to have a serious problem."

He was in charge. He was in charge of her. She couldn't help it. It did something for her. The fact that he wanted to be responsible for her actions, her life, meant something. But it didn't mean he loved her.

One week of training. Sixteen days on the boat. She would hold his hand while they searched for the bad guy. She would have about a month with him and then they would go back to their normal lives. He would smile her way every now and then and she would do her work and go home to a nameless, faceless flat where she didn't know anyone around her and no one cared about what she did or said.

Penny slid into bed, drawing the sheet and blanket around her. She turned on her side, but it was the wrong side because she could plainly see Damon laid out like god's gift to women. And he obviously wasn't cold.

She couldn't help but stare at his male parts. His cock. His balls. They were just right there. His cock was as big as she'd imagined it.

It was flush against his abdomen.

"Sorry. I took a cold shower. I tried to get it to die down." He might say all the right things, but he didn't pull the sheet up. He lifted his hips and let his legs lay open. "But the minute I saw you, it just had its own ideas. I want you, Penelope. I can't help wanting you. Go to sleep and we'll deal with everything tomorrow. You want to stay pure. We'll see how that goes."

She turned to the other side. She wouldn't give in.

No matter how much she wanted to.

Chapter Seven

Sunlight brushed her skin and warmth encased her. So warm. She couldn't help but rub against the strong body she lay next to.

Penny opened her eyes. Sometime in the night, she'd turned and cuddled close to him. Damon's arm was around her, holding her to his chest, her arm around him. Her cheek rested against his heart. She could hear it. Damaged as it was, it still beat strong against her ear. She didn't like to think about what had happened the day before. She'd watched him fall, watched his big body stop and then lose control. Damon shouldn't ever lose control. He needed it so badly.

She knew she should move, but she couldn't help it. She gave herself a moment to let the heat of his body wash over hers. All the reasons to hold herself apart from him were still there, but it suddenly seemed silly to not enjoy the man. She'd denied herself so much. Yes, there would be heartache, but wouldn't it be better to ache than to feel nothing?

"Did you sleep all right?"

Penny looked up, startled, but when she would have moved away from him, Damon's arm tightened slightly. "I did."

He closed his eyes and sighed. "I did, too."

Silence stretched out between them, but it was strangely comfortable. She let herself relax again. "When did I end up here?"

His chest moved as he breathed, and she found herself breathing in time to him. Her heart seemed to synch as well. "After you fell asleep. You tried to take all the blankets. I had to let you close to me just to stay warm."

"I'm not used to sleeping with someone." She let her eyes drift up.

Morning light softened him, making the gray of his eyes seem almost blue as they opened and he looked down at her. "The walking corpse never slept over?"

She stifled a laugh. Damon had a way with words, especially when he was insulting someone. He and his friend Ian had insulted each other all night. She might never understand men. "That's a horrible thing to call him."

Damon smiled a little. "Peter never slept over?"

"He said he slept better alone. He tried once but I snored and he left." That was a terrible thought. "Did I keep you up?"

"With your little snuffles? No. He was an idiot, love." He laid his hand over hers and took a long breath, seeming to settle back in. "I liked sleeping with you. I haven't slept with anyone in a very long time. In fact, there hasn't been anyone at all."

That was a bit hard for her to believe. "Anyone?"

"I haven't actually had sex since the shooting. I was worried the damn thing wouldn't work, but I think it's safe to say it's waking up again." His voice got serious. "I liked it. Last night, that is. I liked holding you. I liked how we kept each other warm. Kiss me, Penelope."

"Damon." It was a bad idea.

"You can't even kiss me? We're going to struggle on the boat if you won't kiss me."

He was right about that. She pushed herself up and looked down at him. He was a deliciously gorgeous beast of a man, every inch of him muscled and lean. His hair had lost its former perfection and a lock of black silk lay across his forehead.

What was she really afraid of? She was afraid of losing herself in him and then being utterly adrift when everything was over. She was afraid of not coming out on the other side of the affair with a whole heart, but she had agreed to this. She'd said yes, and that meant being braver than the old Penny. The old Penny never woke up warm and cradled against a man. The old Penny had accepted far less than was her due.

The old Penny would have given this man a peck and then run away. She didn't want to be the old Penny any longer.

She reached out and touched him, her fingers on his face. Maybe she was looking at everything wrong. Maybe instead of holding back, she should take every moment and revel in it. He looked at her solemnly as she brushed her fingertips along his jawline, his whiskers tickling against her skin. She studied him, taking her time to memorize the way he looked. A sharp blade of a nose. Sensual lips.

He didn't move, didn't say a word, simply allowed her to explore, though she could feel the tension in him. Was he truly afraid she wouldn't kiss him? Could a man like him really want her?

She couldn't know if she never tried. This wasn't a problem she could logic her way out of. She had to feel her way through it.

She let her lips find his skin, first his cheek and then along his jaw. She placed a kiss on his nose and one between his eyes. She smoothed back his hair.

"Penelope, I don't want you to treat me like a boy you're trying to soothe."

She wasn't going to let him rush her. "Hush, Damon. I'm enjoying this."

His eyes flared slightly. "When we're on a proper footing, I'll spank you for that."

Yes, she thought he'd do a lot of things when they were on "a proper footing." It was why she had to enjoy the time she had with him now. "Because I'm a brat?"

She'd read the term, heard Ian complain about his wife being one. Of course, he'd said it all while petting her and holding her.

Those delicious lips curled up in a sexy grin. "I think you could be a spectacular brat, love. If you wanted to."

She wanted to. All her life she'd been the perfect daughter, the one who got good grades and did her duty. Had she ever really grown out of the role and tried being a woman? She brushed her mouth across his forehead and then finally let her lips find his own. Warm, soft, but so firm. He let her have her way, allowing her to play along his skin.

Emboldened, she let her hand drift down, caressing the strong column of his neck and making her way to his shoulders and chest. A light dusting of hair covered his torso, making a neat triangle toward his abs. She traced the flat discs of his nipples, watching them peak the minute she got close. She let her hand move lower to his lean stomach. He twitched under her fingertips. The blanket covered him from his hips down, but it tented, his cock stretching the material up.

"Yes, that's what you do to me." His hands were fisting the sheet underneath him as though he had to hold on or he would reach for her and take over. "Seven months without a whisper and now he wants to play."

He was giving her a gift, allowing her control when he needed it himself. He strained under her hands, his hips lifting when she got close.

This was why she was afraid. Because she didn't want to stop with kisses. She wouldn't want to stop at the end of the mission. She might never want to stop exploring Damon Knight.

"Give me more," he demanded. "Kiss me. Use your tongue. Please, pet. I want it."

She knew she should stop, but she couldn't turn down his plea. There was a desperate quality to his tone that made her feel sexy, desirable. Maybe he was manipulating her, but he couldn't fake the erection. It was difficult to believe that she was the cause, but the evidence was staring her in the face.

She lowered her head back to his and let her tongue run across his plump bottom lip, feeling her power when he shivered beneath her.

More. She wanted more. Her body was starting to sing in the way it only ever had for him. Her pussy softened, starting to pulse and get wet. She couldn't deny it. Damon was her weakness, her odd joy, the one man who could bring her out of herself and into the world. She didn't even want to deny it or him.

She let her tongue surge in, rubbing against his. Never before had she been so brazen, so bold, but then she hadn't ever wanted anyone the way she did Damon.

They kissed, his tongue playing along hers, making her heart beat in a rapid rhythm. Alive. Maybe it was a farce on his part, but it was real for her, and she couldn't let it rush by without reveling in it. Without saying yes to it.

"Let me take over," Damon whispered, his deep voice pure seduction. "I can make it so good for you. We could be good together. So fucking good. Touch me. Touch my cock. Stroke me."

She wanted to see it again, loved looking at him. One last kiss on his lips and she forced herself up.

"Damn it."

She ignored him and pulled at the sheet, tugging it down. He hissed a little as his cock was exposed, but she couldn't miss the satisfied smile on his face. He pressed his hips up, squirming a bit, like she had in the bathroom at her cousin's wedding. Her first real orgasm. He'd given that to her. Didn't she owe him something?

A gasp came out of her mouth as she really caught sight of his cock for the first time. Never before had she had the time to look at her lover. Peter had wanted the lights off and to get it done fairly quickly, but Damon seemed to want to take his time, to revel in it, to treat it like a leisure activity he never wanted to finish up.

His cock was a thing of beauty. Long and thick. There was a drop of pearly liquid seeping from the tiny slit on the tip of his dick. His hips were lean, with lovely notches that proved just how much he liked to work out.

"Do you like what you see?" His voice was low, a hard groan coming out of his mouth.

"You know how beautiful you are." He had to. She was sure a thousand women had told him.

His hand came out, touching a place just below his heart. "I know I'm scarred."

There was a red puckered place right below his heart, to the left of his breast bone. It was a nasty scar, the one that might still cost him his career. That mark was the reason he couldn't run the way he used to, couldn't perform in the field. He should have had a few more years, but the injury had aged him.

It hadn't made him any less desirable. His flaws did nothing but make him more open, easier to get close to. She forced herself to look away from his cock. It was beautiful, but he was more than a hot cock. He was a man who'd been hurt, who had the same strengths and weaknesses as everyone else, who needed more than just sex even if he wouldn't admit it.

She ran her fingers across his scar. He'd almost died. She couldn't imagine what he'd gone through. His best mate had walked in and calmly put a bullet in him. He'd been forced to endure months and months of trying to get back to normal. Everything that made up Damon Knight had been put in jeopardy. She couldn't help but think about the picture in his office. That smiling boy and parents who loved him. He'd lost them so young. He'd been alone in the world. Only a child, but orphaned.

When her mother had died, she'd felt her aloneness and she'd been an adult. Her entire body had ached with the loss, but he'd been truly alone, a child with no one to care for him.

Then he'd opened up and his best mate had betrayed him brutally, the evidence right beneath her fingers.

Damon needed to be healed. Not from his physical ailments, but from the wounds that came from the ones he loved always leaving him.

She leaned over and pressed her lips to his scar. There was a line that moved in and out of the circle. His surgery. Someone had saved his life. Someone had pulled the bullet out of him so he could be with her right now, in this moment.

Her tongue came out to trace the scar. That scar was important. It meant he was alive. It meant he was here.

His hand sank into her hair. He held her hard against his skin. "God, keep your mouth on me. Penelope, I need it. I know you don't believe me, but I want you. I want everything you have to give me."

Though it was so dumb, she licked the scar, trailing over to his nipple and then giving him a baby bite.

Damon hissed and the hand in her hair tightened. "Yes, that's what I want. I want Penelope Cash's bad girl. I want her to fuck my cock. I want her to crave me."

She already craved him. Bad girl. Good girl. Everything Penelope Cash was wanted Damon Knight.

He was laid out for her, his big body a feast for her senses. He released his hold on her hair, giving her some freedom to explore. She let her palms roam across his chest as she kissed her way down. He'd given her something the day before. He'd taught her that she wasn't cold or frigid, that sex could be good with the right partner. She wanted to return the favor.

There were a million reasons why it was a bad idea and only one reason to keep going—because she wanted to. In the moment, that was all that mattered.

"I'm trying to be very good," Damon said, his hands clutching the sheets. "It's difficult for me not to take over. So give me something. Take off that ridiculous shirt and let me see your breasts. I won't let you hide from me."

He'd touched her and played with her, but he hadn't seen her yet.

"Don't," he growled. "Don't tense up on me. I want to see you."

"I don't look like you, Damon." She was overweight, a bit saggy. He was masculine perfection, and she wasn't anywhere close to him.

"Thank god for that. I don't want you to look like me. I'm not into men."

So frustrating. "That wasn't what I meant."

His eyes narrowed. "Then perhaps you should tell me what you meant."

She had the sudden fear that he wouldn't like her explaining all the ways she didn't measure up. He hadn't liked other people talking bad about her. He wouldn't like her talking about herself in a derogatory fashion either. And he seemed to be looking for a reason to punish her. There was only one clear way out of the situation.

She sat up, making her decision. Before she could really think about it, she pulled the shirt over her head and let it fall to the bed beside her. She wasn't wearing underwear since he hadn't seen fit to provide her with any. Penny sat, kneeling over him, waiting for him to say something.

A slow smile curled his lips up, making him look like a lazy pasha whose meal had been brought to him on a silver platter. "What made you change your mind?"

She bit her bottom lip and decided to tell him the truth. This relationship they were pretending to have was all about trust and honesty. "Well, I decided that if I told you what was going through my head, you would very likely get angry with me. You would have spanked me and then still ordered me to undress, so the argument wouldn't have gotten me anything but a sore bum. I decided to skip it and do as you asked."

Pure pleasure was in his grin. "Such a smart girl. We'll get along well, you and I. And, god, your tits are gorgeous. Look at that. Spread your legs. Let me see your pussy."

She could see he wasn't going to be easy to please. He would demand everything from her, but he'd done nothing to make her think he would hurt her. He'd only given her pleasure in moments like these, only praised her. She shifted, moving her knees apart so he could see her.

"Do you always shave?" His voice had gotten deeper, darker.

She shook her head. "No. It's my first time. I did it on Saturday night."

"After you said yes to me." He turned on his side, obviously comfortable with his nudity. "Did you think about me when you were shaving?"

More honesty. "Yes."

"Did you want to please me? Did you shave your pussy thinking it would please your Master?"

She'd done it for several reasons. "I read that many submissives keep to a grooming routine. And yes, I did think about you while I was doing it. I wanted to know what it felt like. I don't pay much attention to that part of my body."

She'd stood in the shower, hot water running over her as she carefully shaved herself and wondered, hoped and prayed even, that she could figure out why a pussy seemed to be the center of so many women's lives.

Then Damon had touched her there and she'd understood.

His hand found his cock, lazily rubbing up and down. "Don't pay much attention to it?"

She couldn't help but watch the way his hand worked over his erection. She might not have spent a lot of time thinking about her sex, but Damon was deeply, comfortably acquainted with his. "I didn't think much about sex. Even when I was engaged, I didn't really enjoy it."

"I thought about you on Saturday, too. Do you know what I did after we spoke?"

"Apparently you researched all of my relatives and decided on a plan to relocate me." He'd worked quickly, too.

He chuckled a little. "Besides that. And I'd already researched all your relatives. And friends. And anyone you talk to on a regular basis. No. I got in bed that night and I did this."

His fist tightened around his cock, pulling back the foreskin, allowing the purple head to emerge. His balls were tight against his body, beautifully large and round. And it was apparent he spent time on grooming as well.

"You touched yourself while you were thinking of me?" She tried to really imagine him lying there, gripping his own cock and thinking about making love to her.

It wasn't love. It was sex. She had to remember that.

"I did more than touch myself." He groaned and his eyes closed briefly. "I had a nice long session. I lay in this bed and thought about all the nasty things I was going to do to you, and I wanked my own cock until I came everywhere. I told you I hadn't had sex in a long time. It felt damn good."

"Why, Damon?" She asked the question on a sigh because she truly didn't understand him. "Why me? I'm not trying to get into trouble. I want to understand."

"Why I want you?"

"Yes. You never paid me much attention before. I don't understand what's changed."

He stopped his slow stroking and turned to her. "I did think about you. Come here. Lie beside me. It's not fun to touch myself when you're right here. I'll talk but I want you to touch me."

She shifted, lying back on the bed, and soon found herself in his arms again. Somehow she'd thought sex with Damon would be wild and crazy. She hadn't expected him to be so sweet, hadn't counted on the real intimacy she was beginning to find with him. She'd envisioned him fucking her and then walking away, not this long, slow seduction.

"Give me your hand." When she placed her hand in his, he pulled it to his cock. "Stroke me."

Though his cock was hard as a rock, the skin covering it was silky smooth. She let her fingers close around the stalk, her middle finger just barely meeting the tip of her thumb.

A long shuddering sigh went through him. "Yes. That's what I want. Keep it up and I'll keep talking. But slowly. I don't want to come yet."

She stroked him, awkwardly at first and then finding a rhythm.

"I always liked you, Penelope. I wasn't good for anyone back then. I'm probably still not, but things have changed. I always found you attractive."

She rubbed her cheek against his chest. "I find that hard to imagine. You didn't date anyone who looked like me."

He chuckled, his chest moving with the laugh. "I took a few women out to lunch at the office. It wasn't anything serious. I didn't really date at all. Not the way you would think of it. I played with subs, but I never was exclusive. I took out a couple of women when I was younger, but I have to lie about so much, it didn't seem to be possible. I was in the Army for the longest time and then I was SIS. I can't have a normal relationship. I have to be able to work, and most women aren't going to understand why I need to leave to go undercover for months or even years at a time."

She understood all that, but it didn't answer the basic question. "Why me?"

"You don't think you're pretty, but you're wrong. And it's more than that. I want what you can offer me. I want all that kindness. I want that innocence. I want to be the one who teaches you how to stroke a cock. You're quite good at it, by the way." His free hand came up, sliding across her belly and up to cup her breast.

Her nipple peaked as his hand ran across it.

She lost her rhythm, her whole body on alert as he touched her.

"But you need to learn to focus, love." His fingertips found her nipple and squeezed tight, a short, sharp shock.

She gasped as the pain flared and then sank into her. "Damon."

He tweaked her again. "Master. We're playing. I'm in charge now, and I want you to stroke my cock. I think that you like this. I think the idea of pleasing me does something for you. And I definitely think you respond to a bite of pain."

Her pussy certainly had. It was as though the pain from his fingers had gone directly to her core, morphing in to pleasure along the way. She gripped his cock again, with more confidence this time, and stroked him.

"That's my girl." Damon whispered the words, almost breathing them into her skin. "That's exactly what I want. I didn't have anything to offer you then, but I do now. I can show you the world. All those things you read about in books, I can make them real for you. I can protect you while you explore. I can take care of you, Penelope. All you have to do is submit to me. I'll treat you like the gift you are."

His words drugged her, made her feel drowsy with wanting. There was absolutely nothing to keep her from rolling onto her back and letting him take her. Then she would be his. For how long didn't matter. She would be his, and she could hold the memory forever.

"Kiss me now." He shifted so their lips could meet and Penny never had to stop stroking him. His free hand moved over hers, covering her as he took over. His tongue traced along her bottom lip, making her shiver.

She turned into him, letting her breasts rest against his chest. He made her feel delicate and feminine against his masculinity.

"Say you'll stay with me."

There was only one answer to that. "Yes."

* * * *

The minute Damon heard the word "yes" leave her lips, he was all over her. She'd said it. Penelope had given him permission, and now it was his turn. His cock was raging hard, ready to go off any second. He tore her hand away because he wasn't going to come in her palm. He wanted to mark her, to make her remember exactly who she belonged to so she wouldn't flirt with Lord Weston again.

He rolled her on her back, making a place for himself between her legs. So fucking soft. She was the damn softest thing he'd ever held. He looked down into those sky-blue eyes and nearly lost it.

He hadn't lied to her. He'd always watched her, but she was the type of woman who should have a husband and children, who went to church on Sundays and always had supper ready. He had nothing to offer her. He couldn't be that man, but she'd walked away from that kind of life the minute she'd told him yes.

He was a greedy bastard and she was a good thing.

One good thing. Sometimes that was all a man needed. She was smart, and after he'd trained her, she would be good in the field. A team. They would be a team and then he never had to leave his job, never had to go back to his pitiful existence.

He kissed her, letting his tongue plunge inside. He would make it good for her, take care of her, make her need him like she needed her next breath.

So she wouldn't leave, wouldn't betray him. So all that sweetness and light would be for him and him alone.

Sex would bind her to him. Sex would bring them closer together.

Sex would feel so bloody good.

Her arms wound around him, her legs spread wide. She was a feast and he was suddenly damn near starving.

He kissed his way down her neck, giving her little bites along the way. Every time he nipped her, she jumped a little, but he could see the way her eyes widened, first in shock and then a sultry acceptance dropped over her. She was relaxing, taking what he gave her and allowing it to grow in to hot desire.

He cupped her breasts. Soft, sweet breasts. The women he'd

been around tended to be in the business, and they were either surgically enhanced or so physically fit there wasn't an ounce of cushion on them. Not Penelope. Penelope was all woman, with curves and hips he could hold on to when he fucked her hard and long. He didn't have to worry about breaking her.

That idiot fiancé of hers had been right. Penelope was strong. She gripped him and he felt it. Her nails sank into his skin. He doubted she even realized she was doing it. Little scratches against his skin. They would be there for hours, reminding him how hot he'd gotten her, how far gone she'd been. The way she clawed at him got him even hotter.

He tongued her nipples, moving from one to the other, softening her up. First something sweet, a suck and lick, and then he'd nip her, dragging that bud between his teeth and biting down, glorying in the way she gasped and moaned. She wriggled underneath him, and he could smell her.

God, he loved that smell. He couldn't get it out of his head since the day before. Delicate but strong, like the woman herself.

He had to taste her. The bit he'd dragged off his own hands hadn't been enough. He needed to get his tongue inside her, needed to spear her on it.

"Has anyone ever eaten your pussy before?" He growled the question against her tits, rubbing himself over the satin of her skin.

"What?"

He loved how out of breath she was, out of herself. When she let go, she was a sensual thing. So buttoned up and proper during the day, she turned into a sexy sub when he stripped her down. He dragged himself up so he was on his knees between her thighs, staring down at her. No one who looked at her in her shapeless cardies and bland skirts would ever imagine that she could look so fucking wanton. "Your pussy. You know that thing you never really thought about before? Has any man ever put his mouth on your cunt? Ever made a meal out of you? Ever fucked you long and hard with his tongue? For that matter, has any woman ever done it? I would love to hear that story, pet."

He expected her to flush and she did, a pretty pink. Her ass would be lovely pink, too, but instead of turning away, she met him, amusement in her eyes. "No, Master. No lesbian loves in my past. And I believe you already know the answer to the other. Peter was fastidious. He wouldn't try ethnic food, much less put his mouth on me there. On my pussy."

Prat. Dumbass, as his American friends would call him. "I'm not fastidious."

Her eyes went dreamy and one hand came up to cup his cheek. "No, you're not. You're dirty, Master. You're a dirty, nasty man. You're going to eat my pussy, aren't you? You'll do all those things you said."

His cock jumped. Nasty words sounded somehow sweet coming out of her mouth. "Yeah. I'm going to do everything I promised."

He looked down at her pussy. Plump. Ripe. Her labial lips were already wet with arousal. Her clitoris was poking out of its hood, all pearly and lovely in the early morning light. She was perfectly smooth. She'd done a damn fine job on herself. He could see her, working the razor over her flesh with the same care and caution she used when breaking a code or translating a document. She'd probably looked up how to do it, studied it so she would be perfect.

"I'm going to teach you. I'll teach you how to be my sub, my perfect partner." He let his finger run across the slit of his cock, gathering the pre-come. He rubbed it into her clit, wanting a piece of himself on her. Later, he would come all over her, rubbing it into her skin. He would come inside her and know she walked around with his come in her pussy.

He'd never had a permanent submissive, never collared one before, but she would wear every mark of his possession.

"Damon, you're killing me." Her hips wiggled, trying to force his finger to rub harder.

No time like the present. She wasn't in charge. He'd meant to ease her into discipline, but that was before he'd realized how much she needed it. "I believe I told you to call me Master. Do you know what a safe word is?"

Her eyes flared. "Yes."

"Pick one."

"Master, I…" Something in his eyes must have told that beautiful brain of hers that this was another fight she couldn't win because she nodded suddenly. "Penguin. It's the first word that came to mind."

"Excellent." He moved off her and neatly flipped her over, exposing the sight of the most gorgeous arse he'd ever seen. "You're not in charge. I'm in charge. You'll take the pleasure I give you and by god, you'll take my discipline."

He slapped her cheeks three times in rapid succession. A sexy gasp came from her mouth.

"Oh my god."

That wasn't her safe word. Not anywhere close. Another three. Hard smacks against those juicy cheeks. She trembled under his hand, but didn't make another sound.

"Can you take four more? That's what you'll get when you try to steal an orgasm from me. You'll get ten this first week because we're in training. It will be so much worse for you later, pet."

"Yes. I can take it." There was a steely will in her voice and then she sighed and settled down, offering her bum to him.

God, she was perfect. He drew out the last four, allowing his hand to settle against her flesh so the heat would seep into her skin, turning to arousal.

When he was finished with the final smack, she collapsed, her back shaking.

A flare of panic hit his system. Had he been too hard on her? He turned her over, praying she wasn't crying. He couldn't handle it if she cried because he'd been too rough.

Her face was flushed, her eyes soft. "Master?"

She wasn't afraid. Relief rushed through him. "Yes, love?"

"I think I'm a freak." A smile flashed on her face.

He laughed long and hard because he hadn't expected that. That summed her up. Unexpected. "Yes, you are. Lucky for you. Being a freak is so much more fun. Do you understand what I want?"

"You want me to be still. You want me to submit."

Such a smart girl. "Yes. I'll tie you down if I have to. Don't think I can't do it. The bed was custom built. You can't see it right now, but there's a whole system under the mattress built for naughty subs who can't hold still. Once I've got you tied down by your arms and legs, I'll be able to do anything I want. I'll be able to torture your sweet pussy." He ran a hand over her mound, feeling how wet she already was. "I'll keep you on edge all day long. You'll be crying and begging for me to let you come."

"I'm quite there already, Master."

She had no idea what he could do to her. "Not yet, you aren't. You've just had a little taste. He didn't make you come."

She shook her head. "No. Never."

"I make you come. I'm the man who makes you come. Say it."

"You make me come. Only you."

He wasn't sure he liked the raging jealousy that went through him every time he thought about that skinny accountant putting his hands on Penelope. He had the deepest instinct to obliterate the man. Had Peter told her he loved her? Had he offered her the life she deserved? It didn't matter because he hadn't been man enough to keep her. It had been easy to find that story. Peter saved his e-mails. He'd talked about how Penelope had gotten so involved in her mother's care that she hadn't found time for him. Stupid boy. He should have taken over. She'd been drowning and no one had offered to save her. No one had walked in and made life easy for her. Her siblings had visited but no one had taken control. He would have moved them both in here and hired a nurse twenty-four seven, costs be damned. He would have made sure Penelope never forgot that she was a woman and not just a caretaker. He would have had her in bed every night screaming out her pleasure, the tension dissolving away in pulse-pounding sex.

He knew what she needed, and he wasn't going to make the same mistakes. He might not be able to offer her love, but he damn sure could take care of her.

Love was for idiots who didn't know what the world was really like. What he was offering her was something far more real. A partnership.

"Only me." He parted the petals of her sex. The need to take her rode him hard. His cock was right there. He was hard and she was wet. It would be so simple, but he had a point to prove.

He would control her through sex, not the other way around. He was the Dom. He was the senior partner.

And he'd promised her a good tongue lashing. He could spend the entire morning eating her pussy. Then he would feed her. He could start her training. He would make her sit on his lap and feed her himself, and then he would take her to the dungeon and start getting her used to impact play.

He would plug her gorgeous bum because he was going to fuck her there. Eventually. But this morning it was all about the pussy. It was all about getting deep inside Penelope. It was all about making the connection that would bind her to him.

Fuck. It was all about coming. It was all about spending himself hard inside her. His dick was pulsing, dying. All he needed to do was thrust up and he would be content.

He placed his head against her forehead. It was such a temptation to just fuck up into her.

But she was so inexperienced. He had to stop.

He rubbed their foreheads against one another. He was close to her. Closer than he'd ever been to a woman. Fuck. She did it for him. He didn't really understand why, but she did it. She called to him. Everything about Penelope Cash pulled him in. He had to take care of her, had to protect her. Even from himself because the idea of spending his come inside her was so fucking tempting. He wanted to bind her to him so she wouldn't ever leave.

Selfish. He was greedy and selfish and he wanted to be more to her.

"Love, what about birth control?" He didn't want to have to stop to ask her about it later.

"I'm on birth control pills. I've been on them for years. I guess I was hopeful."

Fuck. He didn't have to wear a condom. "Love, you got my medical reports."

She frowned. "Well, I read the ones you didn't bury." She huffed out a laugh. "Master, I know you're clean. Will you please make love to me?"

So polite and he didn't want polite from her. "Ask me to fuck you, Penelope."

He didn't want to lie to her. He didn't make love. He didn't even believe in it as a concept. It was something people needed to mask their primal needs for sex and conquest and someone to sleep next to at night.

Penelope's eyes widened and a sexy gasp came from those lips of hers. "Will you fuck me?"

"With pleasure, love." But first things came first. He kissed his way down her body, stopping to nip at her breasts and suck each one hard into his mouth. She was primed. She could handle more now. And god knew he wanted to give her more. "Spread your legs wider."

She didn't hesitate, simply moved her legs farther apart, giving him more room, more access to his pussy. His. She would be his in a way no woman had belonged to him before. She was practically a fucking virgin but here she was giving him everything she had.

He let his fingers play in her labia, drawing the petals apart and watching them fold back together. He fingered her clit briefly, not enough to let her fly. No. He wanted that to happen around his dick. He wanted to feel those muscles clamp down on his shaft, holding him hard and long while he spilled inside her.

One long lick of his tongue had Penelope squirming again, but she quickly settled down. Likely she was remembering the hard smack of his hand to her ass. He licked her again, tasting every inch of her. Spicy and sweet. Penelope. Over and over he licked and sucked and she let him. Only her pleas and gasps and the fresh arousal coating her flesh told him how desperate she was becoming.

"You're doing so well." He breathed the words against her pussy. "Just a bit more."

"You're trying to kill me."

He chuckled. He had just enough sadist in him to deeply enjoy her discomfort. Sucking her clit into his mouth, he let his fingers fuck up into her pussy. Just one. She was so tight. The skinny accountant must have had a pencil dick.

Her body tightened and Damon released her clit.

"Damn it!" Her skin had flushed a deep pink. "Please. Please."

Another finger. It would be rough, but he meant to get inside her. She was so slick, but he would still have to be careful. He let himself feel her heat for another second before pulling his fingers from her warmth.

"Not until I'm ready." He got to his knees over her protests. "And you're to call me Master when I'm fucking you, sub. That's what you're going to be, you understand?"

Her blonde curls shook as she nodded. "Yes. Your submissive. Yours, Master."

Fuck, yes, she was his. But not quite yet. His cock pulsed, muscles tightening. He could feel his heart thundering in his chest. At least if he died doing this he would die happy. No. This was a good thunder. A promise of pleasure and peace, not what had happened to him when he was chasing Baz.

He stroked himself, blood pounding through his dick. He couldn't help but stare at the place where his cock sat right on the precipice of her body. She was so soft and pretty and he was going to tear her up. Yes, that thought got him hot, too. She would be sore all day, likely the first couple of times until she'd adjusted to accommodate him.

His pussy. It belonged to him.

He pushed in, her heat threatening to strangle his cock.

Never before had he taken a woman bareback. So fucking good. He let everything else fall away. There was no mission, no betrayal to avenge, nothing at all except the woman he was sinking into.

"Take me." Little thrusts back and forth. She was so small, but he was determined.

Penelope shifted her hips up, her face determined. "I want you, Master. All of you. I want to take every inch of you."

He pushed in. Another inch. His cock sank in and he dragged it back out. Over and over. He took his time because this was important. Discipline would win this battle.

A long sigh of pure pleasure came from deep inside his body as he finally pushed home. He was balls deep inside her, his fingers sinking into the cushion of her ass. She was everything he'd thought she would be and more.

"Maybe I was wrong. Maybe I should take just a bit less of you," she said on a shaky breath.

Brat. "Give it a minute. You'll get used to me. I promise, love. I'll make this good."

Her hands came up, threading into his hair. "It's all right. I don't know that I'm so good at this part."

It was one of those times that he likely should stop and spank her silly, but he couldn't. This was too important. This suddenly didn't feel like play. He was buried inside her and it was bloody important. "We're going to be very good at this. We're going to practice and I do promise you'll come. I'm going to make sure of it."

He ground his pelvis down, hitting her clit, watching her eyes darken.

Her hands moved restlessly from his hair to his shoulders, as if she wasn't sure what to do with them. He knew.

"Grip my arse." He wanted her hands on him, letting him know how much she wanted his cock.

Those soft hands of hers skimmed across his body until they settled on his cheeks.

"I'm better now." She gave him a hard squeeze.

"No, you're not, but you will be. Hold on tight. Be rough with me. I'll fucking love it. You leave your mark on me. God knows I intend to leave mine on you." With a long sigh of relief, he slid out and then thrust back in. This time she accommodated him, his thrust easy and sure.

Damon let himself go. She was writhing under him, her hands trying to hold him deep. It was a fight, but the best kind. She tried to keep his cock inside and he fought for the friction, every thrust and pull a drag on his cock. He pounded into her, twisting his hips so he caught her clit.

Her whole body tightened, her nails digging into his skin as she came on a long moan. His cock was caught, strangled by her orgasm, thrusting him into his own.

Nothing had ever felt as good as filling Penelope Cash with his come. Over and over he thrust in, giving her every ounce he had inside him.

Finally, a deep sense of peace thrumming through him, he collapsed on her. Resting his face against her neck. His world was filled with her. Her scent, the way her chest moved against his, warm arms around him. He could drown in her.

His mobile trilled.

The room stilled, time seeming to stop. He always answered his mobile because it was always work. He didn't have a bunch of friends who called and interrupted him. He had work and they called when it was important.

"Don't, Damon." Her face was red, her lips tight, and now the tears showed up as though she couldn't stand to have him walk away even to answer his mobile. Their intimacy was fragile.

He ignored it. Fuck whoever was calling him. They would call back. This was his time with her. This felt oddly sacred, and he didn't want it interrupted. He wanted to hold her, cuddle with her and kiss her all over again.

Her mobile trilled.

"They'll go away." He willed them all to go the bloody hell away.

The intercom buzzed, and Ian Taggart's voice came over the speaker. "Knight, get your ass down here. We're wanted at headquarters. Apparently your friend has been causing trouble, and he's after your girl. Let's go."

Baz was after her? Baz knew about Penelope, knew the way to get to him was through her. A sudden vision of Penelope cold and dead struck his brain like a hammer. He was supposed to protect her. How could he protect her when he couldn't stop fucking her long enough to answer his bloody phone?

He was supposed to be in control, but she stripped it away from him. He had to get it back, and he wouldn't do it by cuddling with her. He was trapped between giving her what he knew she needed and keeping distant enough to be effective.

He rolled off the bed and started for the shower. He needed to think.

"Damon?"

"Get dressed. We have work to do." He didn't look back. He really couldn't stand to see her cry.

Chapter Eight

Penny sat next to Damon, their chairs almost touching, but she might as well have been in another country. Nigel's office was silent, lit only with the fluorescents above. There was no such thing as opening a window at headquarters. The windows were treated so no one could see in, every pane bulletproof.

Since the moment he'd gotten the word that Baz was still running about London causing trouble, Damon had shut down. There had been no more caresses or hugs. No kisses. No dirty talk. When he'd come out of the shower, he'd been distant. Not cold exactly. He'd given her an encouraging smile, but he'd held himself apart.

She could still feel his cock deep inside her, but he was miles away.

"Are you all right?"

He'd asked her more than once, but she just gave him a tight smile. He seemed to have shifted to treating her with an awkward politeness, like he hadn't made love to her an hour before. "I am, Damon. Where is Nigel? Why didn't you bring the rest of the team in?"

The Taggarts were sitting outside in the waiting room. They'd ridden over in Damon's Benz. Damon and Taggart had talked quietly, but she'd just looked out the window.

For one brief moment, she'd felt so connected to him, so close. She'd never felt as open and free as she had when Damon had taken over.

She really hated Basil Champion.

"Nigel wants to talk to us first," Damon explained.

The door opened, and Nigel walked through looking like he hadn't slept well the night before. The lines around his eyes seemed to have deepened over the course of the weekend.

He strode straight to his desk. "Harris was discovered with two bullets in his chest early this morning. Champion got through hospital security. A nurse found the body."

He flipped open a folder and tossed it on the desk. Penny couldn't help the gasp that came out of her throat. Harris was lying across a mattress, blood staining the white sheets, his eyes wide open and staring up.

Damon's hand shot out, slamming the folder closed. "You didn't have to show her that."

Nigel's eyes narrowed. "You're the one who made her a field agent."

"Under my command and I will decide what she does and doesn't see. Don't pull that shit with me, Nige. You know damn well I mean to protect her from this. Penelope, wait outside."

Nigel shook his head. "Absolutely not. She has every right to know what's happening. If you're telling me you don't trust her enough, then I'll shove her right back behind a desk. This is serious. We have an agent dead."

"I'm trying to protect her," Damon said, his voice tight.

She knew the job was dangerous. "I'm fine, Damon."

Nigel's fist came down on his desk, the first time she'd ever seen him lose his temper. "She's either your partner or your girlfriend. She can't be both. You told me you could be professional."

She couldn't let Nigel pull her from the op. Somehow, she had to see this one thing through. It was important. She was the only one who knew about Damon's weakness. He wouldn't stop, and maybe the next partner would leave him when he needed her. "No. I want to go on. We're fine."

Nigel ignored her. "Read the note, Damon. Open the folder and read the note that was left on Harris's body. Read the note and then the e-mail that followed this morning."

Damon stood, not looking back at her. He picked up the folder and stepped away from the desk, opening it. A long moment passed, tension thick in the air. Nigel sat in his chair, running a hand through his thinning hair.

Damon didn't say a word, but she saw how his back straightened, his jaw tightening.

Nigel looked over at him. "Is it true?"

"You knew what I meant by training." Damon didn't look up, his voice a harsh grind. "You knew. Don't play the prude now, Nige."

"What does it say?" Penny asked. She didn't like the way the men were looking at each other.

"I rather thought you would be a gentleman about it," Nigel shot back.

"You didn't hire a gentleman, Nigel. You hired me, and you knew what I wanted from her." Now he looked up and there was a bitterness in his eyes she hadn't seen before. "You have no idea what it's like in the field. None. Don't you dare start to judge me."

"What does it say?" She was more forceful this time because she was starting to think she had an inkling and it wouldn't be flattering. Somehow it made her a bit angry instead of embarrassed. Days ago she would have been shriveling up inside at the insinuations she was hearing, but spending time naked with Damon had changed her somehow. There hadn't been anything wrong with it. It had been a lovely thing.

Damon frowned as he turned to her. "Give me your handbag. Where do you normally put it? Is it locked up while you're here?"

What the hell was going on? Her brain was racing. "No. I leave it in my desk. Why would anyone try to steal…" The truth hit her squarely in the forehead. "They didn't try to steal something. They put something on it."

She picked up her bag. It was a simple thing, large and roomy. She'd bought it on sale at H&M about a month after her mum had passed on. It had been an impulse buy because the pattern was so unlike her. Paisley. It didn't really go with anything but she'd loved the colors. The pattern was busy, easy to hide something among.

She ran her hand along the material and on the front of the bag, just below the clasp, she felt it. A bug. Small, wireless. She pulled it off and stared at it, thinking about the man on the other end. "I really hate you, you know. I hope your balls shrivel off and die."

"Penelope!" Damon stood, staring at her with shocked eyes.

"Well, I'm not stupid. Obviously that note has something to do with our physical relationship, and Nigel thinks I'm some schoolgirl who doesn't know the score and he's going to try to protect the sad virgin. First off, I would protest and say I'm not a virgin, but lately I've been thinking I might as well be because the sexual relations I had before don't even fall in the same category. Kissing Damon is sexier than full-on intercourse with other men. I don't want to be protected. I knew what I was getting into. I'm not leaving now that it's getting a bit deadly." She held the small device on her fingertip. "He's trying to break us up, but it won't work."

His eyes flared and for the briefest moment, a look of wonder came across his face. It was quickly shut down and he averted his eyes, looking back to the file. "Keep quiet. Get rid of that thing before you say another word."

Because if he really was still listening, she'd just given away a lot. She'd stood there and pledged to not leave him. She'd given away a weakness.

Tears filled her eyes. She'd just proven how stupid she could be. She'd known he was listening and she'd still talked.

Nigel hit a button on his phone. "Send me someone from tech. And tell our Americans they can come in now if Mr. Smith is through with his debrief. We have a lot to sort through. Unfortunately, this bloody mess has gone international. The Agency is here. You need to read his other demands."

The CIA had sent someone?

Nigel took the device from her, palming it and closing his hand.

Damon stayed where he was, though she wanted so much for him to cross the distance between them. "Keep your voice down until that thing is gone. I swear I'll find the mole and I'm going to make whoever it is pay."

Someone had been listening and watching her every move for days, perhaps months. It made her stomach turn, but she needed to make one thing clear. She moved close to him, her voice low. "I'm staying with you. I don't care what Nigel says. I'm strong enough for this. I can be good for you."

Damon shook his head, a dismissal. "Nigel might be right about this."

"You know I'm right, but I don't know what we can do about it now." Nigel's voice broke through the quiet.

The doors opened and Ian Taggart walked through followed by his wife and a tall, well-built man with brown and gold hair. He was wearing jeans and what looked like a Western shirt and cowboy boots.

"Are you fucking kidding me?" Taggart asked. He'd obviously been brought up to speed on the situation, and he wasn't happy about it.

"Don't, Tag." The new guy crossed his arms as he looked around the room. "We're all getting fucked here. Can we be sure it's safe to talk now?"

One of the techs walked in, a younger man named Marvin who had never once spoken to her until Friday last. He'd walked up to her and asked her about something trivial that might have been wrong with her computer. It had only been a few moments, but she'd turned.

Where had her bag been?

She closed her eyes, trying to remember everything about the encounter. It had been lunchtime and the rest of her group had gone, but Marvin had shown up. She'd stayed to answer his questions. She'd put her bag on her desk, turned and pulled up the update he'd asked about.

"Don't give it to him. He'll destroy it or he'll fake a report that gives us absolutely nothing. He's working with Champion."

Nigel stopped in the act of handing over the camera.

Damon shoved her behind him, as though the man would pull a

gun and shoot her right there.

Marvin was a weasel, but she doubted he was a killer.

"I don't know what she's talking about. That's ridiculous," the tech said, but his hands were shaking slightly.

Taggart stepped up. He was a good foot taller than the tech and had at least seven stone of pure muscle on him. Taggart loomed over the man. "Penny, are you sure?"

Sure? It could be someone else, but the timing worked. If Marvin was supposed to follow Damon Knight's movements around SIS, then he would have known Damon had requested information on her. Apparently Damon had delved rather violently into almost all aspects of her life. Champion would want to know why Damon was so interested in a translator. "When did you request my files, Damon?"

"Late Thursday night."

The timing checked out. "And Friday at roughly eleven a.m., he stopped and asked me about my computer. He had access to my bag. I had it out because I was going to lunch. The rest of the time I have it locked in my desk."

Marvin shook his head. "Anyone could have done it. There are people with keys to the desks."

But instinct pointed to him. She wouldn't have been on Champion's radar before. The minute she'd come into his focus, Marvin had appeared. Sometimes she had to follow her instincts. "Check his computer. He likely has more than one here."

Nigel hit his button again. "I need security."

"No, you don't," Taggart said, his mouth curling up in a deeply gruesome approximation of a grin. "You just need to give me five minutes with him."

"Ian, you promised you would stop killing people. I'm tired of getting blood out of your clothes." Charlotte took Penny's vacated seat and crossed her legs casually.

"No problem, baby. I'll put on a raincoat."

Security showed up. Two large men, much larger than needed to handle a skinny guy like Marvin who just now seemed to realize what kind of trouble he was in.

"I'll talk." He tried to back away, but hit the mountain of muscle that was Ian Taggart. He turned and nearly screamed. "I didn't hurt anyone. I just gave him some files and bugged her bag. God, nothing could be wrong with that. She's dull as dishwater."

Penny gasped as she realized that her bag had been tossed in a chair across from the counter in the washroom at her cousin's wedding. "I made a sex tape." He'd bugged her bag and now her first orgasm was likely on the Internet. "Mr. Taggart, I don't have much money, but I will give you everything I have if you would please murder that man and in a deeply painful manner."

Taggart snorted. "Your girl is vicious, Knight. In a very polite way, of course. And Pen, I'll do him for free. I haven't tortured anyone in a long time."

Charlotte cleared her throat.

Taggart groaned. "Not the same thing, baby."

"Get him out of here." Nigel took over, obviously sick of the interruptions. "The Americans can talk to him later. I'll be down in interrogation in ten minutes. I want him alive, but you can soften him up for me, lads."

Marvin was dragged out of the room.

"Give me the bug. Let Chelsea and Adam research it. You have no idea how compromised you are." Taggart held out his hand. Nigel hesitated. "Ten?"

The cowboy-looking man sighed. "He's under contract, Nigel. To both of us. If you can't trust him, why did you sign him up for this?"

"It's not him I don't trust. I suspect Chelsea Dennis had a lot to do with her sister's business," Nigel admitted.

"And we both offered her a job, so give me a little here. From what I understand, your old man Weston rarely takes his eyes off her anyway, and Adam Miles is completely trustworthy. Let's keep this off the radar, man." He turned his green eyes her way. "Besides, I don't exactly trust everyone on your team, so we're even."

"You leave her out of this, Ten." Damon seemed to be putting himself between her and all manner of danger today.

She was sick of cowering behind him, though she did have to

admit she liked the view. What was happening to her? She was surrounded by predatory animals. She'd just discovered she'd made a sex tape. A killer had been watching her every move, and she was thinking about Damon's very tight arse. She moved from behind him. "My name is Penelope Cash."

The man named Ten studied her. "Yes, I know. I know everything about you. You speak four different languages fluently. IQ of 155. You lived at home with your mother until seven months ago. You apparently really like dirty talk."

Damon took a step the cowboy's way.

The testosterone in the room was really getting to be a bit much for her. "Nigel, could you get rid of that thing one way or another so we can talk? Damon, calm down. He didn't do anything you didn't do. He looked into my background. That's all. He's right about everything. And I really do like dirty talk."

"High-five, Pen." Charlotte seemed to be the only one amused. "Don't we all? So give it up, Nige. Little sis and Adam will tell you everything about the sucker in a couple of hours. And Simon is already going through Damon's place with a fine-tooth comb. We'll be clean by the time we get back."

So at least she could be sure they'd be alone in The Garden. She suddenly wanted to be back there. She wanted to be in Damon's arms. She wanted to be his sub and not his partner because she had the feeling she wouldn't like the decisions he was about to make.

Nigel turned over the bug, and the Taggarts left after Charlotte gave her a long, sympathetic look.

"Are we sure it's safe to talk here?" Damon asked.

Nigel nodded. "Yes. We went into a very quiet lockdown the minute we received the files. My office has already been declared clean."

"Good." Damon turned to her, taking her by the arms. He gestured the cowboy's way. "Penelope, that man is named Tennessee Smith. He's with the CIA. According to the intelligence I just read, not only did Champion execute one of our agents last night, he left behind a note. A note for me. Baz told me he wanted to talk, and he's pressing the issue in the dirtiest way he can think of. He told me he'll meet me in one of the cities we dock in on the cruise and I'm to bring you with me."

"He thinks I'm a weakness for you."

Damon nodded slowly. "Which is precisely why I need to leave you behind. Our relationship ends here and now."

Her heart nearly plunged to her shoes. It was over? So quickly? She'd known it would end, known it wouldn't last long, but she'd wanted her weeks with him. She'd wanted a few weeks where she did more with her life than stare at a computer, translating mostly mundane conversations, listening in on other people's lives.

She knew it was stupid. Just the day before she'd decided to guard herself against him, but she didn't want to go back to the way it had been. She couldn't stand the thought of him glancing her way without so much as a smile, just one of the hundreds of women who had loved him and who meant nothing to him now.

God, she was in love with Damon. It was silly to even think it wasn't true. She'd been in love with him for a very long time.

He stared down at her, his jaw tight. "I won't talk to you, Penelope. I won't acknowledge your presence when you walk in a room. I will pretend you don't exist. This was all about one single operation. That operation is over for you. I can't use you anymore."

She felt tears slipping from her eyes. She reached up and cupped his cheek. "Damon, I want to go with you. I don't care about the risk."

It didn't matter that there were other people in the room. She couldn't be one more person who disappeared on him.

He stepped away, his face going cold, eyes blank. "Penelope, I've done you a great disservice."

"Don't, Damon. I know what you're going to do. Don't."

He didn't look away from her. He looked right through her, like she was already gone, already relegated to some place in his mind where he shoved useless things. "I needed you to obey me. Getting you to believe yourself to be in love with me was the easiest way to go. You know I made a study of you. You were lonely. You had very little experience with sex. It was simple. I do have experience. I knew exactly what to say to you."

Her heart was breaking because she did believe that he would do everything he said he would. He would walk away from her. He wouldn't speak to her again. She would dream about him for the rest of her life and his last words to her would be about how he'd tricked her. "You told me it was real."

He shrugged a bit, an aristocratic gesture. "I lied. Getting in your knickers was the best way to control you. You can't honestly believe I was attracted to you."

"You certainly looked like you were." It came out as an accusation.

A nasty smirk hit his face. "Darling, I can get an erection from a stiff breeze."

So the bit about his cock not working around anyone but her had been a lie, too.

"Don't call me that. Don't call me that again." His endearments meant nothing. They were one more way he'd drawn her in.

Something died a bit. A light that had started to grow inside her dimmed again. It had been foolish of her to believe him. She looked in the mirror on a regular basis. No amount of makeup would ever make her really beautiful. The people at the wedding had stared at them, but not because they looked right together. They stared because they wondered what the hell he was doing with her.

He was good. He'd known exactly how to get past her walls. He'd defended her, built up her self-esteem. He'd been just vulnerable enough to make her think they really did have something in common. She'd started to believe she was good for him.

She'd have to tell her sister and brother it had all been a joke. A joke on her.

"I'm sorry, Miss Cash." He didn't sound sorry. He sounded bland, blank, distant. But then he'd always been. The connection she'd felt had been one sided. Otherwise, there was no way he could hurt her like this. Love didn't work that way. Even friendship didn't work like that.

She'd been safer in her shell.

"Why did you sleep with me? I offered to do the job without sex." She was proud of how steady her voice was. She was calm again. This wasn't anything that hadn't happened to her before. It would likely happen again unless she simply shut down.

"I told you. I was training you to obey me. The easiest way to ensure a woman's compliance is to make her happy in bed. It's so much easier if the woman's never had a real lover. It wasn't some grand romance, Penelope. It's part of my job."

And she knew what he would do for his job. He would kill himself for it so sleeping with a woman he found a bit distasteful was likely simple for him.

He'd needed someone pliable, someone smart but naïve. If she looked at it logically, she was rather perfect.

"Are you all right? You went pale. Do you need to sit down?" Damon was looking at her with something akin to pity.

"I'm fine. I believe I'll go to my desk and clear it out."

He frowned. "You're not fired, Miss Cash."

"Oh, Mr. Knight, I do believe I quit. I expect my belongings back in my home by tonight." She turned to Nigel, praying she got through the next few minutes with some semblance of dignity. "Thank you for everything, sir. I'm sorry it ended like this."

Nigel sat down, shaking his head. "I told you this was a bloody bad idea, Knight. I really hope you're happy with yourself."

"Damon, we have a problem." Tennessee's voice broke through her gloom, and she was suddenly deeply aware that she wasn't alone with him. Two men had witnessed her humiliation.

Damon turned to him, every inch the competent agent. "Of course. We can discuss it after Penelope leaves. I would rather not compromise the mission further."

Tennessee sighed. "You've already compromised it, and now we're all royally screwed. He didn't just kill Harris. He's threatened to out undercover agents across the globe if you don't show up with her."

Nigel cursed under his breath. "Miss Cash, your resignation is rejected. You will keep your cover with Knight. You'll be issued a sidearm this afternoon. Please don't use it on him, though I wouldn't blame you if you did."

Damon cursed.

She shook her head. "No. I can't. I can't be around him anymore."

Nigel passed her the file. "I'm afraid you're going to have to."

With shaking hands, she took the file. "May I read it at my desk?"

"Of course. Take a few moments." Nigel nodded her way. "But I really can't let you leave."

She turned and walked out the door. She was suddenly afraid there was no way out of the trap. None at all.

Damon called out for her, but she kept walking. She might not be done with the operation, but she was certainly done with him.

Tears blurred her eyes, but she brushed them away as she sat down and opened the file. It was time to work. If there was one thing in the world Penelope Cash understood, it was duty.

Chapter Nine

Damon let the door slam shut before rounding on Tennessee Smith. He was killing mad. Her face. Her sweet face had gone blank and he'd known he'd just destroyed something lovely and fragile. Now Ten just happened to mention that it was all for nothing?

"You couldn't have said something when you walked past the bloody door?"

Ten just smirked. "Hey, I always like a little drama, man."

Damon got in his face. "Do you understand what you did?"

"I understand what you did. I understand that you fucked that girl and then broke her heart. That was quite easy to see. Don't worry about it. Baz'll probably kill her, but then you won't give a shit. She's just a pawn, right?"

Rage boiled and he couldn't stop himself. He reared back and his fist met Ten's jaw. He was satisfied with the way his hand cracked, the way Ten stumbled back.

Ten dropped his usual charming-guy act, his eyes hardening. "I'll take that once, Knight, because I think you just figured out how much you fucked up your own life, but don't try it again. You won't like the outcome."

"Knight, you will stand down!" Nigel got between the two of them, his face a bright red. "I told you it was a bad idea."

"I was trying to protect her." He couldn't let Baz have her. He couldn't allow it. Since Baz seemed determined to take everything Damon gave a damn about, he couldn't keep Penelope. Baz had killed Jane without a thought, but he would likely torture Penelope. He would make her hurt.

"You protected her by ripping her heart out and stomping all over it in front of everyone?" Ten asked.

"I had to. You don't understand her. She wouldn't have left me." Penelope would have stood by his side no matter what the cost. She was brave and smart, and for some reason, she'd started to love him. He wasn't a fool. He knew she was attracted to him. He'd used it to his advantage, but it wasn't until a few moments ago that he realized how deep her feelings went. She'd declared to everyone that Baz couldn't break them up, that she was here for him.

He believed her.

Which was why he had to let her go.

Ten snorted, his hand rubbing along his jawline. "It didn't occur to you to talk to her about the situation? To sit her down and give her your logic?"

"She wouldn't have left me." She would have found a way. She hadn't left him in the Tube station despite his direct orders. Baz could have taken her out while she held his unconscious body.

"Well, I doubt she'll give a damn about you now." Nigel moved back to his desk. "What a bloody mess. We need her. Do we know how thoroughly compromised we are?"

Ten glared his way but took a seat across from Nigel. "He doesn't specify which operation he's targeting, but he mentioned Afghanistan and Pakistan. We have twenty operatives in those countries under various covers. Some of them have been working their way into terrorist cells for years. If we have to pull them, it's a massive setback."

"That's unfortunate." Damon couldn't sit. He was too tightly wound. He'd wanted Ten to hit him back, wanted a brutal fight. His hands were still clenched in fists thinking about Penelope sitting out there alone. She'd gone pale. He'd thought for a moment she might faint. "You're going to have to pull them all. SIS doesn't negotiate with terrorists."

"That's not your call, Knight." Nigel leaned back. "He's threatening our operations, too."

"Do you still think he's working for the Chinese?" Damon couldn't resist the gibe. "Do you think the Chinese are behind any of this?"

"I think it doesn't matter who he's working for. It could all be a bluff, but after realizing our tech department's been compromised, I can't call him on it. I need you to meet with him. You have to figure out what he wants and if it has anything to do with the operation on the boat. Given that he's planning on meeting you somewhere in Northern Europe, I would say he does have something to do with this whole Nature's Core mess."

"He told me he wanted to talk about the operation when he cornered me in the Tube." And if Baz was involved, then The Collective was involved. How was The Collective involved with an environmental group?

"All the more reason to run the operation as planned," Nigel explained. "Beyond that, I need you to give me time to figure out what he knows."

"And when we have everything we need on him?"

Nigel's eyes narrowed, staring right into his. "Then I need you to kill him."

Finally someone was talking sense. "Of course." That was a forgone conclusion. He would make it his life's mission to see Baz in the ground. "But Penelope is out of this. And I want those photos destroyed."

His vision had misted over with a red haze of anger when he'd seen the photo Baz had left with his directive. *Tell Damon I want to talk to him or this continues. I'll get him instructions on time and place. And he should bring his whore with him.*

The photo had been grainy, a still from a video. The bug on her bag had caught them in the act. Penelope's legs were spread, his hand on her pussy, her pretty face open. The moment of her orgasm. It was ingrained on his brain. He would very likely die thinking about it. It was their intimate moment, the first time he'd been with her.

And Baz had put it out there for everyone to see. Like it was a porno.

That was what he planned for Penelope. Humiliation and death. He couldn't allow it to happen. She was more than an asset. She was...

He wasn't even sure of what he felt. He simply knew that she wasn't safe around him. His first job was to protect Penelope. Somehow she'd become important.

"She's going on the op, Knight. Nigel promised my bosses that you would take care of this." Ten glared Nigel's way. "Get control of your people. I'm going to talk to Tag, but I fully expect that blonde out there on Knight's arm when he goes to meet Champion. Losing those agents would set US intelligence back by years."

"It won't be a party for us either," Nigel shot back. "We will take care of it."

Ten stopped, staring at Damon for a moment. "He screwed the girl over. I doubt she's going to help us out."

"She will," Nigel replied with surety. "She's been with SIS for a long time. She'll do her job. Miss Cash is loyal."

Yes, she was. Which was exactly why he'd had to break with her in a way that would bust her loyalty to him.

She would have walked beside him into hell, and he couldn't allow that. "She's not coming with me. I won't do the job with her. Do you understand me? I will not work with that woman."

"Is there any way we could find someone who looks like me? I would be willing to spend time with her so she could get my mannerisms down." Penelope stepped into the room, the folder against her chest as though she thought it was a wall to protect her. "If Mr. Knight won't deign to work with me, I'll do whatever I can to help out. I understand how important this is."

Naturally, she'd heard the worst. And his stupid cock didn't care that he'd blown their relationship to hell. His idiotic dick just knew she'd walked in the room and called him Mr. Knight in her soft, polite voice, like he was some character out of a bloody Jane Austen novel. He wanted to hear her call him Mr. Knight while he shoved his cock in her arse.

But she wouldn't let him do that now. Before, he could have taken her in every way it was possible to take a woman. She'd been his from the moment he'd asked her to work with him. That was gone now. He wouldn't meet another Penelope. He'd met his match, and it was done.

"We can put a blonde wig on someone. She's right. Someone else would be better." Anything to keep her far away.

"No. She's going to stay with you for the duration." Nigel sighed. "You're like two children. I have to play the father figure. You will work together. You will play your parts. There will be no substitutions. There's too much at stake. Penelope, you will not walk away from this operation. You will go on the cruise with Knight and you will aid him both in finding the terrorist and discovering what Champion has to do with all of this."

She shook those blonde curls he loved to sink his fingers into. "I'll be what you need."

So fucking brave. She could have been his. All that strength would have been his had fucking Baz not screwed him over. His fists tightened. His. Fucking his. She belonged to him as no female ever had before and she wouldn't look at him.

Because he'd burned that bridge, and he knew damn well no one got second chances.

She was far from him. No matter how close, she wouldn't allow him to touch her. Wouldn't allow him access to her. She'd spread her legs before and welcomed him. She'd tossed aside her every inhibition for him. She'd been his in every way that had mattered.

Now she wouldn't look at him and his insides hurt. Baz had shot him but the fact that Penelope wouldn't look at him was worse.

She stood apart. There was no chair for her. He and Ten were taking them up.

Damon practically leapt out of his seat. She should expect courtesy. From him. From every bloody man in the world. She was a woman. It didn't matter if the man wasn't fucking her. She deserved his chair, his protection.

She didn't move to the seat. It was empty. He felt empty, too.

He wanted to hold her. She'd been so bloody perfect in his arms.

She'd fit against him like he'd been missing a piece of himself and he'd finally been made whole.

He'd lost everyone. But just for a moment, he'd thought he would be okay. He would never get over the loss of Penelope Cash. A flash went through him. She was the one. He didn't believe in love in a tangible sense, but he did think that there were rewards the universe gave out. For surviving, for bravery, for saving those who couldn't help themselves.

She'd been his prize, and he'd lost her.

Like he'd lost everything else.

"I would like to talk to you alone," Nigel said. He wasn't talking to Damon. Bloody hell. An hour ago, it wouldn't have happened. He would have told Penelope no, and she would have stayed at his side so Nigel would have treated them like a team. Unbreakable.

They were so broken now.

"Of course, sir." Her words were a brutal monotone. Nothing like her usual lyrical speech. He loved the way she talked. Her ebullience made his heart beat faster, but there was none of it now. Staccato. She spoke in hard rhythms.

"Excellent." Nigel pulled his chair up. He turned to Damon. "Damon, you will continue with the operation as though nothing has happened. Everything must appear normal. I'll let you know when we get the information on the meet spot. It will likely be at the last minute so we have absolutely no chance to send in a team."

He would wait until they stopped in a foreign port and pull them from their assignment. There would be no time for protection. He would be on his own. He would have to shelter her.

He would have to stay with her. Train her. Protect her.

She would have nowhere else to go. How the hell would he keep his hands off her?

Nigel frowned his way. "I believe I explained I need to speak to Miss Cash alone."

"I would rather stay." He sent Nigel a look he should recognize. It was his arrogant look. The one that said he would accept nothing less than absolute control. He was in control of Penelope Cash. He'd been her handler. He'd been willing to give up everything for her. A man got one girl. One woman who understood him. One woman who could change his destiny. Penelope was it. And Baz had fucked him.

He didn't deserve her. He had to find a way to get her to walk away.

"No." Nigel's frown told him everything he needed to know. "I want to talk to her on my own. She'll be with you in a moment."

Damon stood. He couldn't humiliate her again. Couldn't argue his place with her. He'd blown that.

He schooled his expression. "If Penelope wants it, then yes."

"I do." A quick comeback.

Fuck. She hated him now. But it was all right. She would have hated him the moment she truly knew him. She would have found out how cursed he was. She didn't need to be in his life. He would only bring her hurt and sorrow.

It was better this way.

Perhaps Nigel would explain the world to her. She would understand and walk away. Then things would be the way they should.

He nodded her way and he and Ten stood and walked out.

He had no place with her.

* * * *

"He's broken, you know."

She looked up at Nigel, a bit surprised at his words. "Are you talking about Damon?"

Stupid question. Who else would he be talking about? Damon, who had casually ripped her heart from her chest. Or had it been so casual?

"Do you know how we came to recruit him?"

She shook her head. She wanted to tell him she didn't care. It didn't matter to her, but it did. Because he was Damon. He was her love.

He might never return it. She might move on. But he was her first real love. He mattered. She'd sat at her desk and a few things had occurred to her.

Damon was different. He risked his life every day. He was a hero. It didn't matter that he couldn't love her. At the end of all of it, she didn't matter beyond what she was willing to sacrifice. She had her place. Her stupid heart was insignificant. "It doesn't matter, sir. What do you need of me?"

Nigel was silent for moment. "I want to talk to you as your boss and as a colleague. Do you know how he came to be here?"

She shook her head. She didn't care. Couldn't. He'd shoved her aside like everyone else had. He didn't matter. Her duty did. "It doesn't matter, sir."

"It does because I'm sending you back out there with him. I need to know that you're going to protect yourself."

He wanted to make sure she wasn't just going to spread her legs and offer herself up on a silver platter again. "I believe I have my armor fully pulled around myself this time."

"He can be charming."

"I've seen the real man. I understand. I can do the job."

"Did you know he received the Victoria Cross?"

She shook her head. It wasn't in his records. The Victoria Cross was the highest honor a soldier could receive. "No. I knew about his time in Afghanistan, but I didn't know he'd been decorated."

"Because it was kept quiet. I wouldn't tell you the story now, but I think it's very important for you to understand who Damon Knight is. He was Special Air Service. His unit was charged with taking a VIP into Kabul. I can't tell you who it was. That's the reason the whole affair has been classified."

So it was likely a royal or someone close to the family. The Windsor men served their country, and when the country went to war, the Windsor men went as well.

"You have to understand that the men in those units form a family. When you serve, when you literally depend on your fellow soldiers for your very survival, whether you like the others or not, you bond with them. My old unit meets up at least twice a year. All of us, without fail."

She got the feeling she wouldn't like what came next. "Go on."

"The unit was pinned down in the desert. They fought for days.

He watched them all fall. He lost his entire unit protecting their charge. Only Damon and his charge survived. He took out the enemy, but I rather think he meant to not survive. From the reports, he went a bit crazy. It was bloody. It was suicidal."

She didn't want to soften toward him. Not for a second, but there she was. Damon had lost his parents, then his mates.

What if he didn't want to lose her, too?

"Knight was recruited because he had zero ties. He was cold, perfectly capable of making life and death decisions. Capable of sacrificing pawns when he needs to. I know he seems charming, but it's a mask."

Was it? She was finally settling down. The hurt he'd dealt her had seemed overwhelming, but now that he was out of the room, a few things didn't make sense.

Damon was capable of sacrificing pawns. Perfectly capable of it. For years she'd watched him, worked with him on translations. He was known for being an Ice Man. Baz had been the jokester and Damon had been the brutal one underneath all his suave charm.

So why wasn't he sacrificing her? It was the most expedient thing to do. She was a girl who had been on the periphery of his life for years and only in his bed for a single night. Yet in the time she'd been close to him, she'd believed he gave a damn about her. Was he really that good an actor?

He was a man who had lost everyone. Even his best mate had turned on him. What would that man do if he cared about a woman and she was suddenly in danger? Would he trust that everything would work out? Would he place his faith in the universe that had kicked him time and time again?

Or would he do what he needed to do to protect the woman he cared about? Even if it meant hurting her.

Perhaps she should treat Damon Knight like a language she was trying to learn. The words he said might make a certain sense to her when run through her own filter, but every good translator knew that words had different meanings in different languages. The Sami language of the Nordic countries had over a hundred words for reindeer, each expressing a slightly different thing.

What if Damon was trying to tell her something and she wasn't understanding it because she was putting it through her filter and not his?

"Do you understand what I'm saying?" Nigel leaned toward her. She nodded. "Yes. Damon doesn't have anyone."

No one had ever fought for him, ever put him first. He'd been an orphan and then a soldier and then an operative. His career was about using his body and mind as a tool, one that was expendable.

It would have been so much easier to keep her close, to use her as some weird form of bait. If there was one thing Damon wanted, it was revenge on Basil Champion. The man Nigel was describing wouldn't hesitate to use her to those ends.

"He doesn't have anyone because he's not capable of truly caring for anyone. I know him better than you do. I'm trying to make sure you protect yourself. I wish I didn't have to send you back in."

She sat up straighter, squaring her shoulders. "You don't need to worry about me, sir. We'll be fine."

They would be after she spent some time contemplating what he was really doing, what his words really meant. She needed to see how he acted now that the decisions had truly been made. Context clues. That was she needed.

If he went right back to charming and seductive, back to manipulating her to do his bidding, she would know she was a pawn. It was what a smart agent would do.

He hadn't been acting like a smart agent.

She would have seen that if she hadn't been mired in her own misery. She'd walked out, had a cry, and read the file. She'd known in an instant that she couldn't leave.

And if they had to be stuck together, anything could happen. She wiped her tears and faced the truth. He'd humiliated her and she was thinking about how to win him back. It was pathetic, but it was true.

Nigel sighed a little. "It's not that he's a bad man. This job can twist a person. I've seen it before. Once this is over, I'll make sure he doesn't cause any trouble with you."

"I can handle Damon." Suddenly, she kind of believed it. It was all in how a person looked at the problem. Something fundamental had changed inside her. It changed because she'd fallen in love. Unfortunately, she'd fallen in love with a moody chap, and there wasn't room for both of them to be depressed. Damon was likely brooding somewhere.

She could be wrong. He could have meant every word he said. Only time would tell. Before, she would have simply moved on, believing that she didn't deserve that kind of happiness, but now she was different somehow.

If she was right, she would likely have a battle on her hands, one she had no idea how to win.

"Miss Cash, there's one other thing."

"Yes?" Now that she'd decided the world didn't have to end because Damon had a fit, she was anxious to get back to him.

Who was she fooling? She was anxious to know if there was still a chance. If she walked out there and he tried to smooth things over with a charming smile, she would likely burst into tears.

"I want a report on him and his capability in the field. I don't trust the Americans. They're far too friendly with him. And I certainly don't trust him to tell me the truth."

She already knew more about Damon's fitness than Nigel did. It had been one incident, and she likely would have passed out, too. He'd been climbing up a machine that was going the opposite direction. How many times would that happen? Other than that single incident, he'd been incredibly fit. She nodded. "Of course."

"Be safe, Cash."

She took her file—the one with the pictures of her having sex—and walked out, closing the door behind her. Her heart was thudding in her chest. Did she really want to know? Did she really want that moment when he simply smiled at her and acted as though nothing had happened between them? How would she act?

Was she being a complete idiot? He'd ripped her heart out. She should keep her distance. She should protect herself.

"Penelope? What the bloody hell was that?" Damon took her by the elbow. His normally perfect hair was mussed beyond repair. He looked like he'd been pacing, waiting for her not so he could charm her, but to yell at her. "We can still salvage this. Walk back in and tell him you quit again. You were right to do it. Hell, just get your things and you'll walk away."

No. No charm there. He seemed a little unhinged in fact. The cool, calm operative looked like a mad boyfriend.

Hope sprang up inside her. He was overdramatic, and Nigel was utterly wrong about him. He wasn't uncaring. He felt too much. There was a well of passion under his placid exterior.

"I'm not leaving, Damon." She turned her chin up at him. Everyone was looking at them. "Now, we should get back to The Garden. We don't have much time for my training."

He stopped, his eyes finding hers. A slightly horrified expression hit his face and he took a step back. "I'm not training you. I can't train you."

He was going to be stubborn, and she wasn't sure how to handle it. "You have to. It's our cover. I'm your sub."

He stared at her. "No."

"Yes. Or you'll be pulled off the assignment, too. They won't let you go without me. I'm sorry it's so distasteful for you, but you're stuck with me." She needed time to figure out how to deal with him. She couldn't just come out and tell him he was being foolish. She had to find a way around that massive wall he'd erected.

He seemed to realize everyone was looking at him. He smoothed back his hair and his expression calmed, but the tight set of his jaw gave him away to her. "You're right. We'll discuss this at home."

She followed him out.

He didn't know it yet, but he was in for the fight of a lifetime. She wasn't going to leave him. If she had her way, she might never leave him.

Chapter Ten

"What did he do?" Charlotte Taggart's voice went deadly quiet though Penelope couldn't possibly misunderstand her. Charlotte had carefully enunciated each word.

Penelope turned. They had just left the meeting Damon had called to fill the team in on the new setbacks. She'd been forced to spend hours and hours with him, first clearing up everything with SIS and then having her firearm issued along with her cover identification. Damon simply stood back, watching her like she would disappear on him. She'd offered to take the Tube back. That hadn't gone well.

The long car ride back had been utterly silent without even the sound of the radio to break up the gloom that seemed to sit between them.

She was right. He cared for her. If he hadn't, he wouldn't have fought so hard to keep her safe.

But she had no idea how to break through his reserve.

"What are you talking about?" She hoped Charlotte didn't know what had happened. She'd been out of the room when Damon had thrown his hissy fit. She'd hoped the Tennessee fellow had kept a gentlemanly silence about her humiliation. "Mr. Champion? I thought Damon explained that quite nicely."

He'd set up the meeting from his mobile and the entire team was sitting in the conference room joking and laughing when they walked in. Despite the seriousness of the situation, Ian Taggart's crew was relaxed as though they knew they could handle it, as though they really had each other's backs and that made everything all right.

She and Damon didn't even talk about it.

Now she was banished to the dungeon where Charlotte was going to show her things Damon should be sharing with her.

Charlotte's red and blonde hair shook as she paced down one of the dungeon's brick inlayed paths toward the bar area. "No. I know what Baz did. I'm talking about Damon. What did he do to you? Because when we left you were glowing like a woman who'd just figured out sex is pretty awesome and now you're pale and pinched up again."

"Again?"

Charlotte reached the bar, slipping behind it. "Sorry. It's just you're all tight and tense. And Damon's shut down." Her eyes narrowed as she pulled out what looked like a bottle of tequila. "Unless you were the one who did it."

Suddenly, she didn't really want to be the one "who did it." She got the idea that Charlotte wouldn't like someone who did something bad to her friends. "It wasn't me."

"It was Damon. He's an asswipe just like all men." Chelsea Dennis walked into the bar, her computer in hand. "Sorry, I kind of got the gist of it. Satan had a meeting with Ten this afternoon and I totally listened in on it. If it makes you feel any better, Ten decided Damon's an asshole. Only he said it in a really slow Southern accent."

Embarrassment flooded her system. "No, it really doesn't make me feel better. Were you able to figure out where the bug was transmitting to?"

"Oh, that was easy peasy. It was being sent to a hotel room on Gloucester Road. When the MI6 boys went there, Baz had left it running with a note that Damon better show up when he calls. Well, the sex tape part was also running. He saved the files from the last couple of days. Mostly it was nothing more than you on the Tube and eating sandwiches and cleaning up your house. And the session this morning was just audio and several hours of staring at Damon's really sparse kitchen."

She'd set her bag on his bar before going to bed. Apparently they'd been loud. "Who else has seen it all?"

"Just me and Adam. But he was listening in with me on Satan and Ten."

"Chelsea!"

Chelsea glanced her sister's way. "Adam and I modified our laptops with hypersensitive microphones. I wanted to see if it worked over Skype. It does. Adam says you should give Damon a second chance because he was trying to protect you, but I say we set him up as an escort on the Internet. I can have that website built out in an hour. He'll start getting phone calls shortly after."

Charlotte groaned, pulling out shot glasses. "Use your powers for good, please. Are you telling me he tried to get her thrown off the op? After what happened last night?"

"It was this morning." The words were out of her mouth before she could stop them. It wasn't like she could call up her sister and explain that the man she was in love with had dumped her and hurt her because it was better than getting her brutally murdered by a turncoat agent. *Oh, and I don't actually work for a staid publishing company. I'm SIS. How are the kids?* That would go over well.

And I might have to betray him on a level he'll never forgive me for.

She didn't even want to think about that.

"He made love to you this morning and then tried to get you fired?" Charlotte poured out a nice shot of amber liquid. Three glasses all in a row. "And after you apparently made a sex tape with him?"

"I eradicated it," Chelsea said, taking a seat at the bar.

The man had a complete bar in his house. His building. He owned a whole building. Was she fooling herself? She shook her head. "I don't really drink much."

"That's part of your problem." Charlotte handed her a shaker of salt.

"And I'm the bad influence?" Chelsea licked her thumb and then salted it, picking up a lime wedge with the opposite hand. "He didn't just try to get her fired. He told her he didn't like sleeping with her and he'd done it all for the mission. It was cold."

Come to think of it, maybe she should drink more. The idea of Ian and Tennessee feeling sorry for her made her want to crawl into her shell and never come back out again.

Charlotte's eyes widened. "Bastard, son of a bitch, cocksucker."

Chelsea completed her shot, chuckling a little. "I don't get why cocksucker is a bad thing. You talk about it all the time."

"Stay on topic. And oral is very nice. I'll remove that one from my repertoire. I can't believe he did that. Well, I can. Damon can be a shut-down asshole, but he was totally into you." She frowned. "Damn it. Adam's right. He's trying to protect you. What is wrong with men? Why can't they just say what they're feeling? What would you have done if he'd held your hand and begged you to walk away because he couldn't stand the thought of losing you?"

Somehow, she couldn't see him doing it. "I would have done anything he asked me to. Well, until I could find a way around it. I don't want to leave him alone. He'll get in trouble. He's not thinking straight when it comes to Baz."

And his heart might explode.

Charlotte held up her glass. She didn't bother with the niceties, merely tipped it back and then poured another one. "I knew there was a reason I liked you." Her eyes settled on Penny. "I know Damon pretty well. He's always been very careful with women."

"He wasn't careful with her according to Ten. He made her cry." Chelsea turned in her chair, looking out over the dungeon. The sun had waned and the entire place was encased in twilight. Chelsea looked older than her twenty-seven years. Harder. "He's just like the rest of them, sis."

Charlotte groaned a little, a sure sign that this was a well-worn argument. "Yes, all men are evil. They'll screw a woman in the end."

Chelsea sucked down another tequila shot. "Do you know what I would give to look at a vagina and just want to hit that? I wish girl parts did it for me. Unfortunately, I like dicks. Do you know the

157

problems with dicks? They're attached to bigger dicks."

"She's talking about men," Charlotte explained.

"Yes, I believe I understand. She's not happy with her sexual orientation."

"She's not happy with anything, but that's because she's fighting the inevitable," Charlotte said. "And so is Damon, if you decide to go after him. I've been around that man for a while, and I've never seen him look at a woman the way he looks at you."

Penny bit her bottom lip and decided. She could sit around and try to think this through or she could lean on someone else for a change. "I don't know how to fight for him. I don't even know if I should. When he first said what he said, I was devastated."

"That's because he was an asshole," Chelsea agreed.

She needed to ignore Chelsea if she was going to get anything done. "I don't know how to reach him. Even if it's true, I don't think me talking to him about it is going to change things."

Charlotte waved a hand, obviously dismissing that line of thought. "You can't talk to him. Men are not logical enough. Trust me. I went through hell to get Ian back. I tried to give him a very simple explanation about why I betrayed him and let him believe I was dead for five years, but does he listen to me? No."

Penny had read Damon's very thorough file on the Taggarts. If they could be together and in love, then anyone could. "Then how did you get him back?"

"Sex, of course. It's really the only language men understand."

That was what she was afraid of. "I'm not very good at sex. I don't have much experience."

Charlotte frowned her way. "You're going to be one of those women, aren't you?"

"Here comes the speech," Chelsea said under her breath.

"One of those women?" Penny wasn't sure what that meant.

Charlotte crossed her arms under her breasts, leaning forward. "The kind who spends all their time worrying about what they're not. 'I'm not sexy. I'm not pretty. I'm not worthy.' When you do talk about what you are, it's negative things like 'I'm fat' or 'I have cellulite.'"

She felt herself flush. Yes, she might be guilty of some of that, but it wasn't the whole story. "That's not true. I think I'm smart and nice."

Charlotte shook her head as though Penny had just proven her point. "Only because people tell you that. Do you really believe it? Deep down inside? Or do you keep trying to prove it over and over again? Do you let people take advantage of you because you think the only thing you have going for you is that you're nice?"

It wasn't true. Except it sort of was. She spent a lot of time trying to prove how nice she was. And she spent absolutely no time being nice to herself. That needed to change. She needed to take a real inventory of herself. "I like my eyes. I think they're pretty."

"Yes, they are." When Charlotte Taggart smiled, she could light up a room.

"All the guys think you've got a nice ass." Chelsea leaned on the bar and gave her a reserved smile. "I listen in on everyone. It's for research."

"They like my bum?" She'd always thought it was way too big.

Chelsea giggled a little, her face softening. She was quite pretty when she relaxed. "Yes, I believe Jesse said, in his always intensely literate way, 'Dayum, that's a juicy ass.' But y'all say arse. Why do you do that? It's not very sexy."

Maybe the word wasn't sexy, but apparently her arse was.

"You aren't going to win your man by worrying about cellulite," Charlotte explained. She turned a pointed look to her sister. "Or by treating him like he has the plague."

"He's not mine," Chelsea said quickly.

"Only because you act like a jerk." Charlotte pushed one of the shot glasses Penny's way. "She's got a huge thing for Simon and he totally wants her too. They've circled each other for months and months and they're both irritable because no one's getting laid. Do you want that? Wait, was Damon good in bed? I mean he could be horrible and he could make you feel like shit and then it's a good thing that he dumped you."

"Oh, no, he's very good. And he made me feel good." Her confidence was rising with every word Charlotte said. "We were good together."

They had been. He wasn't closed down with her in bed. When he'd smiled, there had been actual emotion in him. She was sure of it. He was always so controlled, except for today. He'd lost it and it hadn't been all because of Baz. His anger was cold, controlled, but his fear came out in screaming fits and every single one of them had been directed her way.

She knocked back the drink. She didn't drink much because it didn't seem ladylike and she'd wanted to be seen as a nice girl when she was growing up. She'd gotten used to being in control all the time. She'd had to be when her parents were alive.

It burned down her throat, and she practically coughed it up. Both Dennis sisters laughed and Chelsea patted her back. "It's an acquired taste."

But their friendship wasn't. It was easy and simple and she hadn't fit in with another group of women in a very long time. She was always worried about doing or saying the wrong thing, but the Dennis sisters were showing her there wasn't a wrong thing to say.

"I will take another." It was her time now. It was finally her time to figure out who she wanted to be, and she was very certain that one of the things she wanted to be was happy, and that couldn't happen without Damon Knight.

"Can you be brave, Penny?" Charlotte asked, sliding her another shot. "I know it sounds silly, but you're going to have to play a part you're not used to playing. If you want to break through Damon's walls, you're going to have to seduce him and manipulate him and bring him to his knees. You're going to have to change the attitude. In the end, it can't be a part you're playing. It has to be you. You have to fight and fight dirty."

If Damon had his way, she would be safe and he would upend both US and British intelligence and likely get himself killed in the process. He'd always been brave. He'd been through hell and he still was capable of caring about her.

Was she willing to let that go because she didn't like her body? Damon liked her body. If he was her lover, wasn't his opinion of whether she was sexy the only one that really mattered?

"Yes. I can be brave." She'd been nervous about being naked, but it seemed very silly now. She'd been willing to put her life in Damon's hands. Why would showing a bit of skin really bother her?

Chelsea put her head in her hand. "Oh, no. Do you know what she's about to do to you?"

But it was said with a smile and what seemed to be genuine affection for her sister.

Charlotte squealed a little and clapped her hands. "Makeover!"

Maybe she could use one. And she had a bit of money saved so it would be good to have some new clothes. "All right."

"And we'll need some help from my hubby to set the scene, but we can't let him know we're using him so Penny, I'm going to need some serious tears."

She'd held them back all day. It was actually quite easy to let them go. Her tears in the bathroom hadn't even begun to make a dent in her tension, and she got the feeling that she wouldn't be sleeping beside Damon tonight, so there would be no one to comfort her in the night.

Or would there? Maybe she needed to see how he liked being manipulated. As far as she knew, he hadn't moved her things out of his room and she had a keycard.

Charlotte patted her back. "Excellent. You look very dejected. Now, sit over there and look vulnerable. Chelsea, I need you to irritate my husband with a rant about how horrible men are."

Chelsea brightened. "I can totally do that."

Charlotte picked up her phone. Her whole demeanor changed and she went from smiling to screaming harpy in a second. "Ian, your friend is a rat bastard. Do you know what he did? Do you know? Were you in on it?"

Penny could practically hear Ian Taggart quaking in his overly large boots.

Chelsea reached over and covered Penny's hand with hers. "It'll be okay. One way or another. You'll be fine. Damon's being silly. We're not going to let you die."

Funny, she hadn't even thought about the fact that someone wanted to kill her. Love really might cost her everything, but she was willing to take the risk.

* * * *

"Dude, did you seriously dump her in front of everyone?" Jesse Murdoch frowned his way.

Damon still had a headache from the debacle of the morning. It was after supper now, a supper he'd avoided because he hadn't wanted to be in the same room, looking at her sad, gorgeous blue eyes and fighting the need to pull her into his lap. He didn't want to watch Ian feed Charlotte when his chance to do the same with Penelope was gone.

The last thing he needed was Ian Taggart's crew following him about and gossiping. He should have stayed up in his rooms, but then he had to deal with Penelope's things, her clothes hanging next to his, her makeup and frilly feminine things crowding his bathroom.

He looked over at the puppy of the group. The one who had hit on Penelope the first night.

"It's really none of your business." He watched the kettle as though that would make the water boil faster. Given his current stage of rage, it might.

Tag showed up in the kitchen, leaning his big body against the door. "That, PTSD, is what we call a dick move in the States."

Yes, he should have gone up to his apartments and locked everyone out. He just wasn't sure he could look at that bed again and remember just how much he'd lost. He wasn't sure how he was going to sleep in it. He needed to move her into one of the guest rooms. *Fuck.* He needed to figure out how to be able to look into those sky-blue eyes of hers without wanting to apologize and beg her to take him back.

Because that would be dangerous.

"I don't need your input either, Tag." He grabbed the box of tea and set the bag in his cup. He would rather start in on the Scotch, but he didn't trust himself not to get drunk and crawl into her bed again.

Of course, that might solve many problems. Penelope had gotten her sidearm, a Glock 17 that he'd made her prove she could use. If he climbed into her bed, she would likely shoot him. Case closed. Everyone would be happier.

"Too bad because you're definitely going to get my input." Taggart strode into the room. "PTSD, go and finish packing. You have to fly to the Netherlands tomorrow and learn how to make beds and shit. Tell Jake your car is leaving at six."

Jesse and Jake were joining the Royale when it docked in Amsterdam. Chelsea and Simon would travel with the two couples to Dover and board with the new crew there. Cruise ships picked up new members all the time and in multiple ports. Yet another avenue they had to deal with.

Jesse frowned. "I don't know about this, boss. Why do I have to be the guy who cleans up cabins while Chelsea works security?"

Taggart's eyes rolled. "Because she's the computer guru. You got some skills in there you haven't told me about? Trust me, buddy, if the job was walking the decks and knocking heads together, you would be my guy. I need Chelsea to get control of all those security cameras. I need you to search the cabins of the people I tell you to."

Jesse sighed. "Fine. I just want to know when I'm going to get to do something besides clean up and follow after Simon. I'm not complaining."

"Yes, you are."

Jesse didn't have a comeback for that. He shrugged and moved to the door. "Fine. I'll go and watch videos about how to make animals out of towels. That's part of my damn training, Tag. I have to make towel animals."

Tag stopped him at the door. "Jesse, one of these days one of my idiot operatives will inevitably get himself killed because he was too busy texting his wife to deal with the bad guys. I promise you his slot."

Jesse's eyes lit up. "Really?"

Tag slapped his shoulder. "Good things come to those who wait and don't get led around by their dicks. Go."

Jesse trotted off.

It was always interesting to watch Tag deal with his men. Damon never knew what to say. He could manipulate a man a thousand different ways, but Tag had real relationships with them. Crass and argumentative relationships, but friendships all the same.

"Here's hoping he doesn't have an incident while he's gone. I wish I could have gotten him a place with Jake or Simon," Tag admitted.

If there was a problem with the team, Damon wanted to know. "Why does he need a partner?"

"More like a guardian angel." Tag sighed. "He really does have PTSD. I joke about it, but we've had a couple of close calls. Put Jesse in the right place with the right pressures and he can go a little wild. Things got bloody the last time it happened. Simon took care of it, but it's why I have him cleaning rooms. I don't think he's going to knife the vacuum cleaner. And hey, maybe the towel animals will be like therapy."

"If we need to pull him out…" Damon began.

Tag held up a hand. "He'll be fine. Just watch him if things get violent. He forgets where he is. The good news is, I'm keeping him with me in Dallas. You would get to hire your own team if you came on with me. That New York job's looking better and better, isn't it?"

"I'm not leaving fieldwork." Fuck, after today it was really all he had.

"You're a stubborn bastard. And I kind of hate your ass right now because I'm supposed to talk to you." Taggart turned the slightest shade of green.

Damon frowned. They had spent the entire bloody afternoon in the conference room going over every minute detail of the operation since Jesse and Jake were leaving in the morning. It was his last chance to speak openly with them. It had been brutal torture because Penelope had been sitting there the entire time, trying to avoid eye contact with him. "Why? I thought I was clear. Is Chelsea having problems with the files?"

Chelsea and Adam were investigating the names of the passengers on the Royale and any possible connections to either The Collective or Nature's Core. They were supposed to build dossiers on roughly twenty potential suspects. Jake Dean was taking those twenty people and compiling their itineraries for the trip, including all their shore excursions where they might possibly meet up with the man they were attempting to smuggle back into England.

And now Charlotte was down in the dungeon with Penelope going over all the equipment and familiarizing her with protocols.

When they got on the ship, he would be alone with Penelope for days and days, in a tiny cabin where there was one bed and not a bit of privacy.

Tag walked to the fridge and grabbed a bottle of beer. "No. That's going fine. Trust me, Raging Bitch knows how to break apart someone's life in a few keystrokes. I'm talking about Penelope. You do understand what's happening down in the dungeon, right?"

Charlotte was showing Penelope a few hints and tricks. She was going to teach her how to present herself. God, his cock tightened at the thought. "Does Charlotte not appreciate her duties?"

He couldn't imagine Charlotte not taking a liking to Penelope. Charlotte was a kind woman, but if for some reason she didn't like Penelope, he would have to find someone else. He wouldn't leave her with someone who didn't care about her.

This was exactly why he should find a way to get rid of Penelope. He couldn't think straight around her and he needed to fucking think straight.

"Dude, right now those women are downstairs discussing the best way to castrate you. I had to convince her I wasn't the one who told you to dump Penny. My wife is pissed." Tag shivered a little. "When I left her, Charlie was plotting, man. Things go bad when Charlie plots. And she told me I should come up here and talk to you."

Damon shook his head. "About what?"

After a long swig of beer, Tag coughed a little. "Feelings and shit."

What the hell? "You're kidding, right?"

"Dude, women do that shit all the time and when you marry one, they expect you to do it too. But we're not going to. We're going to say we did and then we're going to drink some beer and see what's on TV. Because we don't talk about shit. We shoot people. That's how we show our feelings. Well, I'm going to drink beer and you're going to sip your tea."

Yes, he was definitely going for the Scotch. He reached to the back of the cupboard. After this, he was going to be a loner. No partners. No lovers. No friends. He didn't understand any of it. Not really.

And he didn't want to talk. "I feel angry. That's how I feel."

He took a long swig. Why had he said that?

Tag shook his head. "It doesn't matter. Choke it down, man. Push it back. You're good. You don't have to do this."

But maybe Charlotte was right. Another drink of Scotch and it burned nicely in his belly. "I have feelings for the girl."

He'd never seen Tag go pale. "Should I call Adam and Alex? They will get on a speakerphone and you three can cry to each other and maybe have a sing-along or something."

He gave Tag his middle finger. "Fuck you. I did what was right. It was right for her. It was right for me." The last part was a lie, but one he needed. Maybe if he said it enough, he could make it true.

"It was a dick move."

"What was I supposed to do? Tell her the truth?"

"You could have started with that. It might have been better than telling her she's fat and shit."

Damon felt his whole body stiffen. "I didn't say that."

Tag waved that explanation off. "It doesn't matter. When you sleep with a chick and then dump her the next day, she's coming to one conclusion. She's fat. They are really concerned with weight. I don't get it. She's hot. Once Charlie's done with her, she'll have every Dom here panting after her. Don't worry about it."

"She's quite lovely. I certainly didn't dump her because I don't want her, but I can't bloody well tell her that. And you're a good one to talk to me about this. Tell her the truth? Did you tell Charlotte the truth when she came back for you? You're a hypocrite."

Tag pointed an accusatory finger his way. "No. You do not get to play that card with me. You call me after Penny's lied to you and betrayed you, blown up your career and pretended to be dead for five years. Then you can whine to me about your love life. You should have told her why you don't want her in the field with you. Because she's fuck-all good in bed and you don't want to lose the best pussy you've ever had."

Tag had weird ways of communicating, but Damon got the point. "I don't love her."

A vomiting sound came out of Tag's mouth. "I didn't say that."

But that's what he was talking about in his brutish way. "I feel some responsibility for her. And Baz's hatred for me has already cost one young lady her life. I can't do it again."

He wasn't going to admit more than that to anyone.

"Why does he hate you?" Tag leaned against the counter, his blue eyes becoming very serious.

"I don't know. I suppose it's because I outshone him." Baz had always been competitive, and he'd resented the fact that Damon was the senior agent.

"Did you and Baz ever share women?"

Where was that coming from? "That's a bit private, mate."

"Nothing's private right now. He's brought you into this and it's personal. Knowing why he's coming after you will help us catch him. He's not thinking with his head either. He's running on emotion. I watched the video Chelsea captured from the CCTVs before she dumped it. The one at the station. I couldn't hear what he was saying, but he was taunting you."

Taunting more than just him. "He had some nasty things to say about both of us. It was why I sent her away."

He hadn't just been trying to protect her feelings. He was trying to save her life. If he really was honest with himself, he hadn't wanted her to see how damaged he was. Hadn't wanted her to see him struggle. He wanted her to see him as a heroic, strong operative, not the aging, wasted piece of shit he'd become.

"I find it interesting that he left you alive, too. He hates you, but he couldn't pull the double tap on you. He's been trained well enough to know to take out both fucking lungs or to go for a head shot."

He hated how cold he got when he thought about that day. He was supposed to be over that. He was alive. He wasn't supposed to be stuck in that horrible moment when he'd realized nothing he'd done had really made a difference. He'd been stuck there all this time. Except for the moments he'd spent with her. He hadn't been thinking about how useless he was then. He'd been thinking about how hot he could make her, how she came apart in his arms. He'd been thinking about how right it had felt. "I believe he intends to do the job properly this time around."

"Why does it have to be you? He should want to talk to Nigel."

"He mentioned setting something up with Nigel. I believe he wanted me to be the go between." The whole conversation made him uncomfortable. He wanted to forget about Baz for a while but the one thing that might have done it wasn't available to him now. Fucking Penelope would take him away from everything, but he couldn't do that anymore.

Tag shook his head shortly. "I think that was an excuse. I think you're the one he wanted to see. I would bet he's been tracking you the whole time. Now he's murdered an operative and will only deal with you. I think he changed his plans in the middle of that meeting because he watched you with her."

"He changed his mind because he wants Penelope." A sick idea played at the back of his brain, a thing that had always been there, but he'd refused to acknowledge.

"It isn't Penny he wants, is it? Tell me something. Was the girl he murdered before really just caught in the crossfire? According to the reports, she was found in the kitchens on the conference floor. He came in through the elevators. He knew where your office was. So why didn't he go there first? Why didn't he just take you out? She wouldn't have been able to stop him. As far away as she was, she likely wouldn't have heard a thing."

Sweet, subby Jane. He hadn't loved her, but he'd liked her. "She was my frequent lover. I topped her on a regular basis."

"Was Basil Champion in love with you?" Tag sounded softer, more sympathetic than Damon had ever heard him.

He stood there for a moment, wishing Tag wasn't so damn good at reading people.

"Yes." *Damn it.*

"Were you lovers?" He held his hands up when Damon shot him

168

a nasty look. "I'm not judging. I'm asking. I couldn't care less who you fuck, though in this case it might be important."

It was important, though Damon had tried to avoid it for years. "No, we weren't lovers. I never even acknowledged that I knew he was attracted to me. And yes, we shared some women. I suppose in the back of my mind, I thought he should really see me as I am. I was never going to return his admiration. I like women."

Women like Jane. God, he was crazy about women like Penelope. No. That was wrong and he needed to stop pretending to himself. There were no other women like Penelope. He was simply crazy about Penelope, and it would get her killed.

Because he'd never dealt with it. Never wanted to. Preferred to avoid the confrontation.

"That explains things. I need to know this shit, Knight. It changes how I deal with the op."

"How so?"

Tag put his beer down and crossed his arms over his chest, a sign of his stubborn will. "It means my main job will be to protect Penny. She's innocent in all of this. Ten wants me to bring Baz in, but I won't do it at the cost of her life. I got out of the Agency so I wouldn't have to make decisions like that ever again."

Things were happening far too quickly. Taggart was pushing him. He needed time to think so he tried to direct the conversation back to something that would get Tag off his back. "I thought Charlotte got you kicked out."

"Hell, no." Tag's gaze was steady. "But she taught me I wasn't really that man. I was becoming something before I met Charlie, something dark, something like Ten. Something like you."

"Like me?"

"You'll make the hard decisions, Knight. You'll send your men in to die if you think it serves the bigger purpose. Here's the honest truth. I don't want you to take me up on the New York job. Charlie's pushing me to give it to you. I don't think you can handle it. We're a team and we don't leave our men behind no matter fucking what. It's why I'll watch after Penny. You have your job to do. You have to take him down. I'll consider Penny part of my crew. I talked to

Adam and he can switch up the paperwork. Let her go in with Simon. They'll pose as the couple and you'll do his job on the ship. You can concentrate on what you do best. You can still meet with Baz and she'll go with you, but we'll protect her."

His whole body went hot with rage at the thought. "You want her fucking Weston? You think he's so much better than me? You think he doesn't fuck up?"

"I thought you wanted her out of this."

He wanted so many things but he wasn't going to get them. "I want her to never get on the boat. I want her to forget she ever knew me, but it won't matter to Baz, will it?"

"Nope. It would be worse if you tried to leave her behind. Then he would know how much you care about her. Even if she doesn't. Come on. Let me take over when it comes to her."

It was probably the right move. He couldn't tear her apart if she was with Weston. He wouldn't have to make the hard decisions Tag had talked about. He could shove her to them, give her over, and just worry about himself.

He could become everything Tag accused him of being.

But just for a while, he'd been something more.

"No. Watch out for her, but she stays with me. If you try to go above my head and get Nigel to move her, I'll remove you from the operation altogether. Are we understood?"

A smirk curled Ian's lips up. "Good to know. Maybe I was wrong about you not being right for the New York job. You know you don't always have to accept the long, slow slide into crap, Knight. Sometimes it's all about finding the person who won't let you go dark. When you find that person, you can't let them go." He shivered a little. "God, that was gross. Can we be done with this now and you tell Charlie that I'm a perfect angel and you're the devil who broke her friend's heart?"

"Sure."

"Charlie's the one who set her tits free, though. By the way, they look good. Totally real. It's the only way to go. See, I feel so much better talking about your girlfriend's tits than the emotional crap."

He ignored the idea that Penelope was his girlfriend and

concentrated on the fact that she was apparently being allowed to run wild. "What the hell is your wife doing?"

A grimace took over Tag's face and he ground the word out. "Makeover."

Damon didn't understand. Penelope was lovely the way she was. Yes, she was understated, but he liked her that way. Perhaps a better grade of clothing was called for but nothing more than that. "She doesn't need to be made over."

A long sigh left Tag's mouth. "Apparently when a chick gets her ass dumped, all the other chicks swarm in and there's tears and tequila and makeup and really low-cut shirts. That's why you should avoid her tonight. Although her tits looked good."

He was losing his bloody mind. "You are going to have to explain that to me."

Tag cupped his own chest in a deeply juvenile gesture. "Tits. Breasts. Women have them. They're fun to play with."

"Why would you know what Penelope's breasts look like?" Damon asked through gritted teeth.

"Cause she's naked downstairs. Charlie's makeovers can get out of control. Did I mention the tequila?"

He forgot about the glass and just took a swig from the bottle. It was going to be a long damn night.

Chapter Eleven

Penny woke up warm and happy, cuddled up next to Damon, his arm wrapped around her as he cradled her against his chest. She breathed in his scent, loving the masculine, woody smell that seemed to cling to him.

Without moving her body, she lifted her eyes up to look at him. He seemed younger sleeping, as though his cares had all fallen away. She wanted so badly to reach up and brush her hand against his jaw. It was covered in the beginnings of an inky black beard. He would get rid of it as soon as he woke up and showered, but she liked how it looked. Less civilized.

So ridiculously gorgeous it made her heart skip a beat.

He'd been passed out in bed when she'd finally made her way upstairs. Charlotte had enlisted the aid of the other women of The Garden, and her makeover had turned into a party with Chelsea and the Dom in Residence's two subs, Lora and Anita. Penelope found them charming and open and more than willing to talk about the lifestyle and everything involved. It had been such a difference from the bland discussions she'd had with other women. They had laughed and talked about sex.

After a couple of tequila shots, Simon and Jesse and Ian had escorted them all to the nearest clothing store where Penelope had bought a bunch of clothes she would never have thought to even try on before.

It had been such fun. By the time she'd used her keycard to let herself into Damon's rooms, she'd been ready for a fight. She'd come up with all her reasons for staying close to him.

He'd been asleep wearing nothing but a pair of boxers and his socks, a half-empty Scotch bottle next to him. Some super-agent he was. She'd pulled his socks off and tucked him into bed, then got ready and climbed in next to him.

It hadn't been more than two minutes before he was rolling over and cuddling up to her and murmuring her name.

At least he was honest when he was asleep and drunk. She rather thought she would get a fight out of him this morning.

His hand moved along her side, and she felt a little moan leave his chest, though his eyes didn't open. He sighed and Penny looked down. Sure enough, there was his morning mate. His cock was tenting up the sheet admirably.

Brave. Bold. That was the way she was now. Penny, the Brave. Penny, the woman who boldly stroked the cock she wanted to keep forever.

She let her hand run down his ripped abs to feel the tip of his dick as it stretched out of the top of his boxers. It reached almost to his navel and was so thick she could barely get her hand around it. Would it fit in her mouth? She wanted to try. She'd loved the way he'd licked and sucked her pussy. She wanted to pay back the favor, to learn his taste.

She wanted so much more, but she doubted he would let her have anything other than the physical for now. If he would allow her even that.

She wouldn't know until she tried.

"What are you doing, Penelope?" His voice was a sexy rumble.

She forced herself not to move. Calm. Patience would win this battle. Patience and playing her part. Except she was beginning to understand it wasn't a part. It was who she'd never known she was. "I was thinking about playing with your cock, Master."

He hissed a little. "I meant what are you doing in my bed."

He hadn't moved an inch, hadn't shifted away from her or pushed her back. He simply lay there, waiting for her answer.

It was an easy one. He hadn't spoken much to her after the episode in Nigel's office. "I did what you told me to. You told me I was to sleep in your bed, and I wasn't allowed clothes."

His eyes closed briefly. "Naturally, you're naked."

"It's what you commanded, Master." Charlotte had explained that men like Damon grew deeply aroused with the idea of command and obedience. He needed to think he was in control of her and the situation. To a point.

"And if I ordered you to leave me alone?"

That was exactly what she was afraid of. "I would leave you alone, though I fear it wouldn't help in our mission."

"I want you out of the mission."

She sat up. This was exactly what they should have done yesterday. He'd been an arse, speaking in front of everyone, but then it was obvious to her that he didn't know how to handle simple emotions and allowances had to be made. "I have to go with you."

He turned on his side, his eyes so serious she wondered if he wouldn't simply toss her out now. "You don't. You can quit and go somewhere else. Tag's crew can have new identification for you and you can be out of this entirely."

Such an idiot. She didn't bother to pull the sheet up. The instinct was there, to cover herself, to hide from his view, but she'd started to think she did that a lot. If she always hid, how could anyone ever really know her? "I'm not giving up my whole life, Damon."

"It would only be for a while."

She knew what that meant. "Until you kill Baz or he kills you."

"Yes." His eyes weren't on her face now. He was watching her breasts, and it wasn't with distaste.

She felt her nipples peak and not from the chill. "And if he kills you? You don't think he'll still come after me?"

"I think it would be less likely." He cursed softly under his breath and turned on his back again, his forearm covering his eyes. "I don't know. I don't intend to allow him to kill me. It would be easier to do this alone."

"I don't see how."

His hand fisted in obvious frustration with the entire conversation. "Because I'll spend all my time trying to keep you alive. Can't you see that?"

"No. I'm trained, Damon. I'm sorry I'm not your perfect partner, but I'm the only one you have and you need me. This is about more than me. We could spend the next few days arguing and fighting and wasting time."

His eyes came open again and there was something nasty and predatory in them. "Or we could do what? We could fuck? You want to fuck the arsehole who humiliated you yesterday? I thought you had more spine than that."

She let the words roll off her. She reached out and soothed back his hair. "Not particularly. I'm hoping I can find the Damon who made love to me before."

"He doesn't exist. I told you what I was doing." But even as he said the words, he was still under her hands, allowing her to comfort him.

"I know. I understand. You don't love me. You don't really want me."

His lips turned down in a fierce frown. "Fuck. Penelope, I do want you. Damn it. I enjoyed fucking you, but that's as far as it goes. Do you understand that I'm likely to get you killed? Why do you want to screw the man who's going to cost you everything?"

She couldn't help but roll her eyes. He really did love a good drama. "We need to work on your pessimism."

"We need to work on your realism. Do you think he won't kill you? Do you think he won't do that to try to hurt me?"

"Would it hurt you?"

His hand moved so quickly she was shocked when his fingers clamped around her wrist like a manacle. "Is that what you're looking for? You're looking to see if there's anything under here? You want me to love you, Penelope? You think if I love you then anything that happens to you would be worth it because some man loved you."

It was really hard not to slap him silly, but she had to remember why he was doing it. He'd never been loved before. His parents had died when he was so young, and he'd been raised in boarding schools. He'd lost his unit. He didn't trust anything or anyone. Patience. She couldn't tell him that some man loving her wasn't worth her life, but loving him just might be. He wouldn't understand. Loving him had made her stronger. "I was just wondering if my partner would give a rat's arse if I died in the field. I was trying to figure out what my position is. Do you want me to leave because you don't trust me to help you or because you'll feel guilty if I die? You were very plain to me. You don't love me. You will never love me. My ears work, Damon. I'm very good at understanding what words mean. So no, I'm not looking for you to love me."

If he called her on it, what would she say? Her mind was racing, trying to keep up with the drama she found herself in. He was being stubborn and obnoxious.

And quite fast. He rolled on top of her, pinning her down, making a cage of his body.

"Then what do you want?" He growled the question, pressing down on her, forcing her to take his full weight.

God, she wanted that. She could feel the length of his cock pressed to her pussy, only the thin material of his boxers between them. This was what she really wanted. He wouldn't listen to words, but somewhere in the heat of sex, he might find the connection she was offering him. "I want to do my job and serve my country, Damon."

"You're going to fuck me for Queen and country, then?"

She tilted her hips up, forcing his cock right against her clit. "No. I'm going to fuck you because it feels so damn good. You're an excellent tutor. You taught me to crave it. I want to make a deal with you."

His chest rubbed against hers. "I'm listening."

"Teach me. You have to anyway or we'll blow our cover. I like this lifestyle. I think I fit into it. I think I could be happy here. Consider me a submissive you're training. From what I understand, you didn't have to love them. You just had to want them."

"I can want a lot of women. I like a variety."

She didn't like the faintly cruel way he said it. Her insecurities rose up. "So you like fat women, too? Is that what you're implying, Damon?"

He was off her and turning her over in a heartbeat. She felt cool air against her backside and then the sharp sound of flesh smacking flesh. She screamed into the pillow because he meant business with that slap. Two and three came in rapid succession. She would likely have moved to get away from him, but his big hand was on her back, holding her down.

"If there is one thing I will teach you, it's that you will not denigrate yourself in my presence. You know your safe word, but you should think before using it." Four and five and six.

It was a breakthrough. He was touching her, taking her in hand the way a Dom would with his wayward sub. But why did his breakthrough have to blister her poor bottom? "You said it yourself just yesterday."

Seven and eight. He spread out the smacks, lighting up every inch of her bum. "I never said that."

"You said you weren't attracted to me."

"I bloody well lied and you know it. I like you. I even admire you. I don't want you to mistake that for love. I don't want you to sacrifice yourself when what I can give you isn't bloody well worth it." Nine and ten and then she lost track. She'd pushed his buttons and he was showing his true colors, and if he needed to spank her to do it, then she would take it.

Besides, it wasn't so bad. The first couple hurt—they all hurt really—but somewhere along the way she felt herself getting wet and excited even as she gritted her teeth against the flare of pain.

"You won't protect yourself so I have to. Do you know what he'll do to you? You're putting yourself in danger, and I won't have it."

He finally stopped, the smacks ceasing suddenly. He put his hand on her arse cheeks, softly this time, as though soothing away the hurt. A long moment passed where she cried softly into the pillow, allowing the experience to wash over her.

"Penelope? Are you all right?"

She was better than all right. The tears felt freeing somehow. She bottled so much up, but the two times Damon had spanked her had been a revelation. "Yes. I need this. I just realized how much I need this."

He'd been honest with her—as honest as he knew how to be.

"I can't convince you to leave me?" The question came out with very little hope, just a sad sigh from him.

She couldn't give him all the reasons why. He wouldn't accept them, but she could be honest about one piece of the truth. "No. You of all people should understand. My job is all I have, too. I know it seems dull to you, but I feel like I mean something because of it. I don't mean anything to anybody. Even when my mum was alive, god, she didn't recognize me at the end. She actively fought me trying to help her. If I run away from this, I have to give it up. I won't leave this job. It's the only thing that makes me feel alive."

Except you. Except this.

He rolled her over, and she'd never in her life felt more vulnerable than that moment when he stared down at her, no expression on his face. He was remote, unattainable. He could ruin her with a few callous words. He could lift her up with well-placed ones. It was frightening just how much he meant to her, how much power he had over her when he was so damaged himself.

His fingers came down to brush her tears away. "You crying damn near kills me. I don't know why. I've watched women cry before. I've made women cry before. Something about your tears wrecks me. And yet I want them. I want you to cry because you're bloody beautiful when you do it. Because I want your tears. I want them for me. I'm a greedy fucking bastard, and I want you to cry for me."

Because he couldn't cry for himself. Likely hadn't since he'd been a child. He seemed to study her for a moment before speaking again. "I won't go easy on you. And I don't want you to think we'll be together when this is done. I've decided I don't want a partner. Never again. If you like, you can have access to The Garden. I'll give you a full membership and I'll vet anyone you play with, but I won't touch you again after this is done. I know you won't believe me, but it's for your own good. I'm not the man for you. I'm the man who'll make you cry, and I don't want that. I think you deserve better than that."

She would take it. It was a step in the right direction. At least he admitted he cared about her. "I want this time, Damon. I want the training. I promise I won't beg you to keep me in the end. If you walk away, I'll somehow manage to survive without you."

His eyes closed, but when he opened them again, he relaxed and rolled off the bed. She thought he was going to leave her, walk away and go about his business. He would leave her to Charlotte and Chelsea.

He shoved his boxers off his lean hips, kicking them aside and stroking his big cock. "Fine. If this is the way you want it, I'll teach you. Your first lesson is how to suck my cock. Get on your knees and show me what you know."

She scrambled off the bed, her backside aching, but it was a pleasurable thing now. Her heart started to pound in her chest, excitement driving her. "I don't know very much."

She sank to her knees, trying to emulate the position Charlotte had taught her the night before.

He loomed over her like a decadent dream. "You will when I'm done with you."

She licked her lips, ready to learn everything he could teach her.

* * * *

She was going to kill him. He might not make it to the meeting with Baz. He'd just let Penelope give him a heart attack.

He'd fallen into bed after hitting the bottle far too hard. His head was aching, but it was nothing compared to the pain in his cock.

He knew he should turn her away. He should be brutal with her, force her away. Save her.

Her eyes came up, staring straight through him, and he knew he was a bastard, son of a bitch. Selfish. He put a hand in her hair, letting it sink into her curls. He was so selfish because he couldn't do it. He couldn't say the words that would make her hate him forever.

179

Fuck. He didn't even want to.

His cock strained toward her like the fucking thing had a brain and knew where it wanted to be.

"Spread your knees farther apart." He was supposed to be training her to be his submissive. Not his bloody partner. *His.* Now that he finally realized he was stuck in this mess, several realities occurred to him, the chief one being that she belonged to him for the duration. At the end of this operation, he would give her up and make sure that she never saw fieldwork again because he wouldn't trust anyone else with her safety, but for now, Penelope Cash belonged to him.

His to train. His to fuck. His to pleasure. The word beat through his system like the most addictive of all drugs. *His. His. His.*

Her teeth sank into her plump bottom lip as she moved, spreading her knees, showing him her pussy.

His pussy. It was his for the time being. Tag had been right about that. It was his pussy, the best he'd ever had. At heart, he supposed, men were still animals fighting for the right to mate with their chosen female. No matter how nicely he dressed, he wasn't really civilized. Penelope Cash had proven that to him once and for all. He was just an animal driven by instincts. The instinct to fuck, to protect, to possess.

"How much experience do you have?" The question came out casually, but inside he really wanted to know. He wanted to know how many men had been stupid enough to know the sweetness of that gorgeous, bratty mouth only to allow her to get away.

"None when it comes to this," she offered, wiggling a little.

"None?"

"I told you. Peter didn't think it was sanitary." Her lips curved as she said the words. Before when she'd talked about her ex, there had been a layer of sadness, of embarrassment. There was nothing but a little naughtiness now. Her tears, those sweet tears, had dried and she was ready for play.

He tightened his hand in her hair, pulling her gently back so she was staring up at him. "What do you think? Did you like it when I sucked your cunt? Did you like it when I fucked you with my tongue and ate that pussy until I had my fill?"

"Yes, Sir."

He tightened his hold until she hissed slightly. "What do you call me?"

"Master."

He would only be her Master for a brief period of time, but she would use his proper title until he had to let go. He would get everything that was due to him while she was his. She was wiggling again. Despite the emotion of the morning, he found himself smiling. "Is there a problem, love? You seem to be a bit uncomfortable."

"Yes, Master."

"Tell me what's paining you. Tell your Master what part of you aches." He knew, but he wanted to hear it from her lips. Spanking her felt good and right, and he wouldn't do it unless it was for her pleasure and his, or she spouted shite like she had earlier. He wouldn't allow her to talk poorly of herself. Not while he was her Master.

She frowned, her mouth going into the sweetest pout. "My bum hurts, Master. It still burns a bit."

He stroked his cock, wanting to draw this out. "You should remember that feeling, love, because every time I hear you speak like that about yourself, I'll make sure to set your arse on fire. Am I understood? You want my training, you'll play by my rules."

"Yes, Master." She was watching his cock, her eyes on the head as he stroked himself. So responsive. She was completely untutored, her sensuality only just emerging. It was a gift he didn't deserve, but fate had shoved her into his hands.

"Is a sore bum your only problem, love? Do you have a wet pussy as well?"

She nodded. "Yes, Master."

God, he loved hearing those words out of her mouth. "You'll get no relief until you give me what I want. Lick the head."

Penelope leaned forward, her mouth coming open with a sweet obedience that had his cock swelling further. Her tongue came out, swiping across the head of his dick, licking up the pre-come that had beaded there. She didn't hesitate, didn't pull away, simply lapped at the slit on his dick, tasting him with honest, open curiosity.

He held his ground, though it was hard to stay on his feet. The pleasure was so intense as she ran that sweet tongue all over the head of his cock.

"I like how you taste, Master."

Fuck. "Suck the head. Take me deep."

She leaned forward and worked her mouth around his cock. It was awkward but endearing how hard she worked.

"That's right, love. Do you know how good your mouth feels? Run your tongue all over me." He set his hand in her hair again, threading it tight this time. She was a natural, not because she was perfect, but because she wanted it, wanted him. That was all he needed.

Over and over she worked his dick, taking more each time, with the same diligence she probably used when she was translating a document.

"Take more." He pulled gently on her hair and reveled in the way she shivered. He could smell her arousal.

His cock was past hard. He'd moved into completely new territory. All the blood in his body was rushing to his dick, and it made him a little light-headed. He shoved his hips toward her mouth, gaining another inch before allowing her to drag back almost all the way out of her mouth. She tickled his slit and then began her excruciatingly slow pass over his flesh. Her eyes were closed, but there was peace on her face, the same peace he'd seen in natural subs serving their Masters.

She would need this. Even after he was gone, she would need to submit to a man who had her best interests at heart. Not everywhere. She would need to be a full partner in their regular life, but in the bedroom, she needed this.

He wouldn't be the man to give it to her.

Ruthlessly, he shoved the thought away. He would deal with that when he had to. For now, he was going to take everything she had to give him. He would be selfish and soak up her sweetness.

"More." He wanted the back of her throat. He wanted every inch of his cock inside her.

She licked and sucked and worked him until she'd gotten to his base.

His eyes rolled into the back of his head. "You have to stop."

With regret, he pulled out of her mouth because he didn't want to come yet. He wanted inside her. He wanted to be on top of her.

"Master, I don't mind. I want to swallow you." Her eyes were wide as though she was worried she'd made a mistake.

"And I want to fuck you. Who's in charge? Get on the bed and spread your legs for me. You'll get a belly full of my come, but not today. Right now, you'll get on that bed and wait for me. You'll take me when I want, how I want. This is how the relationship is going to go. You will obey me or there will be punishment." He had to give her one more way out. "Think it through, Penelope. I'll be hard on you. While you're with me, you're mine and I'll want you three times a day. I won't care that you're sore or sleeping. I'll wake you up and get you ready for me. I'll take you when the mood strikes me and when I feel like it, where I feel like it. If I want to shove your skirt up in a coat closet, I'll do it and you'll present to me and make it easy. So if you don't want that, walk out now. I'll find a way around this."

She looked up at him and, for a moment, he was worried she would do just that. She would stand up and get dressed and walk out of his life forever and he wasn't ready. God, he might never be ready for that. He wanted this time with her.

Rising from her knees, she went up on her toes, bringing her lips to his chin. She kissed him there, an oddly sweet affection. "Yes, Master."

She turned, showing off that outrageously hot arse of hers, climbed on the bed, and then slowly spread her legs.

Time seemed to stop, just for a moment, as he looked at her. Presentation. The sweet offering of a submissive to her Master. Charlotte Taggart had been talking about more than castrating him. She'd told Penelope exactly how to get to him. He was being manipulated by a translator who had never been in the field, never even had a real lover in his mind. Penelope was up on her elbows, her legs spread wide. It should have been a tawdry display, but not for her. No. She didn't look like a whore. She looked like a temptress offering him so bloody much more than sex. It was innocent and sweet and just the slightest bit false because she knew exactly what she was doing to him.

"Master?" Her voice shook just slightly as though worried her game was up.

"Who does it belong to?" It didn't matter. He knew he should walk away and it didn't matter because Ian was right. That was his pussy and he couldn't walk away from it, from her. He might find the strength later, but he couldn't now. He couldn't devastate her a second time and he damn straight couldn't disappoint himself. He wanted her more than he'd ever wanted anything in his life.

"You." She met his eyes. "It's yours for as long as I am."

He fell on her, using none of his usual grace. He wasn't an animal in bed. He was always controlled and slightly cool, but not this time. This time his need to brand her beat through his veins, forcing him to spread her legs farther and make a place for himself at her core. With virtually no finesse, he slammed inside her, his cock unable to wait a second more.

She would fight him now. She would see him for what he really was, what he always tried to hide.

Her nails sank into the skin of his shoulders, the pain biting through him with abandon. Her legs wrapped around him, enveloping him. She wasn't pushing him away. Penelope was fighting to keep him close to her.

He took her mouth as he forced his cock high into her pussy. His tongue slid against hers, dominating her, fighting for control. She didn't just lie back. She gave as good as she got. Her tongue pressed against him, her mouth allowing him access. The hard points of her nipples rubbed against his chest, and he couldn't stop the growl that came out of his throat. He let his weight push her into the mattress as he began to thrust in and out.

He wasn't thinking about the future or the bloody past. There was only Penelope, his sub.

He let go, pounding furiously into her, not giving a damn about anything but sinking his come deep inside her. Over and over, he fucked as far as he could into her. She thrust her pelvis up, taking him deep as her hands slid to his back, leaving her mark there.

She came first, nearly screaming into his mouth. The tiny muscles of her cunt tightened, milking his cock for all they were worth.

He held her tight and rode it out, giving up his come in long jets, letting it find a spot deep inside her body. He'd never taken a lover without a condom and never would again. Only from her would he find this connection, this amazing sensation of nothing being between them.

Pulsing pleasure swept through his body, and even though he was empty, he couldn't stop his hips from moving against her. He simply let his body sag onto hers, let her run her hands through his hair, soothing him.

His heart pounded, blood rushing through him. Alive. He felt alive when he was with her. Not cold but warm and happy.

If she died, he would let Baz take him.

Fuck. He was going to get her killed because warm and fucking happy didn't work on an op. Cold. Calculating. He needed to be the same agent Ian Taggart talked about—the one who made the hard decisions. Not the one who slept with his head cradled to his sub's chest.

He rolled off her, utterly unsure how to handle things. "That was good."

A stupid thing to say, but he couldn't think of another way to break the moment between them. He didn't want to hurt her again.

She laughed a little. "Yes, it was. Now you feel free to run away, Damon. It's all right. I'm fine. I understand that this is all about sex and this is how all of our sexual sessions end, with you taking a shower and going about your business. I intend to do the same."

He turned to look at her. She was smiling slightly, utterly unlike what he'd expected. He'd expected tears and regret, but she looked satisfied and relaxed and slightly amused with him. It rankled. Had she not felt what he had? "Is that right?"

"You can't help it. You're a very foolish man." She rolled off the bed with a casualness he wouldn't have suspected she possessed.

"But I'm taking the shower first this time. You left me without hot water last time. I'll meet you downstairs. We have a conference at eleven, right?"

She stretched, not seeming to mind that she was naked and had the faintest pink sheen to her arse. His cock rumbled again, stiffening as he watched her move. It was perverse. It was exactly what he should want. She was accepting the limitations of their relationship, but he was getting irritated at the very thought. Had she just used him for sex? "Yes."

"Excellent. There's time for breakfast then." She walked away, not bothering with the robe at the end of the bed. "See you later, Damon."

He watched her walk away, unable to take his eyes off her. What the hell had just happened?

He heard the shower turn on and wondered if he'd created a monster.

Chapter Twelve

Penelope shifted in her corset, trying to get used to the feeling of not being able to breathe at all. In any way. She stared at herself in the mirror, for once not hating the way she looked.

She was more confident in her body. Sex with Damon every night and every morning and sometimes in the middle of the day had gotten her used to being naked around him. Since the debacle in Nigel's office, almost a week had passed, and Damon was as remote as ever. Except when he took her to bed. Or against a wall. Or on top of his desk.

He'd taken to calling for her in the middle of the day. She would walk in thinking they were going to work and he'd immediately order her to strip, and his cock would be inside her the minute her clothes were off.

He gave her everything in those moments. And absolutely nothing but his polite charm outside of them.

It was frustrating.

"You look gorgeous," Charlotte said, giving her a wink as she joined her in front of the dressing room mirror.

"I look half naked." More than half really since Damon had ordered her to wear a piece of floss between her arse cheeks.

Chelsea snorted a little. "Enjoy it while you can. You'll probably be fully naked by the end of the night." She started to move, but her leg seemed to slip. She caught herself with a wince.

"Are you all right?" At first Chelsea had seemed dauntless to her, unapproachable, a bit cold. Over the past few days, Penelope had come to see beyond the façade to the vulnerable young woman beneath. Chelsea didn't like to show it, but she cared about the people around her. Even though she called one of them Satan.

"It's just my leg. Nothing new. I'm fine." Chelsea rubbed her thigh through the PVC she wore.

"No, you're in pain," Charlotte said, reaching for her sister. "Are you going to take something?"

Chelsea shook her head. "No. If I start taking pills, I might not stop. I can be honest about that much. I need a session. Do you think…"

Charlotte nodded. "Yes, but Jake and Jesse aren't here and Damon is working with Penny tonight. It's Ian or Simon."

Chelsea's eyes closed briefly. "I'll go back upstairs and try propping it up."

Charlotte's hands formed frustrated fists at her sides. "Damn it. Ian won't hurt you. He even told Simon to drop his requirements when you need a session. Do you know what it takes to get that man to interfere with another Dom?"

It was hard to think of Simon Weston being a Dom. He was always so smooth and civilized. He wore designer suits, but tonight she was going to see him in leathers.

"What are his requirements?" The minute the question was out of her mouth, she wanted to call it back. It wasn't her business, but she was so curious.

"Naked, of course." Chelsea frowned as she straightened up and looked at herself in the mirror. "He wants to see how bad my scars are, I'm sure."

Charlotte sighed, an annoyed sound. "I think he wants to see your breasts."

Chelsea huffed a little. "Not so sure about that. You know how much he likes crippled girls. I'll go talk to Satan myself. See you in a bit. Try not to get naked too fast, Pen. Make the man work for it."

Charlotte shook her head as Chelsea walked out of the dressing room toward the dungeon floor. "She's going to be the death of me."

"What did she mean about crippled girls?" She seemed to struggle with minding her own business, but in the days she'd spent at The Garden, she'd settled into comfortable friendships and she was fascinated by the women around her.

Charlotte pulled out her blush and eyed Penny critically before she started applying the light pink color to her cheeks. Penny stayed still. Charlotte was an artist and Penny had recently become her favorite canvas.

"She thinks Simon is holding a torch for a woman named Avery."

"Avery Charles?" She'd been his target in his last SIS operation. He'd infiltrated the organization she worked for, a charity that was headed by a man who dealt arms to war torn parts of Africa.

"Avery O'Donnell now. She married one of Ian's men. She just had a baby, a boy named Aidan. Don't move or I'll mess up." She swept the brush across her cheek. "Chelsea's decided that Simon is only interested in her because she reminds him of Avery. I explained that Avery is practically a saint and she has next to nothing in common with her except that they both suffered injuries to their legs. Simon doesn't run around trying to rub himself all over every girl on crutches, so I'm pretty sure he's interested in Chelsea for Chelsea, though the way she's treated him, I have no idea why. I think we can safely say he's a masochist."

"I remember that op. Simon liked Avery. He thought she was innocent and he wanted to make sure she didn't get hurt, but he never mentioned a deep and abiding passion for her."

"Well, try telling my sister that. Sometimes I think I did more harm than good by taking her with me. Open your mouth a little." She pulled out the gloss and started painting it across Penny's lips. Intimacy. She'd learned more about friendships and intimacies in the past week than she could have imagined. Intimacy didn't have to mean sex. Intimacy was really revealing herself to another person, opening herself up and allowing the people around her to change her in small ways, to let their strengths become her own.

"Taking her with you when you went on the run?" She asked after the gloss was on. She'd learned the whole story of Charlotte and Ian over the last couple of days. It made her problems with Damon seem simple.

"Yes. Although I didn't have a choice at the time. We had to get away from my father's organization. We did not have to become international information brokers. Oh, sure, it protected us and gave us power and crap, but I think Chelsea got addicted to it. It also allowed her to hide away and live in front of her computer. I should have taken her to the park and forced her to socialize with the rest of the puppies." She took a step back and smiled. "You look awesome. Are you ready for this?"

Damon had walked the dungeon floor with her the night before, but they hadn't played. During the afternoons, he'd taken her to his "toy room" and allowed her to be acquainted with the various tools he employed. He'd sat beside her as Ian had presented a class on Shibari, tying up Charlotte in intricate designs.

But tonight, they were playing. She and Damon. In public.

"I'm ready." She wasn't so sure she could say the same about Damon. He'd enthusiastically shagged her at every opportunity, but he seemed reluctant to play. He let her sleep next to him, but still took his own shower. He'd moved into the guest bathroom, leaving the master to her. He dressed in another room as well, as though sharing the mundane intimacies of life was too much for him.

Or he was simply holding himself apart so he could leave her when he'd promised to.

She'd hoped that sex would bring them closer, but it was a false thing. It felt perfect when he held her, but the distance between them afterward was becoming impossible to handle.

She heard the insistent thud of industrial music coming from the dungeon. Trying to push aside her problems with Damon was hard, but she was determined to enjoy the night. It was her first time to play, her first time to really be in the dungeon in something other than an observational capacity.

"Come on. Let's go see what trouble my sister's gotten herself into. She doesn't do well in dungeons without someone to speak for her. Seriously, I've thought about shoving a ball gag in her mouth before we leave the locker room at Sanctum." Charlotte took her hand. "Why didn't Damon give you shoes?"

Because he was being somewhat kind. That was what Penny thought. "I'm not good in high heels."

"Or it's because he likes you being so much smaller than him." Charlotte always seemed to look to the most romantic explanation of everything.

They left the light of the dressing room and were immediately enclosed in the soft night of The Garden. A full moon was shining down and the jasmine was blooming from the walls.

"Gosh, it's so pretty here." Charlotte looked up, wonder on her face. "Do you ever wonder how a man as dark as Damon came up with this place?"

Every moment of every day. She breathed in the scents of the dungeon. Jasmine and loamy earth, and leather with the faintest hint of sweat and sex. Cobblestone was cool on the flats of her feet. Since meeting Damon, she'd become aware of the world around her in a way she hadn't before. The ivy that wound its way across the dungeon would never have caught her attention, but now she saw it. Green, shiny, alive. It crept up the walls and across the floor, invading the space and bringing it to life.

She caught sight of Damon. He was standing beside Ian, both men in leather pants, vests, and boots.

Was she fooling herself? She wanted to cross to him, to sink to her knees in front of him and know that he wanted her there, but she worried she was setting herself up for more heartache.

And then he turned, his eyes catching hers and just for a moment, they lit up, his mouth opening a bit, his whole body turning toward hers. He shut it down, but there had been lust and something else in his eyes for that one minute. It was the same look he'd had on his face the first time he'd brought her into The Garden. Pride.

He was proud of her.

"Oh, girl, you are one of us now." Charlotte put an arm around her and impulsively kissed her cheek. "Let's go and join our intensely obnoxious men."

Penny nodded. She'd gotten far more comfortable around Ian Taggart. She'd learned he was mostly bark. Oh, she was sure when the man really decided to bite he would rip a throat out, but there was an actual fully functional heart under all his cursing.

If a man like that could let go and be happily married, why couldn't Damon? God, she'd just thought it. She'd admitted what she really wanted. To be Damon's wife.

His face had lost that momentary wonder and was back to what she'd come to think of as his Dom face. Gorgeous, just the slightest bit chilly. He gestured for her to come to him.

She did because no matter how cold he seemed, she'd caught glimpses of the real man and she would risk heartache to find him again.

She crossed the distance between them, praying she looked natural in her very little clothing. She was used to covering up, but she'd discovered that all those clothes formed a barrier between her and the world. She'd practically turned into a nudist in the comfort of Damon's apartments.

Damon stood at the edge of a crowd of ten or fifteen people. The Garden, she'd discovered, was very exclusive. On the nights it was open, there were never more than twenty or thirty people in the club, including the staff.

As she joined him, she heard the *thud thud thud* of a flogger hitting flesh. A woman was chained to the St. Andrew's Cross, her body already sagging.

"Holy shit," Charlotte said. Her husband's hand covered her mouth, and he dragged her close.

"Don't you say another word," Taggart commanded quietly. "I had to negotiate for her. We got her down to her leggings, but I couldn't let her leave the bra on. If Simon hit the metallic parts, it could really hurt. She's fine. Let them be. Let them work this out without your interference."

Simon wielded what looked to be two floggers, one in each hand. He moved to the music, allowing it to guide his strikes in a pulsing rhythm. His wrists flicked, snapping back and forth, the sound of the falls striking her skin reaching a crescendo.

It was a beautiful dance and Penny watched, utterly fascinated by the way Simon handled the scene. He stopped suddenly and ran a big palm down Chelsea's back. He was so much larger than the brunette that his palm took up almost all the space between her shoulders. He leaned in, seeming to say something to his partner as he cupped the nape of her neck.

She simply nodded and he stepped back, his hand coming out to request another instrument. Ian stepped up, handing him what looked like a furry black glove.

"It's called a vampire glove." Damon whispered into her ear, dragging her against him. He slid an arm around her waist, cradling her back to his front as he quietly explained. "The material is extremely soft. Simon's been warming her up with a deerskin flogger. Her skin is getting very sensitive. Watch."

Simon ran the glove across her back, and Chelsea seemed to sigh and rub against it. Then suddenly she stopped, shuddering and moaning softly.

"There's a row of metal studs hidden in the glove that Simon will manipulate to keep her off balance. They won't cut her skin, but she will feel it. If she wasn't so stubborn, he would run that glove all over her body and there wouldn't be an inch of her skin that didn't feel alive."

Penny turned her head up, speaking softly to Damon so she didn't disturb anyone. "Why does it help with the pain?"

"Some people get endorphins from enduring, rather like a runner after a marathon or someone working out. I would bet she's actually quite submissive, but she won't allow herself to practice in real life. So she finds her subspace in bits of time when the pain becomes too much to handle. If she were my sub, I would put her on a regular yoga routine to keep her flexibility up. I would get her out from in front of the computer and force her to deal with her issues, but she's quite vocal about not taking a Dom even though I think Weston would accept her in a heartbeat."

Simon put the vampire glove down and selected another flogger.

"Oh, he's getting a bit nasty now," Damon whispered. "That one's pure leather. It's softened up a bit, but do you see the small knots on the end of a couple of the falls? Yes, that's going to sting a bit."

Chelsea stiffened the first time he struck her with it and then after a long shuddering breath, her head fell forward. He found his rhythm again, moving to the music as he struck her shoulders, arse, and hamstrings. He avoided the spine, focusing on the big muscles. After the first sting, Chelsea seemed to go completely limp, her body moving easily with the strikes, but not fighting them at all. She accepted everything Simon gave her.

Charlotte was watching, her eyes never leaving her sister as she hung from the cross. Ian had an arm around her as if he thought she needed support, or perhaps he was worried she would intervene.

He alternated between flogging her and running the vampire glove over her sensitive skin.

Penny relaxed back against Damon. Every now and then he would point out something Simon was doing and why he was doing it. He seemed very dismissive of the fact that she was wearing heavy leggings.

Chelsea was wrong, she realized as she glanced around the crowd. No one would judge her. There wasn't a single perfect body in the building. Most of the men had scars. It did nothing to take away from their attractiveness. If anything, Penny found she liked them. It let her know these were men who had fought.

Many of the women would be considered overweight by society standards, but their Doms seemed to like them that way. Chelsea had a few curves, but she wasn't heavy. She was a pretty woman, especially when she smiled. No one would make fun of her for her scars. Not here.

Yet she clung to those leggings, even when she was willing to take off her shirt to be tied down.

Simon finally placed the flogger on the table and went to untie her.

"Charlie," Ian barked his warning as his wife stepped away from him.

"It's only if she needs me." Charlotte moved forward, clutching Penny's hand.

As they moved closer, she could hear Simon talking in low tones as his hand found Chelsea's hair, stroking her. "You did so well, love. So well."

Chelsea seemed to be shaking herself back to consciousness. "Oh, is it over already?"

Simon chuckled. "Of course not. I need to take a look at your back. I need to make sure I didn't leave marks. Let me take you to the aftercare room and give you a good rubdown. You'll sleep so well."

Chelsea shook her head. "No. I feel fine. Better than fine actually. You're very good at what you do."

His hand tightened in her hair. "Do you know how much better this could be if you let it? Do you know how I could make you feel? Give over to me, Chelsea. Let me take over. You won't regret it. I can make you feel so much."

Penny wanted to move away, to give them this intimate moment, but Charlotte wouldn't move.

Chelsea shook her head and started to pull at the bindings that wrapped around her wrists. "No. Let me out. I want out now. I don't want aftercare. I don't need it."

"Chelsea," Simon started.

"Get me out of these, Weston. I'm done." Her voice rose, losing the dreamy quality she'd had before and becoming panic tinged. "Charlotte!"

"I'm sorry, Simon." Charlotte moved in, her hands going up to untie her sister.

Simon stepped back, his face going blank. He began cleaning up, ignoring the woman he'd just lavished so much time on.

And when she likely thought no one was looking, Chelsea turned and stared at Simon's back, longing plain on her face.

So afraid. She was so afraid. It was plain for Penny to see because she'd been there. She'd been mad about Damon Knight for years and she was sure she'd had that very look on her face a million times when he walked across the room, paying her absolutely no mind.

She had this chance. She wouldn't get it again.

Where had Damon gone? She looked and he'd moved with Ian into the bar. The two men were sitting together, Ian's brow furrowed, his agitation obvious.

She walked back to him, dropping to her knees and taking her place at his feet. A week ago, she would likely have been horrified by the idea, but it didn't make her less of a woman. Kneeling at her lover's feet didn't mean she was a doormat. It was play and an offering of sorts. It meant she was willing to be what he needed her to be.

He looked down at her, his eyes widening slightly, and then his hand came out to touch her hair.

The power exchange was just that, she realized. She didn't have to give up herself. She exchanged one power for another.

Penny wrapped her arms around his leg and felt him relax. He guided her head to his lap and continued to talk.

Penny rested against him, promising herself it wouldn't be the last time.

* * * *

Damon petted his sub, allowing the peace he always seemed to feel when she was being sweet and submissive to wash over him.

Ian, on the other hand, was obviously not feeling his calm.

"She shouldn't interrupt him. I've warned her time and time again. I'm going to spank her ass silly. She won't be able to sit for a week. What's the worst torture device you have? Come on, man. You've got to have something really good. You're British. You still have actual dungeons."

He let his hand play in the softness of Penelope's hair. "Your sister-in-law obviously has problems that she isn't ready to deal with."

"Because Charlie won't let her. I swear sometimes she treats Chelsea like her toddler instead of her twenty-seven-year-old sister." He sat back. "Simon could do her a world of good."

The way Penelope was doing him a world of good. But then he and Chelsea had the same problems. "It only works if she lets him."

He understood Chelsea's issues. He couldn't allow that trust and affection to truly grow between them because it would be that much harder to break from her when the time came.

He wasn't sure how he would handle seeing her at the office. What the hell would he do when she eventually found a smart man and settled down? Would he catch a glimpse of pictures of her husband on her desk? Her children?

He didn't even want children. He'd always known he wouldn't have any. The world was too cruel, too mercurial, to bring something as vulnerable as a child into it. No, he wouldn't do it. Wouldn't even consider it. Still, he wondered what her children would look like. Serious girls with her sweet face and smart mind.

Dumb boys who needed their mother to keep them in line because their father would rather play with them. Like he hadn't been able to play as a child.

He shook off the ridiculous maudlin thoughts.

"Don't spank her too hard," Damon said, his eyes going back to Weston. He was cleaning up his scene space, his spine perfectly straight and not a hint of expression on his face. Poor bugger seemed to have fallen for the wrong girl.

Of course, he could say the same thing for his Penelope. She'd fallen for the wrong man. At least he thought she'd fallen for him. Sometimes he couldn't tell. Sometimes he thought she might be perfectly happy to get rid of him at the end of the operation.

Until he commanded her to come to him and she went with such open willingness that he felt like fucking her was finally being home. Sliding into her body was like finding his place in the world.

Ian ran a frustrated hand through his hair. "I know. We have to get on the boat tomorrow and I need her fully functional. I thought this would be fun, man." He huffed a little. "I thought it would be like a second honeymoon. Then you have to fuck it all up by having a crazy stalker asshole. Kill him when you get the chance because it's screwing with my sex life."

Trust Tag to make him chuckle. Still, it was easy to see the man had changed. He gave a damn about the people around him. Damon remembered when he was cold, calculating. Tag laughed now. He joked. He had a life.

Was there a life out there for him, too?

"What scene are you running tonight with blondie there? By the way, you look lovely, dear." For all Tag's crudeness, he'd always been kind to subs.

"Thank you, Sir." Her arms tightened around his legs. "Was I not supposed to talk? Are we in high protocol?"

He hadn't spent enough time with her. He knew it. He'd spent all his time getting his cock inside her and not enough time preparing her. "Calm down, love. We're going in as a fairly new couple. Ian and Charlotte are going to pose as our sponsors. If anyone asks, we're still feeling our way. It means that we might have to go to some of the seminars."

Tag snorted a little. "I can't wait to see you in *Protocol 101* or *Plug Your Sub's Ass in Ten Easy Ways*."

"Why on earth would they want to make it easy?" A good plugging should be work.

"What?" Penelope's head came off his lap.

He eased her back down. Actually, it might be fun to shock her a bit. "I signed us up for *Extreme Figging*."

"I know what that is, Damon. You are not shoving ginger up my bum."

They had to get a few things straight. He might not have spent enough time with her, but he'd been very plain in his rules. One of them was never to tell him what he couldn't do, and certainly not in his own bloody club. "Over my lap right now."

Her head came up, a gorgeous pout on her mouth. "I'm sorry, Master. I meant to say that I don't think I would enjoy having ginger shoved up my bum and could we please talk about it?"

Not working on him. "If that's what you meant, then that's what you should have said. Do I treat you with disrespect in front of our friends? Do you know the rules about how to act when we're on a dungeon floor?"

She nodded, already sniffling a little. God, she was beautiful. "Yes."

"What will happen if you do that on the boat?"

"Damn it." She shook her head. "And now I cursed. It would blow our cover or at the very least draw unwanted attention to us. I'm sorry, Damon."

"I'm not going to spank you for cursing, love. It would be the height of hypocrisy. I curse quite a bit myself, but try to keep it to a minimum while we're working and certainly when we're playing. And yes, it would draw attention to us. So over my lap. It's a count of twenty."

"But I apologized."

"And you can do so again after you've received my discipline." He kept his tone quiet but firm. She was nervous about being in public. He knew damn well she wasn't scared of the bloody spanking. He'd spanked her several times and every one ended in his cock up her cunt and her screaming out his name. No. She was looking around. Just because Charlotte had talked her into a new wardrobe that showed far too much of her breasts didn't change the fact that she was nervous. Being naked for him was one thing. He was her lover. This was public punishment, and she'd better bloody get used to it.

Tag didn't make things easy on her. He simply grinned her way and waggled his eyebrows lasciviously. "I'm looking forward to watching."

"What are you doing, you pervert?" His wife walked up, her heels clacking against the stone floor. "Are you two being mean to Penny?"

He wasn't having a bloody minute of that garbage. There was no way he was going to spend the evening placating his sub's friend. He was grateful to Charlotte for befriending Penelope, but she tended to stick her nose in where it absolutely didn't belong. "Tag, forget what I said about not spanking her. If she interferes with me the way she did Weston, I'll chuck you both out of this club and you can spend the night on the street for all I'll care."

Tag reached out and grabbed his wife's hand, and she was over his lap in a heartbeat, his hand raining down on her bum. "I've given you an enormous amount of rope, baby, and you are hanging yourself with it. Do you come between a Dom and his sub?"

"She isn't his sub." Charlotte's breath hitched as Ian's hand came down on her ass. "Chelsea isn't Simon's."

"And she never will be because big sister likes to interfere. She had a safe word. She could have used it. What did you think he was going to do to her?"

The Taggarts continued, dealing with their family drama through spanking. He had his own domestic dispute.

Damon patted his lap. "We're up to thirty now. Every second you delay adds to the punishment. We have a long ride to Dover in the morning. You can be as uncomfortable as your stubbornness allows."

She nearly jumped in his lap, but then he noticed that when Penelope finally decided to do something, she tended to leap in with both feet. He had to catch her or she likely would have rolled right off his lap and onto the floor. He found himself with an armful of Penelope, and he'd been right about how lovely she would look in a thong. Her cheeks were round, and he couldn't help but lay his hands on them and give them a nice squeeze.

He brought his hand down in a sharp arc, enjoying the sound of the smack and the little squeal that came after. He rained down on her, keeping a careful count. He'd told her thirty. She'd done her level best not to make it thirty-one, so she would only get thirty.

But he could spank her all night, really. He laid them all over her cheeks, snapping the string of her thong in between spanks. Her skin got a hot pink sheen to it and she clutched at his ankles, her breath coming out in sexy pants.

He let his hand work, delivering discipline to her arse and the curvy backs of her legs. He stopped when he reached thirty and held his palm flat on the last place he'd spanked, keeping the heat against her flesh. It was definitely time to get her more used to public sex.

There was a party on the Royale tomorrow night, and he suspected it would get a little crazy. He intended to firmly cement their cover before they got to Helsinki.

He let his hand slide down to rub between her legs, shoving her thong aside and finding the warmth of her arousal. He didn't have to shove his fingers hard. They slipped between her legs, her wetness making it an easy glide past her labia and into her pussy.

Penelope shuddered sweetly.

"You liked your spanking, didn't you, you bad girl? You liked having the nasty Dom slap your arse silly." He fucked his fingers deep, finding her clit with his thumb and pressing down but not enough to make her come. "Thank me for your spanking."

"Thank you, Master."

"Thank me for getting you hot and wet and ready to fuck."

"Thank you, Master, for getting me hot and wet and ready to fuck."

To his side, he caught sight of Charlotte on the ground between Ian's knees. His leathers were open and his wife was making up for her interference in a very nice way. She sucked his cock in long passes of her mouth.

It was a damn fine idea, but he wanted more from his sub. "Ask me to fuck you, love."

She tensed. Not a good thing.

He pulled his fingers out of her pussy and smacked her sensitive cheeks again. "Is there a problem?"

She took a long breath and then her head came up, her decision obviously made. "Will you please fuck me, Master?"

Brave sub. God, if he had half her guts, he would be so much better for it. He helped her up, chuckling at the surprise on her face as she caught sight of the Taggarts working out their marital issues through oral sex.

"Get used to it." He set her on her feet between his legs. "You'll see much more on the boat. And no. I won't fuck you."

Her face fell.

He spoke again quickly, so she didn't misunderstand. "But I would very much like it if you fucked me, love. Right here. Right now. In front of everyone. If you can't do it, I understand, but it's going to make our cover difficult to keep. I think you'll like it. I want you to think about it. Think about all those people watching you. Think about how every man is going to want to be me, with his cock up inside you. They'll all be thinking about how gorgeous your tits are and how lucky I am to have a sub who serves me so passionately."

It was obviously getting to her because her eyes had dilated and her breath had picked back up.

"Yes, Master." She gave him one of those smiles that did weird things to his insides. "I'll fuck you. Right here. Right now."

Chapter Thirteen

Penny couldn't help the way her hands shook. She had to get it under control. She was safe here. No one would make fun of her. No one would think twice about her having sex here.

Charlotte wouldn't even notice. She was too busy swallowing her husband's incredibly large penis. She had to look away or Damon might get offended.

Desire brought her the bravery she needed. Damon was always in control, but he was offering it to her this time.

"You can't take your Master's cock while wearing all those clothes."

Damn it. Well, she knew she'd have to do it sometime. If she couldn't do it here, she would have a struggle on the boat. "I need help."

He grinned at her, and she was happy she hadn't given him trouble. He seemed relaxed, his cares chased away for the moment. He reached down into his boot and pulled out a knife. "I can help you with that."

It was such a pretty corset, but it looked like she wouldn't be getting back into it that evening. Damon had bought her several more for the trip so she wouldn't need to repair it right away. She loved the fact that he'd selected them and the underthings he allowed her to wear. She would never let him pick out the clothes she wore on a regular basis, but the idea that he picked out her intimate play clothes made her feel warm.

He neatly sliced through the laces of the corset, and Penny could breathe again. The corset fell to the floor.

He sat back in his chair, his legs wide, appearing to all to be the decadent king of his castle. "Now the thong."

His hands worked to undo the laces of his leathers and his cock sprang free. He gave Taggart a run for his money. Her mouth always watered, no matter how many times she saw it.

Penny shoved the thong off. Sure enough, there were eyes on her. She caught Simon Weston staring, an amused look on his face, but she didn't think he was laughing at her. He was likely thinking he'd never once thought to see stuffy Penelope Cash standing in the middle of a BDSM club with her knickers off. And she'd never thought to watch him flog someone, so good for them both. She gave him a saucy grin.

Damon frowned at her. "I don't want to know who you're looking at, do I?"

He was so cute when he was jealous. "Not at all, Master."

She climbed on top of his lap, her heart starting to beat hard in her chest. He'd taught her how good this could be, and now she was a bit addicted to sex—well, she was addicted to Damon.

His brows came together in a *V* despite the fact that his cock was already poking at her. "It's Weston, isn't it? He's looking at you."

Leaning over, she kissed him where his brows met. "I'm naked. You told me everyone would be looking at me. I think you like it because you know I don't want to be with anyone else."

His hands found her hips, moving restlessly against her skin. "Is that right? I thought you were looking for another damn Dom."

The growl in his tone gave her great hope, but she had to play the game for now. "I'm trying to stay in character, Master." She reached in between them and gripped his cock. He liked it when she was a bit rough, so she squeezed him before guiding him to her entrance.

"You're too bloody good at staying in character," he

complained, but his chest was working now, dragging air into his lungs. "Take me inside. Take me now."

She let herself sink down on his cock, glorying in how full she was when he was inside her. Nothing ever felt as good as that moment when he invaded. The stretch reminded her how much she was taking from him, more than sex, more than some dumb job. He gave her more. He gave her strength.

She balanced on his shoulders, letting gravity do its job. When her so sensitive cheeks met the leather covering his thighs, she sighed. Her whole body was on edge, primed.

One hand moved up to the nape of her neck, sliding along her spine, and suddenly she wasn't thinking about the fact that she was naked in front of a dungeon full of people. She was only thinking of him. What had Simon said to Chelsea? He'd told her he could make her feel so much more. It was likely what had frightened her, but it didn't scare Penny. Damon made her feel. Before him the world had seemed gray, and now it exploded with colors so vibrant, it made her blink to look at it. Yes, it was frightening to feel when she'd been numb for so very long. It also meant she could feel pain with such clarity, but she'd never known pure bliss until Damon Knight had made her his.

Freedom. He'd given her freedom. He pulled her down for a kiss, his tongue surging into her mouth. Who would have guessed the most freedom she'd ever found would come from being tied to another human being? She'd spent most of her life serving others. This was the first time she'd felt at peace with her nature.

Without giving up the kiss, she moved her hips up and down, sliding along his erection.

He broke off the kiss, but his lips moved to her chin and neck, lavishing affection there. "Keep it up, love. Don't you stop no matter what I do."

That made alarm bells go off in her head. His hand moved between them as she kept moving on his cock. Pure pleasure sparked through her as he toyed with her clit, but not enough to send her over the edge.

"That should do it. Normally I would use lube, love, but you're so bloody wet, I don't need it. I just need that juicy pussy of yours."

She nearly came out of her skin as he touched her arsehole, pushing in, rimming it gently. "Oh, my god."

"No, love. Just your Master, and I will have this from you. I'm going to fuck you right here when you're ready. You'll wear a plug to sleep tonight. I'll have you ready for me in a few days."

She felt herself clench down.

He slapped at her sensitive skin. "Don't you keep me out. You let me in. I told you not to stop. Do you need another spanking, love? I can do this all night long or you can ride my cock and take your orgasm."

He would do it. He would haul her off him and spank her again and begin the process over and over until he got what he wanted. With a low moan, she forced her hips up. As she sank back on his cock, she was forced to take his finger as well.

It didn't hurt, merely felt foreign. A jangled pressure warred with the pleasure in her pussy.

She could handle it. She fucked him, taking cock and finger, forcing them deeper inside her until she couldn't stand it a second longer and her muscles tensed and flooded with orgasm. Her arsehole was clenching over and over, now trying to keep him in. Her pussy clamped down on his cock, and she was suffused with sensation. She rode the orgasm out, working her hips until he finally joined her.

His pelvis tilted up, and she felt the hot wash of his come as he flooded her. His head fell back and his finger slipped out of her, but he held her with his other hand, caressing her back and bringing her close to him.

She'd just screwed her partner in front of a crowd and she didn't give a damn. It had been good and right, and anyone who thought differently was just wrong. She let her hands slip around his neck as she rested on him, their breaths mingling.

After a while, he kissed her and gently moved her off him. "Sorry, love. We both need to clean up and then I want to watch the fire play scene with you. They should be setting up now. Do you want a glass of wine? We're not going to play anymore so you can drink, though don't think I'm done fucking you yet."

She stretched. "Should I get someone to relace the corset?" The idea of getting back into it wasn't pleasant.

He stared at her. "No. You're fine the way you are. I could get a leash for your collar if you need something more."

Sarcastic brute. "I think I'm fine, Damon."

"Go to the dressing room and clean up. Meet me back here directly. I'll have some drinks and snacks for us, and we'll spend the rest of the evening watching."

She walked into the dressing room, visions of sitting in her Master's lap while he fed her playing through her head. She headed to the shower and turned it on, hearing a telly playing in the background. There was a salon of sorts in one part of the dressing room where subs met and mingled before going out to the dungeon floor.

She washed off quickly, thinking about how little time she had left. The cruise would only take twelve days, but everything would be over the minute they caught the man they were trying to find. It could all end abruptly. Damon would be on the next private plane to London, and she might find herself alone.

And then she would have to decide what to do with the rest of her life. She only knew one thing. If Damon couldn't be brave enough to be with her, she wouldn't lie down and die. She wouldn't run away. She would smile at him and make him watch as she found her life. She knew what she wanted now. She wanted it all and she prayed she had it with Damon, but if he wouldn't, she would be in this club, at the job, dating, searching for the right man.

She dried off, trying to shove aside the morbid thoughts. She had to go and meet her Master, and she had to do it without a stitch on. She started toward the exit when she heard sniffling.

Chelsea was sitting in the salon, staring at something on the telly, but it was obvious she wasn't watching it. She'd showered and changed and looked utterly miserable.

"Do you want me to get Charlotte?" Penny asked quietly.

Chelsea started a bit and turned, then laughed even though there were tears running down her cheeks. She brushed them away. "No, I don't want to interrupt her evening any more than I already have. I should have safe worded out, but it seemed like a wuss thing to do. I guess calling out for big sis isn't much better though. Well, it didn't take long for you to get naked."

She held the towel up, not wanting to offend her. "Sorry."

Chelsea waved it off. "Don't be. It's fine. It doesn't bother me. I'm glad Damon's treating you well, but if that changes, you should know I came up with a plan to make his life a living hell. I wrote an algorithm that will upload orders to every takeout place in a two-mile radius in his name. He'll be answering the door and explaining himself every thirty minutes for at least twenty-four hours."

"That's terrible." Chelsea seemed to spend most her time planning methods of destruction.

Chelsea shook her head. "No. It's actually a hobby of mine. I like to code, and manipulating the Internet to ruin lives is just plain fun. I'm fine, Pen. Really. I'm just in subdrop. I'll be cool."

Subdrop. It was what some people in the lifestyle called coming out of subspace. Some subs took it harder than others. She'd watched how other Doms handled bringing their subs back to the real world. They cuddled them and talked, making the transition easier on both of them, but Chelsea wouldn't allow Simon to take care of her.

"Is it always this bad?"

"No." Chelsea took a long breath. "Not at all. Honestly, I don't sub out. Not really. I kind of thought it was a myth. I relax, but I don't just go somewhere else. Naturally Simon is the one who does it for me."

"Why don't you give him a chance?" It was obvious she was in love with the man.

Chelsea's face tightened with obvious pain. "Look at him, Penny. He's a Greek god and British aristocrat all rolled up in one hot Dom package. He's actually in line for the damn throne. Oh, there are a whole bunch of people in front of him, but his family is connected in ways I can't even understand. My father was a criminal. Hell, I'm a criminal according to a whole bunch of intelligence agencies."

"I don't think he cares about that." Though his father was the Duke of Norsley, Simon had never put on airs. He spent more time with his oil baron Texas cousins than with the aristocracy from what Penny had been able to tell.

Chelsea simply shook her head and laughed bitterly. "Do you know what he's doing on the boat? What his cover is? He's the dancing instructor. Because the bastard knows how to waltz and tango. I'm not joking. The thought of that man being with me is utterly ridiculous. I can't even walk straight. For god's sake, I'm a virgin."

She was a twenty-seven-year-old virgin? "Chelsea..."

"I know. It's pathetic. I'm sorry. I blame the stupid subdrop. I didn't mean to wreck your evening. I had a crappy childhood. I never got to go to junior high dances and cry in the bathroom, so I'm making up for lost time." She sighed and gestured to the telly. "At least my house didn't burn down. Someone's having a worse day than me. Apparently that town house blew up or something."

Penny glanced up, ready to open a discussion with Chelsea because it was stupid to think she wasn't good enough for Simon. She was going to give her the lecture of a lifetime, but something caught her eye.

Right there on the screen, a newswoman was speaking into a microphone as she stood outside what looked to be the smoldering remains of a town house. It seemed to have been gutted by the blaze, but the porch was still there. A firefighter walked from the front door in full gear. He stepped out on the stone porch she knew so well. The stone pots had been left behind. Likely Damon had thought they were part of the house, so he hadn't packed them up when he'd moved her from her mum's home. Penelope remembered the day her father had brought them home. Two large planters with lion's head designs on the front. Her mother had laughed, saying they were atrocious, but they'd sat there on either side of the door for twenty years.

Her mother's house, the house she'd grown up in, was gone.

"Penny?" Chelsea sat up, concern on her face.

"That's my house." Tears pooled in her eyes. "He burned my house down."

Basil Champion meant business, and it seemed she was his next target.

* * * *

Damon stared at the charred wreckage that used to be his sub's home. Penelope was speaking to the fire brigade investigator, but the man's boss would be getting a call from Nigel in the next few minutes that would shut everything down. The fire would be declared an accident, insurance would compensate her, and people would forget.

SIS wouldn't forget. It would go on record, another mark against former agent Basil Champion.

He suspected Penelope was just now realizing what loving him could cost her.

"Bad business, Knight, but I'm glad you're here." George Cash had been in town, seen the news, and rushed over. He'd been the first of the family on the scene, but Diana and her husband hadn't been far behind. Diana and Penelope had cried, hugging each other.

He only had Penelope. If The Garden burned down, she would be the only one there to offer him comfort, and Baz was making it impossible for him to accept it.

This was his way of letting Damon know not to get too close because he could take it all away.

He managed to shake George's hand. "Yes, we heard about it on the telly and got over here as fast as we could." It suddenly occurred to him that he had explanations to make. "Don't worry about photos or mementos. I had them all moved to a storage facility when Penelope moved out."

Cash's shoulders squared. "She's moved in with you?"

"Just while she's looking for her own place." He didn't want to leave her trying to explain their situation after he was gone. "It isn't permanent."

"That's surprising. I actually don't like any of this. Penny hasn't dated since her fiancé left, and now she's moving in with someone we don't even know. I find it odd that she just introduced you and suddenly it seems as though her whole life's been upended. She was living here just last week. The place was full of Mum's stuff. It should have taken a month to move it all on her own."

"I have connections." It was the only explanation he was willing to give.

"Yes, I'm sure you do. Again, thanks for bringing her out, but you should know, I'm going to check into you, Knight. She isn't unprotected, and I won't let anyone hurt my sister." He nodded, taking a step back before he turned and joined his family.

Leaving Damon utterly alone. Cash was a good chap, but he had no idea what he was up against. Penelope wasn't being threatened by a Lothario who would break her heart. Baz would likely cut it out and mail it to Damon.

Ian Taggart strode up. Damon had left him behind to get the club shut down. Weston was still there, watching over it. He wouldn't put it past Baz to use the destruction of Penelope's home as a distraction to attack the club.

"Any sign of him?"

Damon shook his head. "None. You should get back. I'd feel better if Weston had backup."

"He does. He has Charlie. Don't think my wife won't take out your fuckwad for you. She's been itching to get back in the game. Chelsea's taken over the CCTVs around The Garden. They're safe."

He was glad Tag was optimistic. He couldn't help but glance back at Penelope. She was leaning on Diana, and the minute George got to her side, she pulled him close, too. He'd studied her before. She'd been more closed off. At least he'd been able to do one good thing for her. As she accepted herself sexually, she was opening up to the people who cared about her. He watched as George seemed confused at first and then hugged her fiercely.

"Is she all right?" Tag asked.

"She just had her childhood home gutted. No. She's not all right."

"You know it's not your fault."

"I'm the one who brought her into this. I'm the one he wants to punish, and he'll use her to do it."

Tag shook his head. "You're fucking up, brother. She's stronger than you think. I hate to give advice."

"Then don't."

"It makes me physically ill, but I'm going to because you asked so nicely."

"I didn't ask at all."

Tag simply ignored him. "Give her a chance. Let her stand by you. She wants to. That woman is crazy about you, and I think you need her. Don't let Baz fuck this up."

As if saying his name had conjured him, Damon's mobile trilled. Unknown Number. He didn't need to guess. He flipped it on. "You've been busy, Baz."

Tag frowned. "Tell that fucker I'm going to kill him."

A low, nasty chuckle came over the line. "Oh, how I love the Americans. Tell me something, Damon. How is your evening going?"

There was no point in trying to find a way to trace the call. Baz would use a burner, a prepaid non-traceable mobile. The minute this conversation was over, he would toss it in the nearest garbage bin and move on to the next. "What do you want?"

"You can't handle what I want, can you? So I'll have to take what I can get. Did you play with her tonight? Did you make her prance around the dungeon, showing off those tits of hers?"

"I'm only going to repeat myself once more and then I'll hang up. What do you want?"

"Do you think you're in a position of power here? Do you think you're superior to me? You're not, and I proved it tonight."

"All you proved is you can use a lighter and gasoline. I'm finished here." He started to pull the phone away.

"I know who you're looking for on that boat. I know his name. I know what he looks like."

Damn it. Now he had to talk to the bastard. "I'm listening."

"We're on the same side in this, Damon. Neither one of us wants what could potentially happen."

A few things fell into place. "What exactly does the The Collective have to do with this?"

"His name is Walter Bennett. He was a virologist working for one of the companies I represent. He worked in this very distinguished pharmaceutical company's level-four lab."

Fuck. A biosafety level-four lab was for the most virulent of pathogens—the hemorrhagic fevers and small pox would require the over-the-top safety measures found in that type of lab. "So he managed to get a sample past security measures?"

"I'm afraid so, and you know as well as I do that this opens up my employers for rather expensive lawsuits and some nasty press. We would like it back. I'll trade the list of operatives for the package. Be careful, Damon. It's a bit like Pandora's box. You do not want to open it."

Baz wasn't telling him anything he didn't know. "If you know so much, why don't you take this Bennett man down yourself? Leave SIS out of it. I know you've run operations like this before on your own."

"But it's so much more fun with you."

He wouldn't give him a damn thing. "I need more information."

"And I'll get it to you. I'm going to meet you somewhere in Europe. I'll let you know where and when a couple of minutes before it happens. I don't want you to have time to plan anything, after all. You should know though that I'll be watching you and your whore."

"Leave her out of this, Baz."

"You brought her into it."

"And you can let her go. I don't have to bring her with me. I'll leave her here and this can be just you and me."

"It was never just you and me. You always had to bring some slut into it. Do you think I didn't watch you? I always watched you. I saw exactly how you looked at her. Like she was a sweet lamb and you were the hungry wolf. Did you think she could save you? Did you think she would save your disgusting soul? Does she know some of the things you've done?"

Every word burrowed into him, a time bomb waiting to go off. He glanced over and Penelope turned slightly toward him. The minute she caught sight of him, a tremulous smile curled her lips up.

She needed him and she didn't even know all the people he'd killed. Oh, she'd likely read his mission reports, but they were cleaned up and sanitized to the point that she couldn't conceive of the blood on his hands. Yes, he'd done it for his country, but there had always been a part of him that enjoyed his work, enjoyed dealing death to the world's worst criminals. She would be shocked if she really knew him, if she could see past the placid surface to the killer underneath.

He turned away from her. "She was assigned to me. You should know me better than this, Baz. I have no intention of keeping any female long term. I'm not built that way. As soon as the op is over, I won't work with her again. She's not field ready, and I don't think she ever will be."

"She can't understand you. I'm the only one who ever understood you."

Damon's stomach rolled. Baz was going to play this out to the end, and all Damon could do was go along. "You were my partner and you betrayed me."

"You betrayed me, Damon. Over and over again. You're the reason everything went to hell and don't ever tell yourself differently. If you'd just….it doesn't matter."

"It does. Let me dump her. This should be just you and me." Play to his ego. Play his game. Get Penelope out of it.

"No. She comes with you or everything's off. Do you understand? If you show up at the meet spot without her, I'll kill her. You won't be able to hide her from me. Maybe I'll play with her a bit. First, I'll kill that brother of hers. Does he really think that haircut looks good on him? I should take him out now just for crimes against fashion."

His blood chilled. He looked to Ian. *He's here*, Damon mouthed. He let his eyes find Penelope.

Tag nodded shortly and proved how much he'd changed, how much he understood exactly what Damon was feeling. Most agents would have immediately started looking for Baz, but Ian strode to Penelope, taking her hand and speaking quietly to her. Within seconds, Tag had all of the Cash siblings under cover.

"No, you don't care about her at all." Baz's voice was a silky evil over the line.

Where was the blighter? Damon looked around him. He could be anywhere, likely in one of the buildings surrounding them. "Why don't you come down here and talk to me? This doesn't have to be bad between us. Taggart is gone. Just you and me. We'll talk this out."

A low chuckle filled his ear. "Talk is all you ever wanted to do. Offer me something better, Damon."

"We'll go somewhere private." He would promise the bastard just about anything to get in the same small space with him. He needed to get him somewhere he couldn't run from. He needed to even the odds. "We're close to any number of hotels. Meet me at one."

"If only I thought you were serious, but I'm not a fool. Enjoy your whore tonight. I'll be thinking of you. I've got to get out of here. I had to kill someone to get a good seat to this show. God, I hate the elderly. But then I pretended it was your girl when I was strangling her to death. Good night, Damon."

The line went dead, and Damon cursed. He looked around but there was no way to know which building Baz was playing his murderous games in. He hated this feeling. Weak. Stupid. Vulnerable.

There was nothing to do except plan for their next meeting when Baz would again have the upper hand.

He strode to the car. There wasn't anything he could do here either. Penelope's home was gone, and he had next to nothing to offer her.

"Damon?" She got out of the car and rushed to him, throwing her arms around him.

He pushed her back. "Get in the car."

"He's here, isn't he?" She didn't fight him, simply got back into the car that Tag had already turned on, ready to get them all away from here.

Damon knew he should get in the front seat, but she moved over and put her hand out, willing him to come to her. There were tears in her eyes.

Now would be the perfect moment to show her how cold he was, to prove he didn't really give a damn about her. That he had nothing to offer her. He was cold and dead inside.

Except he wasn't when it came to her. She'd lost her home and he did have something to give her. He got into the backseat, gathering her close. "Go ahead and cry, love. It's all right now."

She wept into his shoulder, moving so she was in his lap as if she couldn't stand to be even that far from him.

His arms tightened, and he realized Baz might be right. She just might be the death of him.

Chapter Fourteen

Penny looked out over the dungeon and was deeply thankful that she seemed to have found her sea legs. The entire ballroom had been transformed into a massive play area. There were St. Andrew's Crosses along the walls, areas with spanking benches, and a couple of spots for master riggers to help with suspension play. Several subs had been intricately tied up in Shibari designs and placed on display in the bar area.

A couple of big dungeon monitors stood by the lifts and stairs. The rules were very plain. No intoxicated play. Jake Dean stood by the lifts. Apparently he'd been pressed into security duty. He looked big and slightly mean despite the fact that he was wearing a sunny yellow polo shirt and khaki pants. He'd already tossed two men out, his eyes lit with a certain glee. The rules of the dungeon and play spaces below had been explained in the meet and greet. Two drinks allowed in the bars inside the dungeon. Anyone attempting to get around it would be escorted to the non-play area of the ship.

"Are you all right, darling?" Damon eased up behind her, his hands finding her hips and sliding around her waist. He put his head close to hers, his mouth against her ear. "If you're sick, this is over."

She had to fight the urge to groan and roll her eyes. Her Dom was the touchiest thing. Over the last forty-eight hours, he'd found roughly four hundred reasons to end the op. First, he'd worried about her mental state after the fire. He'd held her the whole night, but in the morning claimed she wasn't rested enough and they would have to cancel. She'd simply hauled her bags down to the car and then gotten her bum spanked for carrying her own luggage.

Then he'd claimed they'd lost her papers. She'd easily found them in his laptop bag.

As the boat had rolled out of Dover, past the glorious white cliffs and pebbled beaches, she'd discovered that being on a massive floating ship didn't particularly agree with her stomach. At the first sign of nausea, she could have sworn she'd seen Damon jump up and down with joy.

Luckily Charlotte had gotten her some Dramamine, and she'd been perfectly fit for the meet and greet.

"I'm fine, Master." She put her hands over his. He really was a foolish man. But he seemed to be right about a few things. They didn't work together well since Damon seemed to find it impossible to think about anything except ways to get her off the boat. "What did you find out about the couple below us?"

Though they'd checked the room for bugs twice already, Damon preferred to whisper in crowded rooms, somehow thinking Baz was everywhere at once. They'd spent the day checking out the ten names Chelsea and Adam had targeted as their best bets to meet Walter Bennett. Six had connections to known Collective companies—although Damon insisted there were likely many more they didn't know about. One was a reporter who had written a lengthy magazine article about Nature's Core. Two had recently been in places that hosted Nature's Core rallies.

And one Chelsea had just said was obviously something called a skank-ho and was likely a criminal who should be shoved off the boat. Chelsea had offered to do it herself. Penny discounted contestant number ten because she'd seen her put her hand on Simon's ass as he instructed her on how to do the rumba. Chelsea had a bit of a vindictive streak.

She'd read everything she could on Bennett, had tried to memorize his face, but he could have undergone plastic surgery. She looked over the crowd, wondering which of these men were waiting to take Bennett's place.

Damon's hand traced her curves and ran back up to her breasts that seemed barely encased in a too-tight corset. His words whispered against her ear. "I discovered that Tiffani Hall enjoys large anal plugs and apparently likes very much to play the pony to her Master's rider. There was absolutely nothing there past sex toys and an inordinate amount of cherry flavored lube. I stole a tube. She won't miss it. Do you like cherry? God knows I do. You still have one, you know. I'm going to take that cherry. You're almost ready for me."

His hand ran down to her backside, cupping her cheek and reminding her that he'd been prepping her for that bit of play. Anal sex. He seemed a bit obsessed with it.

"That sounds like fun, Master. Can you be serious for a minute?"

"I am serious. I'm seriously thinking about fucking your tight arse. I'm trying not to be serious about the rest of it because it's likely to end in violent death. Both of ours, most probably. So I would like to spend my last days with my cock in your arse."

He was making her insane. He'd taken the tactic of shutting her out of the professional part of their relationship. She'd returned from a class he'd sent her to only to discover the entire crew had gotten together to discuss logistics without her. When she'd confronted him about it, he'd just kissed her and tossed her on the bed and explained that it had been "organic," and then she hadn't been able to think about anything but the way he was devouring her pussy.

"Damon, please, you can't shut me out of this."

"I'm not shutting you out." He licked the shell of her ear. "This is your job, love. You're here to give me cover. That's all. We could break up, you know. You could stomp off and throw that collar you're wearing in my face and everyone would believe it. The way you frown at me all the time has given me a bad reputation. Charlotte heard someone talking about the sweet-faced sub and her mean Master. I'm the mean Master."

"I'm not taking off my collar, Damon."

"Then you have to put up with this." He gripped her hips,

rubbing his erection against her bum.

Yes, she'd rapidly learned that being Master Damon's submissive meant taking Master Damon's cock at least three times a day. The man was utterly insatiable, and he didn't seem to care that they might not be alone when he got it in his head to have her. On the long drive from London to Dover, he'd hiked up her skirt and screwed her in the backseat while the Taggarts argued about whether or not they should bring someone named Phoebe back a Harry Potter souvenir.

"Who are our targets?" There was no point in arguing with him. At least he'd shoved aside the arctic treatment she'd gotten before. She preferred perpetually horny, pessimistic Damon to the cold, distant Dom.

"I told you. I'm targeting that pretty hole of yours."

"Damon, please."

He smacked her left cheek hard, his brows furrowing. "What did you say?"

There were certain things he insisted on. He would let her get away with a lot, but he had his own protocol. "Master."

"Better." He sighed and drew her back into his arms. "You're turning into a workaholic."

"How can I since you never let me work?"

"Fine." He swept her hair aside and went back to nibbling on her ear. "Do you see the girl in the black corset?"

"Seriously?" That described almost everyone.

"The one with dark hair and the blue stiletto boots that she can't bloody well walk in."

Ah, yes. She'd noted the woman as well. She seemed a bit out of place. "The reporter, right?"

"Yes." He let his hands delve into her corset, pulling on her breasts so he could play with her nipples. "The Dom is her boyfriend. He hasn't got a clue. If that bastard's ever wielded a flogger, I'll eat my own shorts."

"You don't wear shorts."

He chuckled a little. "That's because I want to be able to fuck you at any given moment, love." He sighed. "Fine. You seemed determined to take something fun and make it into a drudgery."

How had he ever gotten his double *0* status? "We do have a job to do. What's the Dom's name again?"

"Robert Tilman. Chelsea can't find a connection with anyone in The Collective or Nature's Core for him. As far as we can tell, they've been living together for over a year. They fight a lot if their e-mail and text conversations are any indication. They've only just joined a club in London. The Cave. It's a touristy piece of shite. I wouldn't even call it a starter club."

She stared at Robert for a moment and had to admit, Damon was right. He looked uncomfortable. Most of the couples around them seemed deeply at ease with their roles, while Robert and his sub kept switching positions and trying to find where they should be. The reporter, whose name was Candice Jones, kept tugging at her knickers, which were oddly conservative given that many of the subs were naked.

As she stood and watched with Damon, Candice reached up and tugged on her Dom's hand, pulling him down and frowning his way.

If she did that to Damon in a dungeon, he would put her over his knee before she could take another breath, but Robert just shook his head at whatever she was saying. She'd seen the expression on Robert's face a million times. It was the same slightly constipated look that her sister's husband had when he was trying to please her and couldn't figure out how.

It was not an expression she would expect to see on a Dom.

"They're pretending."

"Very good, love." His fingers twisted her nipples to that sweet spot just before pain, the exact amount of pressure it took to get her pussy nice and wet, and her blood flowing through her veins with a pulsing rhythm. She was rapidly becoming addicted to Damon's brand of dominance. It was a sweet combination of discipline and indulgence.

What would she do if he followed through with his threats to give her up at the end of their operation? She'd become suspicious that his constant desire had something to do with having her as many times as he could before he let her go.

Or died. Her Master wasn't a "glass is half full" sort of man.

"Why are they here if they aren't a real D/s couple?" She felt like she could safely ask the question since she'd been in an actual D/s relationship for a week. It hadn't been long, but it had been immersive. She really was Damon Knight's submissive. She'd surrendered utterly to him.

"That's a very good question. I think we should find out. Unless you would rather play. There's an empty spanking bench."

She knew exactly what he would do. He would spank her senseless, fuck her until she couldn't breathe, and carry her upstairs and tuck her in. Then he would put a guard on her door and come right back here and do the damn job himself. "Tempting, but I think we should figure out if they're our targets. We dock in Helsinki tomorrow. The switch could happen at any port."

He growled against her skin, giving her a good nip that let her know how frustrated he was. "All right then. I'm going to go talk to Tag. You stay here. Simon is at the stairs, Jake is at the lifts, and I'll be right over there." He kissed her cheek and stepped away, moving toward where the Taggarts stood watching a whipping scene play out.

She hugged the wall, though she didn't really have to. No one bothered her. Her collar protected her from unwanted attention. She reached up and touched the silver chain Damon had placed around her neck. He'd clasped it around her, not allowing her to touch it until he was satisfied with the way it laid. There was a small heart with a diamond in the center that touched the hollow of her neck. She wanted to keep that damn chain around her neck forever, but might only have these few days with him before he went back to being the cold, shut-down agent he'd been before.

Although she held his fate in her hands, and he didn't even know it. She could save him from himself by telling Nigel he wasn't fit for duty. Not physically or mentally. He was too emotional. That would be a bitter irony for him. The one time he got emotional, the object of his feelings betrayed him.

She couldn't do it. No matter what it cost her, she couldn't hurt him like that. He'd never recover.

She stared at the couple in front of her, keeping them in her sights, forcing herself to focus on the problem at hand. Candice was a pretty woman, probably in her mid-twenties. Robert looked to be roughly the same age.

They were watching a scene with a Domme and her male submissive. The Domme had her sub tied to a St. Andrew's Cross, his naked body on display. She was whipping him with a singletail and now she tugged at his balls, squeezing them until he squawked before she went back to flicking the whip in her hands.

Candice's eyes widened and then she turned away. Her boyfriend went green. Penny had to stifle a laugh. A few weeks before perhaps she would be the one turning green, but she stood there feeling not an ounce of concern for the sub. Yes, he cried out, but she could read him. He actually relaxed as his Domme handled him. He liked the pain. She understood him. The Domme tenderly kissed him between snaps of the whip, likely telling him how good he was, how proud she was of him. Despite his occasional grimaces, the sub practically glowed with pride.

It was so blatantly obvious that neither of her two targets understood. Robert stepped back away from the crowd. He had to put a hand on her shoulder to get her attention. She was shaking her head, her hand over her mouth.

The two stepped back to the wall, and Robert set down the leather bag he was carrying. Like most of the other Doms in the dungeon, he carried his own kit. Unlike other Doms, he hadn't checked it at the entrance until he needed it. He'd spent the whole night clutching it. He let it drop as he found a place against the wall. He slumped into the seat, but his sub frowned at him and he immediately surrendered the seat to her.

It was time to listen in.

She glanced over and Damon was deep in conversation with Ian Taggart. Charlotte stepped away from them at her husband's nod and began walking toward Penny. So she had a babysitter.

Although it was a bit like asking the fox to watch the hen house.

The minute Charlotte joined her, she glanced over at the targets. "What's up with that?"

"I think they're tourists."

Charlotte grinned. "I love hearing you spout lingo."

Penny sighed. "I'm not a tourist anymore. I passed tourist when Damon used that slappy thing on me."

Charlotte laughed. "I'm so sorry about that. Ian made the thing. I like to call it the Fucking Bastard, but not around him because then he uses it on me. It's a repurposed fire hose. He's obsessed with pervertables. I don't let him go to home improvement stores anymore. I sent him for a new light switch, and he came back with fifteen things to torture me with. So, the tourists aren't liking the dungeon much, huh? I've been watching them all day. They're really out of place. And what the hell is in that kit that he won't let it out of his sight? He had it with him at dinner. And the pool."

She and Charlotte looked at each other, understanding obviously dawning. "We need to get into that kit."

"Okay." Charlotte's eyes trailed over to the men, but they'd stepped away, conferring in a quiet section of the bar. "I really should go and talk to them."

Yes, it was what they should do, but unfortunately, their targets were about to be on the move. Candice stood up, a distressed look on her face as she pulled at her corset. She had another couple of words with her boyfriend and stalked off toward the bathroom. "If we wait too long, we're going to lose them. It would be easier to get the kit here. Everyone's watching scenes, not each other. And I don't know that those two will be back in the dungeon for the rest of the trip."

"Damn it. We're both going to be spanked, you know. Okay, we're going to have to run a distract and dash, and I think it has to be you. The distraction that is," Charlotte explained. "I think I scare him. I know Ian does. We tried to talk to them earlier by the pool and that dude practically ran away."

Penny's stomach dropped. She wasn't good at flirting. "You want me to talk to him?"

Charlotte nodded. "Yep. Just bat your eyes and ask him a couple of questions. Like you don't know anything. I'll get that kit and then go straight to our rooms. When I'm free and clear, you get the boys and meet me. Maybe it's nothing and then I'll find a way to get it back to him, but I'm suspicious."

Penny was, too. She glanced back to where Damon was talking to Ian. Neither man was looking her way. If she stepped away to talk to him, she and Charlotte would likely lose the chance.

And no matter what he said, this was her operation, too. "All right. Go and get in place. We might not have much time before she comes back."

Charlotte winked her way. "Not a problem. Just give him a sweet face. He's been flirting with anything with breasts all day when his girlfriend isn't looking."

Charlotte strode away, having not a bit of trouble with her five-inch heels. She was a bombshell of a woman, but Penelope had learned that bombshells didn't work for every man. Sometimes a round pixie with a nice big bum was called for, and that was when she went to work.

She sent another slightly nervous glance her Dom's way before she slipped her collar off. She needed to seem available. Hopefully Charlotte would work quickly and she could get it back on before Damon even noticed she'd stepped away. He might forgive her for working without him, but she doubted he would forgive taking off her collar.

Shoving the silver necklace into her bodice, she drew a deep breath before walking toward the target. Oddly, it wasn't as hard as she would have thought. She'd never seen herself as a femme fatale until Damon had shown her she could be sexy.

He stood in the back of the room, his kit in his hand. Every now and then he glanced toward the bathroom before watching the scene in front of him. He'd moved from the Domme and her sub to a Dom who was plugging his petite sub with what looked like an elephant penis.

Just as she was going to move past him, she forced a slight stumble, moving her body toward him. Sure enough, he dropped the kit and caught her.

"I'm so sorry." She kept her voice down, not wanting to draw attention away from the scene. From the corner of her eyes, she saw Simon moving toward her, but he stopped, likely noticing Charlotte in the vicinity.

"It's all right." Robert gave her an open smile and helped her back to her feet, his eyes going straight for her breasts. "I don't know how you ladies walk in those heels without killing yourselves anyway."

She flushed a little, showing him her bare feet. "I'm just clumsy."

"Oh, don't talk bad about yourself now, love. I've heard that can get you in trouble in a place like this. What's a pretty girl like you doing in a dungeon?"

She bit back a groan. "Oh, I'm just here with some friends." Charlotte was being cautious, waiting back while one of the dungeon monitors walked by. *Damn it.* Naturally they showed up when she needed a clear path. She glanced back and Simon moved away from his post.

"Jerry?" Simon called out.

The DM turned and walked back by, rushing to get to Simon, who started pulling him out of the way as he spoke.

One problem down.

"Those blokes are kind of scary." Robert gestured to where Simon had the DM by the stairs, likely explaining some imaginary story. She'd always wondered about Simon out in the field. He seemed so urbane, but he had incredible instincts.

"They are. It makes me wish I'd come with my boyfriend." She needed him to think she was free to flirt. He seemed touchy.

"I thought you had to have a partner to get on the boat."

"That's only for men. Women can come in singles." It was sort of true. From what she'd learned, there were some unattached Doms, but they were teaching classes and running the dungeons. It was time to really get his attention away from the kit at his feet. Charlotte was moving in. "You know, in case a couple wants to be adventurous."

Robert's eyes widened. "Adventurous? Bloody hell. Are you talking about a threesome?"

Unfortunately, he practically yelled the question. Several heads turned.

"Sorry." He went back to whispering.

But Charlotte had been forced to back off. *Bugger.* She quelled her frustration, forcing what she hoped was a seductive smile on her face. "Yes. Sometimes we singletons get lucky and find a couple to play with. I saw your sub. She's very pretty."

His mouth curled up in the first real smile she'd seen out of him. "That's brilliant. Actually, Candy and me like to play like that. It's probably why we thought we'd like this kind of thing. She read that Grey book one too many times, if you ask me. I don't think they crushed some bloke's balls in that book though."

Charlotte very carefully reached down and had the kit in her hands as she moved back toward where Simon was still talking to the DM. He held the door open for her as she slipped away.

Brilliant. Now to get back to Damon and then up to their cabins. She smiled a little. "I haven't read it, but it sounds interesting. Well, maybe I'll see you around."

He reached out and caught her. "Hey, don't go. Let's go up to my room. We can have a good time."

"Or you can take your hands off my property this bloody minute before I fucking cut them off," an arctic voice said from behind her.

She closed her eyes. How to handle this? Damon wasn't exactly being professional, but she couldn't explain why she'd disobeyed him here in the open.

"Hey, mate. She's single. She told me herself." But Robert seemed to have some sense of self-preservation since he'd taken his hands off her.

"Do you not have a bloody brain in your thick head? Can you not see the collar around her throat? In this world, that means she's taken and I can slit your throat for touching her."

Penny flinched and kind of prayed she wouldn't have to turn around because he was going to be angry with her whether or not he was happy with the outcome of her endeavor.

Robert backed up. "She's not wearing a collar."

She felt Damon's hand grip her elbow as he whirled her around. He had to know she was working. She was sure he would be upset, but she hadn't counted on the utter rage she saw stamped on his face.

"Hey, Damon. Do you need me to get a bench ready?" Ian

Taggart stood behind him, his face in a forbidding frown.

"I'll take the sawhorse. And get my kit. I have to deal with my sub. I fear if I take a hand off her, she'll disappear again. Where the fuck is the collar I put around your neck?"

For the first time, she was actually a bit afraid of him. And oddly aroused. He'd done his job far too well. He'd trained her to respond to him, and even when he looked like he might truly take a pound out of her flesh, she was already warm and wet. "It's in my corset."

The time for prevarication was over. Especially when she realized everyone was looking their way. Everyone in the dungeon. All of the scenes had stopped.

The dungeon monitor, who had been talking to Simon, elbowed his way through the crowd. "Is there a problem?"

"My submissive decided to see if she could find a more pleasant Dom," Damon said, his jaw tight.

Penny shook her head. "No, I didn't."

Robert held his hands up. "She offered a three way with me and me girlfriend. She didn't say anything about being attached."

The DM glared at her. "Are you trying to get away from him?"

"No."

"Do you have a safe word?"

"Of course she does," Damon bit back.

The DM looked disgusted with all three of them. "Then I suggest you make her say it because you just ruined everyone else's scene with this one. I should ask you to leave the dungeon and not come back."

Horror settled in her gut. She couldn't get them kicked out of the dungeon. They needed to be here. "I'll do whatever I need to. Please don't kick us out."

"Are you so ill-trained that you speak to him and not me?" Even in the low light, she could see how red Damon had turned.

It was time to play her part to the hilt. She fell to her knees, head down, and knees wide apart. Tears were starting to fall because she'd screwed up so horribly. He couldn't think she was really trying to pick up that man. But then she thought about it and perhaps in the moment, he could. He didn't trust anyone. Not really. There was always a part of Damon that would be waiting for her to betray him, like everyone else had. He'd learned the lesson young, taking it into his soul like an education on how the world worked.

How could she prove she loved him when he didn't believe in love at all?

"Don't think that will save you." He turned to the DM. "I would rather she didn't spend the rest of this ridiculously expensive holiday in our cabin. Allow me to make up for the scene. I think this crowd would love to see her cry a bit."

There was a general consensus that her ass should be something the Americans called grass.

It didn't sound pleasant, but she'd nearly wrecked their cover and she had to make it right.

The DM stood over her. "Eyes up, sub." She looked up and there was some small amount of sympathy in his eyes. "Tell me your safe word."

"Penguin." She couldn't stop the tears from falling.

"Use it if you have to." The DM nodded Damon's way. "Let me know if you need anything."

"Get up," Damon growled.

She turned her face up to him. "Damon…"

He hauled her up and immediately laid five hard smacks on her arse, lighting her up with pain. "You don't seem to learn."

"Master." She could barely talk because he'd meant business with those smacks. Her hands were shaking and she gave serious thought to spitting out her safe word and ending everything here and now. He was barely leashed.

But that would get them kicked out. She had to trust him. She had to trust that he knew what he was doing.

"Hey. Where's my bag? Oh, fuck me." Robert started to panic, looking about for the kit Charlotte was likely rifling through at this point.

Damon started to haul her toward a raised platform.

"Please, can we talk?"

"Not a word from you. I suppose this proves you meant what you said to me. You're going to happily hop away and find some other bloody man to take my place."

"Damon, that's not fair."

He stopped and forced her to turn. "When are you going to learn that nothing in this life is fair? Nothing at all. You dance through life treating it like it is a tea party."

She tried to pull away from him. "How can you say that? I know very well life isn't fair. I spent years learning that."

She'd watched her mum try to please her absent father and then when she'd finally started to find a life without him, her disease had taken over, making her final years a living hell.

"Yes, and you're going to learn again, aren't you? Maybe this time the lesson will stick." He hauled her along until she stumbled a bit. He turned and cursed. For a moment she thought he would just drag her across the floor, but he leaned over and lifted her up, cradling her to his chest though his face was a cold mask.

He strode to the sawhorse, a long apparatus she'd seen used at The Garden. Taggart had kindly adjusted it, apparently knowing exactly how high to place it.

Damon set her on her feet, her heart pounding in her chest. He pulled a knife out of his boot and neatly sliced her corset off. He really was hell on her wardrobe. "Give it to me."

She was holding it to her chest because everyone was looking at her. The entire dungeon seemed to have moved to this one place, silently staring up at her in utter disapproval.

Shame washed over her.

"I said give it to me." Damon tapped his foot impatiently.

She couldn't have it out with him here. Couldn't. They had a job to do and it seemed she was the only one thinking straight. Tears pierced through her as she passed him the ruined corset. Her collar fell to the floor with an audible thud.

She'd been naked at The Garden, but it hadn't felt like this. She started to reach for her collar, but Damon was faster.

"I'll decide if you get this back." Damon tossed the corset aside, moving close to sink his hand into her hair. With a bite of pain, he tugged her head back so she had to look in his eyes. "Even when I'm brutally angry with you, I want you. Don't stand there and think you're anything less than gorgeous. Fuck, Penelope. I'm blindingly mad and I still can't leave you like this. I can't let you think you're less than perfect."

And just like that she was comfortable again. "Please, can we talk?"

He shook his head. "Not until we're done. And then everything is going to be different. Ian? Tie her up for me. I need a moment to calm down."

He stepped away, leaving her with Taggart, who softened slightly the minute his back was turned from the crowd. "Where did my wife go and what did she steal? I'm not crazy in love with you the way Damon is so I can figure out that you two decided to do some work without us. She's getting her ass spanked, too. If you don't want him to ruin the thong, you should probably hand it over."

Somehow after what Damon had said, it was fairly easy to step out of her last bit of clothing. It hadn't really covered her anyway. "He's not in love with me. And Charlotte took the target's kit."

Ian grinned slightly, though it merely made him look like a happy predator. "The one he's had with him all day, even at the pool?"

Penny nodded. "Yes. The reporter went to the loo so we thought it might be our only time."

"I need you to hug the sawhorse. Find a comfy spot." Taggart held up a nice length of rope. "He has to go through with this, you know. He lost it and now he has to play the badass Dom. He has no idea how to handle himself. Give him some slack, okay?"

She nodded because it was obvious Damon was in over his head. She settled herself over the sawhorse. The long apparatus was padded, the plastic cover touching her breasts.

Taggart knelt down, looping the rope around her wrists with a practiced hand. The knot was tight, but not so much it would cut off her circulation. "He might say some things he doesn't mean because that man is terrified of what could happen to you. He's used to losing people, and he can't stand the thought of losing you. And I swear I'm going to beat the next dude who forces me to play Cupid. I'm not good at it."

But he was good with a rope. And apparently a spreader. He grabbed a spreader bar and she found her legs spread wide, her ass in the air.

Oh, god, this was going to hurt.

Taggart swiftly locked her ankles into the spreader bar. She was caught and there was no way out except to say her safe word and possibly get both herself and Damon locked out of the place they needed to be. She had to endure whatever Damon was about to give her.

She had to hope it was worth it, that Charlotte had found something that could help them.

Damon stepped up, putting a hand on her. His voice was steady now. "Thank you, Master Ian."

"You're welcome. You all right to do this?" Taggart asked.

Damon kept his tone low. "I'm fine. You know I have to do this or we'll lose access to the dungeon. I'm perfectly in control."

"Try not to make it so she can't walk," Taggart said. "We have a tour of Helsinki tomorrow."

"I promise nothing."

She could hear the frown in Damon's words. She watched as Taggart's boots moved out of view, and she couldn't see anything but the floor in front of her.

"I apologize for the actions of my submissive. Her disobedient, reckless behavior reflects on me and my weakness."

She hated how desolate he sounded. "Master…"

She nearly screamed at the pain that flashed through her whole system as he brought something horrible across her ass. It hit her with a *thunk*, moving up her spine and speeding along her every nerve ending.

"Do not speak. Do I need to gag you?" Damon moved around the sawhorse. She could see his boots as he stood in front of her.

She shook her head because she wasn't speaking again.

"Excellent. Perhaps you'll learn to obey me." He knelt down, his voice lowering. "You think I'm doing this for show, but I'm not. I didn't tell you to stay where you were for my happiness. I did it for your safety. And you took your collar off. I don't care what you thought you were doing or why. The minute you took that collar off you put yourself at risk. The minute you stepped away from where I'd left you, you put yourself in the bloody line of fire, and I won't have it. You will understand that when I'm done with you, love." There was a paddle in his hand. A nasty looking round paddle.

He stood back up and almost immediately she felt the paddle on her backside.

"You don't need to count. I'll let you know when I'm done." He smacked her three times, each one harder than the last.

Tears dripped from her eyes. She'd cried more in the last week than in the years before, but it was oddly satisfying. She'd learned that emotion wasn't a flat thing. It could be multicolored, with more sides than a prism. The pain ached, flaring and causing her to bite her lip against the cries in her throat, but the tears were purifying. They were a release she'd needed for years. She'd been so numb before Damon. She'd smiled and been kind, but it was mostly because she'd been taught to do those things.

She felt it now. Her kindness flowed from an open soul and she never wanted to close it again, never wanted to go back to that place where pain was just pain, where tears were an annoyance, where she had no idea who she really was.

He'd opened her up in more ways than one. Because she was tied down, she had no choice but to endure because she wasn't going to say her safe word. The spreader bar kept her open, leaving her pussy on display for him.

He was watching. He wanted her like this, needed her naked, and there was nothing wrong with it. He loved her body. He'd proven it over and over again.

He needed this. She needed this.

Penny relaxed and felt the pain, but also a deep peace. A floaty feeling came over her as he continued to paddle her. He struck her arse, her thighs, smacked right between her legs where her pussy felt the reverberation of the slap.

Every now and then, he slapped right on her pussy, making her gasp and squirm.

She lost track of time. Heat suffused her, making her skin feel more like a tether than flesh, holding her to the place where she floated along, holding her to Damon. Her partner. Her Master.

Her Master was so scared. She had to give him what he needed. She had to give him this. He could be so indulgent with her. He would spend hours pleasing her, making sure she was happy and satisfied. In the time she'd been his sub, he didn't let her carry her own anything, insisting on bringing her coffee in the morning, on making sure she had the best of everything. It wasn't hard to give him her submission in this. Their needs dovetailed beautifully.

The smacks finally stopped. She had no idea how many he'd given her as she started to come out of the pleasant place she found herself in. Her arse was on fire, but she welcomed it. It meant she'd endured. She would enjoy the ache in her cheeks even when they walked the streets of Helsinki.

He moved in front of her, his boots coming into view. When she held her head up, she could see the spanking had done something for him, too. While her pussy was aching and needy, his cock was straining against the laces of his leathers. Not for long though, as he quickly undid his pants and his cock sprang free. "This is for me. Open."

She immediately licked at the head of his cock, tasting salt and Damon.

His hands gripped her hair, tightly but not enough to hurt. He always seemed to know exactly how to handle her. He squeezed and her scalp lit up. "Relax. I'm going to fuck your throat. You take what I give you, love. Show me you can obey when you want to."

She gave over and suddenly found her mouth full of him. He invaded, pressing his dick in past her lips and teeth and over her willing tongue. He thrust in ruthlessly, and she had to remember to breathe.

He pressed in until she'd taken the whole of him. His grip never wavered, keeping her exactly where he wanted her. She was tied down and held for his pleasure. And it did something for her. She was slick and wet.

When he'd shoved his cock in as far as it would go, he held himself for a moment. "Fuck. You feel so damn good. You almost make me forget."

He dragged his dick out and then forced himself back in. Over and over he fucked her mouth, his thrusts getting hurried and losing the precision she'd come to expect from him. He seemed to let himself go until finally she felt him swell against her tongue and he came. She heard him groan and curse just before he coated her tongue with his release.

She swallowed furiously, not wanting to lose a drop.

He panted above her, his hand softening on her hair. He finally pulled his cock out and straightened his leathers. "I'm going to release you now. We're going back to the cabin, but you should understand this, Penelope. If you disobey again, even in the slightest way, I'll have you right back here. I'll tie you down and let every Dom in the dungeon have a go at you. Do you understand?"

Her whole body went cold as his words washed over her. He would let every man in the room…

"Penelope?"

He would? It took a moment for it to really settle in. She'd taken everything he gave her because she loved him. Because she loved what he did for her. Because she loved who she was when she was with him.

And he would give her to any man in the dungeon who wanted to take a turn?

"Penelope?" His voice hardened. "I need you to tell me you understand the punishment waiting for you if you disobey me again."

Her safe word was right there on the tip of her tongue. She wanted to scream it at him, but she wasn't in physical danger. No. There wasn't a safe word in the world that could save her heart from breaking.

"Yes, Master." She forced the words out though they were bitter on her tongue. She blinked back tears because she wasn't going to let him see her cry. They'd felt like a healing balm only moments before. Now they would show far too much of her soul.

She'd counted on his possessiveness. She'd come to view it as his version of love. She'd been so foolish, thinking he just couldn't say the words. It had been there in the back of her mind that she could teach him.

She shivered. God, she was naked in front of a crowd and the man she loved had just promised to allow her to be gang-banged in front of them if she didn't follow his rules.

She shrank away from him the minute she could. When her hands and feet were free, she forced her stiff body to stand up, covering her breasts.

Damon frowned her way. "Are you all right? We should go in the back to one of the aftercare rooms. I was rough on you."

Numbness was starting to flow through her veins, a welcome thing. She was able to stand tall. No matter what happened between her and Damon, she still had her job. "I'm fine. I would rather retire to our cabin. I would like a shower if that pleases you."

Her words were like stones, falling from her mouth. Flat. Cold and hard.

"If you like." Someone had passed him a robe. He held it out, but she couldn't stand the thought of him wrapping it around her. He would hug her, like he always did, but now she knew it was a meaningless gesture.

She took the robe from his hand and quickly wrapped it around her body, grateful to not be on display a second longer. What had seemed loving a moment before now made her feel vulnerable.

Years of doubt rushed back in, blocking the progress she'd made. She stared at Damon. He really was beautiful, and she wasn't close to his league.

What had she been thinking?

He closed his kit, zipping it up. Her collar was in his hand. "I'd like to put it back on you."

She was safer with it on, but the idea repulsed her a bit. Would he take it off before he let another man have her? Or was it so meaningless to him that it wouldn't matter?

She nodded, turning and holding her hair up, forcing herself to stay still while he clasped it back on.

"Are you sure you're all right? I should look at your skin. I don't think I raised welts. I could be wrong." For the first time, he sounded deeply unsure of himself.

"No. I'm fine. We should get back to our friends." The mission was important. Her feelings, his feelings or lack thereof, didn't matter. She'd been an idiot. She'd spent more time thinking about how to continue her relationship with Damon than focusing on the reason she was here. That time was done. She would obey Damon and do her job and then walk away at the end.

He'd wanted to teach her how dangerous it was to be close to him. She'd finally learned the lesson. She couldn't fix him. She couldn't heal him.

"All right." He picked up his kit and stepped off the stage, turning to hold his hand out to help her down.

Stubbornness bought her nothing. She placed her hand in his, but she'd never been further away.

Chapter Fifteen

Damon held the lift door open for Penelope when it arrived at their floor. She stepped out with a calm detachment that deeply worried him.

He'd been too rough on her. He should have stepped away and given himself a few hours to calm down. The sight of that bastard touching her had sent him into a rage.

He'd known immediately that she had disobeyed because of some mission related event, but there had been a deep disconnect between his brain and his mouth. His mouth had let his anger talk. He'd heard himself spouting shit about her finding another Dom, and he couldn't stop himself.

"Where did Charlotte go?" His words were even and measured now. Now that it seemed to be far too late.

"She was going up to her cabin. She was going to meet us there." She'd explained what had happened on the way up the lift, her voice flat and monotone as she told the story of how they came to have Mr. Tilman's kit. "Mr. Taggart should be there by now."

Whenever she started talking like a Jane Austen heroine, he knew he was in trouble.

"Penelope, do you understand why I had to punish you?" He reached out and grabbed her elbow or she would very likely have kept right on walking.

She didn't meet his eyes. "Yes, of course. We would have been disinvited from the dungeon if you had not."

"But you're angry with me. Damn it all. Did I hit you too hard?"

Her eyes were as blank as any doll's. "It's fine, Damon. I think I just realized what you've wanted me to all along. This isn't the life for me. I'll obey you from now on. I won't attempt to use my own brain. I'll remember at all times that you're in charge."

He should be jumping with joy because apparently he'd finally gotten through to her. All it had taken was a minor paddling and she wilted.

And then he'd been stupid enough to threaten to let all the other Doms spank her, too. Lesson number one in the Dom book was to never threaten something he wouldn't go through with. He couldn't stand it when another man touched her. He certainly wasn't going to allow one to spank her, but he'd been so angry with her the threat had just popped out.

Anything could have happened. She'd taken off her collar. She'd lost herself in the crowd. He had no idea what Robert Tilman was capable of. If he'd caught her trying to steal his kit, he could have quietly carried her off and slit her throat and Damon would have gone utterly insane. He'd had a vision of her, broken, dead, cold. His Penelope was always so soft and warm, and he'd seen her rigid and trapped in the horror of death.

He wouldn't survive it. He'd known in that moment that he couldn't live through her death, and he'd do anything to prevent it. Hence his idiotic words.

He couldn't work with her. He couldn't think about anything but her when she was around. Since that first moment he'd gotten a taste of her, he'd lost his bloody mind to anything except her.

"I want to look at your bum. I want to make sure I didn't hurt you." He thought it had gone well after he'd calmed a bit. Yes, he'd spanked her hard, but he'd tested her. He'd felt her arousal, her relaxation. He'd thought she slipped into subspace. Even through his irritation with her, he'd felt a deep satisfaction because of the trust she placed in him.

And then she shut him out.

"My bum is fine, Damon." Her lips moved, but there was no

expression on her face. That killed him. She was always so vibrant, smiling or with a mischievous light in her eyes that only he seemed to be able to see. "Could we please get some work done? I would like to know if I endured that for something."

"Then I did hurt you." Something didn't add up.

Her face flushed, her blue eyes narrowing as she snarled his way. "Yes, Damon. Hitting someone with a paddle hurts. My arse hurts. It will likely hurt for several days. Are you happy now?"

He'd never seen her angry before. He was shocked to find that what he really wanted to do was get on his bloody knees and beg her forgiveness.

But if she hadn't been able to take that scene, he'd been wrong about her. Or she was attempting to manipulate him. She'd done that before. He let himself go cold. If she didn't want aftercare, who was he to complain? She'd disobeyed the rules. She'd put herself and their operation in danger. It wasn't his place to apologize. "Not at all. I didn't enjoy that scene any more than you did."

Except he'd rather thought they had both been enjoying it. After he'd slapped her ass silly and still been able to smell the arousal coating her pussy, he'd decided to take it a step further and fuck her mouth. She'd been enthusiastic. She'd sucked him down like a starving woman.

Was she mad he hadn't given her an orgasm? Did she think sulking would fix the problem? He hadn't expected that from her.

"Well, the good news is you won't have to suffer through it again."

He tightened his hand on her. "I meant what I said."

Except the part about allowing other Doms to get a smack in. It was a common enough punishment at both Sanctum and The Garden. Some subs enjoyed it. No hands were allowed because most Doms Damon knew didn't share even the touch of their sub's skin, but paddles and canes and floggers were all on board. Hell, for some subs' birthdays, he'd arranged spanking parties, but he couldn't allow it with Penelope. He had hard limits, too, and letting someone else touch her was his. But he couldn't tell her that. He needed to stay in charge.

"I believe you." There was such accusation in her eyes that he nearly folded and just apologized.

He was saved from that fate by the door opening down the hall and Tag stepping out, a grim look on his face. "I was just coming to find you. Pen, you all right?"

She nodded. The smile she plastered on her face didn't come anywhere close to her eyes. "Of course. What did you find?"

Tag gestured them inside the cabin he shared with his wife. It was the cabin next to theirs. The balcony between them had been opened to form a long outdoor space.

"I've got Jesse on his way here," Tag explained. "Chelsea, too. Simon and Jake are herding our targets. Jake is going to have a talk with Rob, and we'll get the reporter. Though from what I hear, I should have sent Pen down because she's totally into threesomes."

Jealousy flashed through his system. Tag held the door open, and Penelope entered.

"Dude, chill." Tag held a hand out, his voice going low. He let the door close. "You have got to check the caveman. She wasn't trying to fuck the guy."

"I know. She wouldn't do that." Damon shook his head. Why did everyone seem to think he was accusing Penelope of cheating? "I might kill him though."

"Okay, that's slightly healthier, but seriously, she's pissed. What the fuck did you do?"

Yes, he'd certainly figured that out. "I spanked her with a paddle. Her arse is red, but I didn't break the skin. I doubt she'll even bruise. I fucked her mouth. I told her if she ever did it again, I would let every Dom in the room paddle her and see how she likes it."

A chuckle came out of Tag's mouth. "That's going to go so well. You'll go insane when the first one touches her."

Damon felt himself flush. He never used to get embarrassed. "I know. It was stupid. Now she says she understands this isn't the lifestyle for her."

"It isn't for everyone," Tag said with a sigh. "Give her some time. Some subs freak out after their first intense scene. The good news is Baz is likely to try to kill us in Helsinki tomorrow, so she'll

241

probably forget you spanked her."

His stomach turned. If she wouldn't even look at him, how was he going to protect her? "Don't remind me."

"And if Baz doesn't kill us, the unholy amount of smoked fish they'll offer us might. Man, I know why Northern Europeans are so skinny." Tag started to open the door again. "Pull it together. You're going to endanger every single one of us if you can't control yourself. You could have handled that situation in a way that her punishment would have been private."

"Really? So if Charlotte had done the same thing and you found her with another man, you would have been perfectly calm?"

"Not at all. I would have thrown down with the fucker, target or not. But then I admit freely that I love my wife. Last I checked, Penny was just your unwanted partner and part-time fuck buddy. So check yourself, man."

Sometimes he wanted to plant his fist in Tag's face.

He couldn't love Penelope. He couldn't. The people he loved died. He followed Tag into the suite and couldn't help but take in how perfectly the soft, fluffy robe suited Penelope. Soft and sweet as candy.

Penelope's lips finally curved into an actual smile. "We were right."

Charlotte was standing beside the bed that dominated the room. "Oh, yes. Look. I think that's our guy."

He glanced down at the table where the contents of the kit had been placed. There was a small photo of a man. He was roughly thirty with thick glasses, dark hair, and a ready smile. Damon picked it up and turned it over. There was writing on the back. *Walter Bennett.*

Their guy. So the reporter was the contact. Or they had more trouble than he'd thought. "What else did you find?"

Charlotte sat down on the sofa, wincing slightly. "Sorry. Ian took a moment before he let me go through the kit. My ass is a little tender."

Penelope sat down beside her, but there was nothing on her face. She'd shut down the minute Charlotte spoke. She was right back to blank professional. "There was a thumb drive under his flogger."

Ian picked it up. The flogger was black and looked to be cheap leather. It wasn't custom made. He'd likely bought it at a toy store. "I wouldn't use this on anyone."

Penelope stared at the flogger and when Ian set it down, she picked it up, touching the falls. "It isn't soft. Why are they so stiff?"

"Because he's never used it before. It's strictly ornamental." Damon jumped on the chance to be her mentor again. "The leather should be treated so it has some flexibility. The one I use on you is actually deerskin. It's more for the thud than a sting. I'm not sure this would give you either."

She laid it back down and turned her attention back to Taggart. "Have you tried to open the drive?"

"Password protected," Charlotte said. "That's why we need Chelsea. We're going to have her in your cabin while we talk to our reporter."

There was a knock on the door and Chelsea entered. She was dressed in her security uniform. "What's up? This is my sleep time so it better be good. I get to share a cabin with eight other chicks. I want to kill myself. Oh, and nice move, sis. It was quite the distraction."

Charlotte grinned. "You know me. I like to give a good show."

Taggart chuckled as he passed Chelsea the thumb drive. "There are cameras everywhere on this ship. When Damon rifled through the target's cabin, he wasn't on camera, but they would have caught him breaking into the room. So we gave them something better to watch."

"Security is a bunch of peeping tom perverts," Chelsea complained. "I swear, they must test these guys for voyeurism before they hire them. There aren't cameras in the cabins, but they're all over the balconies. When I needed to turn their attention away from Damon, big sis and Satan here just went at it on the balcony. No one noticed when Damon slipped into a room that wasn't his own."

"You better destroy that tape," Ian said. "Well, after you make a copy and give it to me."

Chelsea rolled her eyes, took the drive, and slipped out after Damon handed her the keycard to their cabin.

He had zero doubt she would break the code in no time at all. If only he could make her break Penelope's code so she would make sense to him.

He stared her way, but she didn't spare him a glance.

This was why he didn't have girlfriends. He didn't understand women at all. She'd been comfortable in D/s. She'd opened up more in the last week than he'd seen her in the years he'd known her. When they had been on that stage, she'd been hot and ready for anything. Now she thought she could make him feel guilty?

He just wished he knew what he was supposed to feel guilty about because he was feeling bloody bad about everything now. Perhaps she'd been acting, playing along so he wouldn't leave her behind.

That was stupid.

"Hello? Knight? You with us?" Taggart sat down beside his wife.

"Of course." He was losing it. Focus on the job. If Penelope no longer wanted him, he would just have to deal with it. Perhaps she was telling him the truth. She'd seen the real him and she no longer fooled herself that she could care for him.

It was better. Really it was.

He forced his brain away from her.

The sound of a keycard engaging made him turn just in time to see Jesse Murdoch begin to head inside.

"And you're sure it's here?" a female voice asked.

"I saw her run away with it. She stole the bag and I followed her here," Jesse replied. "This is my floor so I have the key. That's when I called security and then talked to you."

"I just want the bag and then I need to get back to my boyfriend. I don't get why security needed to talk to him. I don't want to involve security. My not-so-brilliant boyfriend will keep it with him from now on," Candice complained as she started into the short hallway.

She stopped when she saw the group around the table.

Damon stood up.

"What's this?" She tried to turn but Simon was right behind her.

"Fuck."

Simon caught her, putting a hand over her mouth. "Don't scream. I don't want to have to gag you, but you should know that we have everything we need to ensure this talk is very uncomfortable for you."

She'd been wearing an ill-fitting corset in the dungeon. She'd changed somewhere along the way and now looked extremely young and somewhat fragile in jeans and a T-shirt covered by a cardie. Her eyes were wide with terror. He had to figure out who she was really working for.

"My name is Damon Knight. I'm with SIS. Can you nod if you know what that is?"

She nodded. She was a reporter. She should understand how her country's intelligence worked, but he was often surprised at some people's stupidity.

"If my colleague removes his hand, will you scream?"

Her head shook. Either she was an excellent actress or she was scared. Either way, he thought there was a chance she would keep her head about her.

"If you do scream, he's going to tie you up and keep you that way until we sort this out. Simon, let her go." There was no reason to be uncivilized if he didn't have to.

Her hands were shaking as Simon took a step back. "You're MI6? Really? You're a real bloody double *0*?"

"Yes, though I'm afraid you'll have to take my word on it since we don't carry badges."

"We don't need no stinking badges," Taggart said with a smile.

"How do I know if I should talk to you then?" She might have gone to a posh university, but her accent gave her away. She'd been raised in the country.

And she was cautious. He couldn't blame her. "Because I'll very likely torture you if you don't." He could be uncivilized when it was called for.

Tears started rolling down her cheeks. Penelope sighed and stood up. "Come here. He's not going to torture you. He just likes to have everyone afraid of him. Come sit down and we can get this sorted out. It's obvious you're not in league with terrorists."

"It's not obvious to me." Did Penelope think she would wear a sign?

Candice Jones practically tackled Penelope in her haste to get away from him. He was just charming all the ladies this evening. He had to admit, conducting an interview in his leathers was a new experience.

"Is he really with the government?" Candice turned to Penelope as though she'd figured out she was the only person in the room who hadn't recently killed someone.

"Yes. I am as well. Can you tell me how you know Walter Bennett?"

Candice's jaw practically locked.

Penelope reached out and picked up the shot of Bennett. "Your boyfriend is carrying around a picture of him. We've got the thumb drive as well. We'll know everything very soon. How about I tell you what I know?"

"That isn't necessary," Damon explained.

Penelope sighed. "Damon, something's obviously wrong. If she's trying to blow up the London underground, I would be very surprised."

Candice's eyes went round. "What are you talking about? I'm a reporter. I don't want to blow up anything except a story. Walter wouldn't do that. He's not like that. At least he doesn't seem to be the type."

Clever girl. What might have taken him an hour to pry out of her, Penelope had gotten her to give up inside a minute. "According to what we know, Walter Bennett works for a pharmaceutical company."

"I'm not going to get a big story out of this, am I?" Candice asked, frowning.

"No, you're very likely going to spend some time in prison if you don't start talking," Damon explained.

She sniffled and clasped her hands together on her lap. "About a year ago, I did an exposé on a group called Nature's Core. I became friendly with a couple of them. Two weeks ago, the leader of the

Core called me. He said he had a massive story for me, but he wouldn't tell me what it was about."

"Not even a hint?"

She bit her bottom lip, sighing. "No. He just said that I had to help him smuggle a man into England and that it would be dangerous. People would try to kill him."

"That man was Walter Bennett?" He settled in across from her, fairly certain she wasn't going to break out any martial arts moves on anyone.

"Yes. I've talked to him over the computer a couple of times. He seems harmless enough. He says he's got something really important, but he won't tell me what it is until we meet. I was supposed to find a way to meet with Walter and to get him on this boat without having to use his passport. He's paranoid. He thinks someone from his old company is trying to kill him."

Yes, Baz would very likely kill the bloke. "What company did he work for?"

He already knew the answer to that, but he wanted to see what Candice knew or if she would lie.

"Agro Pharma is what I was told. I looked him up, of course. I didn't just believe him. I did my research. He's a virologist who's been working in DNA coding on some of the nastiest strains in the world. He worked at CDC in Atlanta for a couple of years after he graduated from Johns Hopkins."

"But then the lure of big money was too much, huh?" Taggart asked.

Candice nodded. "That's how it seemed to me. He's been working in their Geneva campus for the last two years. It's one of the only private BSL-4 labs in Europe. Nature's Core has been watching Agro. According to my source, they think Agro is working on some nasty bioweapons."

He looked over at Taggart, who nodded. It was something of the same story they were getting from their handlers and nothing that went against what Baz said.

"Why you?" He had an inkling, but he wanted her thoughts.

Her shoulders moved up and down. "I guess I was the only

reporter they trust."

Penelope leaned forward. "If he has pure intentions, why wouldn't he go to the government?"

She pushed a hand through her hair as she spoke. "I don't know. I just wanted a big story, all right? My career hasn't exactly been smashing. My editor wants to move me to the society pages. He thinks I'm not smart enough to work anything but debutante parties. He thought my piece on Nature's Core was a fluff piece, but I'm going to show him. It was my idea to use the boat. I've gone on a couple of cruises and the security isn't the best."

"And if you're being used by a terrorist to get into England?" Damon was well aware he wasn't using his charming voice. "How is that going to affect your career? When you abet a terrorist, I think you might get relegated to something less pleasant than society weddings."

"He's not a terrorist," she shot back.

"How do you know that?"

She pointed to the picture. "Look at him. He's a geek. Geeks aren't terrorists."

"You've obviously never met my sister-in-law," Taggart said.

His wife sent Tag a nasty look, but it was so much more than Penelope sent his way.

There was a knock and Simon let Chelsea in. She moved past him, obviously trying not to touch the big guy. "It's all porn and pictures of naked chicks."

Candice gasped. "Hey, that's mine. You're not supposed to look at that."

Chelsea tossed it to Damon. "This is not the droid we were looking for, boss. I'm going back to bed before the spa staff gets in. They smell better than the maids, but god they love to talk in like fifteen different languages. This assignment sucks."

Jesse grinned her way. "Hey, I saw one of the head waiters hitting on you. Nice."

Simon frowned. "Staff isn't supposed to mingle in that fashion."

Chelsea gave him back a nasty look. "Oh, we're only supposed to sleep with guests, huh?"

She turned and stormed out.

Damon was getting sick of the soap opera, but Tag just grinned as though the world was his entertainment.

"Sorry." Jesse held his hands up. "I was just teasing her. It wasn't like she took him up on it. She doesn't look at anyone except Simon, and even then it's only when she thinks he's not looking."

"Could we deal with the problem at hand?" Simon asked. "If she doesn't know anything, then we need Walter Bennett and we need him damn soon."

"Look, I'm obviously in over my head. This was a stupid plan. I should have known it was too good to be true." Candice wiped away tears.

The last thing he needed was another crying female. "When are you meeting with Bennett?"

She sniffled a little. "Tomorrow. I'm meeting him at someplace called the Rock Church. It's in Helsinki. I'm supposed to be there at three. It gives us just enough time to get Walter on the boat. He looks a bit like Rob. Rob is going to spend a couple of days with some mates from university and then fly back in time to pick us up from Dover."

Bennett bore a nominal resemblance to Tilman. They were roughly the same height, same coloring. If Bennett took off his glasses, he would likely be able to use the card the cruise company had assigned to Tilman. He wouldn't need a passport if he didn't go into the ports that required them and he wouldn't need to show one to get back into England. He would be flying utterly under the radar.

"I'm going to need you to make that meeting. I'll let you talk to my boss tonight so you feel more comfortable with me, but I need you to cooperate until I can take Bennett into custody and figure this mess out. Is that understood?"

She nodded, tears still in her eyes.

"Penelope? Would you take her to our cabin and use the sat phone to contact Nigel? He's going to want to talk to her." He could give Penelope something to do, take her mind off whatever was bothering her, make her feel like one of the team.

She stood up and gave Candice a smile. "Yes, I can certainly do that. And while we're at it, I'll order us some tea. Charlotte, should we leave the men to their plotting?"

So she saw right through his plans. He found it rather frustrating. "Someone needs to talk to Nigel."

"Of course." She walked by him, clutching her keycard. Candice and Charlotte followed.

"Dude, what did you do? Because Penny looked pissed." Jesse seemed to be very good at stating the obvious.

"He punished her for doing her job," Simon said, pulling his jacket off. "I was watching over them. Jake and I were both there."

Taggart shook his head. "Don't you get in the middle of this because you're pissed about Chelsea. She was given very specific instructions. No matter what she and Charlie say, this was not going to be the only time for us to get that kit."

"They were fine," Simon bit back.

"They're not your subs, Weston." Damon was sick of people questioning his rights. It was his right to keep Penelope safe. She bloody well belonged to him. She was wearing his collar. Well, when she thought to keep it on she was wearing it. "Penelope might be SIS, but she's not a trained field agent. She's only here because I need cover and Baz is a bastard who never learned how to play well with others. So I will make the decisions concerning her."

"Until the operation is over. It looks like you scared her away from the lifestyle. How hard did you hit her?" Weston asked.

Taggart stood up, apparently ready to get between them. "Stand down, Simon. I get it. You're frustrated and pissy, and I can't let you take that out on him."

"But I want to so badly, boss."

"Step away. Go back to your job. Tell Jake to bring Tilman down here. We have some plans to make. And you stay away from Chelsea tonight."

"I think I'll stay away from Chelsea altogether. You're right, boss. I've been frustrated over nothing. I think it's time I moved on. And Knight, Penny's my friend. Don't think this is over. If you hurt her, I'll take you apart with my bare hands and I'll enjoy it. I'm not your employee anymore." He turned and walked away, letting the door slam.

Jesse groaned. "Damn it. I'll go after him. I don't want him doing something stupid." He held his hands up. "I know, boss. I'm usually the one doing stupid shit. I swear I'm going to roofie them both and get it over with."

He followed Weston out of the room.

Taggart shook his. "Yeah, he doesn't understand how a roofie works. I'm going to keep him away from the pharmaceuticals. So, how do you want to play this?"

"Well, we need to figure out how big this church is and where to place everyone. We know we can get Bennett on the boat, but perhaps the best thing to do is to take him into custody and get him on the first plane back to London."

Then his time with Penelope would be over. How long would it be before she moved out? An hour or so? Would he even get a chance to talk to her?

He suddenly knew he couldn't do it. He couldn't go back to England and ignore her. He needed her in ways he'd never thought possible. He needed her in his bed and his life. He needed to know she was waiting for him. He needed to know he had time with her.

"But you have to meet with Baz," Tag pointed out.

Baz. Baz who didn't really understand the meaning of needing someone. It was why they'd actually worked well together. Baz would prefer that he spend the rest of his likely short life alone because he hadn't been able to return his affection. He laughed because actually Baz had been a terrible partner. He'd constantly gone behind Damon's back because he was a secretive fucker who liked to one-up everyone around him. He'd kept things from his handlers, his fellow agents, everyone, so he could pop in at the end and save the day.

Fucker.

"I think I know when I'm supposed to meet Baz."

Taggart growled and threw his big body back on the couch. "Of course. Three o'clock anywhere but the Rock Church."

Suspicion began to play in his head. What if Baz was lying to them all? "He wants Bennett. He knows he has to keep Bennett away from me. What better way than to force me to meet him somewhere else while he scoops up the prize?"

"Do you think he made up the threat about our operatives?" Tag seemed to follow his line of thought.

"You know he was always awful with tech. How hard would it be to get that list?"

"From both agencies, damn near impossible unless he has someone on the inside. Adam could probably do it, but it would take him time. But, again, we know he has some people on the inside."

"People who could get him a list of undercover agents? If he was that well connected, why would he have to wait for Eli Nelson to die to take his place?"

"You really think the fucker's lying."

"I think Baz was always climbing the ladder, and he would do it any way he could. He wants to bring this guy in and he's alone. He knows he doesn't have a shot until he gets rid of me and the team. He found a way to do it."

Taggart shook his head. "How does he know about the meet up?"

"He's been on this case longer than we have. If Agro is a Collective company, I have no doubt they keep a close watch on their employees. If Bennett is going to sell some sort of viral agent, he's likely had to talk to someone about it. I would bet our reporter's phone is tagged."

Taggart was on the small walkie he'd given everyone on the team. "Jake?"

"Yeah, boss?" Jake Dean's voice came over loud and clear.

"Check his phone."

"Already done. He's got a tag and so does she. Tilman is cooperating. He's crying actually. I think I might have been too honest about what could happen to him. I don't know that he's going to be capable of helping us in an undercover capacity."

Fuck. At least his girlfriend seemed fairly calm. Damon leaned in so he could be heard. "Thank you, Dean. Tell him he needs to keep his mouth shut. SIS will want to debrief him when he gets back to London."

Taggart shut off the walkie. "All right, so Baz played the odds and figured out who to listen in on. It doesn't mean he doesn't have that list."

But sometimes an operative had to follow his instincts, and every single one he had was screaming at him that this was just another distraction. "I have to make a call. If he contacts me and tells me where to be at three p.m. tomorrow, I'm going to assume this has all been a distraction. It's typical Baz. I worked with him for years. I've run this play with him. He's got nothing."

"Let me send Jesse and Chelsea in as decoys. They're roughly the right height and size. We dress them up and if Baz shows, Jesse can kill him. He's a rabid puppy who hasn't been able to shoot anyone lately. It would likely help me out in the long run."

"All right. Penelope stays here. I go with you to the church."

"If you can convince her to stay, man, good for you."

"She's my sub. She'll do what I tell her to."

Taggart snorted a little as he laughed. "Yeah, you keep believing that, dude. I'm just going to give Charlie a sniper position. She gets mad when I try to treat her like a pretty toy. Even though she's a really pretty toy. The good news is, she's a gorgeous fuck toy with killer aim."

He rather envied Taggart his relationship with his wife. Charlotte was proven in the field. Penelope wasn't. He couldn't risk her.

He just worried that he was risking his relationship with her instead.

He took a deep breath and stepped out on the balcony, the cool air from the Baltic whipping against his skin.

It could all be over tomorrow. Penelope would be safe.

So why was he still so scared? It wasn't a feeling he liked.

He stepped through the door that led to the balcony of his and Penelope's room. The curtains were open slightly. He could see her sitting at the sofa, speaking into the satellite phone. Her face was soft, blonde hair curling around her jaw. So beautiful.

He couldn't lose her. He just couldn't.

Chapter Sixteen

Penny pulled her sweater around her. Despite the fact that it was summer, there was an overcast sky looming across Helsinki.

She sat next to Damon in the car that had been waiting for them when they got off the boat. Chelsea and Jesse had gotten on the bus she and Damon were scheduled to be on. Chelsea had seemed calm, but Jesse had been treated to what looked like a long lecture from Simon Weston likely on what would happen if Chelsea didn't come back in one piece.

Of course, she'd heard the same lecture from Damon, though she didn't credit it with any deep affection. He simply didn't want more guilt on his hands, most likely. Or he didn't want Baz to have the satisfaction of winning.

Taggart was driving with Candice in the front with him.

She'd tried to get in next to Charlotte, hoping Ian would take the other seat in the back, but Damon had tossed him the keys. He'd crowded in beside her, leaving her no choice but to move to the center and allow him to sit next to her.

She stared out the window on Charlotte's side, watching the shipyards go by. Massive cranes were moving parts into place for what looked like an enormous icebreaker.

Damon moved beside her, his hips touching hers. "Are you sure you want to do this? There's no reason for you to be here."

"I want her," Candice said with a frown in the rearview mirror. "I trust her. I'm not sure I trust you. Operatives like you aren't exactly known for giving a damn who gets taken out in the line of fire. I think you'll be a bit more careful if your girlfriend is around."

Penny had to stop the smile that threatened. She'd known the minute they found Candice that Damon would attempt to find a way to cut her out. He'd sent her off to make the call to Nigel like she was his glorified secretary. That had been a mistake on his part. She'd used the time to convince Candice that she was her best bet on getting out of this alive. It hadn't been hard. The reporter was already the tiniest bit paranoid.

"You talked to my boss," Damon said, sliding his arm over the back of her seat. The car wasn't really big enough for all of them, but neither Damon nor Ian thought it would be a good idea to split them up. So she was stuck with too-big Damon invading her space.

"I talked to someone who said he was your boss," Candice replied.

Damon sighed. "But you believe her. You understand how utterly insane that sounds. You believe that Penelope is an undercover agent but you question me."

"I think you're probably a really good liar," Candice said primly. "And you won't give me an exclusive."

Penny forced herself not to lean into him. He was so strong and warm against her. She'd woken up plastered against his body this morning despite the fact that she'd hugged the side of the bed before falling asleep. She'd woken up and just for a minute, she'd forgotten about what had happened the night before. She'd started to lift her face up for her morning kiss. Damon had sighed as though he'd been relieved, his hand stroked her hair back and then...

She'd rolled out of bed and gotten into the shower before she could make a complete fool of herself.

"Candice, I'm sure you'll be allowed some access since you're involved and cooperating. I'll make sure to give you any information I possibly can."

Damon leaned over, his mouth close to her ear. "Don't promise what you can't deliver."

It seemed a warning, or perhaps he was simply reinforcing his lesson. She'd promised herself she could fix him but he didn't want to be fixed, very likely didn't even see himself as broken in the first place. "How do you know Baz won't have men waiting in the church?"

The last thing she wanted to talk about with Damon was broken promises. He hadn't made her any so why did she feel so betrayed?

"We don't," Taggart said from the driver's seat.

Damon sighed, a frustrated sound. "Baz struggles to work with anyone. He prefers to work alone, but more than that, he really is paranoid. He didn't even trust me. Most of the time he went off on his own and tried to one-up me. If he had a team with him, he wouldn't have needed a distraction. He would have swooped in and taken the prize. The group he works with has more than enough resources, but I suspect Baz is attempting to make an impression. His group might not even realize he's got the target in his sights. Baz would be afraid they'll send someone else in and then he would get cut out. It happened to him more than once during his time with SIS."

"But don't worry." Penny felt it was her job to keep the reporter calm. No one else seemed to want to do it. Damon just pointed out how bad the situation was and Taggart growled at everyone. It was only through her efforts that the woman had remained calm and somewhat helpful. "You'll be perfectly safe. You were smart to choose a tourist location. I think even Mr. Champion would likely think twice about opening fire there. He needs to stay under the radar. We all do."

The car had come equipped with their handguns, thanks to Simon. She'd checked hers and watched as Damon had strapped weapons onto his body, her eyes greedy for any hint of skin.

After today, it would be over and she wouldn't have to fight her urges. Being close to him and not being able to touch him was making her crazy. She didn't trust herself to not give in. There was an ongoing argument in her head about simply accepting who he was and never disobeying him. She could do it.

She would come to hate herself and him.

"Do you think he's already there? Waiting for Mr. Bennett?" Penny asked.

Damon nodded. "I think he's certainly got eyes on the place. We have to be very careful. We need to stay with a tourist group. I'm going to stay close to Candice. I have the cap Robert is supposed to wear."

"But Baz knows you."

"And I know how to keep my head down. It will be fine."

Penny wasn't so sure, but he didn't leave her with a choice.

Ian turned down the street. Helsinki was laid out in front of her, clean and neat. As he stopped at a light, bikers lined up in the lane beside them. A green and yellow train barreled by.

They drove in silence, Penny lost in her own world. She knew she should be thinking about the upcoming operation, but she couldn't seem to forget the fact that Damon would be out of her life soon and she wasn't sure how to handle it. How she could watch him every day?

It was time to think about changing her career.

Long before she was ready, Ian pulled into a small underground parking garage. Everything had been arranged, likely by Nigel or someone from Taggart's organization. Simon was standing by a van with the cruise line's logo on it. She hadn't seen him leaving the boat, but knew it was his shift off and he and Jake were supposedly going sight-seeing while Jake was helping pick up supplies for the kitchens.

At least they had backup.

Simon stepped forward, his big body in a jacket that likely concealed the weapons he was carrying. "It's a clusterfuck of a situation. I don't like it at all. Is Jesse off all right?"

Damon nodded. The information from Baz had come through not an hour before. "He'll be fine. He has all the information Baz sent. He and Chelsea are taking a train to someplace called Porvoo. They're supposed to be meeting with Baz in a coffee shop there. I suspect Jesse will get to try some Finnish coffee and have a very boring sight-seeing expedition. They're supposed to wait in town until Baz contacts us with the exact meet time."

Jake nodded. "I think you're right. We showed a picture of Baz to one of the local shopkeepers and he seemed to know him. He doesn't speak a ton of English so I'm struggling with getting him to tell me if he was with anyone, but I think the trip to Porvoo is likely a distraction. He's counting on the threat being so terrifying you can't call his bluff."

"Yeah, well, if it isn't a bluff, we just screwed a bunch of undercover operatives," Taggart pointed out.

Penny shook her head. This very scenario had kept her up most of the night. "I don't think so. The last thing The Collective wants is to have the SIS and the CIA coming after them. They want to stay clandestine. No product or bump in stock prices can be worth having the government turn their attention on them. It doesn't make sense that The Collective approves this method. The minute they cause the death of an undercover operative, they become the enemy. Right now, no one actually believes they exist. They can't want that to change."

"I don't know that Baz will care." Damon checked the clip on his SIG and holstered the weapon. He pulled the cap low on his head.

He wasn't wearing a vest. There was nothing to stop a bullet from taking him out except his wits and speed, and she'd seen that his speed wasn't what it used to be.

"He'll care when his employers decide he isn't worth the trouble. Somehow I don't think The Collective's layoff package is going to include job retraining," Charlotte Taggart said.

Damon held out a hand, helping her out of the car. "We're not going to argue about this anymore. There's no point."

"The Collective sounds awesome. I mean, that's a story. You know?" Candice shook out her light brown hair. "I could really break out with that."

"Or you could find yourself beheaded and tossed into the Thames."

She was going to kill Damon. "He's joking."

Damon frowned. "No, I'm not. They won't take kindly to some reporter sniffing around. Besides, she works for one of the largest media conglomerates in the world. How do we know her newspaper chain isn't a part of The Collective?"

Candice froze. "Oh my god. I hadn't thought about that. What if I'm working for the enemy? Do you think they already know? They're probably watching me."

He seemed to almost delight in baiting the reporter. Or did Damon know he was actually getting to her? Penny put a hand on Candice. "Stop. You can't think that way. It's very unlikely or they would have picked you up and they would be the ones forcing you to bring Bennett in. So stop worrying about it. Stay calm. It's all going to be over in less than an hour."

Candice nodded, taking a deep breath. "All right. And I'll have a hell of a story. Yes. I'll be fine."

Penny left Candice with Charlotte and stepped away, gesturing for Damon to follow her. The minute they were out of earshot, she rounded on him. "Stop trying to scare her."

He stood far too close to her. "I'm trying to keep her alive."

"By terrifying her? She won't be able to stay calm if you don't stop telling her all the ways she could die."

A single brow swept up his forehead. "She doesn't seem to have your fortitude. I've told you all the ways you can die and you're still here."

She wished he wouldn't stand so close, but she couldn't back down now. "I have a job to do. She isn't trained and she didn't take an oath to protect her country. You can't compare us."

"I compare everyone to you." His expression didn't change at all though his voice went deeper. "Why won't you sleep with me?"

She stared for a moment, utterly taken aback. All she could manage was a quick shake of her head as she spoke. "This isn't the time or the place."

He crowded her again, taking a step toward her, forcing her back against the concrete. "It's the only place. It's the only time you've been alone with me since last night. You pretended to be asleep when I came to bed. You locked me out of the bathroom. By the time you came out, the Taggarts had invaded. Did you text her to come over? I noticed you grabbed your phone during your escape."

She had texted Charlotte. She'd done it before she'd stepped into the shower because she wasn't sure she wouldn't end up right back in bed with the same man who threatened to share her with all-comers. "I thought we all should talk before breakfast."

"You thought you could avoid talking to me at all."

Well, he'd fooled her. She certainly hadn't expected him to corner her when they had a mission to perform. He was right. She was trying to avoid him and she still wanted to. "Damon, we need to get to the church."

His mobile trilled and he bit back a curse as he pulled it from his slacks. A grim look came into his eyes as he read whatever was there.

"Who is it?" Penny asked, though she feared she knew the answer. The question was whether or not their game was up.

"It's Baz. He says the meet is at three."

A weird sense of relief hit her. "You were right."

"Yes. And he's waiting in that church. He's not where he tried to send us. He wanted us as far from this church as he could get us." His eyes pinned her as surely as if he'd put his hands on her. "Don't forget what I said. You stay close to Tag or Jake or I'll punish you."

An ache went through her heart at his words. At least he was holding his ground. He'd meant what he'd said the night before. It made it easy to let herself go cold. "Of course. I assure you, I won't give you any reason to lay hands on me ever again, Mr. Knight."

His eyes tightened and it was easy to see he had questions. She regretted her choice of words because it looked like he was willing to have it out right in the garage.

"We need to move." Taggart's voice echoed through the space. "We still have a half an hour. I'd like Penny to try talking to the shopkeeper to see if we can figure out if Baz is alone and where he might be coming from."

A sigh split Damon's mouth. "All right." He stared down at her for a second more. "This isn't over, Penelope."

But it was for now. She watched him walk away. When they caught Bennett, she would get on the first plane back home.

Safe from him. Safe from herself.

* * * *

Damon moved toward the entrance of the Temppeliaukio Kirkko otherwise known to tourists as the Rock Church. The odd building sat in the middle of the Töölö neighborhood in Helsinki. He turned back briefly, looking down the long street that led to the Lutheran church. The shop Jake Dean had found was on the corner. Penelope had stood inside. Speaking in perfect Finnish to the owner, she'd learned that Baz had been in Helsinki for at least four days. He seemed to be staying in the neighborhood and hadn't been spotted with anyone else.

Damon knew he was right. Baz was up to his old tricks, but he could be deadly when he was trying to get ahead. Just because he didn't have backup didn't mean he was any less lethal.

He'd stared at Penelope as she'd easily charmed the shopkeeper. The man had gone from suspicious to smiling and laughing within a few moments of talking with her. That was who she was. Damon could charm a woman into his bed, but he couldn't make people light up the way Penelope could. She was a bit of sunshine walking through the gloom.

He almost wished he'd never gone to bed with her. For years he'd been able to watch her, want her in a general way. Now he craved her.

He forced his thoughts away from his misery.

The church looked like a bunker set into the earth. Concrete marked the outside, the entryway a simple row of glass doors under the long overhang. Just above, a wall of rock looked incongruously ancient in contrast to the postmodern simplicity of the entry. To his left, the wall was covered in green vines, the only spark of color to be seen on the building. The rest seemed a bit bland, all shades of brown or gray.

Simon Weston sat on the bench in front of the vined wall, his big body slumped over as he seemed to study a map. Damon couldn't see his face. He had to admit the man blended in well.

To his right, Ian Taggart hoisted himself up the natural rock stairs formed by the side of the hill the church was built into. He moved up and past the small cross that denoted the building. From his vantage, he would be able to see 360 degrees around the building.

He also made a huge target, but he wasn't alone up there. Tourists were everywhere. It was exactly the kind of spot Baz despised. He preferred to work under the cover of darkness, in the shadows.

Baz was likely already in the church.

The reporter beside him stopped.

"It's going to be all right." He'd been a bit of a bastard to her. He tried to think of what Penelope would say but then he would likely sound like an idiot. "I won't let you die."

Surely that was somewhat reassuring.

She sniffled. "I just wanted a story."

"Well, you're about to get one."

"I think I'm going to switch to fiction after this."

He opened the door for her. "Well, you can write about this."

They moved into the odd gloom of the lobby. Up ahead, he could see the sanctuary and how light filtered in from the roof, but the lobby felt still, like the calm before the storm.

He glanced to his left where some stairs led to the lower part of the church. There was only a small velvet rope keeping the tourists out. Baz could come from there. Or the hallway beyond it.

He caught a glimpse of a man with dark hair walking the circular length of the sanctuary, his head close to the woman he walked hand in hand with.

God, he'd threatened her again with something he could never do. He hated the fact that Jake Dean's fingers were entwined with hers even though he knew damn well the man was in love with his wife, had just had a baby with her. He still wanted to rip Penelope away from him.

"Do you see him?" He kept his head down, turned away from the security cameras.

Candice shook her head. "No." She leaned over, speaking quietly. "I'm supposed to let him find me. We need to go sit on the third row opposite the organ. Apparently this whole place was built to house this organ thing."

He forced himself to sling an arm around her shoulders. How the hell was he going to do his job when even touching a woman like this felt like he was cheating? He wasn't, damn it. He wasn't Penelope's boyfriend, certainly wasn't her Dom. She'd made that clear by rejecting everything he was.

"Is it always this scary?" Candice whispered.

He glanced over at Penelope and Jake. He thought about ignoring the girl. She'd made her bed. She should have to lie in it so she didn't put herself in the same position again. She'd been brutally stupid and let her ambition cloud her judgment. He should leave her to hang, but Penelope chose that moment to put her face up to the sun that had finally come out from behind the clouds, lighting up the sanctuary.

Or maybe it was just her.

"There's nothing to be afraid of. It's going to be all right. You're surrounded by professionals who have zero interest in letting you die." The words were out of his mouth before he could think about them because Penelope would want him to be kind.

Was he going to spend the rest of his life thinking about what Penelope would want him to do? He was finding it difficult to do his job because she seemed to have taken up residence in his brain.

Candice glanced up at him. "Thanks. We should sit down. I don't want him to think we didn't show up."

He stepped into the light toward the left of the church where the side was dominated by massive organ pipes that seemed to be set into the rocks of the wall. It was as though the church emerged from the rock it was built on. The place might have been a bit nondescript on the outside, but it was spectacular on the inside.

Candice moved toward the front of the church. The altar was simple but he was caught with how the light flowed in from above. The church's copper ceiling was surrounded by wood and glass that allowed the sunlight to stream in and light the sanctuary up.

They sat down, pretending to study a guidebook.

It was only a moment before someone settled in behind him.

"Baz is here." Jake Dean's voice was very quiet.

Damon couldn't reply so he simply nodded his head.

"Penny talked to a couple of the docents. She convinced them she was looking for her brother. They said he'd been in more than once and they'd seen him hanging around today." Jake got back up and joined Penelope at the right wall where the faithful were lighting candles.

The sanctuary was filling up, but there was still a hushed atmosphere. People who shouted outside spoke in whispers in the church.

"I don't think he's a terrorist." Candice's words were barely audible.

"We'll figure that out." It didn't matter in the end. He needed to complete this operation so he could focus his attention on figuring out Penelope because he knew damn well he couldn't let her go.

"He told me he was trying to help."

Because terrorists always told the truth. He had no idea whether this Bennett bloke was a terrorist or just looking to sell something nasty for cash.

Or if he was something else entirely.

Once it wouldn't have mattered. He would have brought the fucker in and not looked back because at the end of the day, he was a weapon, nothing more. He was a tool that SIS used. They primed him and pulled the trigger.

But he didn't feel that way anymore. Maybe it was the time he'd spent recovering with the McKay-Taggart crew. More than likely it was the time he'd spent inside Penelope, but he was different now. The man he'd been before Baz had pulled the trigger was dead and gone and someone new had taken his place.

He needed to figure out who this man was. It did matter. What he did mattered because it affected her. The man he was affected her.

"We'll figure it out."

"You won't just shoot him?" Candice asked.

He shook his head. "Absolutely not."

There was a moment of silence. "Thank you."

Someone moved in behind them. This wasn't Jake, though he moved quietly. Damon heard the way the pew creaked under his weight. He closed his eyes as he listened. Male. He wasn't sure why he thought the person behind them was male, but his instincts said it was so. He was breathing in a calm manner, but it was audible. He leaned back against the bench, making it bend against his weight.

"Candice? Is that you?"

Aussie. No mistaking that accent. *Damn it.* Unless Walter Bennett had put on a whole lot of weight and developed a really authentic accent, then they were in a bit of trouble.

Walter had hired some muscle. It was the only explanation. Smart boy. It's exactly what Damon would have done. If he was on the run and knew damn well several people wanted his head on a silver platter, he would have hired some muscle to make sure his head stayed on his body.

Walter likely wasn't actually here.

Slippery motherfucker.

Candice stiffened and started to turn around. Damon put a hand on her thigh to stay her. She stilled. "Yes. It's me. I mean Candice. I'm Candice."

There was a low chuckle. "Hello, Candice. I'm Brody Carter. I'm representing Walter Bennett. You need to understand that he has to know you haven't been compromised. There are a lot of people looking for him."

"From The Collective?" Candice asked.

It took everything Damon had not to curse.

Brody went quiet for a moment and then, "You know about them? Well, Walter heard you were smart. Is this Robert? Do you have all the papers we need to get Walter on board? I've got Robert's plane tickets here."

"Yes."

Damon wouldn't have believed her. Her answer was too quick. There had been a breathy gasp that accompanied it.

"Brilliant."

Shit. The new guy's voice had gone from relaxed to tense in a word. He'd heard the same thing in Candice's voice, but he was too professional to give it away by questioning her.

And then he heard something that made his blood go cold. It was a laugh that held not an ounce of humor. "Oh, that's not Robert Tilman. But then you're not Walter Boy, are you?"

Damon turned. Baz was sitting two rows away, directly behind the massive man taking up the fourth pew. The Aussie had close-cropped blond hair and a square jawline that might have been hewn from the same granite as the church. He had to weigh eighteen stone, and every bit of it was pure muscle. He was built like a brick shit-house, and Damon was slightly intimidated at the thought of having to take the bloke down.

Maybe reason would work. He was their only connection to Walter Bennett. He had just become deeply important, so important that Damon couldn't allow him to fall into Baz's hands.

"Didn't buy my play, eh? Well, I can't win them all. I can, however, murder anyone who could possibly help you out." Baz gave him a wicked smile. "Did I mention you look really good, Damon? Also, I have a high-caliber weapon pointed at this bloke's spinal column."

"Fuck," the Aussie cursed under his breath.

"Hey, stay calm. I'm going to get you out of this. He's with The Collective. I'm not. I'm the good guy in this scenario." Damon didn't look around. He didn't want to tip off Baz if he didn't know how many people he had inside the church.

Out of the corner of his eye, he could already see Jake moving in. He could see Penelope was walking toward the exit, very likely trying to get to the Taggarts.

Baz seemed to be focused solely on his target. "Now, big guy, we're going to stand up. I don't want to cause a fuss, but I will if I have to. Stand up now or I'll fire directly into your back. How do you feel about being a paraplegic?"

Brody Carter's whole body stiffened, but he stood. His face went cold, blank, as he stared forward and Baz leaned in.

"Don't move too fast or I'll fire. Let's walk outside. I've got a car waiting. I have a couple of questions for you. We'll see how long it takes for you to give our mutual friend up," Baz said.

Damon had zero intention of giving up his prize. "You're surrounded, Baz."

Jake was walking down the aisle. Ian was in a sniper position. He didn't need to do anything. His team would handle the problem.

Baz put a hand on Brody Carter's shoulder, his other hand in his jacket pocket. A nasty smile lit his face. "I might be surrounded, but I'm not alone. I figured you might decide to roll the dice. I hired a friend who had one job and one job only."

Cold fear snaked along Damon's spine. He looked toward the front of the church, his eyes seeking Penelope's form, praying he couldn't find her.

She moved into the sanctuary, her body stiff, her pretty face tight. Someone was walking behind her. Damon's eyes focused on his target. A man, roughly mid-forties. He walked close to Penelope, more than likely because he had a gun pressed to her delicate spine.

That body he'd held, found such pleasure in, was in danger. He'd known he shouldn't let her get close. He'd known it would all end badly.

"Step back, Jake." He couldn't allow that man to send a bullet into her.

He was a man who had sacrificed his body for a mission, sacrificed pawns, given up anything to complete his operation. Nothing came between him and the completion of his task.

Nothing except Penelope Cash.

She was his weakness, the one thing he couldn't give up.

Jake's jaw tightened and he stepped back, allowing the Aussie and Baz to enter the aisle. He held his hands at his sides, letting Baz see they were empty.

Baz gave him a wink. "It's not the prize I was after, but it will have to do. We're going to walk out of here very carefully. If I even get a hint of trouble from you, I'll make sure you never walk again. We're going someplace private, and you're going to contact Walter for me. It's time he understood there's nowhere to run. I think I should take the reporter, too."

Candice shook her head. "No."

Baz gave her his best smirk. "Oh, darling, you don't get to say no to me."

Damon went completely still because Baz had never known

when to be satisfied. He just always had to overreach.

Tension slid across Damon as he realized Candice was going to panic. He caught the Aussie's eyes. The massive block of muscle stared at him as though reading his mind. Damon noticed that he wasn't wearing a jacket. His big biceps were on display and there was no way to miss the tattoo on his left arm. A sword with golden wings and the Australian Special Forces motto written in script—*Who Dares Wins*.

Carter was SASR. A commando or a former one at least.

His eyes narrowed slightly, and he cocked his head to the left. He was going to do something, very likely throw a punch over his left shoulder, and Damon would have to be ready when Candice finally broke. Because she was definitely going to break and then all hell would bust loose.

Candice took off, rushing down the pew, screaming for help.

Damon was left staring his greatest enemy down, praying he wouldn't give the call to end Penelope's life.

Chapter Seventeen

"Don't move or I'll fire."

Penny stopped at the words. She'd moved away from Jake Dean because she'd caught sight of a big man walking toward the place where Damon and Candice were sitting. He was huge, somewhat incongruous amid the flock of tourists. He stood out and that had caused Penny to stare. He had at least three inches on Damon and likely five or so stone of muscle. She couldn't tell exactly what the color of his hair was because it was so closely cropped. He looked like someone had taken a massive hunk of rock and carved a man out of it.

He didn't look anything like Walter Bennett, but he was walking straight to Damon. Fear snaked across her skin. Taggart was outside watching over the entrance. Jake was moving through the crowd toward her. Charlotte was keeping the van warm and running in case they needed to get away, and Simon was in front. Damon had no one close.

She had a gun. She could help him.

She felt the press of something hard against her lower back and her blood started to pound. She wasn't the only one with a gun.

She had to stay calm. Jake was twenty feet away, but he'd noticed the big guy, too. His attention was on the man as he sat down in the pew directly behind Damon.

"Don't to be moving." The man at her back spoke with a heavy accent.

Calm. If she stayed calm, perhaps he would as well. "All right. Are you working for Mr. Champion? Is he here? Perhaps you should take me to him."

He stood very close to her. He smelled of tobacco and the faintest hint of licorice. Salmiakki. Her grandmother had loved the salty licorice candy. "You to be staying still."

She switched to Finnish. His accent could be from any of the Nordic countries but the Salmiakki made her think he was from right here in Finland. "I'm not alone here. I don't know what Mr. Champion told you, but you're very likely not going to survive this."

He tensed behind her, replying in Finnish. "You speak my language."

"Yes. And I'm employed by people who won't take kindly to you killing me. Are you with The Collective?" It occurred to her that his answer would tell her a great deal.

He wrapped an arm around her waist. She was sure they simply looked like affectionate tourists. He spoke low and close to her ear, his Finnish coming much more surely. "I don't know what you're talking about. I'm supposed to hold you here until the boss tells me we're ready to go. He wants you real bad."

She was sure he did. "This isn't a kidnapping. I'm not some wayward girlfriend or some rich man's daughter he wants to ransom."

"I don't care. The man is paying me." He chuckled lightly. "Maybe he'll let me have some fun with you before he does whatever he's going to do to you."

Kill her at the very least. Likely in some incredibly nasty fashion.

Her small gun was in her jacket pocket. He hadn't found it yet. He seemed more interested in grinding himself against her backside.

"I've been in prison for a while. It's been so long since I had a woman."

She just managed to not gag. Perhaps it had been better when they couldn't communicate.

She saw the minute he walked into the sanctuary. Basil Champion moved like an elegant predator, every muscle streamlined with deadly grace. He wore a hat over his hair, his head down, but from her vantage point she could see the line of his jaw. It was him.

"Don't try to call out." The gun pressed hard against her spine.

Baz moved behind the big guy. Damon seemed to be talking to him, but he hadn't turned around. He and Candice were still staring toward the altar. Jake turned her way, and she watched as his eyes went wide.

She shook her head slightly. He couldn't come after her now. As calmly as she could, she nodded toward Damon.

Jake turned and started walking toward the front of the church, then turned again, moving toward her. Damn it. No one listened to her. Damon had told Jake to take care of her, and Jake would endanger the operation to help her. She'd seen Damon take Jake aside, and he'd probably given him a serious talk on what would happen if she died.

Why would he take such care of her and then threaten something so nasty? Had she overreacted? Had she allowed her heart to rule her head?

She should be brutally mad at him, but all she wanted was for Jake to leave her behind and back up Damon. Baz would likely keep her alive for a while, but he would kill Damon.

Jake stopped, obviously assessing the situation. Penny didn't have time. She had to send Damon some help. Baz seemed to be talking to them. He leaned forward and the big guy stiffened as though he'd just realized the threat.

She heard Jake curse and his eyes flared as though to tell her to stay where she was. He turned and started toward Damon.

As if she was going to run away with a gun in her back. He needed to save Damon first and then he could come back for her.

Or she could try to get out of this on her own.

Her would-be kidnapper was watching the scene with a single-minded intensity. It was easy to slip her hand into her coat pocket.

"Stay still," he said in guttural Finnish just as the big guy and

Baz stood up. It looked like Baz was making his play.

Damon finally turned, and his eyes went straight for her. His expression didn't change at all, but she could practically feel the panic pouring off him. He held a hand out and Jake stopped short of his goal.

Who was the big guy? A representative of Bennett? Baz seemed to want him so he had to be important.

She did her job, which was to stay quiet and show Damon just how fucked they all were. Except she didn't think they were. Baz had likely been hiding somewhere in the chapel, but he had to take his hostage out the lobby door. He had to get both him and her out of here in order to get away and keep the upper hand.

A long scream split the air. "Help me!"

And he likely hadn't counted on Candice causing a bit of chaos.

Her attacker dropped his hand for a moment as the crowd suddenly surged around them, and without a thought, she moved, bringing her foot down on his and firing into his body. Screams seemed to fill the small space and horror overtook her as she realized her attacker had fallen to the ground at her feet.

Blood began to run, pulsing from his thigh, and she watched as his eyes went from pain filled to completely blank. The acrid smell of smoke hit her nostrils. She'd fired through her coat and it was smoldering. She beat at it with her hands, putting it out as the crowd pushed her along.

Someone stumbled over the body and she caught the slightest glimpse of Jake trying to get to her.

"Get Damon!" She started Damon's way. She needed to get to him. He didn't have anyone with him. She couldn't stand the thought that he was alone.

Jake rolled his eyes as he caught her around the middle and easily hefted her up. "Did you not hear him screaming for me to get you?" Jake started for the exits. "Nice shooting, sweetheart, but now we have to get you out of here and fast. The police are on their way and they'll have surveillance tapes to work from."

She tried to look around, but she couldn't see Damon. Jake forced his way through the crowd, dragging her along. She didn't have more than a second to think about the fact that she'd killed a man. His body was cooling not a hundred feet from her. Yes, he would have killed her. She wasn't upset that he was dead, but being the instrument of it weighed on her.

Damon. She had to think about Damon. She couldn't see him. The sun had come out and she had to cover her eyes as they adjusted to the outside light.

"We're getting you to the van." Jake nodded at Ian, who leapt down from his perch.

"Damon's still in there along with our screaming reporter," Jake said as he hauled her toward the van.

"I heard shots. How many dead?" Taggart asked.

"Just one. Penny got tagged but she showed him her claws," Jake said. Up ahead, the van door opened.

Taggart grinned down at her. "Nice. I'll get Knight. Take off if you need to. We'll meet at the docks."

He ran off. Even as Jake shoved her in the van, she looked back, desperate to see Damon walking out of that church.

It wasn't Damon who ran out of the church first. The big guy shoved his way through the crowd. He hit the streets and started running.

Ian and Simon were going after Damon. He would be safe with them.

She couldn't let their only link to Bennett disappear or it would all have been for nothing.

There was a thud as Candice threw herself in the car. "I can't believe I panicked like that. Should I stay and talk to the police?"

Jake closed the van door. "Nope. We get back to the boat."

"No." Penny moved to the seat next to Charlotte and pointed out the window. "We have to get that man."

Without even a hesitation, Charlotte gunned the engine and took off, a smile of anticipation on her face. "He's a hulk. Who is he?"

Candice sniffled but seemed to be recovering. "He said his name was Carter. Brody Carter. Sounded Aussie from his accent. I think he's Walter's bodyguard. Walter didn't show up."

Charlotte made a sharp swerve to avoid traffic, keeping Carter's figure in her sights.

"Shit." Jake moved in between them, getting to his knees. "Why do I get left with the crazy chicks? Should I point out that our orders were to make for the docks and hook up with the rest of the team there?"

"You can certainly point it out all you like, but this is SIS's mission and you're a hired contractor, Mr. Dean. As the head of the SIS mission is currently not in contact with me, I believe I'm in charge," Penny said primly. "Don't lose him."

"I'm not the one who's going to get her ass smacked. And I am outnumbered unless Candy back there wants to help me take you both on." Jake sighed a little.

Candice shook her head. "I'm pretty much terrified of everyone. But I would like to know where Walter is, and that man up there is the only one who can tell us. I think if we ask him to come with us, he might say no though."

"I wasn't intending to ask him." She reached into her bag and pulled out a covered hypodermic needle. Damon had one as well. They had discussed it earlier and decided that if Bennett didn't cooperate, they would drug him and bring him on the boat a different way, hence the cruise ship van they had liberated and the big storage box in the back. There was more than one way to get on a ship.

"You can't kill him," Candice protested.

"It's just going to put him to sleep." She frowned as they slowed down. He was moving uphill now. "I worry a bit it won't be enough, though. It's dosed for a smaller man. He's much larger than Walter."

"It will work. Shit. I'm probably going to get my ass kicked first though. Why does everyone I fight have to be so fucking big?" Jake asked.

Charlotte swerved and made a crazy turn. "He's going down the alley. I think I can get ahead of him."

She stared at the GPS on the van's dash. It showed where the small side road led. She made another turn and brought the van to a halt.

Jake hopped out just as Carter sprinted from behind the building line. Jake found a way to avoid a prolonged fight. He simply put a

foot out and the big Aussie, who was looking behind him, tripped
and hit the ground with a loud thud.

"Bloody hell!"

Penny got out of the van, followed by Charlotte.

Jake jumped on the guy's back, placing his gun at the base of his
neck. "All right now, you massive piece of meat. We're going to do
this nice and easy."

The Aussie twisted him off with a loud shout and Jake was
tossed in the air, hitting the bricks of the building to his left. A groan
came out of his mouth, but he was back on his feet in an instant and
he never dropped the gun.

"Get the hell out of my way, yank, or use that gun because I'm
not going anywhere." The Aussie was on his feet, bleeding slightly,
but shoulders squared and ready to fight. "And get the women out of
here. I don't want to take them down but I will."

Charlotte stared Penny's way and nodded.

It was up to her. She palmed the needle, flicking the safety cap
off.

Charlotte cleared her throat. "Hey, we just want to talk, Mr.
Brody. Candice is in the van."

She was hiding in the van. Likely crying again.

Carter split his attention between Jake and Charlotte. "I think
I'm done jabbering for the day. We'll find another way."

She couldn't let him do that. She steeled herself. She would get
one shot.

"We can't let you go. Please come with us," Charlotte said.

He turned directly to her and Penny strained to reach him,
shoving the needle into the man's thick neck, pushing the plunger
down.

Carter immediately batted his big arm out and Penny went flying
the same way Jake had. The air knocked out of her lungs as she
brushed the side of the building. She fell to the cobblestones,
struggling to breathe.

"Damn it." Big hands reached down and started to pick her up.
She was surprised to open her eyes and find it was Brody Carter and
not Jake Dean who tried to help her up even though he had a needle

sticking out of his neck.

"Shit-arse job. Hate hurting women." His eyes glazed and he dropped her hands, hitting the ground with a hard thump.

"You okay?" Jake reached out a hand.

Penny nodded, adrenaline still rushing through her system. She got to her wobbly feet.

"Charlotte, see if you can help me get this guy in the van. We need to get out of here. I can't imagine Baz isn't coming this way."

That was when the first bullet flew down the alley.

Penny looked down the long street and saw Baz there.

"Shit." Jake returned fire, putting half his body behind a trash bin. "Get him in there or we leave him behind. You've got ten seconds before my need to get you to safety takes over and there will be no more discussions or rebellions."

Gunfire cracked through the air.

Penny wasn't about to leave the Aussie behind. There had been something about the way he'd tried to help her even after she'd shot him full of tranquilizers that brought out her protective instincts. He hadn't been like the other one. She couldn't leave him to die, and that's what would happen if she let Baz have him. She pulled the needle out of his neck, tossing it away before gripping his wrist. Charlotte took the other one and they started to drag him toward the van.

Sirens began to wail.

"If we all get taken in, who do you think is going to fare better with the cops, Champion?" Jake called out.

There was a frustrated shout and then the beating of shoes against the cobblestones.

Jake left his spot. "Get him in now. We have to go. I have no idea if he's gone for good or if he's just picking a better spot. Your men will have my ass if I get you killed."

Where was Damon? Panic threatened because she couldn't be sure Baz hadn't shot him. He'd been perfectly willing to shoot anyone in the church it had seemed. She hefted the Aussie up, helping to roll him into the back of the van.

Charlotte looked down at her phone. "No time for

recriminations. Ian wants a pickup. Let's go. He's got injured."

Penny's heart sank as she hurried to her seat. Candice stared down at the unconscious man and huddled in the back of the van.

Penny tried to hold it together because one way or another, she would need to get through the next few minutes.

* * * *

Damon's heart pounded in his chest as he burst out of the church. All around him panicked tourists screamed and yelled for loved ones, but he was looking for one woman. Where was Penelope?

He'd attempted to make his way toward her, but by the time he'd muscled to where she'd been last, she was gone.

Was she hurt? Was she lying somewhere bleeding and wondering where the hell he was?

Simon Weston was suddenly beside him. "Let's go. Penelope's been taken to the car. Charlotte's driving. Both of the women are fine. We need to get down the street so we can avoid the police who should be here any moment."

She was fine. Relief flooded through him at the thought. And he could see Baz forcing his way through the crowd up ahead. They'd slowed him down, the throng forming a wall that made it hard to get through. As he watched, Brody Carter managed to bust through and started to jog down the street, his head turning back to see who was following him.

"We have to get the man Baz is chasing. He knows where Bennett is." Without another thought, he took off.

He slipped through the crowd, forcing his way where he needed to. He had seconds before Baz would be through the human wall and then Damon had very little chance of catching him. Even as he picked up his pace, he could already feel his lungs burning.

Baz turned, catching sight of him. A look of pure hatred crossed his face and he pulled his big gun, pointing it straight at Damon.

He moved just in time, rolling to his left.

A man beside him fell, the bullet that had been meant for Damon taking his life.

The crowd scattered and Damon was on his feet again. He couldn't stop, couldn't consider the man who had fallen. Baz had done that. Not him. It was up to Damon to bring Baz down, but he couldn't do it from where he was standing. Fredrikinkatu Street was full of terrorized tourists, and the wail of sirens could be heard in the distance. If he took a shot, he might hit one of them. Too much chaos. It aided Baz.

He could see down the long length of the road, tall buildings on either side. He forced himself to move, to ignore the pain in his chest. He ran through the small park, past the tiny store they'd visited earlier. His feet beat against the cobblestones as the uneven ground threatened his every step.

Baz turned again, firing back. Damon whirled, his head spinning as he felt a burning sensation sizzle along his left bicep.

The road was sloping up now. He had to work harder. Run faster. Push himself. He had to.

He couldn't stop. He had to get that fucker. Penelope would never be safe as long as Basil Champion was walking the earth. Somewhere in the back of his head he knew she wasn't the objective. Protecting her wasn't what he was being paid to do but somehow she'd become his mission. When everything else was stripped away, when he couldn't allow his own stupid history to hold sway, when all he could hear was the thundering of his faulty heart, he knew what mattered. Penelope.

Pain flared as he stumbled a bit.

He could see Baz had stopped at a side street. In the distance, he heard the flare of guns firing. More than one. Was Penelope fighting?

Run harder. Run faster. Don't give in to the pain.

"Come on, mate." Simon was suddenly beside him, the younger man easily catching up.

Damon's vision was just the slightest bit foggy, clouding on the periphery. He didn't let up. He focused on one thing and one thing only. Baz.

Except he couldn't see him anymore.

"It's going to be all right." Simon's voice sounded distant.

Why wasn't he running? What the bloody hell was that pain in his leg? He forced his eyes to open—he wasn't aware they'd been closed.

His chest heaved, trying to get oxygen into his lungs.

"You passed out, mate. One minute you were running and the next you were down for the count." Simon was staring down at him, his face stern. "We have to get you up. The police are already at the church, and they'll be here any minute. Up you go."

His stomach turned as Simon got him on his feet.

Everything hurt. What the hell had happened? Simon slung Damon's arm over his shoulder.

"Come on. We have to move."

"We have to get Baz. He was right there. I almost had him." He'd been closing in.

His legs moved, but he had to think about it. They felt useless. It seemed like all of his effort, all his energy, was spent just trying to breathe.

"Come on, Charlotte," Simon said under his breath as he dragged Damon's useless body into the nearest alley.

"Have to get Baz."

"Baz is gone, Knight. He's long gone, and we're going to get hauled into Finnish prison if we don't get ourselves gone, too. I'm sure it's very clean and polite, but prison is prison." Simon sighed. "Thank god."

There was a squeal of tires as the van they had switched to in the garage stopped at the alley. The side door slid open, and Taggart jumped out.

"What the fuck was that, Knight?"

Simon dragged him along "Not now, boss. He's in bad shape."

Damon started to shake his head. He was fine.

Taggart's boots echoed along the pavement. "Hospital? Did he take fire?"

"No hospital." He didn't need a bloody doctor. Nausea threatened to overtake him, but at least he was breathing somewhat normally again. His legs still felt useless.

Taggart leaned over, shoving a big shoulder into his middle and causing Damon to curse. "Let's go then. We have the package. You owe my wife and your girl big-time, Knight."

If he vomited all over Tag's backside, it would be payback.

The van doors opened and Jake Dean was in the back, shifting something to the side to allow Tag to toss Damon's utterly limp body inside. He was just starting to regain control of his legs as his back hit the floor of the van. The doors clanged closed and in a second, they were off.

He realized what package Charlotte and Penelope had apparently picked up. Brody Carter was unconscious beside him.

Penelope stared down, her hand on his forehead. "It happened again?"

He'd passed out. Like he had in Liverpool station. He'd failed. He closed his eyes and nodded. He kept them closed because he didn't want to see the pity in her eyes.

"What happened, Penelope? How did you get away?"

"Oh, I shot him."

His eyes flew open and he twisted, forcing himself to get the hell up. "Penelope?"

Her face was pale, but she seemed steady. "He would have killed me, Damon. When Candice started running, I smashed my foot across the bridge of his and I shot him. I think I killed him. But it was him or me and I don't think he was likely a very good person."

"I'm so sorry." Candice was sitting on the floor, huddled close to the front, her face blotchy from crying.

Penelope had killed her attacker and managed to bring in both of their assets.

He reached out for her. It didn't matter that she was angry with him. It didn't mean a thing that she didn't seem to want him anymore. She needed comfort, and he was damn well going to provide it. She was still wearing his collar. He'd brutally failed to protect her. He could at least offer her this.

If she rejected him, he might die.

She went into his arms the minute he opened them. She was soft and warm and he hadn't realized how cold he'd been.

"I killed him." Her body shook as she cried, and he tightened his arms around her.

"It's all right, love. You did so well." She'd been more than he could have hoped for. But she was gentle at heart, and it would hurt her that she'd been forced to kill. "You did the only thing you could."

She simply cried into his shoulder. As they moved deeper into Helsinki, Damon held on and prayed he could be enough for her.

Chapter Eighteen

Standing in an alley near the docks ten minutes later, Damon forced himself to move though every single muscle in his body ached. He had to face certain truths. He was damaged. His body was ruined. Possibly beyond repair. He might look all right on the outside. He might be able to fake his way through looking fit, but he wasn't. He'd lied to himself, to everyone. He'd hidden from the fact for the last six months, but it was brutally true and he'd discovered something else about himself.

It didn't matter. He didn't even care that he'd lost consciousness, nearly wrecked the operation. All that he cared about was the fact that Penelope had held onto him briefly and then shut him out again.

"Are you sure this will work?" Taggart asked.

Jake Dean used a crowbar to force the crate open. "If it doesn't, we won't be any worse off than we are now. I already called Chelsea. She's back on board. She and Jesse cut their trip short once they confirmed it was a distraction. She's worked the system. They're expecting crate number 1021009 in housekeeping. It's supposed to be a new shipment of organic cleaning equipment. Jesse's back on board, and he's going to sign for it. He's waiting for the crate and then we'll move it to storage and get him back out again with no one the wiser."

Him being Brody Carter, who was still unconscious. Simon wound rope around the bugger's massive wrists and Taggart held out a ball gag setup that would have made the subs spit and scream his way, but it would totally work for what they needed to do.

There was more than one way to get on the boat, and they were using it.

If only he could get Penelope to look at him.

She'd clung to him, crying into his shoulder and holding him tight, but when the van had stopped and they'd had to get out and be cruise ship passengers again, she'd pulled away from him.

He couldn't stand it. He hated not touching her, not being close to her.

It shouldn't matter. They had the package. Everyone on the crew was fine. The cops weren't waiting at the boarding level of the ship. It was successful despite the fact that they didn't have Bennett or Baz. He should have been okay with it, but he didn't give a shit because Penelope wouldn't look at him.

"Should we stay here and look for Walter Bennett?" Penelope asked quietly.

At least that was a question he could answer for her. She wouldn't allow him to do much else. "That's not a good idea, love. After the debacle at the church, we have to be worried about the police. We need to question Carter and it's going to be easier to do that on board, where we can control our surroundings. He knows where Bennett is. If we need to come back to find him, we will. But we'll come back with a full team and support."

They stuffed Carter in the crate, his dead weight a massive burden. Jake brought in a handcart and they got the crate on wheels. Jake nodded toward him, waving him off. He and Simon would board on the cargo level with the shipment. The rest of them had to get back on the boat with smiles on their faces like they'd had a brilliant time in Finland. Charlotte and Penelope had been trying to fix Candice's makeup. She looked pale but walked solidly ahead of them.

His chest still ached with every breath. He kept his footsteps steady, but he had to think about it, had to focus. There was a small wound on his left bicep that still stung a bit. He was wearing Taggart's jacket to cover up the small stain on his shirt.

"Are you all right?" Penelope asked as they moved toward the cruise terminal. All around them happy tourists flocked to buy candies and small souvenirs to take back to loved ones at home.

He had no one who cared where he'd been or what he'd done. No one who cared truly if he lived or died. He'd had Penelope, but he'd ruined that somehow. "I'm perfectly fit."

Candice looked back. "Can I go to my room?"

Damon nodded. "Yes. But don't leave there. We might need you."

"I would like to talk to the big guy, if I could. I'm worried about Walter. I've never met him, but after talking to him for weeks, I feel like I know the bloke. I'm sorry about panicking." Her cheeks flushed as they moved onto the gangway that led to the boat.

Penelope put a hand on her arm. "Everything turned out all right."

He pulled his keycard out. It was everything to the ship—key, passport, credit card.

She nodded and went silent as they headed through security. The tourists were all talking about the terrible things that had happened at the church, but Damon didn't engage them. Even Candice went silent as she handed over her card and was buzzed through. She waved as she headed up the stairs toward her room.

He and Penelope walked to the lifts and found themselves blissfully alone for a moment. Charlotte and Ian were heading to the cargo decks to pick up the package. The interrogation could be a long process.

It would be the perfect time to hold her tight and reassure himself that she was alive and all right, but she stepped away from him. He pushed the button for nine.

"I won't let you punish me. I know I didn't do exactly what you said, but you can't expect that I would allow you to do that to me." She stared straight ahead at the ridiculously ornamental doors to the lift.

"Of course." He stood to the opposite side, not wanting her to think he was going to attack her. Punishment in D/s was consensual despite the meaning of the word. The submissive had to allow herself to be corrected or it was abuse, and he had no intention of abusing her. He'd been too rough, gone too far, and now she would lock away that part of herself that he could have freed had he not been such a ham-handed idiot.

She sniffled though she still didn't turn his way. "I'll be honest, Damon. I didn't expect that of you."

She shouldn't have expected anything from him at all. He shrugged slightly. "It happens all the time at The Garden." She should truly understand how rough he could be. "I've done it to submissives before."

The door opened and he allowed her to walk out first. She moved with stiff accuracy. "Well, it's no wonder you don't have a full-time sub. I suspect they don't like to be shared in such a manner."

There were so many reasons he'd never had a full-time sub, the chief one being he'd never had one move him the way Penelope did. "It's common enough. Jane enjoyed it. She thought it was fun. She would close her eyes and try to figure out which Dom was spanking her. I'll be honest. I wasn't going to go through with it. It was a stupid thing to say. I tried to come up with ways to let them spank you that didn't involve touching you at all. How silly is that?"

She stopped. "Spanking?"

He shook his head, reaching for the keycard again. At least the operation would be over soon. He could get Penelope off the boat at their next port. He wouldn't have to lie next to her at night and wonder where he'd gone wrong. "Like I said, it was stupid of me. I was very angry. No. I was scared. I was scared of losing you so I threatened you with the worse thing I could think of."

"Allowing other Doms to spank me." She seemed to struggle with the words as though they didn't fit properly in her mouth.

"I wouldn't have." He had no idea what to say to her. How was he supposed to tell her how much he was going to miss her? How much he wanted her to stay with him? How much he regretted not being the right kind of man for her?

In the end, he simply turned and started down the hall. The ship would be moving again soon, and he had preparations to make. He needed to think things through. Bennett had to be found, and the Aussie was the only connection they had now.

Unfortunately, Aussies weren't known for being gentle, cooperative souls.

"Damon?" Penelope was a good ten feet behind him.

"Come along. We need to get ready." He frowned her way as she stood there. "I won't touch you, Penelope. You have my word. You might think very little of me, but I won't hurt you again."

"Damon, it's not that," she began.

A couple of stewards walked through the narrow hallways, shoulder to shoulder, interrupting whatever Penelope might have said.

"Did you just see that? What the hell?" the taller of the two asked.

"I have no idea, man. I'm keeping my eyes closed until this cruise is done. These people are freaks." He flushed when he realized they weren't alone. "Evening, sir."

Damon nodded and allowed them to move by and then he saw what they were complaining about.

Ian Taggart had the big Aussie gagged, his hands behind his back and his shirt off. Charlotte walked next to him, a crop in her hand.

"Bad sub. You are a bad, bad sub and there will be punishment. You never talk to your mistress that way." She slapped his ass with the crop.

Carter's head came up, and he looked Charlotte's way. He seemed to be trying to talk around the bright red ball gag that was strapped to his mouth. He struggled, moving his shoulders hard and to the right, trying to buck Taggart off him.

"You need some help with that one, Tag?" It was a good excuse to end the painful conversation with Penelope. He hurried down the hall, but noticed Carter's head was back up.

He made some incomprehensible sounds.

Charlotte leaned over. "We'll get it off you as soon as we make it to the cabin. It's going to be okay, Mr. Carter. And besides, I'm having fun playing the mistress."

She lightly tapped his rear with the crop.

"Don't get used to it. You're going to be the one taking the crop tonight, Mrs. Taggart. Get his other side, Knight. He's a heavy son of a bitch." Taggart hauled him back up.

Damon moved to Carter's right, but he seemed to cooperate a bit more. His feet didn't drag now and he stood straight, walking along.

Penelope moved to get the door to their cabin open. She held it while they managed to get Carter inside.

"This is what the world is like in my dreams," Tag said with a smile on his face. "An all D/s world where it's perfectly normal for an almost seven-foot dude to get his ass cropped by a Domme. Wouldn't everything just be better this way?"

Charlotte shut and locked the door. "I'm sure it would be better for you, babe. I, on the other hand, like wearing clothes from time to time. Don't laugh. You know I do. And if you had your way, we'd all just run around naked."

Damon did see a couple of flaws in Tag's plan, though Penelope always being naked and available for him was a tempting idea. But they had bigger things to deal with than Tag's dream world.

Of course, he likely wouldn't see her naked again.

Carter slumped to the couch.

"Damon? Can I talk to you?" Penelope caught up to him.

He wanted to avoid "the talk." She seemed ready to finally give him the chat where she told him never to touch her again. Thank god he had a job to do.

"Later. It has to wait." He turned his attention back to their guest.

It was time to lay his cards on the table and figure out if he had a winning hand. He looked down at Carter, though not far. Even sitting the man was as tall as a lot of men standing.

He stood in front of the Aussie, crossing his arms over his chest as he began. "My name is Damon Knight. I work for British intelligence, SIS or MI6, if you prefer. I would like to take that gag out of your mouth so we can have a pleasant chat."

"Damon, please do keep it friendly." Penelope put a hand on his arm, the first time she'd willingly touched him since the dungeon. She looked right up at him. "I don't think he's the bad guy."

He hated the fact that she could manipulate him, but it didn't matter. It was exactly that—a fact and there was nothing he seemed to be able to do about it. "Why do you think that, love?"

He would soften, listen to her, very likely give in to her just to keep her looking at him.

"I shoved a needle in his neck, and he seemed horrified that he hit me."

Anger flared through his system at the thought. "He hit you?"

Carter outweighed Penelope by a good seven stone. He could likely crush her without even thinking about it. What had she been thinking going after the man? She should never have been in that position. She'd been forced to kill and then to attack a man three times her size.

He couldn't do anything to the man she'd killed, but he could deal with this bastard.

Carter shook his head and he nodded Penelope's way.

Penelope put a restraining hand on Damon's shoulder. "Damon, I had just attacked him. He can be forgiven for lashing out a bit."

Damon didn't have to forgive him. He didn't even want to. He wanted to pull the big bloke's head off with his bare hands.

"He kind of freaked when he realized she was a chick," Charlotte explained. She held the keys to the cuffs in her hands. "It was weird. He tried to help her up. I think Pen's right and he's a big old softie under all those muscles."

Carter grunted in obvious disagreement.

"He's got a Special Air Service Regiment tat on his forearm. I seriously doubt he's a softie." Taggart inspected his left arm. "Unless it's just decorative."

Carter grunted again, his eyes flaring.

"I think that means no," Charlotte said.

"Can we at least talk to him, Damon?" When had Penelope started to smile at him again? She was looking at him with an amused expression on her face, the one that he'd mistaken for affection before.

It looked like he would have to forgo thrashing the bloke. Penelope seemed to have taken to the bugger like he was an overgrown house pet. "I'm going to remove the ball gag. If you shout out, I'll have to replace it."

Gingerly, he released the gag and pulled the rubber ball from Carter's mouth. Charlotte was right there with a towel, wiping off the guy's chin.

"Hey, I know what that feels like," she explained. "And hopefully I didn't really hurt you too much with the crop."

Carter moved his jaw, stretching it out a bit. "Not at all, though I have to say I'd prefer to be on the other end of that crop when it comes to a pretty bird like you, sweetheart." He turned to Penelope, his face serious. "Did I hurt you?"

Fuck. He really did seem upset. He was giving Penelope soulful eyes. His mouth turned down.

Penelope shook her head. "I'm perfectly fine, thank you. How about you? I'm so sorry I had to use that needle on you, but you didn't seem like you wanted to stop and have a chat."

"I'm just glad you didn't get hurt, luv." He gave her a smile that changed his face from slightly scary to something resembling handsome. Despite the big scar he had running along his left cheek, the Aussie wasn't hard on the eyes. A woman like Penelope might like him.

Oh, there was going to be none of that. He might have to deal with the fact that he'd lost her, but he wasn't going to watch her flirt with someone else. "All right, Romeo, if you're done flirting, perhaps we can get on with it."

Carter turned distinctly predatory the minute he focused on Damon. "Listen up, you pommie bastard. You've got a few roos loose in the top paddock if you think I'm giving you anything."

God save him from Aussies. It was bad enough to be surrounded by Americans. "You think I'm crazy? Mate, I'm not the one working for a terrorist. Are you angry with the crown? Is that why you want to help Nature's Core hit London?"

"What are you talking about, you fuckwit?" Carter shook his

head. "You think Walt is a terrorist?"

At least he wasn't denying he had a connection to Bennett. "I think Walter Bennett stole something very important, and he means to sell it and he doesn't care who gets hurt in the process."

"Bite my arse." Carter sat back.

"Oh, Ian. I like him. Can we keep him?" Charlotte asked, obviously amused.

It was nice someone found the situation humorous.

"Absolutely not. I don't think he's housebroken, baby," Taggart shot back.

"You're former SASR? I assume you aren't current." He would have to go about this a different way. He needed the man's cooperation. Unfortunately, the room was really small. He required a bit more space to really get his torture on. And then there was the fact that Penelope would likely object if he started pulling the man's fingernails out one by one. So he had to appeal to his reasonable side. If he had one.

"I got out three years ago," Carter said. "I was in the service for almost twelve years. Took an IED in Afghanistan. Apparently having a skull that's more metal than bone means I can't serve anymore. I wasn't ever much good at anything else."

"You a mercenary?" Taggart asked, his voice serious for once.

Carter frowned at the word. "Nah. I'm a bodyguard. I cop the bullets. End of the day, I'm just dumb muscle. And I sure as shit don't hire out to terrorists. Tell MI6 to get better intel." He shrugged against the cuffs holding his hands behind his back. "And what bloody right do you have to hold me? I'm a private citizen."

"In the post 9/11 era, that doesn't mean a thing if you've got the wrong connections and you know it. We have places we can take you, Carter. Places you don't want to go." Places that would take far too long, but he couldn't come out and say that.

"Damon, that seems a bit rude. Mr. Carter, we really are trying to help," Penelope said. "We only know what Candice has told us. The intelligence we've heard leads us to believe that Mr. Bennett is attempting to smuggle something dangerous into the country. I find it hard to believe a decorated officer such as yourself would help him."

They'd been able to find out a lot about their captive in the short time between when they picked him up and when they'd made it to the boat. Brody Carter had been highly decorated, his service record unblemished. His career had been cut short by his injury. He'd been working private security for the last couple of years. They'd asked the questions to see if he would lie.

"Even decorated officers can go bad when they feel they've been wronged." Damon seemed to be the bad copper in this scenario, but the good news was he was perfectly comfortable with the role. "Did you decide to help with the attack after you realized your military career was over?"

"I'm not helping with any bloody attack," Carter shot back.

Penelope reached out, putting a hand on his knee. "Could you please tell me what's really going on? Because I don't believe for a second that you would hurt innocent people. You couldn't hurt me and I was attacking you."

"I can hurt people. You have no idea how I've hurt people in the past, luv. I've killed more than my share. I just don't like hurting women. It makes me sick, to tell you the truth. But your boy there is wrong about Walt. He isn't bad. He's trying to do the right thing, but none of us really knows how to do that anymore." He got quiet for a moment. "Is that bloke there really Ian Taggart?"

He knew Tag?

Ian stepped up. "I'm Taggart. I run a firm called McKay-Taggart."

Carter stared at him. "You used to be a Green Beret. You knew an SASR officer named Harrison Craig?"

Tag nodded, his lips curling up with humor. "Hell, yeah. I know Harry. He gave us ground support on a couple of NATO missions. How the hell is he?"

"He was my half brother and he died a while back, but he always told me if I got in trouble that I should trust you. Fuck a duck, mate. I tried calling your offices but they said you were out of the country."

Ian put a hand on the big guy's shoulder. "Your brother was a good man and an excellent soldier. I'm sorry to hear he passed. Harry told you to trust me so I need you to listen to me. Damon's a good man. You haven't heard of him because most of his military time was classified. He's going to take care of you."

Carter shook his head. "I can't trust anyone but you. And if you're working for the government, I won't even trust you. I want to hire you. Outside of the CIA. What Walt has, no government should own. Fuck, mate, no one should have it."

Instinct started to pulse through his system. Something was wrong and it always had been. The Collective wasn't working with them. If they really had the trouble they said they had, why wouldn't they be working with the agencies?

Baz wanted whatever Walter Bennett had back.

Nature's Core had always been peaceful.

Candice was an idiot and no terrorist in his right mind would use her.

But a dumbass scientist who thought he was saving the world just might.

"What was Agro developing? What was so dangerous that Bennett thought he had to risk his life to steal it and expose it to the world?"

It was the only thing that made sense. Bennett had zero ties to any terrorist organization.

Carter's face froze.

"Please, tell us," Penelope pleaded. "We want to help."

Carter's eyes went to Taggart.

"I promise I'll do whatever I can to protect you and Bennett, if you deserve it," Taggart replied.

Carter's eyes closed briefly and for a moment Damon was certain he would spout some crazy Aussie curses and be done with all of them. But finally he looked straight at Damon. "All right then. It was too much to hope for anyway. Walt's been working for Agro on a system that helps identify the DNA of a virus. I'm not smart like him but apparently it's important to get the DNA of emergent viruses. He's been working in the real tight labs. And that was when he found it."

"Found what?" Damon asked.

"Apparently even when we eradicate a virus, it never really goes away. The way he explained it, we just made it so it's hidden. Like it's behind a barrier because we immunized whole generations and now it's behind that wall."

Cold fear ran up his spine because he had an idea of what Carter was talking about. "And they want the wall to come down?"

"No one immunizes for it anymore. Not since 1972. And the immunization thing….it don't last forever it seems. Everyone is vulnerable now."

Fuck. Smallpox. Mandatory vaccines had ended in the seventies and the medical community considered it eradicated. But a dirty company like Agro could come up with a million ways to make a buck off something like that. "You're talking about smallpox."

Carter nodded.

Taggart shook his head. "The CDC has enough vaccine stored to immunize everyone in the States against smallpox if we have to."

"This isn't the same virus you've read about," Carter explained. "Agro made it stronger. Smarter. More resilient. They figured out a way to weaponize it. And only they have the vaccine. They're going to take out large swaths of the Third World. They plan to scare the crap out of the rest of us and then charge us through the nose to save the world. Millions will die so they can make a buck. Do you understand?"

Penelope gasped a little. "He was trying to warn us?"

"He still is. It's why I took the job. Walter Bennett isn't the enemy. Agro is. Walt got out with all the research. He wiped the drives. He took the samples and destroyed them. He wrecked his entire career because he couldn't stand the thought of all those people dying for corporate profits. He took an oath, you see."

Bennett was a virologist, but he was a doctor, too. He'd had to make a Hippocratic Oath, and it looked like he took it seriously.

And Damon had another mission.

He was going to save Walter Bennett. Penelope looked up at him, her eyes shining like he was some kind of hero.

He was going to save the whole bloody world if he had to.

293

Chapter Nineteen

Penelope shivered while she waited for Damon to return. He'd taken Carter to an empty cabin Jesse had procured and that Chelsea was securing from the cameras' view. After a long discussion about what was going to happen next, they had decided to call it a night.

Carter and Walter had another meeting set up. According to Carter, he was supposed to vet the reporter in Finland. If she checked out, Carter would give them the meet spot in Berlin and travel there himself. Carter was supposed to meet Bennett and Candice at the Holocaust Memorial in the heart of Berlin, and they would have gotten Bennett on the boat from there.

They wouldn't be getting back on the boat for the last leg to Amsterdam. They would be headed straight for the British Embassy.

In two days' time, this mission would be over and her relationship with Damon could come to an end if she chose.

She didn't choose. Not at all.

She'd been wrong. Wrong about everything. When he'd said he would let every Dom in the room have a turn at her, he'd meant a spanking not a massive gang bang. She'd been stupid.

The trouble with translating foreign languages was sometimes the person interpreting had to make a judgment call, and all too often it involved the translator's own cultural prejudices.

Damon spoke a different language. Oh, he used all the same words, but it was different because he had no idea how to talk about what he felt. She had to look past his words to find what he truly meant. She'd been doing it since the moment she began her relationship with him. For the most part, she'd done a good job, but when she screwed up, she really screwed up. She'd made a call and it had everything to do with her insecurities. She'd allowed them to lead her to a place where she'd shut Damon out and he'd had no idea what to do with the behavior. Now that she looked back, she realized he'd actually done his best. He'd asked her about the problem.

It was more than he would usually do. She knew Damon and he would simply walk away from situations he didn't necessarily understand on an emotional level. He'd done his best. He'd come to her and tried to talk about it. Yes, he'd put it in sexual terms but that was Damon Knight's language.

He'd asked her in his low, careful voice why she wouldn't sleep with him anymore. It was tantamount to asking her why she didn't love him now.

She'd left him alone. She'd done what everyone else in his life had done, and she had to make up for it.

Penny pulled off the sweater she was wearing and wrestled her bra off. She'd made the mistake of putting her own insecurities over his words instead of really looking at the situation and evaluating how to translate him.

He was a man who was always in control, but he'd allowed her to manipulate him. Every step along the way, he'd backed down. Now that she looked at it with a wiser eye, she could see that he'd tried to rein her in, but when she bucked against the restrictions, he'd allowed her to have her way. Yes, he'd spanked her, but he hadn't done what she would expect him to do. He hadn't locked her away or shut her out. He'd made love to her. He might call it sex or discipline but it was how he expressed his caring. He treated her like she was precious, like she was everything he needed to breathe, to live.

She'd ignored what he did in preference to what he said. She'd heard the words and not questioned the meaning of them. It was a fatal flaw for a translator.

Every step of the way, every dumb word that had come from his mouth led her to one thing.

Damon Knight loved her, and he had no idea how to say it.

He knew one language though. He understood the language of submission. It was a gift she could give him.

She shimmied out of her slacks, tossing them to the side, and took a long breath.

Had she ruined it? Had she driven him away?

They were in the middle of a crisis but all she could think about was getting Damon back. She'd vowed that she would walk away if she couldn't win him by the time they got back to England. She'd promised that she would let him go, that she would salvage her pride.

She sank to her knees, allowing them to spread wide.

Fuck her pride. She wanted her man, and he was worth fighting for. No one had ever fought for Damon Knight. His parents had died and his family had fallen away. He'd found himself in situations beyond his control. His country wanted him as long as he was capable of serving it. But only one person had loved Damon enough to give up everything for him. She was his woman. She wouldn't ever give up on him. She would fight for him with every breath she had left in her body.

The ship moved beneath her, jostling softly under her skin. She barely noticed it now, but when she was still and quiet, she could feel the way the boat plowed through the waves. Motion. She'd been in motion since the moment she met Damon, moving to this moment when she finally made her choice.

Time passed, minutes going by, but she found a certain peace in waiting for him, in staying in position for her Master.

Finally, she heard the cabin door open.

"Are you sure about this?" Her heart skipped a beat as she heard Simon's voice trailing in. She'd expected Damon to return alone. "I don't know that I like the idea of leaving the bugger alone."

Her first instinct was to leap for her clothes, but she stayed in position. Her submission wasn't determined by who walked into the cabin she shared with her Master.

"I think he'll be fine," Damon said. "We need for him to trust us and quite frankly, we need to be able to trust him. If what he says is true, and I think it is, we're all in this together and we have some hard decisions to make about where this information goes."

"All right then. I'll get back to the dance floor. I'm apparently teaching a bunch of subs how to tango tonight." Simon chuckled all of a sudden. "Well, I didn't expect to see that. Hello, Pen. You're looking quite lovely this evening."

Damon huffed, a surprised sound. "Penelope? Weston, get the bloody hell out of here. Move. Now."

She heard the shuffling of feet and then the door closing with a hard click as Damon locked it. She kept her head down because it was up to her Master to either accept or reject her gift.

Tears pricked her eyes because she'd been so foolish. He wouldn't share her. Never.

His loafers came into view. They were normally perfectly polished but now they sported scuff marks and a long scratch on the top of the right one from where he'd stumbled trying to chase after Baz.

Accepting him meant accepting the fact that he would likely die in the field one day. It was a part of who Damon was. She wanted to beg him to quit, to retire and settle down with her, but she couldn't. She had to accept Damon for everything he was—hero, protector, stubborn arse. She loved everything about him.

"You should get up now, Penelope. I'll get your clothes." His voice sounded strained, harsh even.

She tensed, her heart clenching. Had she ruined everything? "Damon, please."

He stepped back, his hands out as though she was a dangerous creature and he needed to put space between them. "No. I'm not going to let you use me like this."

"Use you?" She stayed still though she wanted more than anything to look up and plead with him.

"Yes. It's what it would be. You think you can use me for sex for the rest of the mission? I'm not interested. Get your clothes and we'll talk. I'm going to explain to you exactly how this is going to go from now on."

Fear gripped her for a moment. "I'm sorry, Damon. I didn't understand."

"But you do now." He reached for the Scotch he'd had delivered earlier and poured himself far more than he usually did. "You understand what it's like."

"No, I didn't understand you." And it was obvious he didn't get what she was trying to tell him.

His foot tapped impatiently against the carpet. "Penelope, you will be quiet for a moment. I say that as your superior and not your Master. We both know that was only for show anyway. Put on your bloody clothes."

She wasn't sure where this was heading, but she wasn't about to go backward. And he seemed to have real trouble concentrating on anything but her breasts. "I'm perfectly comfortable this way. And if you're just my superior and not my Master, then I think I'll make the decisions about what types of clothes I choose to wear."

A bitter huff came from deep in his chest, and he took a long swallow of the Scotch. "Fine. You seem determined to punish me for something. Well, you'll find I'm made of sterner stuff than that."

Her heart softened. He looked so lost. "Damon, I can explain."

His jaw straightened, a stubborn look coming over his face. "I don't want to hear it. It doesn't matter anymore. We're starting over again. I pushed you far too fast and into a world you don't have a real interest in. Fine. When we get back to England, we'll play it your way. We'll date. I'll take you to a nice restaurant and treat you like a lady."

She smiled at his words. It was ludicrous, but it was sweet to hear. "I don't think that's going to work."

"It will. If you prefer vanilla sex, I can handle it. I'll give you vanilla sex and we can work the rest of it out."

He couldn't even look at her while he said it. Poor Damon. He had no idea what had happened because she'd broken his cardinal rule. She hadn't been honest with him. If she'd been brave, she would have called him out the minute he said the words and they would already be through this, but she'd been a hurt coward and she'd let Damon stew in his worry for far too long. Now he had it in his head to change his entire life for her.

But he claimed he didn't love her.

They didn't speak the same language. Men and women rarely did. She'd accepted that, but now she knew she'd forgotten something. Languages could be learned. They just had to be practiced.

"I love you, Damon."

He turned, nearly knocking his glass over. "What?"

"I said I love you, Damon." He would need to hear it many, many times before he got the meaning.

His eyes tightened, focusing on her. "I don't understand."

She rose to her feet and walked to him, peace filling her. This was what she should have done in the first place, but she was too used to hiding behind a wall. "I know you don't, but I'm going to teach you."

"Damn it, Penelope. I don't understand a bit of this and I really don't like it."

He was confused and he hated it, and she hated that she'd placed him there. He looked so hard on the outside, so polished and smooth like nothing could touch him, but inside he was quite tender. Inside he was still a boy praying that someone would take care of him, love him enough to stay.

She reached out and touched him, cupping his gorgeous face in her hands. "I'm so sorry, Master. I broke trust with you. You said something that hurt me, and I didn't ask you about it. I took that hurt and put it up like a shield between us to protect myself. It was wrong of me and I hope you can forgive me."

He shook his head as though trying to clear it. "What did I say?"

She moved closer, brushing her pelvis against him. She sighed when his hands came out to skim the curve of her hips. "You told me if I disobeyed that you would allow every Dom on board to have a go at me."

Pure confusion was on his face now. "I explained that."

"Yes, you explained that you meant they could swat my arse. But that wasn't what I heard."

His hands tightened as realization seemed to dawn. "You

thought…you bloody well thought I would let them fuck you as a punishment? You thought I would let other men use you?"

She was probably in for a few bad moments because there was a righteous indignation in his tone. Perhaps he would handle it a bit better if she showed him just how sorry she was. She took a step back and found her position once more, spreading her legs as wide as she could and allowing her head to fall submissively forward. Her Master had been overstimulated. Between the torture she'd put him through and then all the terror at the church, he'd likely had enough.

"I asked you a question." Yes, his frustration was right there in his voice.

"Yes, Master. That's what I thought." Her arse was already starting to ache, and he hadn't even touched her yet. She let herself cry because it seemed to move him and because she was done with all the games. The day had been perfectly dreadful and she needed to cry, to let it all out. She loved this lifestyle. It had all gone badly when she had played it vanilla. Kink couples had to talk. They had to communicate about everything and she'd broken that rule.

His hand came down, fingers finding her chin and tipping her head up toward him. His face was tight as he looked down at her. "And you didn't think about talking to me about it? You thought I was the type of man who would share my submissive with every bloody cock in the place and you didn't once think about asking me why?"

Put like that it really did sound bad. "I thought about it, Master. Once. Perhaps twice."

"Those tears aren't going to save you. Are you mine?"

An easy question. "Yes."

"Say it again."

She smiled up at him. He really did like that particular word. "Yes."

He shook his head. "No. Not that. What you said before. I want to hear it again."

"I love you, Damon." She hoped he could see to her soul so he would know just how much she meant those words.

"I will never share you with anyone." His voice was rough with emotion. "Do you know what it took for me to not put a bullet in that arsehole who hit you today?"

It wouldn't ever matter that the man was defending himself. Damon would try to protect her, defend her, avenge her if need be. "I thank you, Master, for being so indulgent."

It had been an indulgence on his part, and now she could see how much he'd bent for her.

"Not again, Penelope. You will not go in the field again. There's no reason for it. Your gorgeous self is staying on this bloody boat until I come back for you. Is that understood?"

"But I was good in the field." Except for a sore shoulder where she'd hit the brick wall, she was perfectly fit.

"Penelope."

Just one word and she knew she'd pushed him to his limit. "Yes, Master. I'll stay on the boat or wherever you put me."

It was better that way. Damon spent all his time trying to keep her safe. He needed to focus on the job at hand.

"I don't like it when you won't talk to me."

Translation. *You hurt me.*

"I'm sorry, Master. I won't do it again."

"You have to tell me what you feel. It's important to D/s."

Translation. *I need honesty to feel close to you.*

"I promise. I'll be honest. Even when I'm hurt. Especially when I'm hurt because I don't think you ever mean to hurt me."

"I do mean to hurt your arse, Penelope."

Translation. *I'm horny, but I'll make you beg before you get my cock.* Yes, she was learning Damon's language quite nicely.

"I can handle it, Master." Her heart clenched a little at the smile that broke over his face.

"On the bed. All fours. I'm not going easy on you because you decided to cry prettily and apologize."

She scrambled to obey. That needed no translation, though she knew some of it was bluster. He'd never harmed her. His version of torture brought about the sweetest pleasures she'd ever known.

"I want you to understand something. After this is over, I'm not letting you go. You're mine, damn it, and it's going to stay that way.

You're going to keep that collar on forever. And if you ever take it off, you won't bloody well appreciate the spanking I give you. I swear every smack will be from my hand and when I get tired, I'll switch to the flogger." His hand came out, cupping her arse. "Who does this belong to?"

"It's yours, Master. It's all yours." Everything she had or was or had been belonged to him. Everything she would be was his. For as long as she lived.

She tried not to think about it any other way. Damon was reckless, stubborn. He would likely die long before her, but she wouldn't stop loving him. She would just wait until the day she could join him again.

He smacked her, his hand covering her cheek with heat and that flare of sensation that got her moaning. Once, twice, three times. "You will not shut me out." Four. Five and six. "You will talk to me when you're angry. I'm your Dom. I'm your lover. You will tell me what's wrong." Seven and eight and nine.

She thought about mentioning that what was wrong right now was that her arse was on fire, but decided to hold that bit back. "Yes, Master."

She cried, letting it all out. The day had been dreadful despite the fact that it had turned out all right. Now that she was here with him, she could let go.

"That's right, love. Let it all out. Let it go. You're safe now."

She lost track of the number of times he spanked her. It didn't matter. What mattered was their connection and the fact that she didn't have to hide her pain. She cried and cried, the tears purifying her in a way she'd never known possible.

After what seemed like forever, he stopped, pulling her up into his arms. He shifted her around.

"Don't ever leave me." Translation. *I love you. I missed you. I can't live without you.*

She saw him through her tears. She saw how vulnerable he was. He'd made himself vulnerable for her, only for her. "I love you, Damon. I won't ever leave you."

His mouth slammed on hers, his tongue surging inside. His arms caged her, holding her to his chest so her nipples rubbed against the fabric of his shirt. His hands moved lower, cupping the cheeks he'd recently set ablaze and dragging her against him, grinding his erection on her. "I need you."

"You have me." She let him press her down to the bed, the ache in her bum strangely erotic. She spread her legs, her pussy already wet and warm. The spanking got her primed for her Master.

He was up on his knees, staring down at her. "Do you know how beautiful you are to me?"

"You make me feel that way." No one else had ever made her feel like Damon did.

He tore at his slacks, his usual grace deserting him in the heat of the moment. He fumbled a bit, shoving them down and freeing his cock. "Don't think that just because I give you an orgasm means all is forgiven. You're going to be my slave tonight because it seems I'm going to be yours for the rest of my bloody life."

It was a fair exchange in her estimation.

He didn't bother to get undressed, merely tossed his shirt to the side and stroked his cock before falling on her.

He kissed her like a starving man, inhaling her. He made a place for himself between her legs, his cock homing in on where it wanted to be.

She gasped as he pushed his full length inside her in one long pass.

So full. It didn't matter how many times he fucked her, he always managed to take her breath away.

He held himself still, allowing her to get used to just how big he was. This was the moment that made all the bad stuff worthwhile. This moment when they were together, when nothing was between them.

"Take me." He pulled out and fucked his way back in. "Take everything I give you."

She reached up and let her hands find the muscular cheeks of his rear, her nails sinking in. If he hadn't tied her down, then she knew he wanted her with him. Her Master didn't want her still and silent when he fucked her. He wanted to make her moan. He wanted her passion, and she gave it to him.

All other thoughts fled. The world receded until it was only the two of them. They were all that mattered. Her and Damon.

He moaned and shoved in hard as she cupped his arse. He picked up the pace, slamming his pelvis against hers, hitting high inside her pussy even while he ground himself against her clit. "Come for me. You come for me, Penelope. My Penelope."

She worked his cock, straining for the pleasure she knew was waiting for her. Over and over again, he took her higher until his cock hit that magic spot and she went flying.

She cried out, letting the pleasure take her. The orgasm crashed into her like a rushing wave, sending heat through her veins.

Damon stiffened on top of her, his gorgeous face contorting. Another spark of pure sensation went through her as he flooded her with come, holding himself tight against her body, keeping them connected.

He collapsed against her, their chests nestling together. He kissed her again, his mouth lazy against hers.

"I'm not done, love. Not even close. I want everything. I'll have everything from you before the night is over," he whispered against her mouth. His tongue traced the seam of her lips, making her start to shiver and shake all over again.

Penelope sighed and wished the night would never end.

Chapter Twenty

Damon stared down at her body. Flushed with her recent orgasm, she was the most beautiful thing he'd ever seen.

And he really wanted to punish her some more.

"Turn over. Arse in the air." He was well aware his voice was harsh, but he couldn't seem to control it. Like all things when it came to Penelope Cash, he wasn't in control. Not really. He could play at it, but he'd been hers from the first moment he'd touched her, the first time he put his lips on hers and realized what it meant to kiss a woman with his whole being. He'd fought it, likely would still have a few battles with it, but he wasn't willing to ever walk away.

He could have it all. He could still work and he could have Penelope. All he had to do was be more careful. Knowing Penelope was waiting for him would make him think before he did reckless shit like today.

But she needed to understand that he could only be pushed so far.

She smiled up at him, a lazy gorgeous thing. "You're going to torture me, aren't you?" She flipped over, moving with a slow grace as if she wasn't really worried about what he would do. "I did say I was sorry."

He moved from the bed, but couldn't take his eyes off the way she presented herself to him. Her knees were wide, her cheeks in the air. He could see her labia. It was rich and creamy and still had his come coating it.

He was so hard he could barely breathe. He sent a small thanks to the universe that his heart could survive sex with her because he'd rather die than give it up.

"I require more than your apology." She'd put him through hell. It was stupid because he was a man who had actually been tortured by people who knew bloody well what they were doing, but he'd rather have his balls crushed by Afghan terrorists than spend another day thinking he'd broken her.

Her lips curled in a serene smile. "Yes, Master. What are you going to do to your poor sub?"

"I'm going to show you who's boss. I'm going to take that pretty arse and make it mine. No one else's. God, Penelope. How could you possibly think I would share you? I can't stand it when other men look at you." He kicked his pants and shorts to the side. He wouldn't need them for the rest of the night. He might just keep her naked and in bed until they reached Berlin.

He loved how she shivered. "Damon, I was insecure. I still am. I love you so much. I couldn't stand the thought that I meant nothing to you. I know that's wrong now. I won't make the same mistake, but you should know, my insecurities will likely come up again."

"Then I'll have to slap your arse silly until we get rid of them." How did he make her understand? How did he tell her that of the hundreds of women he'd slept with, she was the only one to really engage him? Well, for starters, he would never mention that there had been hundreds of women. He wasn't a bloody idiot. "I only want you, Penelope."

He grabbed his kit out of the drawer and found what he was looking for. He set aside the toys he would use later on the small bedside table and then pulled out his prize. He'd prepped a pretty purple plug for her. Her favorite color. It looked good on her. It would look damn fine forcing her tiny hole open in preparation for him. She'd slept with a plug a few nights when they were in London, but it was still so small, so tight. He would be the only man to ever touch her like this.

"That's good because I only want you, Damon."

He frowned her way. He was indulgent, but this was the only place he had any real control and he wasn't about to give it up. He swatted her arse, right down the middle. Her squeal made his dick jump. "What do you call me when I'm fucking you?"

"Master. I call you my Master."

"That's right." His sub. She was his and she would remain his. He reached down and touched the silver collar around her neck. He would replace it with something better, more expensive. His sub deserved diamonds. "Relax, Penelope. I'm going to open you up a bit."

He lubed up the plug and then took a look at the petite hole he was going to fuck. Pretty and pink, and so tight he could already feel it strangling his cock.

She took a deep breath in, and he loved the way her spine straightened as she waited for him. She didn't protest as he placed the plug against the rings of her hole, teasing it in tight circles.

He stared at that sweet hole, watching it fight him. He would win. She didn't stand a chance against him. Patience was all that was required, patience and a steady hand. He had both. "Tell me what you're feeling."

He loved to hear her talk about sex. She sounded like a dirty Victorian heroine.

"Pressure, Master. It feels weird and jangly and I don't want it, but I know I really do."

Because she trusted him. Because she knew he wouldn't hurt her. He pressed in a bit, gaining a centimeter before drawing the plug back out again. Her gasp of relief was short-lived because he pushed the plastic back in, deeper this time.

"I'm larger than the plug, Penelope."

"I know that. Believe me, Master, I'm thinking about that fact right this very minute." She panted a bit as he rounded the plug's tip around her, the rings of her muscles tightening in a vain attempt to keep it out.

"I'll fit, love. I'll fit just fine." His dick strained up, pre-come pulsing from his slit. He'd had her not five minutes before and he was already dying to be inside her again. He couldn't imagine a time when he wouldn't be desperate for her.

He pressed in again, her hole opening beautifully and the plug sliding in halfway. He held it there, allowing her to get used to the feeling. "I can fuck you with the plug inside and you'll be so full. You'll be packed tight and you'll scream for your Master."

She moaned as he forced the plug deep, burying it inside to the flat head that kept it anchored.

"Turn over. Don't you lose that plug or I'll know you need a bigger one."

She moved carefully, gingerly twisting her body while clenching her cheeks together. The expression on her face was so sweet as she concentrated on doing his biding.

And she looked scrumptious. He hadn't eaten all day. Not speaking to her had set off his appetite, but now it was back with a vengeance. "Spread your legs."

"Master, if I spread my legs, I'll likely lose the plug."

Ah, the joys of torture. "That's exactly what I intend for you to do, love. I intend for you to lose that plug and then I'll smack your arse and maybe get out the ginger lube. That will teach you not to lose my plug." He climbed on the bed, letting his hands slide up her legs. Curvy and petite. He loved how small she was compared to him. Feminine and yet solid. She could handle everything he wanted to give her.

Her whole body tightened. "You want me to fail. You want to punish me."

It was his nature, but he liked a fair fight for the most part. "If you concentrate very hard, you can keep it in." He licked his lips as he stared down at her pussy. So pretty.

A little laugh huffed out, making her chest rise and fall, her nipples peak. "You're going to make it hell for me to concentrate, aren't you?"

No one ever said she wasn't smart. He moved her legs apart, cautiously, giving her the chance to adjust. Now that he was here, he kind of wanted to see her succeed. She was biting her lip, trying so hard. She tackled tasks he set for her with the single-minded determination of a pure type-A personality.

"Oh, yes, love. We're going to play a game. I'm going to lick you and suck on your clit. I'm going to bite your nipples and make a feast of you, and if you keep the plug in, you'll get a prize. If you don't, you'll get a bigger plug."

"And what does my Master get?"

"Oh, your Master gets to taste you, and either way he's still going to shove his cock in your virgin arse and fill you with his come." He had to admit, the game was stacked in his favor. Either way, he won.

His cock split her labia, resting against her clit as he stared down at her. The eager bugger wanted back in, but he wasn't in charge right now. Damon reached down and palmed her breasts, cupping them before he took her nipples between his fingers. He had more toys to torture her with.

"I think you're beautiful, love. I mean for you to understand that. You'll be even prettier with a bit of jewelry." He reached for the clamps he'd set up. Tweezer clamps with a T-chain running through them.

"Oh, Master." Her face tightened as he rubbed her nipples between his thumb and forefinger.

He leaned over and tongued her nipple, loving the way her skin tasted, inhaling her clean, feminine scent. He sucked the tip into his mouth, pulling hard. Her body tightened under his, her skin heating up. She moaned a little, her legs restless.

He switched to the other nipple, tonguing and sucking. When he was satisfied with her squirming, he got back to his knees. He took her nipple in his fingers and pinched down, bringing the blood to her peak before slipping the clamp on.

She gasped, her eyes widening.

"Very nice." He played with the opposite nipple, toying with it before attaching the jewel. "See. You don't need anything else. Well, maybe one more thing."

He held up the final clamp, perfectly satisfied with the way her eyes widened.

"Where does that go, Master?" She asked the question with the deep suspicion of one who worried she already knew.

There was no point in telling her when he could show her. He got to his belly because he wasn't going to pay any less attention to her clitoris than he had her nipples. It deserved some love before he tortured it.

He licked her clit, a long, slow pass of his tongue. He could still taste himself on her, knew his come would be inside her for a good long while.

"Master. Please, Master," she panted out her pleas.

That was what he wanted to hear. He wanted her breathy cries, wanted her desperation. He wanted to hear her beg him. He wanted her so far from any worries or cares that all that existed in her head was pleasure.

He suckled her, letting his fingers part her flesh. She was still so wet, so warm and soft from her previous orgasm. Her clit was swollen, extended from behind its hood. It poked out, desperate for another bout of pleasure.

But he wasn't giving it to her just yet.

He suckled her, taking her clit between his teeth and biting down gently.

She screamed. "Please. Please, Damon. Please more."

And she graciously gave him the chance to punish her. He reached up and gently pulled the chain, making the clamps bite into her nipples.

Penelope gasped, losing her breath. "Master. Master. I meant Master."

"Then you should say Master, love." He gave it one more yank before setting it back down. The T-shaped chain looked beautiful against her skin. He smoothed it out, drawing the lower line down her sweetly curved belly toward the place where he would soon clip it to the final piece of jewelry. "For a woman who speaks so many languages, you seem to have a bit of trouble with English."

"As long as I speak Damon Knight fluently, I think I'll be all right, Master."

So he spoke a different language, did he? She was probably right and he was fine with it. As long as Penelope could understand it, he didn't give a damn if anyone else could.

"Are they too tight?" He focused on her clit again.

"They're making me crazy, Master. It feels like you're everywhere."

That was the point. He wanted her aware of him. In her nipples, her pussy, her arse. He wanted to touch her everywhere at once.

He suckled her clit one last time before easing the clamp on. Very gently, he tightened it until it was a pearly jewel, throbbing just for him.

He got to his knees, looking down on his work. She was writhing, her muscles clenching, her pretty face desperate but filled with trust. She wasn't fighting him. She was waiting for his pleasure, his discipline, anything he wanted to give her.

No one had ever trusted him the way Penelope did, and he had to do everything in his power to be worthy of that trust.

He couldn't do that if he was bloody well dead because he wasn't smart enough to know when to hang it up.

He shoved the thought away because he didn't have to make any decisions now. He couldn't imagine not being an operative, but he also couldn't imagine life without her. The job required long times away from home. The job sometimes required him to fuck for information.

He couldn't ever take another woman. How was he supposed to fuck a target and then come home to Penelope?

"Master? Don't. Not now." She reached for him. "Stay with me."

She understood him, saw him in a way no one else could, not even himself. She knew when he was drifting and knew how to bring him back. He had to make a few things clear. He touched the chain, tracing it with his fingertips. The metal was cool and her skin warm. The chain twinkled with polished beauty but she was the real gem. He'd been so cold, hard, until he'd managed to fasten himself around her warm heart. "I won't let you down. We have things to work out, but I won't let you down. Not ever."

Her hands covered his, holding the chain to her body. "Say it,

Damon. Say the words for me."

He frowned. He knew what she wanted. He just didn't know if he should give them to her, didn't know if it was right. "Penelope, I'm not sure that I believe them. I want you. I care for you. I need you."

"You don't have to believe them. I believe them. Damon, I can love enough for both of us. Say them. Say them for me. Say them because I need to hear them."

When she put it like that, he couldn't refuse. "I love you, Penelope."

"I love you, my Master." The tears shining in her eyes were worth the little lie.

If it was a lie. Maybe he just didn't understand. She'd said she spoke his language. He should try to speak hers. "I love you. I love you."

Maybe, if he said it enough, he would believe it. Maybe he would believe he was capable of more than fighting and killing, that he was capable of nurturing her, of giving her a home she could be happy in.

Maybe if he said it enough, he would believe he could give her a family.

He couldn't hold back a moment longer. She'd been a good girl. She'd held the plug through everything. She'd been steadfast.

"Turn over for me." He helped her turn over, getting her to her hands and knees.

"Oh, god, Master. The chain."

It was pulling on her, forcing her to focus on her nipples and her clit. "Tell me if it hurts."

Her back moved with a chuckle. "It hurts. It aches. I need more."

She was perfect for him. And he would give her so much more. He reached for the lube, finally able to give his dick some small relief. He lubed up his hand and stroked himself, preparing for her. He gently pulled out the plug, watching her hole struggling to keep it now. He brought it out by the base and placed it on the stand, his whole being focused on making this good for her.

He needed to take her every way he could, to push past any

barriers that were still between them. He wanted to bind her to him in every way a man could bind a woman.

With a long sigh, he pressed the head of his cock against her sweetly puckered hole. She moaned as he rimmed her with his dick.

"Open for me. I won't let you keep me out. Press back against me. Take me inside, Penelope." Heat was already coursing through his system. The pressure was building and he wasn't inside her yet.

Penelope straightened her back, her arse moving toward him.

He slipped inside, just a bit, but he wouldn't give up his territory. With ruthless intent, he gripped her hips and began to impale her on his cock, the tight hole fighting him all the way.

He fucked his way inside, her muscles already threatening to milk his dick.

She clenched around him. Pleasure raced along his skin. Little thrusts. He kept them tight, giving her time to adjust to his size. His whole consciousness faded to the point where only their connection mattered. His whole world was Penelope and the pleasure they shared.

"Master. I can't. You're too big."

He reached down and jingled the chain and she cried out again. He slid home. "You can handle me."

Her head fell forward. "You're killing me. I'm so full. I can't breathe. I can't even think."

Because he was stimulating her everywhere. He pulled the chain gently, toying with her clit. Penelope responded with a low moan, clenching around him. "I don't want you to think. I want you to feel. Feel me."

"I can't feel anything else. Oh, god, Master. Please move. You have to move. If you would just move I think…"

She could breathe? Oh, he was going to show her. He dragged his cock slowly back out.

"Oh, my god." Her whole spine straightened, her body moving back toward him, trying to get his dick back, fighting for the sensation. "It feels so good."

That was what he wanted to hear. He pulled out so just the tip of his cock remained within the tight ring of her muscles. He stroked her back, soothing her as he tilted his pelvis up and fucked his way back in.

He gave over to the pleasure, moving in and out of her, letting the world fall away because nothing else mattered. He lost himself in her, giving and receiving pleasure because she was his.

He finally understood that meant he was hers. He belonged to Penelope Cash and that was a good thing. Before her, the power exchange had been a mere transfer of responsibilities. It was a contract that could be easily broken.

He could never break with her. He could never be complete without her.

Damon felt her body shake with her orgasm. She called out his name over and over. Damon. Not Master. He wouldn't punish her because in that moment he was hers. Her Damon. He'd hidden behind Master because he understood the role in a way he'd never understood himself.

Now he realized he liked being Penny's Damon. He wasn't exactly sure who that man was, but he intended to find out.

The minute she relaxed beneath him, he let go. His balls drew up, come exploding from him in a hot wash of joy and pleasure and connection unlike anything he'd felt before. He pumped into her until he had nothing left to give.

Peace settled on him as he moved out of her, drawing her to her side as he fell to the bed. He settled her on her back, admiring the way her skin flushed and her breasts moved with the force of her breaths.

He hated to do it, wanted to see the marks of his possession on her always, but he couldn't leave them there.

He slipped the first clamp off, delighting in her squeal and the way she squirmed as he eased the pain with his tongue and lips. He moved to her other nipple, and she didn't fight him at all. Her hands found his hair, holding him to her breast.

"I love you, Master."

He looked up at her. "Damon."

A soft smile spread on her lips. Her hands smoothed his hair back. "I love you, Damon."

"I love you, Penelope." The words came easier.

He rather thought that had been her point in making him say them. He chuckled as he kissed his way down the chain.

* * * *

Two days later, Penny sat in the suite Damon had rented for her and the rest of the team in Berlin. She wished she could spend time enjoying the city, but it looked like this would be a very short trip. After a three-hour train ride from the cruise terminal, Damon still wasn't done going over and over all the logistics with the afternoon's operation. Penny gave her Master her surest smile. He was so nervous. It made him a bit crabby with everyone.

"Do you understand what I'll do if anyone deviates from the plan?" Damon asked, looking sternly at the man and women assigned to keep her company.

Damon had told her it was so she wouldn't be lonely, but she rather thought he was leaving them behind as bodyguards.

"Yeah, yeah, you'll murder me in cold blood," Simon Weston said, rolling his eyes. He turned to Ian Taggart. "Why am I babysitting the women?"

"Because Jake let the girls run wild last time," Taggart announced.

"Hey, I could stay behind. I'm good at watching a couple of pretty ladies." Brody Carter looked a bit more cheerful without his hands cuffed behind his back and his mouth ball gag free.

The Aussie had proven perfectly charming once he realized they weren't the enemy. They had been careful to keep him in one of the cabins and out of the sight of the ship's many cameras just in case. He seemed to spend all of his time either eating massive quantities of food or working out. She had to admit she and Charlotte had spent a nice afternoon watching him do one-armed pushups. He was a lovely man.

But she would never let her Master know it. He was a tad possessive.

"I believe you're required at today's mission. I think Mr.

Bennett would be a tad surprised if you didn't show up," Penelope said. She put a hand on Damon's shoulder. She'd discovered she could calm him down by touching him.

She'd had to do a lot of calming during their days at sea. When he wasn't on top of her, he was pretty much coming up with all the ways the mission could go wrong and she could die. She'd had to promise to stay at the hotel in Berlin. Then he and Taggart had decided that Charlotte should stay with her.

Now she and Charlotte needed a bodyguard and they'd decided Jake was too indulgent.

"I'm merely saying I could be more helpful in the field," Simon said with a frown. "Charlotte can handle this. For that matter, Penny is quite smart. I think she can bloody well lock her door and stay in her room."

Ian frowned his wife's way. "Leaving Charlotte in charge is a very bad idea. She could blow up the hotel while we're gone."

Charlotte smiled. "I would yell at him but he's right. I can't help it. It's fun to cause trouble."

"And he's not watching me." Chelsea shot Damon a grumpy look. She was nearly lost behind a mountain of computer equipment she was hooking up. "I don't need a bodyguard."

"I'll make sure Simon knows he can let you die," Taggart said.

Chelsea sent him her middle finger. "When I hack into the CCTVs, if I see you being horribly murdered on one, I'm just going to watch, asshole."

Charlotte rolled her eyes. "You two make my life complete."

God, she hoped her brother and sister got on with Damon. "I really would be all right here with Chelsea. I can help her monitor the CCTVs. I promise I won't try anything crazy."

Candice looked up from her computer. "I would feel better if we had a man with us."

Chelsea rolled her eyes. "Why isn't she at the airport?"

"Because Walt wanted to talk to her," Brody replied. "And I don't like the thought of her being on her own, what with that boyfriend of hers up and leaving like he did. She cried all day when she found out he left the boat in Helsinki. We have to protect her.

That bastard in Finland knows what she looks like."

Candice smiled the Aussie's way. "At least there are some real gentlemen left. Like I said, I would actually feel better with two guards. I think you're going to scare Walter off if he sees too many of you."

"He won't realize we're not tourists. Now if you're all done complaining about the plan, let's go over it again," Damon said.

The room groaned collectively.

"I just think it's a little sexist," Charlotte said. "You're leaving the women behind. What if Walter Bennett would feel better talking to a woman? We're far less threatening."

"And far more unpredictable," Ian said. "No. You stay, Charlie. After that shit you pulled with the van last time, it's going to be a while before I let you go into the field alone again."

Charlotte stood up. "We wouldn't have Brody if I hadn't pulled that shit with the van."

The Taggarts squared off. "We damn near lost Damon because of it. And you and Penny are staying behind because Damon and I can't think about a goddamn thing but our women when you're in danger."

Charlotte softened. "Oh, sweetie. See, you can learn." She went on her toes and kissed her husband. "Fine. Penny, Candice, and I will get in-room massages. I didn't even get to go to the spa on the boat. Oh, and let's order room service. SIS is paying, right?"

Penny needed to calm her Dom down. She put a hand in his and nodded to Charlotte. "Why don't you go ahead and call for tea? Simon takes his with milk and sugar. The least we can do is properly feed our poor guard. I'm going to say good-bye to this one."

The men had to leave in fifteen minutes. She didn't like the thought of Damon out there, but she had to get used to it. He wasn't going to stop working anytime soon. She would spend every day they were apart worried that he wouldn't come home, but she was determined to not waste the time they did have.

She led him back to the bedroom. He was dressed in khakis and a polo, ready to blend in with the rest of the tourists who would throng around Berlin's sights. "Calm down."

He stopped, staring down at her. "Is that any way to talk to your Master?"

Oh, he was on edge. She gave him her big sub eyes and bit her bottom lip. She'd noticed it seemed to do something for him. He'd kept her in bed for almost two days. She'd learned a lot about how to distract him from his troubles. "I'm sorry, Master."

He sighed, his head shaking ruefully. "You're going to be the death of me."

She hated that word. She wrapped her arms around him, praying she didn't have to hear the word "death" for a long while. "You'll be careful?"

His heart beat against her ear. The steady sound had become her whole world. His hand soothed down her back. "I think it's going to be all right, love. Carter is sure he can talk Walter into coming in. He called Candice because he got it in his head that they couldn't touch him if he went public. We're going to convince him there's another way. He can talk to the press without giving away the information."

"I just want you back safe."

He tilted her head up. "I will be back before you can finish your tea. And dear god, don't let Charlotte bankrupt me. I don't think Nigel will let me expense personal masseuses."

A long moment passed between them.

"I love you, Penelope." He said it without prompting now. She'd read somewhere that it took a human being about eight times to memorize something, to commit it to memory. Damon seemed to be well on his way.

"I love you, too." It was so easy now. He'd been tentative at first. His face would tighten every time she said it, ask her to say it again. Now he often said the words first.

He was educable, her Dom.

There was a knock on the door and Taggart's voice came through. "Damon, we need to go."

His eyes closed briefly and he put his forehead to hers. "I won't be long. In a couple of hours this is all over, and we'll get on a plane for London tonight. We'll be back in The Garden before you know it. You're living with me now, you know."

She smiled. He couldn't help but be a bit bossy. "Well, I better because I don't have anywhere else to go."

His arms tightened. "Your place is with me."

She nodded. Her place was with him for as long as they had. She didn't mention that if he kept it up, she might be a widow before her time.

Her arms wound around him. She wouldn't think that way.

He kissed her again and then he was gone, walking out the door with Brody Carter, Taggart, Jake, and Jesse. He would stay close to the Aussie. The others would be in the area, staking the place out.

And she was going to spend the entire afternoon worrying.

There was nothing for it. This was the way her life would be from now on. She would kiss him and send him off and pray he came home to her. Women had been doing it from the beginning of humanity. They sent their warriors off with a heavy heart. Unfortunately, her warrior had a damaged one, but that wasn't a fight she could win.

She stood by the window overlooking the magnificent Brandenburg Gate. The *Platz* surrounding it was mobbed with tourists out on a lovely summer day. The sun shone, making everything around it seem crisp and clean.

"He's going to be okay." Charlotte put an arm around her, leaning into her as she looked down as well. "He's not going in alone. Ian will watch his back."

But Taggart wouldn't always be there to watch his back. Perhaps if Taggart and his crew were around, she would feel better. But they would be back in America and Damon would be on his own. Still, she nodded, not wanting to spend the next few hours crying.

"Ladies, the tea should be here in a moment." Simon smiled at her, seeming to forget the fact that he'd railed at being left to babysit. "Chelsea, how many headphones do you have?"

Chelsea's eyes came up warily, as if Simon was a tiger who would attack at any moment. "Two or three, but only two that have communication capability. If you want to sit in front of that monitor, you can talk to them through these."

She held out a pair of state-of-the-art headphones that would be connected to the communication devices each member of the team had placed in their ears before they left. Simon reached out, his hands brushing hers as he took the headphones from her. Their fingers touched, lingering slightly before Chelsea pulled away and her shell came snapping back down.

"Thank you," Simon said in his smoothest tones.

Chelsea frowned. "Don't screw up my system."

Charlotte groaned, shaking her head. "You really know how to make a moment special, sis."

"That's not my job." She touched something on her computer and then she wasn't talking to the people in the room anymore. "I've taken over the few CCTVs here. Apparently this is a country that doesn't like being watched. Something about the former USSR and occupation and crap. Get over it, people. How can I watch you if you don't have cameras everywhere? Get me back to England."

"What coverage do you have?" Penelope asked, not wanting to debate the long history of abuse of power that had plagued Germans from World War II until the Berlin Wall had come down.

"Well, it's shit. It's mostly from private shop owners but I can get some coverage. Satan, I have you in my sights. I can see Jesse. I've lost Damon and the big guy. No. I have them. And they're gone." Chelsea groaned her frustration.

Simon put the headphones on, chuckling lightly. "Thank you so much for leaving me here, Tag. I'll pay you back somehow. No. We're not going to be able to see the meet. There's no camera there. We can't see anything but the area around the memorial."

Chelsea stiffened suddenly. "Oh, shit."

"What?" Penny asked.

Chelsea shook her head. "Probably nothing."

Simon frowned her way, pulling his headphones off. "What is it, Chelsea?"

She bit her bottom lip, her hands flying across the keys of her laptop. "I couldn't monitor all the sites I would normally monitor while I was on the boat. I was stuck with their crappy Internet and downloading the proper browser onto their systems would have outed me."

"They don't use Google?" Penny asked.

Chelsea snorted slightly. "Google is a search engine, hon. I'm talking about a browser and not the kind a normal person uses."

"I thought you gave up brokering information." Simon stood up, looking perfectly ready to discipline her.

Charlotte held a hand up. "Whoa, boy. Ian asked her to monitor some of the old sites. He wants to have an ear to the ground."

"But it's not the ground she's monitoring," Simon argued. "She's on the Deep Web. He's got her out there with terrorists and traffickers."

"And intelligence agencies," Chelsea pointed out. "I can handle myself, Weston. But unfortunately Walter Bennett can't. Mother flying fucker. Someone's been talking." She closed her eyes briefly before touching the button that connected her to the team. "Damon, you might have a problem. I can't promise anything, but the Agency and MI6 aren't the only interested parties anymore. And there have been hits on your information and Tag's. Sixteen in the last twenty-four hours. And I'm finding chatter about the boat and Berlin."

Penny's stomach dropped. If the word was out, there would likely be several governments and organizations who would love to have the information Walter Bennett was offering.

There was a knock on the door. Candice seemed lost in her computer. Charlotte was staring at the monitors. It looked like she got to play hostess. Simon and Chelsea were talking about all the ramifications of trying to get Bennett out of the country if other agencies were after him as well.

She clenched her fists. It was hard to be the only one without a task. Well, she was British and they damn well knew how to handle a crisis. Tea. There was nothing she could do except make sure everyone remained calm, and tea would help.

Penny stepped out of the main room of the suite and answered the door. She ushered in the room service men.

They pushed a cart along. A cart they needed to push into the suite, and then there might be questions about why they had an army of computers set up. No one had thought of that. *Yes, thank you, Super Spies.* She gave the two men her best smile.

"I'll handle it. Sorry, I'm afraid my husband isn't completely dressed, if you know what I mean." Better to let them think she was having an orgy than spying. She initialed the bill and left them a decent tip, hoping they wouldn't walk away talking about the crazy Brits and their sex party. The last thing she needed now was a curious staff.

"Of course, Miss Cash," the larger of the two men said in heavily accented German as he turned and left. She locked the door behind them.

She pushed the cart through the marbled foyer and into the main room. Everything smelled delightful but she doubted she could eat a thing.

Candice looked up, closing the top of her computer. "I'll help you."

"Who do we think is interested?" Simon was asking. He had his headset on so she couldn't hear the other side of the conversation. She imagined Damon was using a lot of curse words.

"Definitely the Germans. God, I can't even pronounce that," Chelsea complained.

"*Bundesnachrichtendienst*," Penny said, looking at the screen. Chelsea had pulled up what looked like a series of messages written in German.

Chelsea sighed. "Oh, I forgot. Penny, please come work with us. It would take me forever to run that through damn translation software, and half the time it comes out as gobbledygook. I'll print it out so you can see it more easily."

Thank god, something she could do. "All right." She could already hear the small printer starting to spit out paper. "I speak most of the Northern European languages. I'm starting to learn Mandarin and Pashtun. I'm not excellent at either but I can likely pull enough information out."

Candice set a cup of tea in front of Simon, who immediately took a long sip. She passed out the rest, pouring it with the expert hand of a woman who had served more than a few times.

Charlotte shook her head. "I'd rather have the coffee. I know. I'm a horrible American. I'll get it."

Candice shook her head. "I don't mind. I can't do much else. Cream and sugar?"

Penny pulled the printout into her hands and immediately started working. She walked out toward the balcony. The rest of the group was talking and she needed some silence.

Warm sun stroked her skin as she looked down at the words, her mind making sense of the puzzle.

What Chelsea had found was the discussion between two operatives about something they had heard from informants. One of Walter's colleagues had been talking. A woman. She sighed. Walter had kept in contact with a German woman from his lab, and she'd reached out to the authorities with what he'd told her.

Damn it. She also knew he would be in Berlin today. She was going to have to call Nigel and likely get more than just SIS involved. This could become an international incident.

She looked out over the *Platz*, wishing she could catch sight of Damon. He was in such danger. He was an intelligence operative working on foreign soil. If the Germans caught him, he would at least be in for a long, possibly uncomfortable interview. If Nigel wasn't willing to negotiate for him, Damon might disappear. It wouldn't matter that England and Germany weren't enemies. No one would want to admit they had the information on the bioweapon.

How had the waiter known her name?

The question flipped through her brain, stopping all other thought. The suite was under an assumed name. Damon had paid for it with a safe card, one set up with SIS. Her name hadn't been involved in any way.

Yet he'd thanked her as Miss Cash.

Bugger, the Germans were already here.

She pushed through the door and then her stomach threatened to roll.

Simon was slumped over the desk, his tea dripping onto the carpet below. Chelsea's head was thrown back. Charlotte had slipped to the floor.

Not a one of them was conscious. *Please don't let them be dead.*

"You really should have some tea," Candice said. She stood in the middle of the room, a gun in her hand. Though her voice shook slightly, she held the gun like she knew what she was doing.

"Did you kill them?" Tears filled her eyes, but she was determined to remain calm. She had to figure a way out of this. She could handle Candice. She had to.

"No. They're just asleep and you should be, too. I don't want to do this, but do you understand how hard it is to move up in my world? If you aren't gorgeous and don't have great connections, you end up on some bloody town paper reporting nonsense about local gentry. That's not going to happen to me."

"Miss Jones is getting a promotion. You see, my employers run several of the world's largest news agencies," a familiar voice said.

Terror threatened to take over. She wasn't dealing with German intelligence. Oh, it was so much worse.

Basil Champion stepped into the room.

"Hello, Damon's whore. It's so good to see you again."

Chapter Twenty-One

Damon tapped the communications device in his ear. "Chelsea? Are you there?"

"Hey, I hate to pull you away from all your talk, but Walt's going to be here any minute, and he might run if he hears you talking to your bloody self," Carter said.

Technology could be so frustrating. He forced himself to focus. Chelsea would get it back on line. She seemed very competent. And he had to hope they weren't supremely fucked. "We have a slight change of plans."

He needed to keep the Aussie calm.

Carter couldn't help but draw some notice. The man was at least six foot seven. Germans weren't small people, but everyone looked a bit tiny compared to the Aussie. Damon wasn't used to being forced to look up at anyone. "What's gone wrong? Damn it. He should be here any minute."

"We're going to need to get him to the embassy." Both the British and the American Embassies were in the plaza behind the Brandenburg Gate. The American was closest and Taggart had informed him that Tennessee Smith was inside, awaiting the outcome. Or more than likely waiting to see if he could get his hands on the package. Apparently he wasn't the only one.

Damon had to hope their plan went down properly. The addition of the American operative put a kink in everything, but Ian assured him that Ten was in. Tag and Tennessee had spoken during the train ride to Berlin. Jesse and Jake were ready to do what needed to be done. They'd been forced to think on their feet. Not even the women knew what he and Ian had decided to do.

Which was good, because some people might consider what they were about to do treason.

Brody Carter wouldn't. He'd been the one to come up with the plan in the first place. Too often soldiers only followed orders and not their consciences. This was not going to be one of those times.

"The Germans are looking for Walter. And they very likely aren't the only ones. Before our system went out, Chelsea said she found some communications between Walter and some German woman."

Carter cursed, pulling on his ball cap as he shook his head. "Horny bugger. I told him he couldn't contact anyone. Damn it. She worked in his department."

"The good news is she didn't knowingly work for The Collective. The bad news? She decided to inform on him to her government. I can't imagine this hasn't gotten out. We have to get Walter to the embassy. We could all find ourselves in a German holding tank talking to their intelligence, and they will get him to hand over the goods."

What Walter Bennett had in his hands was a weapon of mass destruction. Every government in the world would want it. Every single one of them would kill to get it or keep it out of every other country's hands.

Carter nodded. "All right. We have to find him first. I don't know what the fuck this is."

Damon stared out over the Holocaust Memorial, understanding a bit of Carter's confusion. The Memorial to the Murdered Jews of Europe, as its designer had named it, consisted of over 2700 concrete slabs in a grid pattern. From the outside everything looked uniform, as though the slabs were all of the same height. It was very different when Damon walked through to get to the other side. The ground was uneven, sloping in places. One moment he could easily see the tops, and the next he'd been staring up as though he'd gone underground. He'd walked a straight line to the other side but if he'd gone even once off the line, he would have found himself lost.

That massive maze stood between him and the embassy. He wondered what else would be in the way.

Jake Dean walked by, his eyes on a map of the city. "Comm's down."

"Yes, I got that."

"Jesse's going back to the hotel. Ian doesn't like it. He can't get Simon to answer his cell."

A cold tendril of fear laced through him. "Penelope?"

"Not answering hers either." Jake put his phone to his ear, looking for all the world like he was talking to someone on the other end. "You handle this. We're going to figure out the rest. Tag's on the other side of the…whatever it is. I've got to move to the embassy in case we actually get the package. I have to be in place or this could all go to hell."

"Do you have what you need?" Jake was very important to the plan. He had to be in place.

Jake nodded. "Yes. When Jesse calls, we'll let you know what's happening."

He couldn't panic. Panic was what whoever was causing the disruption wanted him to do. Weston was deadly. If someone attacked the suite, he would likely be able to handle it. For that matter, Charlotte Taggart wasn't exactly a shrinking violet.

And neither was his Penelope. She'd killed a man when she had to. She could do it again.

"There he is." Carter sighed beside him. "God, it's a miracle he hasn't got himself murdered by now."

Carter stepped away, moving toward the trees that lined the road, and Damon got his first look at Walter Bennett. The scientist was a lanky man, looked more like a kid really. Though he knew Bennett was in his thirties, his face was younger, more open than any man who had managed to create one of the deadliest bioweapons in the world should look.

Damon turned away, not wanting to scare the man off, but he strained to listen. He had to stay close because Taggart had no idea the target had arrived. Dean had moved out of his sight line, likely doing long turns around the memorial.

"What the hell happened? I nearly freaked when you didn't call after Helsinki," Bennett said.

"I ran into a bit of a mess. And you're in further than you realize. Why the hell did you talk to Heidi?" Carter sounded brutally annoyed.

"I was lonely," Bennett whined. "I've been hiding here for weeks. I missed her."

God, Carter should have made sure the poor guy got laid because he couldn't seem to go for very long.

"She called the Germans," Carter shot back. "Their intelligence is looking for you. If they know where you are, it's likely The Collective does, too."

"Fuck. What are we going to do?"

Carter sighed. "You're going to listen to a friend of mine. I've got a security team around you."

Damon turned. Walter was starting to back up.

Carter got a hand on him. "Don't try to run. You're paying me to keep you alive and that's bloody well what I'm going to do. I'm going to keep you alive even if it kills me. This man is British intelligence. He wants us to walk over to the embassy."

Walter went pale. "I can't. I can't give this information up to a government."

"But you were willing to give it to the Internet?" It was time to point out a few things to the very naïve scientist. And it was also time to get out of sight. He nodded toward the memorial. The good news about a maze was everyone tended to get lost.

Carter entered first, hauling Walter along easily.

"If everyone has it, then we all have mutually assured destruction," Walter said, his feet tripping slightly as they started on a downward slope.

"That might work when it's two or three superpowers who have nuclear arms," Damon explained. "I'm going to suspect this is easier to get hands on than uranium and a hell of a lot easier to deliver a payload. If you turn it over to a reporter and it gets out, every extremist group in the world will be cooking up smallpox and unleashing it on their enemies."

"I guess I hadn't thought of it that way. God, that sounds horrible. I still don't think I should give it to the British, though. I'm an American."

Damon moved carefully toward the other side. He caught a glimpse of something metallic and turned. A man was moving past, roughly ten rows down. He was holding a Ruger.

So the Germans were here. He would bet his life that man was German intelligence. The man disappeared behind the columns as he moved away.

Damon needed to hurry this along. Carter's eyes had widened. He seemed to have caught the threat, too.

"Nothing is going to matter if we don't get you out of here now. The Germans likely don't want to hurt any of us. They don't particularly want an international incident, but they aren't bloody stupid. They can't allow this information to fall into our hands any more than we can let it fall into theirs. We have one shot. We get to the embassy and then I'll find a way to destroy it. No one should have it. No one."

He would probably lose his job, but that didn't sound so terrible anymore. He would try to play it off as incompetence and not a brutal lie.

Of course he had to get to the embassy first. "Do you have the package?"

Walter frowned, though he seemed to be walking on his own now. "Yeah." He reached into his pants pocket and pulled out a thumb drive. "I brought it with me. I kind of want to get rid of it altogether. I wish I'd never worked on it. It was a puzzle. I've never been able to turn down a puzzle."

Damon didn't care. He just wanted this whole thing over with so he could figure out what had happened with the communications.

"*Wir haben sie gefunden,*" a masculine voice shouted.

Damon turned to his right, and one of the German agents was

moving their way.

"Let's go," he said. He ran forward, turning to the right and then the left.

"We can't get lost in here if we stay together and we bloody well need to get lost," Carter said. "Give him the package."

Walter's eyes widened. "You really trust him?"

"I trust the man he's with and he tells me to trust this bloke. I also think his girl would kick his arse if he didn't do the right thing." Carter put his back against one of the slabs. "We need to split up. There are two things they want. They want the package and they want what made the package. It's still in Walt's head."

"Shit." Walt's hands shook as he passed the thumb drive over. "I wish I never did this."

Scientists had been saying that since they realized their work could be used for mass destruction. They still did it. Damon grabbed the thumb drive. The lives of thousands, maybe millions, were on that drive, and he had to figure out a way to destroy it. He and Taggart had decided hiding it wasn't good enough. They could hide Walter, but the physical information had to be destroyed.

"*Halt!*" A tall man started running toward them.

There wasn't time to debate.

"Get to the embassy if you can or somewhere safe. He needs to disappear." Damon moved again, running into a tourist and forcing his way by. Maybe if they split up the Germans, their odds would increase.

He needed to find Taggart, needed to know Jesse had made it to the suite and everything was fine.

He also had to hope German intelligence wanted to keep this as quiet as the rest of them or there would be a line of cops waiting for him when he hit the street and started for the embassy. He jogged, the world a gray blur on either side of him.

And then his comm came back online. "Hello, Damon."

Baz. He would know the voice anywhere.

He stopped, touching his comm so he could talk. "What the hell are you doing on this line?"

"Oh, I thought it was probably time to talk. After all we've got some business to do. You're going to bring me the package and I'm going to trade for something you like."

His blood went cold. "What?"

"Oh, my gorgeous boy. I think you know."

He did. Baz had Penny, and he was out of options.

* * * *

Penny closed her eyes against the bright light of day as she was pulled out of the van Baz had shoved her in.

"Do you remember what our deal is, love?" Baz asked, his voice silky and smooth. He was dressed for the occasion in slacks and a sport coat, his eyes hidden behind a pair of aviators.

She forced herself to nod. She'd come quietly because he'd been willing to not put bullets in the unconscious team members' heads. "I do."

"Excellent. Because I have friends who can finish the job if I call them. I actually feel a bit sick that I didn't take the chance and off Weston. I always hated that bastard. So far above the rest of us."

"The waiters."

"What?" Baz shook his head and then it cleared. "Yes, of course. The waiters." He stepped behind her. "Of course I could always just shoot you, but I think Damon wants you warm."

She had no doubt that Baz would prefer to murder her in front of Damon.

Baz shoved her a little. "You better hope that your lover isn't lying about having the package."

"You better hope that the German intelligence agents aren't waiting for you." She stumbled but managed to keep on her feet.

"What are you talking about?"

He didn't know? The word about Champion had always been that he could be hyper focused to the point that he missed things he shouldn't. He tended to work alone. He might not know.

"Nothing." She wasn't going to hand him information. "I'm sure if Damon says he has the package that he has it."

"He better." He looked back into the van at the woman who was driving. "Stay here. You don't want to cross me. I got you that job. I can take it away, and you won't like how I get you fired."

Candice, the turncoat traitor who hopefully would die horribly, nodded. "I get it. Just please hurry. I don't know how long I can keep the van here."

"You'll keep it here as long as I need you to, bitch." Baz shook his head. "Good help really is hard to find these days."

"Or it could be no one wants to work with you." It had been that way at SIS. Only Damon had been able to really stand the man, and now she understood why. Damon held himself apart because he believed everyone would leave him one way or another. Baz had offered him company, but Damon hadn't been emotionally involved. It had been the best relationship he could manage.

"No one can keep up with me. Move." He gripped her elbow, forcing her to walk beside him.

She couldn't forget about that gun in his coat. And there was a possibility that she was wrong about the waiters. If they really did belong to Baz, he could still make good on his threat. She had to do everything she could to keep her people alive.

How quickly they'd become her people. A few short days and she knew she would care about them forever.

"Damon could keep up with you." For some reason she wanted him talking. Baz seemed to love to talk. Even if he was insulting her, he wasn't fully thinking about what was about to happen. She needed to keep him engaged. He was moving toward what looked like a forest of cement slabs. The Holocaust Memorial.

If she could get away from him in there, she might have a chance, but she had to find Damon first.

If she ran, what would happen to her friends?

"We're meeting him in the south corner. And he certainly can't keep up with me now. I saw to that. Poor Damon with his damaged heart. It's rather fitting, actually. He's always had a metaphorical one. I just made it real." He stopped in front of a bench. "Sit here."

She sat on the bench, Baz firmly behind her with a hand close to her throat. She was sure they looked somewhat affectionate. Just two tourists enjoying the beauty of Berlin.

"Damon, you're not here," Baz said into his device.

She couldn't see him, but she knew he would be touching the device in his ear, the one he'd taken off Simon's unconscious body. "I guess you don't want her. Well, I wouldn't either. She's a bit chunky. Look, you don't have to take the girl. I'll pay you well. My employers are willing to write you a check. And you know I'd be more than happy to get rid of her for you. It would be my pleasure."

Damon walked out from between the slabs, moving with none of his normal grace. His chest was working, moving up and down as he forced his lungs to take in oxygen.

"Oh, look, you ran. You know, I remember a time when you could run for hours and I wouldn't even be able to tell. You were so fit, so young." Baz's voice lowered, taking on the intimate tones of a lover.

Damon didn't look at him, his eyes steady on her. "Are you all right, love?"

Penny nodded. Just being in the same space with him, seeing that he was alive and whole, brought a calm to her she hadn't possessed before. "Yes. I'm fine. Damon, you can't give it to him. You know that, right?"

Damon's face softened. "You're telling me what I can't do again. It's a pattern with you."

She could see people moving through the columns of concrete in the memorial. She caught flashes of them as they walked through. Why couldn't anyone see that something terrible was happening under their noses?

"Do you have the package?" Baz asked.

Damon nodded.

She had to stop him. There would be far too many lives at risk if The Collective got their hands on that information again. "Damon, don't give it to him. Get out of here."

He could lose himself in that maze. It would be so easy. Even now she saw little splashes of color as someone ran by and then disappeared again.

"But if I leave he'll kill you." Damon was perfectly calm, as though they were discussing dinner plans and not the possible fate of the world.

She needed to remind him what was at stake. "And if you give him that information, thousands will die. You know what they're planning. You have to sacrifice me. You have to. This is a choice between one woman and the world. There is no choice."

"You're right. There is no choice." He held up a small thumb drive dangling from the end of a lanyard. "You are my world, love."

Her heart cried out for him, but she shook her head. "No, Damon."

She wanted him to survive, couldn't stand the thought of living in a world without him, but she couldn't trade her freedom when it meant the deaths of so many others.

Where was Ian Taggart? Where was the rest of the team?

Baz's hand tightened on her shoulder to almost the point of pain. "Well, isn't that touching? It actually makes me sick."

"I don't care what it does to you, Baz," Damon replied. "If you want this, you'll let her go."

"How do I know that's got anything at all on it? That could be a blank drive. I'm afraid I'm going to need more than your word. Where is Walter Bennett?"

Damon shook his head. "He's long gone, and you won't find him again."

"That is a tragedy. I was so looking forward to spending time with him."

"It's not going to happen. You can take the package or you'll have nothing to give your bosses." Damon gripped the drive in his palm, shielding it from view. "I'll go with you, Baz. Take me instead of her. I'm the one you want."

She didn't even try to stop the tears now. "No."

"Shut up." Baz let her feel the barrel of his gun against her back. "If you say another word, I'll do you right here in front of him."

Now Damon wasn't looking at her. He was focused on the man behind her, and she could feel his will. "I know you have a way out of here. You likely have some way to drug me. I'll submit to all of it if you let her go."

"And what if what I really want is for you to submit to me

completely?" The question came out in a menacing purr.

Penny felt her fists clench at the thought of her Damon bowing down to this man. He was proud. Sometimes his pride had been all he had to hold on to in the world. He couldn't give himself over.

"Then I'll call you Master," Damon replied evenly. "If you want, Basil, I'll be your dog. That is what you want, right?"

"You can't imagine what I want from you."

She saw him then. The man who had brought the tea. He'd ditched the waiter outfit and now he stalked closer. She had to strain, but she heard him call out.

"Ich habe ihn. Komm schnell. Der Brite ist in Schwierigkeiten."

Translation. *I have him. Come quickly. The Brit is in trouble.*

She'd thought they brought the drugged tea, but what if they had just been scouting? Candice had drugged the tea. Baz was bluffing. He didn't have anyone else. Her friends were safe and the German agents were about to cause some serious problems for them.

What they needed was a bit of chaos.

Penny gritted her teeth and prayed she could survive the next few moments.

* * * *

Damon tried not to think about how frightened Penelope must be. In a few moments, she would be free and once she was out of the line of fire, he would do whatever he had to do.

Though he rather hoped Taggart would choose to show up sometime soon.

He'd meant every word he said. He would do anything to save Penelope, including giving up the package, but he hoped he didn't have to.

Another bloody gift she'd given him. Hope. He never used to have it. It was so much better to see the world through Penelope's eyes than his own.

Baz stood behind Penelope, one hand on her shoulder and the other behind her back. He could only imagine that Baz was holding a gun on her. The second time in a week someone had threatened to kill her. "You can't imagine what I want from you."

Someone shouted in German behind him, and Damon watched as Penelope's eyes flared. She knew what they'd said and it meant something to her. Her lips pursed.

She was planning something. She might be the translator, but he'd learned to read her body language. He was an expert in Penelope Cash, in the way she looked when she was happy or mad, or just about to do something incredibly stupid that would make him want to toss her over his knee and blister her bottom.

After they made it to the embassy, of course.

He had to keep Baz talking. He'd said something about Damon not knowing what he really wanted.

"You'll have it. All you have to do is let her walk away from this." Damon took a step forward. "Think about it, Baz. You can make your bosses very happy with you and you'll have me on a leash, ready to do anything you want."

The thought made him nauseous, but he would do it. He would be Baz's slave right up until he got the chance to cut the bugger's throat and watch him bleed out.

"Are you offering to fuck me, Damon?" There was no way to mistake how hot Baz's eyes got.

"If you let her go, yes. Haven't you figured it out? Do you remember when we used to talk about the things we were willing to do for our country? I said anything. I was wrong. She's the one thing I can't sacrifice. She's the one thing I'll do anything for. Every man has something he wants above everything else. I want Penelope to live."

A bitter laugh huffed from Baz's mouth. "You don't know a bloody thing. You think I want a quick fuck? I wanted to be the thing you would never sacrifice. I wanted that. And if I can't be that to you, then no one can."

"Penelope!" Damon moved forward, screaming her name.

But she was already on the move. She threw herself to the side, her head ducking down even as Baz fired.

A splash of crimson formed on her right arm, blood blooming.

"*Halt!*" a new voice rang out. A tall blond man moved with the grace of a natural predator. He held a Ruger in a two-fisted grip and spoke in accented English. "You will lay down the weapon."

German intelligence. He never thought he'd be happy to see them.

Baz stopped, his jaw clenching.

Damon reached down and helped Penelope up. "Are you all right?"

Of course she wasn't all right. She'd been shot. But she simply nodded. "I think so. It hurts, but I think it grazed me. The bleeding isn't bad at all."

He looked at her side, and it was more of a burn than anything else.

Taggart walked up behind them with another German in tow. "Thank god. I thought we'd lost him. Damon, this is Agent Eberstark. I told him we'd been tracking Bennett in a joint MI6/CIA mission. I think you'll find that the Agency has been in contact with your bosses, but we can settle everything up once we get this fucker in custody."

Bloody bastard. There was a reason he loved Tag. The man was cool under pressure and he could lie like a pro. Damon made sure to stand in front of Penelope. He didn't want her in the line of fire one second longer. "Bennett, you should give it up now. You're surrounded. There's nowhere to go."

Baz frowned, his gun still up. "I'm not Bennett and you bloody well know it."

The first German stared, keeping Baz in his sights. "I thought Bennett was an American."

"He's turned out to be a master of disguise," Taggart said in a perfect British accent. He grinned a little and was back to sounding as American as apple pie. "British accents aren't hard. He was trying to get to England."

"His accomplice is in that black van over there. She's actually British," Penelope said. "You should arrest her."

Eberstark smiled. "How did he catch you, Miss Cash? I thought you were in the suite. We checked it out to see how many of the team Knight here was leaving behind."

Penelope's hands rested on his hips. "He knew we were about to catch him so he had his partner drug the tea you brought up. He figured out that Damon and I are closer than normal partners so he thought he could use me to get away."

Eberstark nodded. "Ah, well, I would try to save that fucker there, but I'm certainly not sleeping with him."

Damon went still as he felt Penelope's hand slide into his pocket. What was she doing now?

"The game is up, Bennett. We're not going to allow you to sell your work on the black market." Damon needed to get Penelope out of here. The bullets could start flying again at any moment.

Taggart looked over at Damon. "I'm damn glad I found you. Jake's back at the embassy talking to Ten. He knows the plan went all to hell and he's ready to help. I suspect we'll spend a lot of time in debrief with our new friends."

He might not always understand Penelope, but thank god he spoke spy fluently. Jake was waiting for him. He needed to get to the embassy, the American one this time. It was the only shot they had at carrying out the plan to destroy the drive.

"I am not Walter Bennett. They're playing you. Damon's got the package. He's got it in his pocket. Check it." Baz wasn't letting up. Even with three guns on him, because Taggart had his out now, he wasn't backing down.

Oh, his girl was a smart one. He reached into his pockets and pulled them out, showing everyone they were perfectly empty. "Would you like to check my jacket?"

Eberstark shook his head. "Not at all. We'll take this one into custody and have a nice long chat. Taggart, you will come with us? We don't want to cut our allies out of anything, as you would certainly never have cut us out."

The last was said with a definite zing, but then everyone knew the game.

And Baz knew that it was over.

He pulled the trigger and fired straight into Eberstark's body, felling the German agent with a single bullet to the neck.

Eberstark's partner fired back, but Baz was on the move and

now tourists were screaming and running, making the entire park a dangerous mess.

"Go!" Taggart yelled, his SIG in his hand. "Get her out of here. You know what to do."

Damon took Penelope's hand. She was his mission. Getting her out alive was the only thing that mattered. He ran with her, directly back to the memorial where he could lose them both. The slabs started out around his knees, but then the ground sloped down and before long the sun was obscured as they went underground. They raced along the narrow square-set path.

"The embassy is to the left," Penelope said.

"Give me the package, love." He held out his hand. He didn't want her caught with it, didn't want her to have anything at all to do with what was going to happen.

He'd just pocketed the drive when he felt a burning sensation in his arm. He turned and Baz was running across the tops of the slabs.

"If I'm going down, you're going with me, Damon." He took aim, but Baz's right shoulder was thrown as a bullet slammed into him. Baz yelled as he threw himself to the ground.

"Go!" Taggart said. He leapt from one slab to the next. He had to be four or five meters off the ground. "I'll deal with this fuck. If I can find him, damn it."

He took Penelope's hand and broke to the left. His heart was thudding in his chest as he ran up the sloping path. By the time they made it out of the memorial, his breath was sawing in and out.

He would make it. He couldn't see the embassy from where he stood, but it was close. Right behind the building ahead.

Sirens wailed all around him. Another threat. The German police wouldn't care that he had a mission. They would only know that a couple of Brits and a yank had been firing in the middle of tourist central.

If they were taken in, they would have no idea who to trust.

"Run, love. You can go faster than me." He jogged beside her, letting go of her hand.

Penelope didn't speed up. "No. We go together."

He would slow her down. "Please. Go. Get Jake. He's at the

American Embassy. Do you know where it is? Please, love. I need him. I won't be able to make it."

"I love you, Damon." She took off.

He had to try. Damon forced his legs to move. He still had the package. He couldn't give it to her, couldn't give her that responsibility. If they were going to come after someone, it had to be him. Even if it meant he died because he couldn't live in a world that didn't have her in it. Jake knew the plan. Jake would come and get him.

Pain flared through his system as his right shoulder took a bullet. Blood spat from his chest, and he felt his knees weaken and then crack as he hit the stone under him.

His vision blurred as he fell forward. His gun bit into the muscles of his gut. He could already feel the blood pooling.

He was right back there again with blood and death all around him. The first time he nearly died, vengeance had kept him alive.

The vision he had this time was quite different.

"I told you. If I can't have you, no one can." Baz kicked him hard, rolling him over.

One chance. His whole body shook but he had one last thing to do. He forced his finger to pull the trigger.

Baz stared down at him as red splashed across his belly. A dumb look came over his eyes and he started to aim again.

Another crash hit Damon's ears and a hole was suddenly where Baz's heart should have been.

His greatest enemy was dead and the only reason Damon cared at all was because Penelope would be safe.

He let his hand fall to the side, staring up at that brilliant sky. So blue. Like Penelope's eyes.

"No you don't, you bastard." Taggart shoved his gun into the holster, and Damon groaned in pain as Taggart hauled him up. "You hold on, you son of a bitch, because I can't take this slow. They're coming up on us fast. Do you have the package?"

"In my pocket," he managed. "Do you trust Ten?"

Someone was shouting behind them in German. The police had arrived, and they seemed to be after Taggart.

The man didn't hesitate. Even with Damon's weight, Taggart sprinted. "It's going to be fine."

And Damon endured. Pain wracked his system, but he held on.

Damon forced his head up. They were clear of the memorial and the large buildings that surrounded it. He could see the police running, but they were losing ground.

"Damon!" Penelope's voice rang out.

Damon suddenly found himself in the cool of a building.

"Motherfucker's heavy." Taggart eased him onto what felt like a couch. "He took at least two. We need to dig them out."

A warm hand was suddenly in his, and Penelope's face loomed in his vision.

"Damn it. I thought y'all were going to avoid an international incident," a man with a slow Southern accent said. "I'll go try to find a doctor. I swear if you two hadn't managed to bring in the package, there would likely be hell to pay."

Damon's brain was muddled. There were so many faces around him. "The package…"

He had the package. Something about the package.

Tennessee Smith looked straight down at him, his face deeply serious. "Your girl brought it to me. Well, she gave it to Jake who brought it to me. I gave it to the head of the Agency who came here himself, you understand? That's how important it was. We're grateful, of course."

Ten stared down at him, his eyes saying everything he couldn't because they were all being watched. Damon understood that much. *Don't give it away. Keep your mouth shut.*

"Of course."

Ten nodded. "I'll be back with a doc, and we'll see what we can do to smooth things over with the Germans."

"I think you'll find Walter Bennett is dead in the square." They had a shot at Bennett having a life if Ten would just go along.

Ten frowned, his voice going low. "Really? That's the way we're going? Tag, get Miles on it and fast because they'll be looking. I'd tell you to use Chelsea, but she's still asleep."

"Everyone all right?" God, he didn't know what happened. Pain was wracking his system, but he wanted to know what happened to his team.

Penelope was crying, her tears hitting his chest. "Everyone's fine. Stop worrying about that." She turned to Ten. "He needs a doctor. He needs to go to hospital."

She was so pretty when she cried. He held her hand. The last thing he felt as the darkness took him was Taggart pulling the actual package free.

He would destroy it. Damon had no doubt. He knew he should. He'd never trusted anyone. Another thing Penelope had given him. Taggart would take care of things.

Damn, but it was bloody good to have friends. The darkness took him again.

Chapter Twenty-Two

London, England
One week later

Penelope threaded her hands together as she took her seat in Nigel's office. "You asked to see me?"

Nigel stared at her across the desk. "Yes, I did. I need to understand what happened in Germany."

She managed not to wince. She'd been dreading this meeting ever since they'd made it home to London. They were all back at The Garden, recuperating. The McKay-Taggart team had only left a day before. "You read my report."

Nigel nodded shortly, his hand touching a folder on his desk. "Your report was almost word for word the same as Agent Knight's."

"It's the truth." Well, the truth as she more or less knew it.

"Miss Cash, are you aware of what was on the thumb drive Jacob Dean handed over to the CIA? We were told that you gave it to him. According to his report, you took the drive off Knight and brought it to him." Nigel's eyes narrowed.

This was where things got sketchy. Once everything had gone to hell, Jacob had opted to improvise. The moment he'd seen her, he'd caught her in his arms and told her what they were doing. Damon was coming in with the police at his back. There might not be time to change the drives. She'd looked over his shoulder and several men in suits had been watching them. She'd nodded and pretended to put something in Jake's hands. He'd turned and introduced her to the bloody director of the CIA, who only cared about one thing—that thumb drive and the information he thought was on it. Unfortunately, she wasn't sure how much Nigel knew. "Well, I obviously didn't have time to boot up a computer and check it out. I simply did what I was told."

No lies there.

"It was the complete works of some American author named Steve Berry. He writes thrillers about a former secret agent who saves the world on a regular basis. There was a note. It basically said this is what happens when the wrong people get the right information."

She winced a little. They could have been a bit more subtle. "That doesn't seem right."

A smile suddenly broke over Nigel's face. "Oh, I think it seems exactly right." He laughed and leaned back in his chair. "If anyone asks, I gave you a stern talking to. You're terrified and properly chastened."

She breathed a sigh of relief. "Absolutely, sir."

He frowned a bit. "My agents aren't soldiers, Miss Cash. They aren't simply around to follow orders. Oh, I know the higher-ups would love to believe so, but the people who run the world, well, most of them don't have to live in it. It's a sad fact of our lives. Whatever Damon did out there, I'll back him because it was for the best. There is some knowledge that should never see the light of day, that shouldn't be trusted to any government no matter how friendly. For now, the story is that Bennett was trying to sell something he didn't actually have. The records have all been changed and even Agro is going along with it. They don't want the bad publicity any more than we do. As far as anyone knows, Basil Champion was Walter Bennett and the matter is closed. I identified Bennett's body myself. The Germans and the Americans both believe Bennett is dead. Mr. Smith and I have decided to keep our mouths shut about anything we know or suspect we know. Do you have any idea where the real Bennett is?"

Somewhere in Australia, last she'd heard. Brody had called in to let them know Bennett was safe and they were both looking for new jobs. Ian Taggart had immediately groaned and said something about more strays.

"I think we don't have to worry about him anymore. I believe Mr. Taggart has a plan on how to keep him in the fold, so to speak." She leaned forward. "Is it true that Candice was killed in a car accident?"

The German police reports stated that she'd attempted to evade them and driven recklessly, plowing the van into an oncoming vehicle. Though she'd turned out to be a traitor, Penny still regretted her death.

"Yes, I'm afraid that's true as well. Her boyfriend has been brought in for questioning in relation to the incident. I don't think we have to worry about him. The chap urinated on himself." Nigel shuddered a bit. "On to happier things—how is Damon recovering?"

He was a bear, her Master. He was cranky and crabby and gloriously alive. "He's doing well." She forced a smile on her face. "He should be ready to work again very soon."

It was the one thing about her future she didn't like to think about.

"As to that, Mr. Knight's health is exactly why I called you in," Nigel said. "I told you I wanted a report on his fitness for duty. You haven't sent it yet."

Because she didn't want to. Because she wanted him safe. Because she couldn't stand the thought of losing him. And yet, she couldn't betray him. "I will have it on your desk in the morning."

"And what will it say?"

She took a deep breath. She'd made her decision about this a long time ago. "That Agent Knight is ready for fieldwork."

"Oh, darling, that is such a lie," a familiar voice said from behind her.

She turned and Damon stood in the doorway, looking gorgeous and polished in his tailored suit. He didn't look like a man who had almost died. He looked every inch the seductive, deadly agent. "Damon?"

His lips curled up. "I followed you, love. I couldn't let you do this alone. And as for her report to you, Nigel, she's going to tell you the truth."

Nigel smiled slightly. "And what is that?"

"I'm utterly unfit for service, sir. My lungs were damaged, my heart as well. I shouldn't ever run past a moderate jog, and I tend to lose consciousness when my heart rate gets too high. The lucky thing is I'm perfectly fit in bed."

"Damon!" He didn't have to mention that.

"Well, you seem ready to send me into the field, but you treat me like an invalid when we're in bed together. She's held me off for days." He sank into the seat beside her. "It has to stop. It's all madness."

Nigel didn't bother to cover his laugh. "Well, should I get a desk ready for you?"

Damon shuddered. "Absolutely not. I'll have my resignation to you as soon as possible. Nigel, I can't thank you enough. You've been damn good to me over the years. I intend to give you a slight discount on my services in the future. I'm opening the London office of McKay-Taggart."

That was news to her. "I thought he wanted you in New York."

"I told him to bite my arse," Damon said with an arrogant grin. "It was London or I'd compete against him. He made the right call, although he's tough when he's bargaining. We already have our first two employees. I hope you can translate Australian."

Brody and Walter. It looked like Walt was going to work his second life to its fullest. She smiled. "I think I can manage it."

He was quitting. He would never be completely safe, but if he was running the office, he could mitigate the risks. Tears sparked in her eyes.

He was hers.

"Nige? Could we have a minute alone?" Damon asked.

Her boss rolled his eyes but stood. "I suppose so. I'm losing Penelope, as well, I suspect. Good luck to you both. And I'll expect a twenty-percent discount, damn it. Contractors."

The door closed behind him.

"I'm not giving him more than fifteen," Damon said. "I love you, Penelope."

He said it all the time now. He didn't hesitate. Neither did she. "I love you, too. Oh, Damon, do you think you can be happy?"

He took her hand in his, warmth spreading across her skin. "Do you know I've almost died twice?"

Oh, she would never forget that. "Yes."

"What they say is true. Your life passes before you, except the second time, it wasn't the life I'd lived that passed in front of me. It was the one I could have. It was a life with you. I saw what we could have, Penelope. We could have a home and children and a right brilliant old age. We could have love. I want that life. I want it more than I've ever wanted anything."

He got to one knee and she gasped. She'd expected him to ask her to live with him. She'd known he would want her to take his collar.

She hadn't expected this.

He pulled out a ring. "This is all I have left of my mum. My granddad gave it to me before he died. I used to hide it in my socks. Even at boarding school, I kept it close. I was so afraid of losing it." He pressed it into her palm. "It's yours. Even if you tell me no, it's yours. This ring belonged to the only other woman who ever loved me, and I want to give it to you."

Translation. *Will you marry me?*

"Oh, yes." She threw her arms around him. "Yes, Damon. That ring is mine."

And he was hers.

She kissed her man.

Damon's hands tightened and suddenly she was on Nigel's desk. "Damon, what are you doing? Damon, you can't do that here." The entirety of SIS was outside the door. Nigel could walk back in at any time.

His eyes heated up and he spread her legs, making a place for himself. She could already feel his cock hardening against her. "When are you going to learn? Don't tell me what I can't do."

He proceeded to show her that he could.

* * * *

347

Dallas, TX
Two nights later

Simon Weston poured himself a Scotch and looked over at his cousins, thinking about the question J.T. had just asked. How had his trip gone? Well, he'd finally gotten his hands on Chelsea, and she'd pushed him away again.

And then he'd looked like a complete idiot for drinking drugged tea. He was so glad they'd caught that crazed-idiot Candice and arrested her. She could report on the current state of the British prison system. "My stay was perfectly pleasant, thank you."

He wasn't about to tell them how he'd fucked up again. He blamed Chelsea. He'd been watching her the whole time or he might have noticed his drink had been roofied. Even as the drugs had taken effect, he'd reached out to her.

And she'd ignored him. Again.

J.T. Malone rolled his dark eyes and took a swig of beer. Simon only kept it in his fridge for his cousins' visits, which were occurring more and more often, but then he'd expected to see them since he was living so close. "I talked to Aunt Maura. She said you barely stopped by. Were you doing the spy shit?"

"It's not shit, asshole." Michael reached out and swatted his twin. "Just because you're happy behind a damn desk doesn't mean the rest of us are."

His cousins fought as often now as they did when they were all kids. He would get sent to Texas during long school holidays. His parents were lovely people, but he'd really enjoyed the freedom he'd found on his uncle's ranch. His uncle ran Malone Oil, one of the wealthiest companies in the world, but no one would accuse David Malone or his sons of being aristocratic. No one treated him like royalty on the ranch. There was no pressure on him to bring glory to the family name there. A break from the pressure of being one of the Duke of Norsley's heirs had been a good reason to come see his cousins.

The other being that he genuinely enjoyed their company. They were more his brothers than his own brother. Clive never even knew he did the "spy stuff," much less complained about it.

"I'm in private security now." He went to the big floor to ceiling windows that showed a spectacular view of Dallas. In the distance, the lights from Reunion Tower blinked like a giant Christmas ornament.

"You work for Ian Taggart," Michael said, walking up behind him. "I might be a SEAL, but we all know who Tag is. And we know he works for the Agency."

Tag might work for them from time to time, but he always stayed true to himself. It was why Simon followed him. If there was one thing he'd learned over the years, it was to answer to his own conscience always.

What had Shakespeare said? *Every subject's duty is the king's, but every subject's soul is his own.*

That summed up the utter shit a soldier went through. He was done being a good soldier, a good son, a good agent. Being good had gotten him nowhere.

"Well, I only work for Tag. How about you? I heard the Agency is sniffing around you." Tag had told him. Michael was a SEAL and a highly decorated one at that. He was smart, and there was a darkness about him that spoke of deadly grace. He was the opposite of his sunny other half. J.T. was an open book, every emotion out there worn on his sleeve. Michael's waters ran deep.

Simon was worried for his cousin. He was worried about what would happen if the Agency got their hooks in him.

J.T. frowned fiercely. "What the hell? You're not joining the fucking Agency. My brother is not becoming some damn CIA agent. You're supposed to get tired of playing soldier and come the hell home."

Michael gritted his teeth. Simon was fairly certain this wasn't the first time they'd had this argument. "Big brother, keep your damn nose out of my business."

Yes, that was what he needed to complete his evening. He needed a Malone brothers smack down. "You two keep it down or you can head back to Fort Worth. I'm not in the mood to play referee. Why the hell did you come all the way out here anyway?"

J.T. put his boots on the coffee table. "We wanted to see if you nabbed that nerd you were after. You were in Europe with her. We thought you might take the chance to make your move."

He wished he'd never told his cousins about Chelsea. Too much Scotch. He should quit while he was ahead. "She's not a nerd."

Michael shrugged. "Hey, nerds can be hot."

She wasn't hot around him. She was cold as ice. Except every now and then he saw it in her eyes. He saw her longing. She wanted a Master and he wanted to take care of her.

"I work with her. Nothing more." The bell chimed just in time to save him from a conversation he'd rather not have. "I'll be right back."

He'd ordered Chinese earlier—before his cousins had arrived. They were like locust. He would be lucky to get a noodle or two. He reached for his wallet as he opened the door.

Chelsea stood there, glancing nervously down the hallway. "Simon, I need to talk to you. Can I come in?"

He was dumbstruck. She avoided him like the plague and now she showed up on his doorstep looking like sin on two legs. She was wearing tight jeans and a V-neck sweater that showed off her breasts. "Why?"

She bit her bottom lip, sending his hormones into overdrive. "Because someone's trying to kill me."

He opened the door, letting her in and wondering if he'd ever let her leave again.

Simon, Chelsea, and the whole McKay-Taggart team returns August 19, 2014 with *A View to a Thrill*.

Author's Note

I'm often asked by generous readers how they can help get the word out about a book they enjoyed. There are so many ways to help an author you like. Leave a review. If your e-reader allows you to lend a book to a friend, please share it. Go to Goodreads and connect with others. Recommend the books you love because stories are meant to be shared. Thank you so much for reading this book and for supporting all the authors you love!

A View to a Thrill

Master and Mercenaries, Book 7
By Lexi Blake
Coming August 19, 2014

A Spy without a Country

Simon Weston grew up royal in a place where aristocracy still mattered. Serving Queen and country meant everything to him, until MI6 marked him as damaged goods and he left his home in disgrace. Ian Taggart showed him a better way to serve his fellow man and introduced him to Sanctum, a place to pursue his passion for Dominance and submission. Topping beautiful subs was a lovely distraction until he met Chelsea, and becoming her Master turned into Simon's most important mission.

A Woman without Hope

Chelsea Dennis grew up a pawn to the Russian mob. Her father's violent lessons taught her that monsters lurked inside every man and they should never be trusted. Hiding in the shadows, she became something that even the monsters would fear—an information broker who exposed their dirty secrets and toppled their empires. Everything changed when Simon Weston crossed her path. Valiant and faithful, he was everything she needed—and a risk she couldn't afford to take.

A Force too Strong to Resist

When dark forces from her past threaten her newfound family at Sanctum, Chelsea must turn to Simon, the one man she can trust with her darkest secrets. Their only chance to survive lies in a mystery even Chelsea has been unable to solve. As they race to uncover the truth and stay one step ahead of the assassins on their heels, they will discover a love too powerful to deny. But to stop a killer, Simon just might have to sacrifice himself...

Dungeon Games: A Masters and Mercenaries Novella

Masters and Mercenaries, Book 6.5
By Lexi Blake
Coming May 13, 2014

Obsessed

Derek Brighton has become one of Dallas's finest detectives through a combination of discipline and obsession. Once he has a target in his sights, nothing can stop him. When he isn't solving homicides, he applies the same intensity to his playtime at Sanctum, a secretive BDSM club. Unfortunately, no amount of beautiful submissives can fill the hole that one woman left in his heart.

Unhinged

Karina Mills has a reputation for being reckless, and her clients appreciate her results. As a private investigator, she pursues her cases with nothing holding her back. In her personal life, Karina yearns for something different. Playing at Sanctum has been a safe way to find peace, but the one Dom who could truly master her heart is out of reach.

Enflamed

On the hunt for a killer, Derek enters a shadowy underworld only to find the woman he aches for is working the same case. Karina is searching for a missing girl and won't stop until she finds her. To get close to their prime suspect, they need to pose as a couple. But as their operation goes under the covers, unlikely partners become passionate lovers while the killer prepares to strike.

Their Virgin Secretary

Masters of Ménage, Book 6

By Shayla Black and Lexi Blake

Coming April 15, 2014

Three determined bosses…

Tate Baxter, Eric Cohen, and Kellan Kent are partners for one of the most respected law practices in Chicago. But these three masters of the courtroom also share a partnership in the bedroom, fulfilling the darkest needs of their female submissives night after night. Everything was fine—until they hired Annabelle Wright as their administrative assistant.

One beautiful secretary…

Belle felt sure she'd hit the jackpot with her job, but in the last year, the three gorgeous attorneys have become far more than her bosses. They're her friends, her protectors, and in Belle's dreams, they're her lovers, too. But she's given her heart to them all, so how can she choose just one?

An unforgettable night…

When her bosses escort her to a wedding, drinks and dancing turn into foreplay and fantasy. Between heated kisses, Belle admits her innocence. Surprise becomes contention and tempers flare. Heartbroken and unwilling to drive them apart, Belle leaves the firm and flees to New Orleans.

That leads to danger.

Resolved to restore her late grandmother's home, she hopes she can move on without the men. Then Kellan, Tate, and Eric show up at her doorstep, seeking another chance. But something sinister is at work in the Crescent City and its sights are set on her. Before the trio can claim Annabelle for good, they just might have to save her life.

* * * *

Excerpt:

One year, two months, and four days. Four hundred thirty days all totaled, but Tate hated to calculate their time together that way. It depressed him. Ten thousand three hundred twenty hours wasn't much better, considering that was how long he'd gone without sex. Because that was how long it had been since he'd first laid eyes on Annabelle Wright. She'd walked into his office with her resume in hand, and he'd just stared, dumbstruck. He didn't believe in love at first sight, but he'd found lust in that single glance. Oh, yeah. He'd taken one look at the goddess applying for a job and known exactly why he'd gone to the gym five times a week since he'd turned seventeen.

But love? He'd taken a whole week of consideration before deciding that he had fallen in love with Belle. After all, he was a careful man. He liked to think things out.

"Indulgence leads to chaos. Dominic is going to rue the day he let his sub run wild." Kellan frowned at Kinley, then swiveled his gaze toward the dance floor. "Who is that?"

Tate followed Kellan's line of sight and scowled. Belle danced with some overgrown ape whose smile seemed way too friendly. She looked gorgeous in her emerald cocktail dress. Its V-neck and body-fitting lines showed off her every curve. She wasn't a tall woman, but those crazy-sexy black shoes she wore made her legs look deliciously long. Tate had no idea how women maintained their balance while walking on those high, thin heels. He was pretty sure, however, they would look great wrapped around his neck.

The only thing he didn't like about the way Belle looked was the animated expression she turned up at the lug hanging on her. Then she laughed—a sound that always did strange things to his insides.

Eric slapped a big hand across his back. "Chill, buddy. That's Cole Lennox. He's a PI here in Dallas. We've used his company before. He's happily married. I don't think he's trying to mack on our girl."

Tate still didn't like it. "Why isn't he dancing with his wife?"

He was rational enough to know that jealousy was a completely illogical response in this situation. Technically, Belle wasn't his. She'd never even gone on a real date with him. They'd had lunch exactly fifty-two times over the last year, but they'd mostly talked about work. He'd taken her to happy hour fifteen times, where she always ordered vodka tonics, Cîroc, or Grey Goose, with a half a twist of lime. They'd still talked about work. And the weather. None of that counted, though, because she'd treated him like a colleague, not a boyfriend. He hadn't kissed her yet or made his intentions clear, so he had no right to be jealous that Belle danced with another man. For once, he didn't care if he made less than perfect sense.

Kellan pointed to the other end of the floor. "He can't. His brother is dancing with her. They're twins and I've heard they share."

"Really?" Tate sat up and sent a challenging glance to Kell and Eric. "I'm seeing a picture here. The Lennox twins married the same girl. Those three oil tycoons over there have one wife, and we all saw the three royal princes walk in with their bride. Hell, the whole board of Anthony Anders decided to marry the same woman. But it can't work for us? Explain that."

That was the argument Tate had heard from Eric and especially Kellan for the past year, ever since the night they'd sat around the office and each admitted they were crazy about their new secretary. Administrative Assistant. Office Manager. Belle changed her title more than once. She took exception to the term secretary, but Tate thought it was kind of hot.

Kellan sighed, turning toward him. "Just because it works for some other people doesn't mean it would work for the two of you."

"The two of us? Really? You're still going to play it that way?" Eric challenged. "Tell me you don't want her, too."

Kellan's eyes hooded. Tate had made almost a scientific study of his friends in an attempt to really understand them. Kellan had four major expressions that he used like masks. This particular one Tate had named "stubborn asshole." Kellan used it a lot.

"Of course I want her. I've never denied that. She's a beautiful woman, not to mention lovely, kind, and very smart. If I was interested in getting married again, I would be all over her. But I'm not, and I doubt she's the type of woman to have no-strings-attached sex."

"I want strings." Tate needed to make that brutally clear because his partners seemed to constantly forget. They should take notes during their conversations the way he often did. But again, no one asked his opinion. "I want to be tangled up in all her strings. She's the one. I get that what we want is unusual, though it really doesn't seem that way today. I swear the two dogs are the only non-ménage relationship here. Belle might be surprised that we all want her, but she's not going to be shocked. She's fine with Kinley's marriage."

Eric sighed. "Maybe, but we need to be careful. She hasn't dated anyone since she started working with us."

Tate knew that very well since he'd been keeping an eye on her. Hopefully she never knew the extent of his observation because what he'd done was illegal. And possibly a little stalkerish.

"There's some reason for that," Eric went on.

Didn't they get it? "Because she's waiting for us to make a move."

"Or she's just working hard and isn't ready to settle down," Kellan pointed out. "She's young, man."

"It's not like we're old."

Tate didn't feel old. He was thirty-two. Given that the average life expectancy of an American male was seventy-six, that didn't sound old. Then he did the math and realized that he was forty-two percent of the way through his accepted life expectancy. Forty-two percent—closing in on half. When he looked at it that way, he did feel old. He refused to waste another second.

"That's it." Tate stood and straightened his tie. "I'm going in."

God, he hoped he looked halfway decent because he often got rumpled and didn't notice. He would probably still be wearing pocket protectors if he hadn't become good friends with Eric in tenth grade.

He'd tutored Eric through rudimentary algebra, and Eric had taught him that jeans weren't supposed to hit above the ankles. They'd been a weird duo, the jock and the nerd. But their relationship meant more to him than any other. His parents were cold intellectuals who told him he'd failed by not going into academic pursuits— because yeah, Harvard law had been a breeze. His brothers cared more about their experiments than their family. So Tate and Eric had stuck together like blood, and Kellan had joined them after college.

But Tate realized in that moment that he needed more. He needed Belle. So did they, but she had to come first. "I'm going to do it. I'm going to offer her my penis."

Eric's head hit the table and he groaned. "Dude, how do you

ever get laid?"

So he wasn't smooth. At least he was honest. "She already has my heart. I would like for her to take my penis, too. Is that so much to ask?"

"If you ask her like that, she'll just smack you," Kellan pointed out.

Frustration welled. He sat back down. "Damn it, that's why we need to go after her as a pack. I'm not good at the smooth stuff."

"By smooth stuff, he means any type of actual communication with a woman." Eric rolled his eyes.

They were totally missing the point. "I communicate fine. She'll know what I want and how I want it."

"Which is precisely why she'll know where she wants to slap you next." Kellan shook his head. "This might be a bad idea, but it couldn't hurt for you to dance with her. Can you do that without asking her to take your penis in marriage?"

He wasn't completely sure. His cock had a mind of its own. "I think I can handle it."

"Good. Go on, then. I'll talk to Eric." Kell sighed. "I guess we really do need to figure out how to handle her. I can't stand the thought of another uncomfortable plane trip back. She didn't talk to me the whole flight down. Taking the hands-off approach isn't working. I get the feeling she's just about ready to throw in the towel and leave all of us." Kellan's eyes narrowed suddenly. "And that asshole isn't married. Go. Make sure he doesn't get his hands on Belle."

Tate's stare zipped to her. Sure enough, a guy was cutting in on Lennox. He leered down at Annabelle, then peered straight at her boobs.

Those boobs were his, damn it. At least he fully intended for those boobs to belong to him. Well, a third of them anyway. "You two work it out because I'm making a move by the end of the night…"

Thieves

A new urban fantasy series by Lexi Blake

"Author Lexi Blake has created a supernatural world filled with surprises and a book that I couldn't put down once I started reading it."
Maven, The Talent Cave Reviews

"I truly love that Lexi took vampires and made them her own."
KC Lu, Guilty Pleasures Book Reviews

Stealing mystical and arcane artifacts is a dangerous business, especially for a human, but Zoey Wharton is an exceptional thief. The trick to staying alive is having friends in all the wrong places. With a vampire, a werewolf, and a witch on the payroll, Zoey takes the sorts of jobs no one else can perform—tracking down ancient artifacts filled with unthinkable magic power, while trying to stay one step ahead of monsters, demons, angels, and a Vampire Council with her in their crosshairs.

If only her love life could be as simple. Zoey and Daniel Donovan were childhood sweethearts until a violent car crash took his life. When Daniel returned from the grave as a vampire, his only interest in Zoey was in keeping her safely apart from the secrets of his dark world. Five years later, Zoey encounters Devinshea Quinn, an earthbound Faery prince who sweeps her off her feet. He could show her everything the supernatural world has to offer, but Daniel is still in her heart.

As their adventures in acquisition continue, Zoey will have to find a way to bring together the two men she loves or else none of them may survive the forces that have aligned against her.

Steal the Light—Now Available
Steal the Day—Now Available
Steal the Moon—Now Available
Steal the Sun—Coming March 18, 2014
Steal the Night—Coming June 10, 2014

About Lexi Blake

Lexi Blake lives in North Texas with her husband, three kids, and the laziest rescue dog in the world. She began writing at a young age, concentrating on plays and journalism. It wasn't until she started writing romance that she found success. She likes to find humor in the strangest places. Lexi believes in happy endings no matter how odd the couple, threesome or foursome may seem. She also writes contemporary Western ménage as Sophie Oak.

Connect with Lexi online:

Facebook: Lexi Blake
Twitter: https://twitter.com/authorlexiblake
Website: www.LexiBlake.net

Sign up for Lexi's free newsletter at www.lexiblake.net/contact.html.

7863505R10211

Printed in Great Britain
by Amazon.co.uk, Ltd.,
Marston Gate.